THE REINTRODUCTION
of Sammie Morgan

a pine bluff *novel*

NANCEE CAIN

Serrated Edge Publishing

Serrated Edge Publishing
PO Box 969
Jasper, AL 35502
www.nanceecain.com

First published July 2019

This is a work of fiction. Names, characters, businesses, places, events and
incidents are either the products of the author's imagination or used in a
fictitious manner. Any resemblance to actual persons, living or dead, or actual
events is purely coincidental

ISBN: 978-0-9995362-3-0

10 9 8 7 6 5 4 3 2 1

Editor: Jessica Royer Ocken
Line Editor: Coreen Montagna
Cover Design by Shannon Lumetta
Interior Book Design by Coreen Montagna

Printed in the United States of America

To the typos
that make it through umpteen rounds of edits and proofreaders.
Your dedication and tenacity inspire me.
And to Coreen, Chantell and Michele
who help me catch the little *&^%@#$!

Chapter
One

"Daddy?"

"What, son?" Matt paused and shifted Luke's four-year-old weight on his shoulders.

"My head's melting."

"Mine is too. I'll be ready for that ice cream cone when we get home. How 'bout you?"

"I love ice cream! Hurry!" Luke shouted, kicking his chest.

"Yeow, easy now." Matt patted his son's leg and grinned.

He'd taken the day off to go fishing. They hadn't had any luck, but it didn't matter. He enjoyed spending time with the boy, something that didn't happen often with the demands of work and school.

Summer had arrived with a vengeance in Alabama. On the last day of May, it was already unbearably hot. Humidity made the air thick and difficult to breathe. Sweat trickled down his bare back into the waistband of his old, torn jeans, and red dust swirled with each step. Luke wrapped his thin, sticky arms around his neck and gave him a kiss.

"I love you, Daddy."

"How much?"

"Lots and lots!"

"Back atcha."

Matt smiled when Luke giggled. The sound of his son's laughter was his reason for living, the only light in the dark tunnel that was now his life.

Coming out of the woods, Matt paused at the unfamiliar car stopped in the middle of the road. Few people drove down Tyler Road unless they meant to be there. He gazed appreciatively at the sight of a woman's round ass as she peered under the hood of the car. When she stood, the vision got even better. Tall with curves, the sight was as welcome as a cool drink of water—and damn was he ever parched.

She mopped her forehead with the back of her arm and dozens of bracelets clinked together. Her hair—a rich, dark auburn color with coppery highlights—hung down her back. She wore a white peasant blouse and hip-hugging jeans, her shoulders and midriff bare and turning pink from the sun. She twisted her hair into a knot on top of her head and fanned the back of her neck.

Matt barely contained his laughter as she proceeded to walk around the car, kicking every tire and using language worthy of his father—and Leroy Tyler was known far and wide as a master of profanity.

"I take it she won't crank?" he asked as he approached.

Startled, the girl screamed and whirled around to face him.

"Holy crap!" She swung away from him, hiding her face. Under her breath he heard her whisper, "Fuck."

"Sorry, I didn't mean to scare you," Matt offered.

"Daddy, it's Esmerelda."

Matt bit back his smile. The girl did resemble a boho version of the Disney princess. Although her hair was more like The Little Mermaid's. He put down the fishing gear and pulled Luke off his shoulders to take a look at the car.

"I-I don't know what's wrong. It started to make a grinding noise and just quit," she stammered.

Pushing her round, retro sunglasses to the top of her head, she finally made eye contact with him, and his mouth dropped. It had been years since he'd seen those amazing Caribbean blue eyes.

"Sam?"

"I prefer Sammie now. How've you been, Matt?"

She held out her hand and gave him a firm handshake as he stared at the girl who'd once been his shadow, tagging along everywhere he went.

"Fine, just fine. Wow, this is quite a surprise. Here, let me take a look." He got in the car, and she was right, it was dead. Getting out, he looked under the hood, which was much safer than staring at the changes in Sam, er, Sammie. She was definitely *not* the tomboy he remembered.

His son held out his hand to her. "Hey. I'm Lukas Tyler, but you can call me Luke."

Matt watched the exchange out of the corner of his eye.

"Samantha Morgan, but you can call me Sammie. How old are you, Luke?"

"Four, almost five. You have a diamond in your belly button. It sparkles."

"Luke " he warned.

She laughed. "You're very observant."

Matt smiled. It actually pleased him to hear Luke conversing with a stranger. Since the accident, the boy had been shy, particularly around people he didn't know. Dropping the hood, Matt turned to face his old friend, still amazed by the difference in her appearance.

Sam Morgan. She wasn't beautiful in the classic sense of the word—not like Karen had been—but she had an arresting face due to those large, blue-green eyes. Freckles dusted her skin. When they were kids, he used to tease her and say she was dotted with chocolate sprinkles, which had never failed to make her mad.

"How bad is it?" She bit her lip and fingered her bracelets.

"I'm afraid it doesn't look good. It's an old car, and you haven't got a lick of transmission fluid, so you've probably blown a seal. Did the light come on, or did you smell anything, hear anything?"

Drawing in a deep breath, she shrugged. "I-I wasn't really paying attention. Maybe a burning smell and a knocking noise."

If he didn't know any better, he'd swear she looked ready to cry. Crying women unsettled him and triggered bad memories. Karen had been a crier. But Sam Morgan cry? Unheard of. She hadn't even cried when she broke her arm falling out of the tree beside his house.

"Look, I still live just a half mile down the road." He gave her a reassuring smile. "And you happen to be in luck."

"How's that?" Her brow furrowed, and she looked off into the distance, as if weighing her options.

"I'm a mechanic. I can get your car towed to my shop for free."

"Thank you. Just how much does a t-transmission cost?" The catch in her voice spoke volumes.

Matt really hated giving her bad news. "It's an old car. I don't know if it'll be worth fixing, but I'll know more after I take a better look at it."

She sighed, retrieving her purse from the front seat. "Just my luck. Is there a motel close by where I can stay?"

Matt chuckled. "You're kidding, right? In Pine Bluff? We're still backwoods around here. The nearest is still the rundown no-tell motel on the county line near The Roadside Tavern. You'd have to go into Harrisville. But don't worry, we'll figure something out. Come to the house. I promised Luke an ice cream cone, and I'm ready for one myself. You can decide what to do there. Still like chocolate?" He picked up the fishing poles and empty basket.

"Of course." Sammie's brows knit together as she watched Luke limp ahead of them.

Matt prayed she wouldn't make a big deal about it. "What are you doing back in Pine Bluff?" he asked, trying to divert her attention.

"Takin' care of business." She pulled her sunglasses back down on her face.

"How's your mother, Ms. Sue Ellen?"

"She's in the car…" She stared straight ahead, but her chin quivered.

"What? I didn't notice—Luke! Hold on!" He made sure his son obeyed before turning his attention back to Sammie. "Is she okay? Is she lying down?"

"I reckon she's good as can be expected. She's dead. I'm bringing her ashes to be with Daddy."

"What? I-I'm sorry." *Well done, Matthew. Insert foot in mouth.*

Sam's mother had been a strange woman who'd always unnerved him, but still…He scrounged for something, anything to say that wasn't hurtful or stupid as they continued toward the house.

"So how many years has it been? How old are you now?"

"About twelve years, I think. I'm twenty-seven."

"Not fair."

"Huh? What's not fair?"

"How come you don't look twenty-seven when I look and feel older than dirt?"

"I don't know, maybe because you *are* older than dirt? I mean, aren't you almost *thirty*." She nudged his arm and grinned.

"Don't remind me." For some reason, that smile made him happy. Even as a child, she'd always had the demeanor of someone much older and world-weary. He should know — he was now cut from the same cloth.

"So, how's Karen?" she asked.

"She died almost seven months ago."

Of all the damn places to break down, why did it have to be in Pine Bluff? The fates were obviously working against her, even if his wife was dead. *Oh my God, you're such a bitch. The man's wife is dead!*

"My turn to feel awkward. I'm sorry. I saw Mrs. Jordan, but she didn't mention it."

On a whim, she'd stopped to see the woman who'd always been so nice to her when she was a little girl. Years ago, Mrs. Jordan's Sunday school class had provided a refuge from her mother for an hour a week.

Matt stared straight ahead and kept walking.

She remained quiet, realizing how much their lives had changed since they'd last seen each other. Lines creased his brow, and a haunting weariness seemed etched in his face. His dark eyes, which were framed by obscenely long, dark lashes, squinted as the three of them walked toward the sun. She'd always envied those lashes. Her own were almost invisible without mascara.

Years ago, when he was her teen crush, Matt Tyler had been a lanky, well-built, good-looking boy. Today, sweat accented the definition of his biceps and abs — he'd filled out nicely. *Beyond nicely...* From the corner of her eye, she watched a drop of sweat streak down his chest and past the dark trail that probably lead to Nirvana as it disappeared into the waistband of his jeans. Her mouth was dry, and it didn't have a damn thing to do with the heat. The bright sun gave his black, wavy hair an almost blue sheen, and one curl fell rakishly on his forehead, just as she remembered. The five o'clock shadow added to his rugged good looks.

Matt's son had the same deep-rooted sadness in his young face. Was the limp something he'd been born with? Something about his quiet determination touched her.

"Hey, Luke. How about a piggy-back ride?"

Luke shook his head and peered at her from under eyelashes as full as his father's. "Nah, you're too big to carry." A shy grin followed.

Sammie laughed. "Good one! Come here." She swung him to her back, and he held on to her neck as they continued toward the home that had once been her sanctuary. She noticed scars on the boy's leg as she walked but didn't ask about them.

As they rounded the bend in the road, the old Tyler place came in to view. A two-story house with peeling, white clapboard siding, it appeared sadly neglected. One green shutter on a top window hung loose, and several screens were missing. A collection of large oak trees, sweet gums, and pines shaded the entire house and yard.

"You still live here?" she asked.

"Yup."

To the left of the house stood the huge magnolia tree she remembered climbing. When they were kids, she and Matt had used it to sneak in and out of the house. Once it had landed her in the hospital when she'd slipped and broken her arm. Sue Ellen—her mother, who refused to be called by anything else—had been furious and blamed it on her heathenish behavior. She'd hauled her to a doctor to make sure she was still "intact." The experience had been traumatizing for her as an eleven-year-old who only had a rudimentary knowledge of the birds and the bees.

The wraparound porch was now littered with brightly colored toy trucks and cars instead of beer cans. An old, gray-muzzled hound dog slept on his back next to a threadbare couch. As they approached, a cat darted through the yard and up a tree. Thirty yards to the left of the house, beyond the magnolia tree, was the large garage. Various vehicles in different states of repair sat parked all around the building.

Beside her, Matt stopped dead in his tracks, and the muscle in his cheek ticked below his left eye. She remembered that as his tell when angry. A shiny black SUV parked in front of the house looked decidedly out of place on the dusty back road. Even Luke stopped chattering and became still. The car door opened, and an older man wearing a well-cut navy suit stood and crossed his arms as he waited on them.

"Son of a…" Matt hissed. "It's time for the weekly torture." He trudged forward as if walking the green mile.

"What's torture mean, Daddy?"

Matt didn't answer.

As they neared, Sammie recognized Karen's father. His hair was grayer, but his eyes were still arctic blue and piercing. The well-trimmed moustache didn't hide the impatience on his set mouth. An aura of wealth and ruthless power radiated from James Howell. He'd always intimidated the hell out of her and made her uneasy. His eyes narrowed as they approached, and the look he gave Matt was one of unmistakable disgust.

"My, my, Tyler. You must be fairly rolling in money to take a day off from work to go fishing." His gaze shifted to her, and his lip curled as his gaze swept her from head to toe.

"Is there a reason for this visit? You're the one who canceled on seeing Luke at the last minute on Sunday." Matt's voice was politely cool, but Sammie could feel the tension.

"I understand you've been leaving my grandson alone with that miserable excuse you call a father. I heard all about his Memorial Day shenanigans with Gig Johnson. I don't consider an alcoholic an appropriate babysitter for a small child, do you?" Even without raising his voice, the threat was unmistakable.

Sammie held her tongue and watched Matt's jaw harden. Anger radiated off him like the heat from the hood of her dead car.

He let out a slow breath before answering through gritted teeth. "Pa's never hurt Luke, and you know it. Besides, I'm in the backyard, working in the shop."

Luke squirmed on her back, trying to get down, drawing the attention of the angry men and dissipating a little of the tension.

"Hiya, Gramps!" Luke called as she lowered him to the ground.

James's face softened for a brief moment. "Hello, Luke. Grandma sent you some goodies." He opened the car and brought out a plate.

"Thanks!" The boy limped over to James and gave him a quick hug and a kiss. His grandfather ruffled his dark hair.

"Go on in the house, son. I'll be in after your grandfather *leaves*." Matt's voice was low, almost lethal. His dark eyes locked with his father-in-law's icy stare. The adults remained silent until Luke disappeared into the house.

Mr. Howell's eyes snapped with anger. "I'm warning you, Tyler. I don't like you or your white trash father any better today than I did the day you married Karen. I've been watching you. Lila and I are preparing to sue for custody, and believe me, *I'll win*. A lot could happen to an unsupervised child, and you know it. You were a pitiful a husband, and you're no better as a single father."

The hatred on Mr. Howell's face raised the hair on the back of Sammie's neck. Matt flinched and paled. He dropped the basket and fishing poles. She stepped back, wondering if he was going to throw a punch. She fingered her bracelets, counting.

"I'll see you in *hell* before I let *my* son go live with *you*. Now get off my property," Matt snarled as his fists balled.

"Whose property? I believe *my* bank holds the mortgage on this dump. Everyone knows your father's a sot. As a matter of fact, I think I'll call my lawyer to see about gaining temporary custody of my grandson while the case is prepared for permanent guardianship. Lila and I can give him more than you'll ever be able to as a two-bit mechanic."

Beside her, Matt's fists released and re-clenched. Heart pounding, she felt cold and clammy. Something had to de-escalate the situation; someone needed to step in and stop them before the altercation became physical.

"Uh, excuse me, Mr. Howell?"

Both men turned toward her, looking surprised by the interruption, as if they hadn't remembered she was there. Swallowing the nervousness lodged in her throat, she pasted on a brave smile and held out her hand.

"Hi, I'm Sammie, er, Samantha Morgan. I'm not sure if you remember me, but I'm Matt's fiancée. Luke's gonna be just fine; I'll be here to take care of him and Pa. You ain't got nothin' to worry about."

As soon as the lie left her mouth, she regretted it. Matt's mouth dropped, and he stared at her as if she'd sprouted horns. His father-in-law looked ready to stroke.

Mr. Howell jabbed a finger into Matt's chest. "Seven months after my daughter's death and you're remarrying? I *knew* it! Were you unfaithful to my Karen with this woman?"

Matt's face turned red and his eyes narrowed as he pushed the offensive finger away. Sammie stepped between them before Matt did something he'd regret.

"Now hold on one second, that's just downright offensive," she said. "I may've jumped the gun saying fiancée. I mean, I'm just so excited to be back after all these years, and well, a girl can dream, ya know? Nothing's set in stone yet. Matt and I reconnected online, and we've been talking for a few months. My mother died, and I was lonely, and um, he was, too." She added quickly, "He's told me how much he's missed Karen…And I'm real sorry, about, er, everything…" Her voice trailed off.

She reached over and took Matt's hand. "I came here to meet Luke and see if we want to move forward in our relationship. Now I realize this has come as a total surprise, and I reckon that's why you're throwing out these threats. But you *know* Matt loved Karen; they were crazy in love. Everyone in this county knew it. Not meaning any disrespect, sir, but your daughter is dead. And life moves on. Don't you want your grandson to have love and joy back in his life? I —"

"How dare you, you little bitch!"

Instinctively, she stepped back. Matt moved toward Mr. Howell, but she yanked his hand, stopping him. He was practically pawing the ground like a bull ready to charge.

She straightened her shoulders. "Hey, you! I ain't gonna tell you again. Watch your mouth! I know this is a shock, but you need to keep a civil tongue in your head, or I'll…I'll sue you for slander. Come on, Matt. Let's go get that ice cream. I need to get out of the sun before I burn like a crispy critter."

Mr. Howell looked at her as if she was a she-devil. She didn't dare look at Matt and dug her nails into his arm, silently counting the cars parked near the garage.

Mr. Howell straightened the cuff on his jacket and sneered. "We'll discuss this later. I'd love to find out more about this…whirlwind *romance*."

Pulling a business card from his wallet, he handed it to her. She stuck it in her back pocket, not knowing what else to do with it. *Are the black spots in my vision from the heat or the enormity of the whopper I just told?*

Mr. Howell glared at Matt as he got back in his car. "This isn't over, Tyler..." The door slammed, and he drove away, spraying gravel in his wake.

"Lawd, he's mean as a rattlesnake."

Hands on his hips, Matt turned toward her, eyes blazing. "What the hell, Sam?"

"*Sammie*. He's an asshole and always has been; some things never change. I just said the first thing that popped into my head. It sure shut him up. Did you see the look on his face? He was gobsmacked! You should be thanking me."

"Thanking you? How the hell am I going to get out of this? James is tenacious and still wants to pay me back for marrying his precious daughter. And you need to watch your language around Luke."

"Excuse me? First off, Luke's in the house, and second, you just said hell, Tyler. *Twice*."

He blew out a deep breath, ruffling the curl on his forehead. "Sorry. You're right. I'm usually pretty good at curbing the language. Luke's a sponge and repeats everything."

"Look, I know Mr. Howell's a jerk, but he seemed genuinely happy to see his grandson. And his grandmother baked him some goodies—"

"Mae baked."

"What?"

"Lila probably doesn't even know how to operate the oven. Their housekeeper baked the goodies."

"Fine. Whatever. My point is, the Howells are probably still grieving, like you are. I can't even imagine..." She stopped before she made things worse and took a breath. "I'm sorry about the fib." She chewed her bottom lip and tapped each finger to her thumb over and over as she waited for his reaction.

Matt stared at the ground, toeing a rock with his boot, not saying a word.

"Look, tomorrow we'll just say we weren't compatible or had a huge fight and break up. Or..."

Matt's brows knit together. "Or?"

"I don't have money to pay to have my car fixed. All I've got in this world is a few hundred dollars. I need a job. Maybe we could work out some sort of trade for my car repair?"

"I don't know." He pinched the bridge of his nose.

"How did Karen, um, you know…"

"Car accident last November, along with our oldest, Elizabeth."

Sammie blinked back tears. Last time she'd seen Matt, he'd been excited because Karen was pregnant. He'd talked about eloping… And now that child was dead, too?

Matt's face had gone blank. He nodded toward the house. "Luke was in the car as well. He was hospitalized for months, went through a couple of surgeries, and then had rehab. I know you noticed the limp." His shoulders slumped, and he closed his eyes. When he opened them, she could barely keep her eyes on the pain she saw there. "He's all I have left. My boy is my world…" His voice trailed off, broken. "I can't lose him."

Sammie nodded, not knowing what to say or how to express her sympathy, much less deal with her tinge of jealousy for a dead woman. *Will anyone ever love me like that?*

The front door opened, and Luke hollered, "Daddy, can I have that ice cream now?" He swung around the front porch column.

Matt's eyes softened. "The question is *may I*, and yes you may. Come on, Sam, I owe you an ice cream cone. We'll figure something out."

Chapter
TWO

As they walked through the front door, Sam gasped behind him. For the first time in months, Matt truly looked at his home. Heat crept up the back of his neck and into his cheeks.

After his father's stroke, he and Luke had moved in, and neither he nor Pa had done much in the way of housekeeping since. Kicking toys out of the way, he sighed as they surveyed the living area. In front of them were two old, brown recliners and a dingy, tan upholstered couch with hideous pheasants on it. To the right of the fireplace was an aging television. Fast-food wrappers, empty glasses, and Luke's toys were scattered everywhere.

He motioned toward the kitchen. It had a black-and-white tile floor, although it was difficult to tell which tiles had once been white due to the black scuff marks. The groceries he'd bought two days ago were on the countertop. The open cabinets revealed a disorderly mess. Probably the only thing keeping the health department away were the clean dishes stacked haphazardly in the drainer.

Instead of sitting in a chair, Luke sat with the carton of ice cream *on* the kitchen table, making a mess.

I wouldn't blame Sam if she left right now. Between working, going to school, and caring for Luke and Pa, he barely had time for breathing, much less housekeeping. He found the cones behind the open cereal box by the sink.

"Son, couldn't you have waited on me?" Matt turned to Sam and added, "Please excuse the mess. Obviously, we weren't expecting company."

"Bachelor pad, I take it?" She grinned.

"I guess you could call it that. After the accident, Pa had a stroke. I sold my home, and Luke and I moved in here—it just made sense with the mounting bills. Luke, run and see if Pa wants some ice cream."

"Okay." Luke climbed off the table and limped away.

"I always loved this house," she murmured. "About my car—"

"Not now," he interrupted.

"But I can't pay for a transmission. Could we work out a deal? Like, I pretend to be your fiancée, and I'll get this place in shape as a tradeoff for fixing my car?" Her fingers tapped one by one on her hips. "P-Please?"

The thought of remarrying made his chest ache. And her look of desperation matched the way he felt: cornered. *Aren't we a pair?* He heard Luke talking with Pa in the other room.

"We'll discuss this later, Sam. I need time to think. Plus, I'm sure you remember Pa. He's more cantankerous than ever and not easy to live with. But at the very least, you can stay in the guest room upstairs tonight."

Immediately he wanted to kick himself. *I'm a dead man if James finds out she's staying here...But I can't just throw her out.* He prayed Pa would be on his best behavior and wondered how he was going to explain all of this; his father wasn't stupid.

Luke walked back into the kitchen, grinning. "Guess what?"

"What?"

"Pa's coming to meet Sammie."

Matt's eyes widened. Aside from his *shenanigans* with his best friend and former bootlegging partner on Memorial Day, Pa hadn't been out of his room in well over two weeks. So much for having time to come up with a plausible story and caution Pa to act respectable—or maybe even take a bath. He scooped ice cream onto a cone and handed it to Luke.

Dear God, at least let him be sober.

Sammie recognized Leroy Tyler as he slowly made his way into the kitchen using a walker, but she found it incredibly sad to see how much he'd deteriorated. His long, white hair was combed straight back, and he now sported a full white beard, yellowed with tobacco and dotted with food crumbs. His clothes were stained, and there was a button missing from his brown plaid shirt. He dragged his right foot when he walked, and the right side of his face appeared drawn.

Still, the same intense, dark eyes he'd passed down to Matt and Luke stared at her with frank curiosity.

The old man patted Luke's head before barking, "Move outta my way, brat."

"Okay, Pa." Grinning, Luke pulled a chair out for his grandfather. He didn't seem the least bit fazed by the man's brusqueness and began eating the ice cream cone Matt had handed him.

Collapsing with a grunt, Leroy asked her, "Do I know you?"

"Yes, sir. I'm Sammie Morgan, Sue Ellen and Petey Sam's daughter." She held out her hand. His grip was weak when he took it. Up close, she could smell the distinct odor of beer on the old man's breath.

"What the hell kind of name is Sammie for a grown-ass woman?"

Sammie smiled. Pa had always spoken his mind, and she respected that in a person. "Well, I used to go by Sam. Don't you remember me? I lived here about twelve years ago. You taught me how to drive a straight shift when I was underage."

"Of course I remember you. Don't be impudent, young lady. You're that redheaded hellion Matt used to run around with. You two, along with that Dylan McAthie, were always getting into trouble and fishing when Matt should've been working. You ever learn not to ride the damn clutch, girl?" Pa raised the eyebrow not affected by his stroke.

"Nope, 'fraid not," Sammie confessed.

"Figures! Women drivers…" He looked her over once again. "You're certainly not as scrawny as you used to be. What are you doing back in this godforsaken place? You ain't hidin' from the law, are you? Sherriff Sanford's a bloodhound. He'll find you, and I ain't having it. I'm halfway respectable these days."

Matt snorted and rolled his eyes as he handed her an ice cream cone.

She laughed, shaking her head. "No, sir. Not since I got pulled over driving your truck when I was fourteen. My car broke down just a piece down the road. I hear you're still the meanest old coot in the county."

She ate her ice cream, ready for anything the old man could throw at her. He'd always been gruff, but he'd been a huge part of her past, too. One time, he'd found her crying in the woods and had sat down beside her. He hadn't said a word, just stayed by her side and let her cry it out.

"Damn straight, I am." Pa's dark eyes twinkled.

Sammie laughed. The old man had always liked her, although he'd probably die before admitting it. She couldn't count the times he'd welcomed her into his home when she'd sought refuge from her own. He never questioned why she was there, just yelled at her and fed her like she was his own. He motioned for her to sit next to him.

Luke stood on one of the dining room chairs, grinning. Chocolate ice cream lined his upper lip. "Look, Sammie! I have a moustache like that *goddamned sonofabitch Howell.*" His voice was a dead-on impersonation of his grandfather's.

Sammie bit her lip to check her laughter, but Pa let loose cackling. "Good one, boy!"

Matt threw the ice scream scoop down. "Lukas Matthew Tyler!"

Luke jumped, and his ice cream plopped onto the floor. Grabbing him by the arm, Matt marched him to the sink where he washed his mouth out with dish detergent.

"I'm sorry, Daddy! Stop!" Luke gagged and sobbed. Matt stopped and gave him a glass of water to rinse. He rubbed Luke's back and helped him dry his face. When he was done, he squatted down, eye level with the boy.

"We've had this conversation before. I don't *ever* want to hear you use language like that again. *Do you understand me?*"

"Pa does," Luke replied, his lower lip trembling. "You do, too… sometimes."

No, no, no, don't argue, just take it and stay quiet! Sammie started counting the visible tiles on the floor.

"What have I told you about talking back to me?" Clearly exasperated, Matt scrubbed his face with one hand. "Look, Pa and I are adults. It doesn't make it any better, but I promise we're going to try harder to not use bad language. Aren't we, Pa?" Matt glared at his father.

"Speak for yourself." Leroy mumbled.

Matt refocused his attention on his son. "Regardless, *you're not* to use language like that, or back-talk me. Do you understand? Next time you cuss or back-talk, you'll be spanked."

Luke nodded, tears in his eyes.

"Now, go to your room."

"I hate you. Mommy wouldn't have done this!" Luke wasted no time limping out of the kitchen.

"Your mother didn't put up with bad language!" Matt yelled back.

He hung his head, looking beat down and tired. He rose and placed his hands on the kitchen counter, taking several deep breaths with his back to his father.

Sammie sat motionless as her ice cream melted down her fingers. Confrontations unnerved her. She'd grown up doing anything in her power to avoid them with her mother.

Matt spun around and walked over to Pa. The tic in his cheek signaled the depth of his anger. "How many times have I told you to watch your mouth in front of Luke, old man? I'll not have him talking like white trash. Do you hear me?"

Leroy cocked his head to one side, looking him square in the eyes. "You shouldn't have punished the boy for speaking the truth. Howell *is* a goddamned sonofabitch."

Sammie remained as still as possible so as not to draw attention.

Matt threw up his hands. "That's not the point, and you know it. I'm warning you. I tolerate your drinking behind your closed bedroom door, but I will *not* have you interfering with the way I raise my son. If this continues, we're leaving." He stomped out the back door, slamming it behind him.

Sammie started cleaning up the ice cream mess and glanced at the old man.

Pa's shoulders sagged. He traced a stain on the tablecloth with his finger, looking tired and defeated.

"I agree with *you*," she said. "Mr. Howell is a hateful old sonofabitch."

Leroy smiled, took her hand, and squeezed it. On impulse, she kissed his forehead.

Matt took out his cell phone and called his buddy to come tow Sam's car. After he hung up, he thumbed through the photos of his family. It was masochistic, but he did it every day—as if Karen could somehow give him the answers he sought.

She never did.

Putting the phone away, he sat at his workbench, tinkering with one of Luke's toys that needed a new screw. While he was embarrassed that Sammie had witnessed Luke acting out, he was more upset with himself for losing his shit. *I shouldn't have been so rough on him. All he did was repeat what he's heard Pa say. And they're both right. James is a sonofabitch.*

Luke's imitation of Pa had been kind of funny, but he was trying his damnedest to raise Luke right. The kid already had the Tyler name going against him. And what if Luke said something like that in front of his in-laws?

From day one, Matt had hated James Howell. But after his children were born, he'd attempted to keep his opinion to himself. Even Karen's feelings for her father had been bipolar. When they found out she was pregnant, she'd fought her father to marry him, but she couldn't seem to cut the ties from being Daddy's little princess, often accepting extravagant gifts from her father despite her husband's protests. It was emasculating never to be able to afford the things she wanted.

Guilt washed over him. *Who am I to talk?* Elizabeth had been his little girl, and he'd spoiled her to the best of his ability.

Dammit, Karen, this isn't fair. I shouldn't be doing this alone. You weren't supposed to leave me...

James's threat to take Luke wasn't new, and it was his greatest fear. Would the Howells ever stop? *If I lose Luke, I might as well give up...* And Sam's bald-faced lie only complicated things.

Why God? Why me? Are you even listening?

Probably not. Truth be told, he hadn't actually prayed since the night of the accident. He'd just been informed Karen was dead, and

Elizabeth lay dying in his arms. His son had been in the next room, fighting for his life. Today, he didn't even know if he believed in God anymore, despite going through the motions of attending church. The only reason he went was to keep up the façade of having his shit together, which was laughable.

He threw the screwdriver across the garage. It stuck to the wall like an arrow in a bullseye. He didn't buy the religious view that one shouldn't question the Almighty. He had plenty of questions. Starting with how the hell do you raise a kid alone? When your wife dies, the funeral home should hand out a manual on how to be a single dad.

Matt scrubbed his face. He couldn't fail Luke. He wanted to be a good role model, not like Pa, who was an impossible drunk and had been ever since Mama died.

Pa had been twenty-five years older than his mother when they'd married. The day of Matt's seventh birthday, she'd died of lymphoma at twenty-four. After that, Pa fell apart and gave up everything — except boozing — leaving him to pretty much raise himself. He'd been "that white trash Tyler boy" and run wild like a feral dog.

Things had finally changed after he met and married Karen. Knowing he was soon to be a father, he'd reassessed his life, settled down, and worked hard to improve himself. He'd built up his business and taken care of his family. When Luke was three, he'd started online and night classes with the goal of being a mechanical engineer.

There was no way he'd allow Pa to pull him back down into the gutter. He refused to give James Howell any ammunition to take his son from him.

Sam's proclamation that they were engaged, or at least involved, had shut James up, but for how long? Prying the screwdriver out of the wall, he felt physically sick as the weight of her words looped in his brain.

Sammie placed her purse on the nightstand and smiled. This was the same room she'd slept in whenever she'd come here as a kid. She'd always loved the old-fashioned four-poster bed.

The room had two large windows, but the view was obstructed by the magnolia tree. The wallpaper was faded, and yellowed eyelet curtains on the windows gave the room a tired, sad feeling. At least it was clean and uncluttered, if a little dusty. She flipped on the window air conditioner and stood in front of it, allowing the cool air to blow over her hot, sticky skin. It hummed in a soothing manner.

Luke appeared in the doorway, sniffling. On impulse, she knelt and hugged the little boy, and to her surprise, he clung to her neck.

"You're okay. Your Daddy loves you. You know that, right?"

He nodded in her neck. "Lots and lots. I'm sorry I said that."

"I know you are. And when he comes back inside, you tell him. And talk about it, okay?"

"Okay." Pulling away, he ran a finger over her rings. "Those are pretty. Are you rich?"

She laughed. "Hardly." She looked over the moonstone and turquoise rings. Sue Ellen had never allowed her to wear jewelry, thinking it sinful. "I think they're pretty, too. They make me happy."

A stray tear slipped down his still-flushed cheek. "Pa says I need to go take a nap. I don't want to. Naps are for babies."

"Why don't you lie down with me? We can pretend to nap."

"How do you do that?"

"It's super easy. We close our eyes and think good thoughts for a few minutes."

"Okay!" His eyes lit up.

After they slipped off their shoes, she patted the bed. He hopped on it and was sound asleep within a couple of minutes. Sammie placed their shoes in a line by the bed. Exhausted, she stretched out beside the now-sleeping boy to contemplate the strange turn of events. He looked so much like Matt it was almost heartbreaking.

She wondered how long it would take Matt to figure out if he could fix her car. Worrying about her future, she tapped her fingers together, lulling herself to sleep.

Chapter Three

An hour later, freshly showered, Matt found Luke awake, though curled up in bed with Sam, who was sound asleep. Quietly placing the urn, her suitcase, and a guitar case down in the bedroom, he put his finger to his lips and motioned Luke to come with him.

Outside the guest bedroom he said, "Luke, I'm sorry for getting so upset with you earlier. You were right. I use words I shouldn't."

"It's okay, Daddy. I'm sorry, too."

How he wished he could forgive as easily as his son. "Why don't you take a bath to get the ice cream off?"

Luke nodded, still agreeable, and went for a splash—literally—in the tub.

After Luke was clean and dressed, he asked, "Can we FaceTime Winston?"

Matt chuckled. "Don't you mean Aunt Eugenia? I mean *Jinx?*"

"Her too. She lets Winston FaceTime. He licks the screen. I can tell her I saw Gramps today."

"She may be in class, but we can try." Matt pulled his phone out. His sister-in-law answered on the first ring.

"Hey, Matt. What's up?"

"Someone wants to talk to Winston," he replied, laughing as he handed the phone to Luke.

"Hi, Luke. How are you?" Jinx whistled and her huge mastiff joined her on the screen.

"Winston!" Luke laughed and waved.

As Luke and Jinx chatted, Matt picked up the dirty clothes in the boy's room.

"Sammie's visiting us, but she's still asleep—"

"Who?" Jinx asked as Matt grabbed the phone.

"Hey, Jinx. Sorry to cut this short, but we're about to head out for some supper. Talk soon?"

"Sure. I have to get ready for work anyway. Bye!"

Thankful to have dodged that conversation, he listened to his son babble about Sammie as they walked downstairs. He held hope that his son's infatuation with her would be enough to get him to agree to a trip into town to grab a pizza and some groceries. Tonight, after Luke was in bed, he and Sam would talk. Settling Luke in front of the television, he went back upstairs and rapped on her open door. No answer.

"Sam?" Peeking in, he found her still sleeping. Luke was right, her bellybutton ring was pretty. "Wake up, Sammie." He spoke gently and gave her arm a little shake.

She sat straight up, clearly startled.

"Sorry. I didn't mean to frighten you."

"Geezus, Matt. You scared the crap out of me." Her hand trembled as she pushed a strand of copper hair behind her ear.

"I came to see if you wanted to go grab a pizza with us. I brought your suitcase and guitar up earlier. I'll take a look at your car tomorrow; it's been towed to the garage." He pointed at the urn now on her dresser. "I didn't know…er, I, uh, put your mom there."

Sammie giggled. "I'm sure she's quite comfy. I need a few minutes to get ready."

"Luke and I will be downstairs. Take your time. We're in no hurry." Matt smiled and left, closing the door.

Sammie hung up her phone, disappointed. Her friend Ashley was broke and getting married. She'd sounded a little relieved that Sammie wouldn't be coming to Nashville. There'd be no loan from her.

She hurried to ready herself for the evening. When she was sixteen, if Matt Tyler had asked her to go eat pizza, she would have died a thousand happy deaths. Her crush had always considered her nothing but a friend, a fishing buddy, one of the guys. Now she was going on a pseudo-date with him because his wife was dead. Life sure twisted and turned in some strange directions. In less than five minutes, she sped down the stairs with her hair pulled back in a low knot at her neck.

"Sammie's here!" Luke clapped. Judging by his appearance, he'd dressed himself.

"Come here. Look at these buttons, silly boy." Sammie re-buttoned his blue plaid shirt and straightened the cuffs on his shorts, again noting the long, pink scars. "There, that looks better. Are your hands clean?"

Luke held up his hands for inspection. "Now do Daddy."

She turned and looked at Matt. Dressed in a pair of blue jeans and a white oxford shirt with the sleeves rolled up, he looked fine. *More than fine.* He'd cleaned up the scruff on his face but left enough to make her wonder what it would feel like against her neck. Standing with his hands in his pockets, he met her gaze with a sheepish smile. He was the most gorgeous man she'd ever known.

"Daddy's buttons are okay," she managed to croak.

"Are you ready to go?"

She nodded and followed Matt to the front door.

"We'll be back in a few hours, Pa."

Leroy grunted an acknowledgment from his bedroom.

"Pa doesn't want to go with us?"

"No, he doesn't leave the house much. He said he just wanted a bowl of cereal for dinner, but it'll more than likely end up being a *liquid* supper, if you know what I mean."

Luke dragged his feet, tugging on his father's hand.

"Stop, Luke."

The closer they got to the car, the more Luke struggled. "No, Daddy." He intensified his efforts to be free when Matt opened the back door.

"Get in the car, please." Matt's voice was calm, but firm.

Luke twisted and turned, trying to get loose. Matt picked him up and sat him on top of the car to peer into his tear-filled eyes.

He spoke soothingly, rubbing his leg. "You can do this, son. Don't you want to go eat with us? We're not going to the doctor, I promise."

Luke shook his head and clamored to get off the car.

"I thought you wanted pizza for supper? You don't want to stay home with Pa and eat boring old cereal, do you? Sharing a pizza with Sammie will be a lot more fun. Please come with us."

Luke cast a longing look at her but shook his head no. A tear tracked down his cheek.

Matt sighed and took him in his arms and hugged him. "Okay, you don't have to go, but we'll miss you." He kissed his forehead and wiped away his tears.

Sammie rubbed the boy's back. "What's your favorite pizza, Luke?"

"P-Pepperoni."

"Are you sure you won't go with us?"

Matt sighed and muttered, "God, I hope James doesn't find out Luke's with Pa alone, again."

"I could stay if you want me to," Sammie offered.

"No, I'll risk it. We'll go into Harrisville instead of Pine Bluff. I don't feel like explaining anything to the busybodies of this small town, and it will give us time to talk. We need to figure out what we're going to do, and we won't be gone that long."

Remaining silent, Luke tucked his head in his father's neck as Matt walked him back to the house. He left him on the porch as he went inside to talk to Pa.

Luke sat next to the old hound dog and picked up one of his trucks. The kid looked like he'd lost his best friend, and it tugged at her heart.

"What's your dog's name? Are you sure you won't go with us?" she asked, sitting next to him.

He shook his head no, not making eye contact. "This is Rufus."

"Hey, Rufus." She scratched the dog's head. "Well, I guess we'll have to pick the pizza up and bring it back here to eat. And maybe next time you'll feel like going."

Hope brightened Luke's face.

Opening the front door, Matt said, "Come on in, son. Pa doesn't feel like sitting outside in the heat."

After Luke was settled, Matt walked her back to the car and opened the door for her.

"Well, ain't you a gentleman. You don't have to stand on ceremony for me, Tyler," she commented, secretly pleased.

It was just like those old movies Sue Ellen used to like. She couldn't remember anyone ever doing this for her.

"Habit."

Karen was so lucky.

He didn't speak for a full minute as he drove. "I go through this every day. Luke hasn't willingly ridden in an automobile since the accident. The day he was discharged from the rehab center, the drive upset him so much he threw up on the way home. I've tried getting him to ride just to the end of Tyler Road, or to visit his grandparents, but he yells the entire way. Twice, I forced him to go to church, and he screamed and carried on like he was possessed. And it didn't let up once we arrived. I damn near lost my religion dealing with him. When I take him to the doctor, he's so hysterical by the time we get there it's a nightmare."

"I'm sorry. I'm sure it's understandable with the accident and all." She took a deep breath before continuing, feeling uneasy. "Look, I misspoke with Mr. Howell, and I apologize. Maybe you could loan me a car when we get back. I'll stay at the motel and find a job…"

"You're not staying at the no-tell motel. I'm pretty sure they rent by the hour and have bedbugs. Where were you headed before you broke down?"

"I wanted a change of scenery after Sue Ellen passed. I was headed to Nashville. I've never lived in a big city. My dream job would be to work at the Grand Ole Opry. I know it sounds silly, but I'm realistic enough to know I'll more than likely end up flippin' burgers." She didn't mention it was her self-imposed therapy to step a little out of her comfort zone of lists and detailed plans.

"Dreams are never silly. Sometimes it's the execution that proves difficult. Or they have to change due to circumstances." Matt sighed. "What've you been up to since you moved away? School? Work? Married?"

"No school. I was a stripper for a New York minute, but I fell swirling around the pole, knocked some dude to the floor, and he threatened to sue, so I was fired."

The car swerved, and Matt glanced over at her. "What? I mean, not that there's anything wrong with being a stripper—"

She laughed. "Geeze, Tyler, I'm joking. Really? Me? A stripper? I mean, look at me. They'd pay me to put my clothes back on. I've worked at a few different jobs. Never married. Sue Ellen and I came back to Pine Bluff once, after I turned eighteen. She added me to her lock box at the bank, and we visited Daddy's grave. It was a quick visit because she kinda fell apart seeing the tombstone." She hushed and squirmed under Matt's brief perusal.

His sunglasses prevented her from seeing his eyes. "You could strip. I mean, not that I think you should be a stripper, unless that's what you want. I don't think jobs like that come with much security…" An awkward silence filled the car, and his ears turned red. "I wish you'd called me when you came in to town."

She shrugged. "It wasn't like it was a social visit. And I didn't imagine Karen would've invited me to dinner or anything. You know, now that I think about it, I've got a key somewhere in the few belongings I kept of my mother's. I don't even know what's in that bank box. There's no telling with Sue Ellen. Maybe it's the bones of her perceived enemies. She didn't have any friends."

He didn't respond to her weak attempt at a joke.

Sammie bit her lip. "You okay? You used to have more of a sense of humor."

He sighed. "I haven't had much to laugh about for…well, forever. James has tried every way possible to get rid of me short of hiring a hit man. And I wouldn't even put that past him. I can't lose Luke. But I'm going to be honest here. I've never considered marrying again."

She flicked her thumbnails together. "Well, of course not. I mean, you and Karen were a love match written in the stars or whatever. It wasn't like y'all swiped left or right, whichever it is on that dating app. Again, I'm sorry I lied. It was just the first thing that popped into my head to stop him from being so hateful. Mr. Hoity-Toity has always thought his shit didn't stink. It was also a low blow to hold your mortgage over your head. It's not right. He's just plain ol' mean and spiteful."

"An asshole for sure."

She stared out the window at the passing scenery. "One time, I remember going to the Thanksgiving dinner your church held for the poor. He and Mrs. Howell were particularly condescending toward me and Sue Ellen. Karen didn't even speak. She never had much to do with me; she was one of the popular, rich lake kids. Her younger sister, Eugenia, was okay. She tried talking to me, but her mother intervened. I got the sense they probably all went home and bathed after volunteering. It seemed more for show, whereas I always believed Mrs. Jordan did things because she cared. You know what I mean?"

Matt nodded, keeping his eyes on the road. "Eugenia goes by Jinx now. She touches base with Luke every few weeks. He loves her dog, Winston."

"Sometimes Sue Ellen would go to the church for our clothes. I hated when she'd come home with Karen's hand-me-downs...They were pretty, but it was embarrassing to wear them to school. Anyway, I don't like being beholden. There's always strings attached."

"I never realized. I'm sorry. And you're right; with the Howells there are always strings attached."

He didn't say anything else, and out of habit, she kept her mouth shut, counting telephone poles. They drove to Harrisville and shopped for a few groceries and cleaning supplies before picking up their takeout order.

The smell of hot pizza filled the car as they passed the seedy "no-tell motel," as Matt called it, on the way home. She was relieved she wouldn't have to stay there. A quarter of a mile down the road, The Roadside Tavern caught her attention. It hadn't changed much at all—still a dive bar. The sign out front said *Karaoke Night Thursdays No Cover*. It had been ages since she sang karaoke. But right now, she had more pressing issues.

"Did you have time to check out my car?"

"Not completely, but honestly, I wouldn't hold out much hope. I'm ninety-nine percent sure it just needs to be scrapped."

She turned and faced Matt, unable to hold her tongue any longer. Living without a plan was not the way she wanted to start her new life. With her car out of commission, she felt on the precipice of being out of control, which could lead to trouble. Uncertainty was her old way of life. She'd lived with a mom whose mental health was a pendulum; all she wanted now was an uncomplicated, simple life.

"Shit," she said. "I don't know what to do. I tried to borrow some money from my friend in Nashville, but she's flat broke. She's getting married in a few weeks." She sighed and whispered, more to herself than anyone, "What am I going to do?"

"I don't know what to tell you. I mean, marriage—that's a little extreme." He shuddered.

"It wasn't exactly in my plans to break down and have to beg an old friend to get married either," she snapped. "But I ain't got a pot to piss in, and I don't know what I'm going to do." Her old insecurities roared through her head. Looking out the window, she began counting fence posts. Dammit, she hadn't counted this much since Sue Ellen died.

"Hey, I know that. And you didn't beg me to get married. I'm sorry. I've just been mulling things over in my head, trying to find a solution to both of our problems. So, you have no family to help you out? Any other friends?"

She snorted. "Nope. We moved from Pine Bluff about a month after I last saw you, one step ahead of the creditors. We moved ten more times after that. I dropped out of school. I did odd jobs here and there before Sue Ellen got sick and died. And here I am, stuck with no money and a vehicle that ain't worth fixin'. Just my damn luck." She rubbed her brow. "Enough about me. Tell me about you and what you've been up to."

"Let's see…I was an irresponsible teenager and got my girlfriend pregnant. You moved without letting me know, which kind of hurt, because we were buddies. Karen and I married. Her parents hated me. Elizabeth was born. Her parents still hated me. My son was born, and a few years later I started taking college classes at night. The Howells continued to hate me. Karen and Elizabeth died, and a piece of me died, too. And her parents still hate me—the end. It wasn't the story I envisioned for my life, but there it is." He glanced at her. "So here we are, full circle, back to you and me."

Sammie's mouth dropped open, and her nails dug into her palms. "Excuse me?"

"Like I said, I've been thinking. You may have bought me some time. We can, as you said, pretend to be a couple until I can find you a reliable, decent used car, and then we'll break up."

She laughed. "I dunno. The more I think about it, the crazier it sounds. I promise, I don't usually do stuff without thinking it through. I just hated seeing that man go after you. I mean, I could get your house clean and look after your son while you're working, but that may not solve your problem."

She sighed, fingering her bracelets. "Anyway, what's your major?"

"Mechanical engineering."

"You're shitting me." Matt Tyler had cut school more than anyone she'd ever known, including herself. "Sorry, that was rude," she added.

Matt laughed. "I know. It shocks a lot of people. Fatherhood changed me, made me settle down and take a good hard look at myself. What do you do for fun?"

"Karaoke," she answered.

"Are you good at it?"

"Tolerable, I guess. What do you do to blow off steam?"

"Torment redheads with twenty questions."

Sammie laughed, and Matt flashed the smile that had melted her heart so many years ago. He pulled into the driveway, and Luke threw open the front door, waving excitedly. He jumped up and down as she pulled the pizza from the backseat. With groceries in hand, Matt headed toward the house.

"You're home! What took y'all so long?" Luke demanded.

"Hey, Matt? Bring out some drinks and napkins, okay?" She placed the pizza on the hood of the car. "Luke, why don't you ask Pa if he wants a slice?"

"Okay." He scurried back inside, pushing his father out of the way in his hurry.

Matt looked at her, puzzled.

"It's a beautiful evening. I thought we'd eat outside." She nodded toward the pizza. "We can sit *on* the *car*."

"Ah, gotcha. Good idea." He grinned before heading inside.

The front door slammed open, and Luke flew down steps but stopped short in front of the car. "Pa doesn't want any pizza. Ain't ya gonna bring it in the house, Sammie?" He eyed her suspiciously as Matt walked past him with two cans, a juice box, and a roll of paper towels.

"Aren't. Don't say ain't—your mother hated that word," Matt corrected as he handed Luke his drink.

The boy refused to move closer to the car, and distrust filled his dark eyes.

"Uh-oh. You're getting the infamous stink eye, Sammie." Matt handed her a Coke and lifted her onto the hood of the car. Grinning, he stood between her legs, his hands still on her waist.

"S-Stink eye?" The feel of his hands on her waist made it hard to breathe.

Matt's demeanor was solemn, but his eyes crinkled at the corners. "Also known as the evil eye. It's known to slay dragons and zap fathers within seconds. Are girls named Sammie immune to it?"

"Must be. It's the power of the red hair."

Matt sat on the hood of the car next to her. Taking a slice of pizza, he smiled and offered some to Luke. "Want a slice?"

The boy nodded and took a small step forward. He stopped three feet from the car and glared at his father, who fell back on the hood.

"I've been zapped by the dreaded stink eye!" Matt moaned.

Luke's mouth twitched.

"Mmmm, pepperoni pizza is my favorite." Sammie took a bite, licking her lips. Holding out her hands to Luke, she leaned forward and offered, "Sit in my lap and have a slice?"

His eyes filled with tears, and his throat bobbled several times. Shaking, he finally took three slow steps toward Sammie, then one step back. She waited patiently, smiling at him. At last he took two tiny steps toward her and raised his arms. Sammie lifted him into her lap, hugging him close.

"You're such a brave boy," she murmured against his dark waves, handing him a slice of pizza. He curled into her, his head resting against her heart, his feet tucked up close to his chest, so nothing touched the car. She kept her arms wrapped around him as he ate and sipped on his juice. She pretended not to see Matt wiping his eyes on his shirtsleeve.

After finishing the pizza, she and Luke attempted to catch fireflies as Matt watched from the front porch.

"It's getting late. Bedtime. No argument, son."

"Ooo-kay." Luke drew the word out but followed his father inside.

After a moment, Sammie trailed after them and went to the guest room to unpack.

As she worked, she could hear Luke chattering away and giggling as he got ready for bed.

"Son! We have company. You can't be running around butt-naked," Matt shouted.

Luke streaked into her room, waving his pajamas above his head. "Come with me, Sammie!"

Laughing at his silliness, she followed him to his room.

The house phone rang. Downstairs Pa shouted, "Matt! It's *he* who shall not be named."

Matt took the call from his bedroom. After a moment his voice rose, and he slammed the door.

"Must be Gramps," Luke whispered. Wise, sad eyes gazed into hers. "When Gramps and Grandma come visit, they go to Daddy's shop with him and yell at each other."

"Sometimes adults do that. It don't make it right, though."

Toys were scattered everywhere, and his sheets were sticky from a spilled juice box. The mess made her skin crawl. On his dresser were clean sheets. Sammie stripped and remade the bed.

He giggled and jumped between the fresh sheets. "This feels good, Sammie!"

"Tomorrow we're going to clean this pigsty, little piggy."

"Oink, oink! Will you read me a story?"

Sammie hesitated. Reading was not her strong suit. "Um, doesn't your daddy do that?"

"Sometimes." His face fell. "Mommy used to read to me. Lizbeth did, too."

At the mention of his mother, Sammie looked around and realized there were no pictures of Karen or his older sister. It was as if his toys had simply been dumped in Matt's old bedroom. Spying one of her old favorite books on the floor, she picked it up and started reading, only tripping every now and then on a word. Luke's eyes grew heavy, and he was out before she finished the story.

When she finished, Matt leaned against the doorframe, arms folded, watching her. He looked tired and pensive. She wondered for a moment if she'd done something wrong. Turning off the bedside lamp, she followed him into the hall, closing the door behind her.

"Thank you, Sam."

"He's a sweet little boy. Are you okay?" she whispered.

He sighed. "That was James on the phone, reinforcing his threats. He says he has an appointment tomorrow with his attorney. I was hoping to buy some time...I don't have the money for a lawyer to fight him, nor do I have the money for childcare or preschool right now. I think if you moved in under the pretense of being my fiancée it would just make things worse. In his eyes, Karen could do no wrong and is irreplaceable. I'm in a catch-22."

"What are you gonna do?"

"I don't want to get married." Matt ran his hands through his hair, pacing in the hall. "But I can't lose my son. God, I can't believe I'm doing this. Sam, I mean Sammie...I'm going to ask you for a huge favor, and I totally get it if you say no—but marry me. Please? As soon as possible."

Sammie bit her lip, trying not to take it personally. She had red hair and freckles and a background that, if delved into, probably wasn't suitable for being a mother or a wife. Karen had been beautiful and confident, even if she had been a bit of a snob. This time around, Matt would definitely be getting the short end of the stick. But he was her friend.

In truth, right now, he was her only friend.

Still, she hedged, seeing how much he *didn't* want this marriage. "This is the twenty-first century; he can't force you to marry..."

"You're wrong. James Howell owns every shady politician and lawyer around. He does what he damn well pleases and always has. And he might not win, but the hell it would put Luke through in the process...I can't risk my boy. I just can't."

"Can't you reason with him? Or maybe with Mrs. Howell?" She remembered Karen's mother as quiet, perpetually in the shadow of her husband.

"No, she's his parrot. She just repeats what he tells her." Matt collapsed on the top step and covered his face. "I don't think she's ever had an original thought outside of what to put on in the morning. And I wouldn't put it past James to lay out her clothes for her."

Sammie sat beside him, thinking. He needed her. She was sure marriages had been built on less, and without a car, her previous plan had fallen apart. But still, some psychiatrist would have a field day with this.

"I don't know. This seems awful permanent for what may very well be a temporary situation. Maybe it's just part of his grieving process to focus on Luke. What if I be your housekeeper and Luke's babysitter?"

"Where would you live? You're broke."

True.

He shook his head. "I know you haven't lived here in a long time. But some things never change. It might be the twenty-first century in the rest of the world, but in Pine Bluff, set your clock back seventy years—especially when dealing with James Howell, who values his family's reputation over anything else. Believe me; I know this firsthand.

"Sammie, I'm so far in debt, I'm drowning. For a while I carried two mortgages—one on the house Karen and I owned and this one. At the time I took on this house, I was doing well. Karen agreed it was a good investment with the land and my shop being here.

"But the accident took more than my wife and daughter. It wiped out my savings. Right now, I haven't got shit except my son. Pa's an alcoholic. I used to run his moonshine for him and dabbled in selling the pot I grew when I was a teenager. Folks around here know this, and they have long memories. Even though I've changed, one slip and everything I've worked so hard to attain will be gone. I can't risk it. To be quite honest, Sammie, I'm worried sick."

She took a moment to let his words sink in. "Okay. So how do we do this?"

He turned and stared at her. "You're saying yes?"

"Yes, but I ain't got a dress." She chuckled at Matt's clueless face. Obviously, he'd never seen her favorite television program about brides buying expensive-ass dresses. "Sure, why not. Friends help friends. And if I can find some sort of part-time job to help out with the bills, I will. I'm not lazy."

"Taking care of Luke and Pa will be more than enough, and a full-time job. We'll get the license tomorrow and marry the next day. If we're a legally married couple, I don't think James will have a leg to stand on. I just have to keep the bills paid, Luke safe, and Pa out of trouble. It'll be great to have your help. But are you sure about this?"

She shoved her girlish dreams aside. There was no bended knee with flowery words, no ring. Instead, Matt looked as if he wanted to throw up. Sadly, the look of desperation on his face was like looking in a mirror. How well she knew that feeling—total loss of control. Maybe this was her purpose...

Before Sue Ellen died, her mother had asked her to sit down at their rickety kitchen table. Prepared for a lecture on sin and God knows what else, Sammie had reluctantly found a chair and waited to see which way the mental-health wind was blowing. She never knew if her mother would be a tearful mess or violent. To her surprise, Sue Ellen had begun *talking*, not lecturing.

"Samantha, you need to always remember where you came from. The good Lord knows being in this world is hard. Greater things await us. But if you stay grounded and figure out what you're supposed to do with your life, you'll be all right here on Earth. You're made of strong stuff, not like me. You got that from your daddy. You and him were the best things to ever happen to me."

She'd held her breath, waiting, but to her surprise, her mother had simply squeezed her hand and they'd enjoyed their iced tea in silence. She could still remember the pattern of the condensation slipping down the glass and pooling in a ring on the table. But she hadn't moved to get a coaster or mop up the water, afraid of ruining the rare moment of peace with the strange woman who'd given birth to her.

Matt cleared his throat, snapping her back from the past. He ran his hands up and down his legs, waiting on her answer. Maybe taking care of this family was what she was supposed to do. She'd help her friend and perhaps find a place to belong.

"Sounds like a plan. Shake on it?"

He rubbed his eyes with the heels of his hands and his shoulders sagged. The sound of Pa's TV from downstairs was the only noise breaking the strained silence.

At last he held out his hand, looking like he was about to strike a deal with the Devil himself.

"Like a business deal kind of thing?" he croaked.

"Yep."

She wasn't a fool. No one could replace Karen Howell.

Matt gazed out the window, feeling much older than his twenty-nine years.

A flash of copper hair caught his eye, a white cotton gown billowing as she swung higher and higher in the air. *Sammie.* The name fit her now. Watching her brought back memories of them sneaking out of the house as kids. She'd just been Sam then, the funny tomboy who'd hung with him, Dylan, and Alan growing up. She could out-swear most of them and never shrank from a dare. She'd fit in so well, they'd never thought of her as a girl. She was just their friend.

And now his *friend* was about to become his *wife.*

It seemed like a lifetime ago that she'd left. She and her parents had moved to Pine Bluff when she was eight and he was ten. Her father had been killed a week after they moved here in a freak accident at his job, and her strange mother had isolated herself, leaving her daughter to her own devices. Sam had been skinny with freckles and sported the worst haircut he'd ever seen on a girl. She'd been destined to be tormented.

She'd started school the last week it was in session, which he'd always found weird. Who moves and puts a kid in a new school with only a week left? That first afternoon he'd found her shouting an impressive string of obscenities and beating on Bubba Kelton, the biggest bully in the school. No one stepped in to help her, so he did—not that she really needed it. She'd already managed to black Bubba's eye and bust his lip.

Their friendship had started on the walk home when instead of thanking him, she'd berated him for not letting her finish the fight. Pointing out that her fifty pounds had been no match for her hundred-and-fifty-pound tormentor had earned him a cussing that would've made his old man proud. But that summer she became his shadow, and over time, his best friend.

Sammie hopped off the swing, and he soon heard her soft tread on the staircase.

Is this the right thing to do? Did he have any other choice? If he didn't have his son, he might as well be dead.

He stood at his dresser and pulled open the top drawer. He took out a frame—his favorite photograph of Karen, taken the day they took Elizabeth home from the hospital. In it, she glowed with love and happiness. With his index finger, he traced the contours of her face, remembering the love they'd once shared.

After a moment, he removed his wedding band and placed it with the framed picture in the bottom drawer of his dresser. He shut it firmly, closing the door on that chapter of his life.

Chapter
Four

Matt descended the stairs, yawning. His eyes felt like they'd been polished with sandpaper. He hadn't slept a wink last night, worrying over the changes about to occur in his life.

From the kitchen, Luke screamed.

He picked up his pace and found the boy standing on a chair next to the stove, laughing as Sammie expertly flipped a pancake.

"Yay, Sammie! Do it again!"

"You damn near gave me a heart attack, son," he barked.

Luke looked over his shoulder and giggled. "You said a bad word!"

Goddammit. Luke was right. He'd probably cussed out loud more in the past twenty-four hours than he had in ten years.

Sammie's hair was twisted on top of her head with a clip. Wearing no makeup and dressed in jeans and a T-shirt, she was the complete antithesis of Karen. The only time Karen hadn't been made up was when she went to bed. And Karen would've admonished him for his language.

"You timed that right," Sammie said. "Breakfast is almost ready."

"Thanks," he mumbled, pouring himself a cup of coffee.

Glancing around, he realized she must've been up awhile. The kitchen looked like a different place from yesterday. The counters were clear and the cupboards closed, the groceries put away.

"Luke, sit down before you break your neck."

"No. I'm helping Sammie."

"What have I told you about back-talking?"

"Relax, Matt. He's fine. I'm watching him. Sit and enjoy your coffee." She plated four perfect pancakes and directed her attention back to Luke. "How about we make your last one look like Mickey Mouse?"

"Really?"

"Watch. See? There's his head and now his ears." Sammie steadied Luke's hand and helped him pour the batter.

His son's sunny disposition was a direct contrast to *his* mood—and the weather outside, which was gray and dreary. He felt like that fox he'd once found in Bubba Kelton's stupid trap: ready to gnaw off his paw. A gust of wind slammed the house, and the trees bent with the impact.

Behind him came the scraping sound of Pa making his way toward the kitchen, cussing up a storm. Matt rubbed his forehead. There were times he wished he could run away from all of this.

"Language, Pa," he warned, knowing it wouldn't do a bit of good.

"I'll cuss if I damn well want to. Luke knows better, don't you, boy?"

"Yes, sir. Daddy said a bad word, too." Luke climbed down from the chair and brought a plate of pancakes to his grandfather, beaming.

"Snitch," Matt muttered.

"Did you make these? Or Sammie?" Pa asked, cackling over Luke's tattling.

"Both of us!"

"Sure beats cold cereal." The old man grinned.

Luke returned with another plate for Matt.

"Thank you." Matt smiled and received a hug in return.

Luke pulled out his chair and sat down. Sammie handed him his plate with the mouse-shaped pancake.

Pa and Luke doctored their plates with enough butter and syrup to cause a sugar coma.

"Damn, these are good, missy," Pa announced.

Matt sighed. Correcting Pa's language was a losing battle. The pancakes *were* delicious, but his nerves were as taut as one of Sammie's guitar strings. How should he tell his family he was remarrying? Perversely, he hoped James would stroke when he found out. That would solve all of his problems. The entire situation was nothing but a damn mess.

Sammie walked over to pour the old man a cup of coffee and refill his. "I think we need a no-cussing jar." She returned with her own plate.

"What's that, Sammie?" Luke asked with a mouthful of pancake.

"Don't talk with your mouth full, son."

"Anytime anyone says a bad word, they have to put a quarter in the jar."

"Pa will be flat broke in a week," Matt observed.

"Damn straight," he replied.

"Pa, stop. It isn't funny."

Luke giggled, Pa guffawed, and Sammie snickered. Matt shook his head but ended up grinning.

Sammie dug in the pantry and came back with an old pickle jar, which she placed on the table. "Pony up, old man. A quarter for every bad word. This goes for all of us. The *really* bad words will be fifty cents."

"Like ain't?" Luke asked.

Sammie frowned. "You're just wantin' me to go broke. Yes. We'll include that word, too."

Thunder rumbled in the distance. Matt watched as Sammie moved her hands to her hips and waited. To his surprise, Pa pulled a quarter out of his pocket and slammed it in the jar. She returned to her seat.

Matt nodded. "I like this idea. Luke, this money will be yours. When it's full, we'll put it in a savings account for college. With Pa around, I anticipate you earning a full ride in no time."

"Does that mean I'll be rich?"

"Quite possibly," Matt assured him.

"Shit." Pa glared.

"Ahem." Sammie's eyebrow rose.

Pa dug out another quarter, and Matt laughed outright.

He wiped his mouth and pushed his empty plate back. "By the way, Sammie and I have an announcement."

Sammie sucked in a deep breath and paled as she glanced around the table. Pa paused eating, but Luke continued swirling his pancake in syrup.

"Eloise Jordan is going to come by today and visit for a while."

"Yay!" Luke beamed.

Pa's eyes narrowed. "That's your news? Eloise is a nice woman, but so what?"

Matt willed himself to sit still under Pa's scrutiny. "Well, uh, Sammie and I are going to the courthouse to get a marriage license, and tomorrow, we're getting married."

Pa swiveled to look at Sammie. "Are you pregnant?"

"Pa! She just got here yesterday." He glanced at Luke, who licked his fingers, unfazed by the news. It was an ironic analogy of this entire sticky situation.

"Then why?" Pa persisted. "You haven't seen her in years until yesterday."

"Online—we've talked online." The lie fell readily from his lips, no different than when he'd been a teen lying about his whereabouts. Which was a little disconcerting—he'd worked hard to be a better man.

So of course, he added to it. "And on the phone."

"Luke, if you're done eating, would you go pick up your toys in your room and make your bed?" Sammie asked quietly.

"I don't want to."

"If Sammie asks you to do something, the correct answer is *yes, ma'am*," Matt advised him. "Take your plate to the sink and be sure to wash your hands before touching anything else." He managed to keep his tone level.

"I want Mom—"

Matt interrupted, "Please don't say it. Just do as you're told."

Luke huffed and disappeared down the hall, leaving the adults in an atmosphere reminiscent of a nuclear holocaust.

"Matt, he's just a kid." Sammie folded and refolded her napkin.

"What in the hell is going on here?" Pa asked.

"We're getting married. That's all I'm going to say on the matter."

"I think I'm entitled to an explanation. I live here, and I'm your father, dammit."

"Matt—"

"Hush, Sammie, this doesn't involve you!" As soon as the words were out, he realized his mistake.

"Well, it sure won't involve me if I say no!" Bright red stained her cheeks, and her freckles stood out. Leaping to her feet, she threw down her napkin and stormed out the back door, slamming it behind her.

"Way to go, son. If you're marrying the woman, how the hell does it not involve her? This has to be the most asinine thing you've ever done. It's right up there next to marrying Karen."

"Shut up and put a quarter in the jar." Matt hurried after his soon-to-be wife, unless he'd fucked it up already.

Sammie's hair blew wildly in the wind as dark clouds moved across the sky. Far from frightening her, the energy of the impending storm felt empowering. Nature was something she knew she couldn't control, and that was freeing. She was angry but had long ago learned to walk away from confrontation. Moving toward the dilapidated fence, she watched the stately pines sway as she took a minute to calm and center herself.

Not that it was a real marriage, but Matt should've included her in telling his family. She sure as hell would've done it differently. She didn't want Luke upset; that kid had been through enough.

Footsteps approached, and she turned and crossed her arms, waiting. Matt looked haggard as he trudged toward her. He stopped and stood with his hands on his hips, looking everywhere but at her.

She pushed her disappointment to the side. What had she expected? All her life she'd longed for love that wasn't dependent on the swing of mental illness. The closest thing she'd had was her father's love for eight short years. Matt didn't love her. She needed to remember that. He cared about her, but was it enough?

Maybe it would be best to cut my losses and find a way to Nashville.

"Look, Sammie, I'm sorry for what I said...the way this is going down. Honestly, I don't know what I'm doing. This is crazy, us getting married—"

"No one is forcing you to get married. I'll leave."

Matt tilted his head back and looked at the swirling storm clouds.

"That's not what I meant. Or maybe it is...I don't *know*. I'm telling you as my *friend*, I don't know what to do. All I know is I *can't* lose Luke. I feel like I'm stuck in that movie where the same day repeats over and over," he shouted. "Don't you remember how small Pine Bluff is? As soon as word gets out, the countdown will begin to see if that white trash Tyler boy knocked up another girl. Shit, it's not fair to you. Dammit, it's not fair to *me*. I had dreams. I wanted to finish school, get a good job, and overcome the labels this town has stuck on me."

He stooped and sat on his heels, pulling up blades of grass. He threw them to the ground as if they were his long-forgotten dreams. When he spoke again, his voice was flat.

"I don't have the money to fight James. He hates me and blames me for everything from Karen's pregnancy to her death. He's hellbent on ruining my life. This is a personal feud between us, and I shouldn't ask you to get involved. I'm not perfect. And I'm probably a lousy father, but I'm not unfit like James claims."

He rubbed his face, and his shoulders sagged. "I know I screwed up telling Luke and Pa. And I know I'm asking too much, that I'm being selfish, but please, don't leave...Marry me."

Sammie's heart slammed so hard in her chest, it hurt to breathe. She could do this for her friend. "I'll marry you, Matthew. I owe you this."

He stood up, looking puzzled. "Owe me?"

"For being my best friend when I lived here. You might've been *that white trash Tyler boy*, but I was *crazy Sue Ellen's kid*. As you've said, we're friends. We'll get married, but even if it's not really real, you can't make decisions without me. We're a team, Matt. Like business partners."

The wind picked up and thunder rumbled, closer now.

"You're sure?" Matt shouted above the wind and a crack of thunder overhead. Huge raindrops began to fall, and in a matter of seconds, it became a torrential downpour.

She nodded.

Stormy, dark eyes met hers. She wasn't sure if it was rain or tears glistening on his lashes. They were both soaked to the skin, but the storm didn't compare to the tempest of emotions swirling between them.

"We won't let Mr. Howell win," she shouted.

Lightning streaked the sky, followed by another deafening clap of thunder. They both jumped, and Matt looked up at the clouds. When he looked at her again, his gaze moved to her now-hard nipples in her soaked T-shirt.

Trying for nonchalant, she held out her hand, watching the water cascade down his face. "S-Shake on it?"

"Shake on it?" he parroted, still staring at her breasts. "Fuck a handshake."

He pulled her to him, kissing her with a savage intensity that matched the storm. Shocked, she stiffened at first, but as the kiss deepened, her body molded to his and she savored the kiss she'd always dreamed about.

"Matt, we need to stop. The storm…"

"I know," he whispered, kissing across her jaw.

A sheet of rain whipped against them.

"I'm sorry. That probably crossed a line." He looked confused and sad.

"I'm not," she replied, breathlessly, as thunder boomed again. She doubted he even heard her.

The sound of the dinner bell ringing from the back porch permeated her lust-induced haze. Leroy and Luke stood watching them. Even from this distance, she could see the smirk on Pa's face.

"Shit," Matt breathed against her forehead. "I fuckin' hate living with my father."

She giggled. He grabbed her hand, and they hurried toward the house. Pa went back inside before they reached the porch.

Luke scrunched his face. "Ew, were you kissing?"

Matt didn't answer, instead shoving a dollar in the no-cussing jar.

"Thanks again, Mrs. Jordan. I appreciate you staying with Luke and Pa. The weather's let up, so at least you won't have to drive home in the rain."

"I didn't need a damn babysitter," Pa complained.

Unfazed, Mrs. Jordan laughed. "Who said you did? Can't old friends visit? You're just mad I beat your pants off at gin rummy."

Matt prayed she didn't mean that literally. She and Pa had grown up together, and it was rumored they'd dated years ago.

"Next time we'll play poker." Pa winked with his good eye.

Blushing, Mrs. Jordan said, "Leroy, you old rascal! Luke and I made some cookies. I've missed this sweet boy. Maybe someday he'll feel comfortable enough to come back to Sunday school."

Matt didn't hold high hopes. "Say thank you, son. And then go feed Rufus."

"Thank you, Mrs. Jordan." He gave her a hug before limping off to feed the dog.

Mrs. Jordan looked at Matt and then Sammie and shook her finger, smiling. "A wedding! You two sure kept it quiet. I'm so happy for you." She turned to Sammie. "Young lady, you didn't mention a word when you stopped by the other day."

Sammie shrugged and bit her lip. "Well, uh, I wasn't sure until I got here."

Mrs. Jordan ran a finger over the moonstone ring. "I like that you didn't go traditional on the engagement ring…" Dropping her hand, she rummaged through her purse to pull out a handkerchief embroidered with blue flowers, which she handed to Sammie.

"I'm so sorry Sue Ellen didn't live to see this day. I know when my daughter, Cathy, got married, it was one of the happiest days of my life. I want you to have this as your something old, something blue. Do you have something new? Well, of course — your rings. Will the band be plain? You can return this if you'd like and we'll call it borrowed, but I'll turn right around and give it back to you after the wedding. Will that work?"

Rings! Matt jammed his fists in his pockets.

Sammie's cheeks were bright red, her eyes shiny. He hadn't given any thought until now about the traditions of a wedding, or Sammie's family and friends.

"Thank you, Mrs. Jordan. This means a lot to me." The women hugged, and Sammie walked her to her car.

Matt paced in the living room. What the hell did he know about wedding planning? Last time he'd been in this situation, Karen and her family had done everything; all he'd done was show up, much to her father's disappointment. And Pa's. But he'd bought Karen a small engagement ring and a simple band. Of course Sammie should have a ring, to symbolize their partnership...

He wanted to puke. And run. Not necessarily in that order.

"Sit down, son. You're wearing a hole in the carpet."

"There isn't any carpet. It's hardwood."

"You know what I mean. So why are you and Sam in such a damn hurry to get married? Have you really been going to school or have you been sowing some wild oats? If it's the latter, that's fine, but have you talked to the boy about getting a new mama?"

When Matt was a kid, his father had taken him to the lake and thrown him in to teach him how to swim. He'd been terrified and gone under a few times before getting the hang of dog paddling. Right now, it was the same damn feeling, but instead of the shore being within sight, it felt as if he were in the middle of the Atlantic Ocean.

Sammie walked back inside, her gaze moving between him and Pa.

"Y'all okay?" She started tapping the fingers on her right hand to her thumb. It was a habit he remembered from when she was a kid. She'd do it whenever Sue Ellen went off her rocker.

"We're fine." Matt glared at his father. Thankfully, Pa kept his mouth shut. "I need to explain all of this to Luke..."

"Do you want me there?" Sammie asked.

"I think it best if I do it alone — no disrespect or anything, and not to leave you out."

The look of relief crossing her face almost made him smile.

"Okay. I'll start some supper. I'm thinking something light, like BLTs?" As she spoke, she straightened his books on the coffee table.

"Sure, that's fine."

"Okay, good." She fled to the kitchen under Pa's watchful eye.

"Mind your own business, old man," Matt muttered on his way to find Luke.

He found him on the back porch, playing with the yard cat and singing to Rufus, who was blissfully sleeping through the ABC song and the chorus of "Help me, Rhonda."

"Hi, Daddy."

Matt sat next to Luke and rolled a dump truck back and forth as he tried to figure out what to say to his son.

"Good job on your ABCs."

"I like the Rhonda help me song. It was Mommy's favorite. Can I name that outside cat Rhonda?"

Matt's stomach knotted. "It was? I, uh, guess I didn't realize that." *I wish someone would help me.* "May I, and sure. I guess that's a good name for a cat. Do you like Sammie?"

He peered at the cat and realized it was a boy. Oh well. If a boy could be named Sue, a male cat could be named Rhonda.

"Sure. Do you?"

"Yeah, I do. Did you know she can bait her own hook?"

"With real worms?"

"Yup."

"That's cool. Can we go fishing tomorrow?"

"Not tomorrow. Would you like Sammie to stay here?"

Luke continued to pet the cat, whose tail was now flicking. "Sure. She makes good pancakes. Is she your girlfriend?"

"I, uh, guess you'd call her that." Matt stayed his hand, and the cat jumped off the step with an agitated tail swish. Rufus picked up his head but soon returned to his nap.

"I have two girlfriends: Angela and Kenzie." Luke turned his attention to his trucks.

"Two, huh? That could cause you a heap of hurt, son."

"Nah, Pa told me it was good not to get tied down to just one girl. He calls it playing the field. Girls are all the same anyways."

Great, Pa's offering dating advice to my four-year-old. "No, they're not. They're like flowers — kinda the same but different. And you need to handle 'em gently."

"What do you mean?"

"You don't want to hurt their feelings."

"What kind of flower was Mommy?"

Memories of Karen flashed like a newsreel — laughing at the dinner table, crying when Elizabeth started school, playing in her parents' pool with the kids, and holed up in a dark room not talking.

"Mommy was an orchid. She was beautiful but had to be handled with care."

"Lizbeth?"

"I'd say she was a daisy, bright and cheerful."

"What about Sammie?"

"Hmmm. I think Sammie's a sunflower. She's strong and a survivor. The point is, they're all flowers, all beautiful in their own way, and you have to take care of them differently. So be careful with Angela and Kenzie. Okay? You don't want to hurt their feelings. And really? Being friends is a lot easier than dealing with girlfriends. Trust me on that one."

"Okay."

"Anyway, Sammie's gonna stay here and help me take care of you."

"Like Mommy?"

Guilt engulfed him. *Oh shit. What's gonna happen to Luke if Sam leaves? What if this doesn't work out?*

"Uh, kind of, yes. You know your mother loved you more than anything in this world, right?"

Luke gazed up at him and smiled. "She loved me lots and lots. Lizbeth did, too. Even when I went in her room."

Matt blinked back tears. In the midst of the epic fights that used to spring up between his children, he never once thought, *I'll miss this pandemonium.* But he did. Every damn day. The house was too quiet without his daughter.

As if sensing his mood, Luke stopped playing and crawled into his lap, hugging him. "Don't be sad, Daddy. Sammie will take care of you, too."

"Okay." He smiled against his son's hair and held him for a few minutes longer.

Chapter
Five

Sammie washed the dinner dishes, mulling over the part of the conversation she'd overheard Matt having with Luke. *Sunflowers are so common compared to orchids…*

Matt appeared at the doorway, hands in his pockets. "I need to ask you something."

"Yes?"

"I didn't think this through. I mean, about Luke."

She turned around but kept her eyes on her bracelets, fingering them one by one. *Is he worried I'll be like Sue Ellen?* "I'll be good to him…"

"No, I'm not worried about that. It's just…he's gonna get attached. I don't want his heart broken if something happens. Maybe this was a dumb idea…"

"I ain't plannin' on going anywhere. I mean, well, we're friends. Pathetic as it sounds, you're really my only true friend, aside from Ashley in Nashville. But she and I aren't that close. And Mrs. Jordan—she's always been nice to me." She counted the tiles on the floor. "I'm rambling. I'll do whatever you think best."

Matt didn't speak for a few minutes, staring a hole in the stack of bills in the basket on the counter.

"I just can't hurt Luke. He's been through so much."

"Matt, no matter what happens, I'll do right by your son. I promise."

"Okay. You're right. We *are* friends. We can make this work." He let out a deep breath and squared his shoulders. "I'm sorry to be waffling back and forth. I'm going to go make sure Dylan got his ministerial credentials online. I'll be back later."

"Sure, sure." She giggled.

"What's so funny?"

"Come on, Dylan McAthie, Mr. Rockstar-who-thinks-he-is-God, as a minister? That's about as believable as me being a college professor."

Growing up, Dylan and his older brother, Rob, had spent summers here on the lake with their grandmother. He'd raised as much hell as Matt had. And from what she'd read in the tabloids, he hadn't stopped.

"Go have fun." She wiped down the counter, still giggling.

"What?" Matt shifted on his feet, nervous as a long-tailed cat in a room full of rockers.

"I bet y'all are really going to have a wild bachelor party," she teased. "It'll be all over the *National Intruder*, so make sure you ain't doing anything stupid." She sighed and dug two quarters out of her pocket and deposited them in the jar. "I'm having more problems with that word than any other."

"Don't worry. I'm a father with responsibilities. About as wild as I get is having a full-sugar, caffeinated cola. See ya later." He paused at the door and looked back. "And, Sam? Thank you."

"No problem."

"Shit, man, I thought you were fuckin' kidding me. You really want *me* to marry you?"

Seated in Dylan's in-home studio, Matt suffered his friend's laughter for a full five minutes before he finally obtained his online license.

"Daddy! Rory won't leave me alone." Angela McAthie shrieked. She raced in with her baby brother fast on her track.

Matt grinned, but seeing the brother and sister tussling made him sad, too. Angela was close to Luke's age, and Dylan's wife, Jennifer, had brought her over to play every few weeks since the accident. A former nurse, Jennifer had been a huge help in reassuring him that Luke's acting out about cars wasn't abnormal considering what he'd experienced.

Jennifer ran in to shoo the children out, apologizing for the interruption.

"Guess what, Jen?" Dylan said.

"Do I look like I have time to play guessing games? Rory, stop tormenting your sister! Angela, stop being a drama queen!"

"I have a new career," Dylan replied, handing her the freshly printed certificate.

"Oh, really? It better not be tonight. I have plans. You're not getting out of staying with your own children. You promised." She frowned as she read, and then her mouth dropped open. "Is this some kind of joke?"

Matt shook his head, wondering for the umpteenth time if this was all a huge mistake. "No, I'm, uh, getting married, again. Dylan's going to perform the ceremony, and I'd like you to be a witness, tomorrow."

"You are? Why not get married at church?"

"Pastor McClain's on vacation."

"But Dylan? *A minister?*"

Jennifer laughed so hard she had to sit down. When she started hiccupping, Matt pinched the bridge of his nose. *Maybe there's another way to get out of this fiasco with James…*

An hour later, with Dylan and Jennifer on board for the wedding disaster of the century, Matt climbed in his truck and headed to Walmart's jewelry department. The sales girl looked to be Sammie's size and helped him find what he hoped was a simple wedding band that would fit.

It was dusk, but instead of going home, Matt drove straight to Gig Johnson's, Pa's old bootlegging partner. He needed some fortitude for the rest of the evening.

It's time to say my goodbyes.

"Hey, Gig, let me have a pint of wildcat."

"Is this for your Pa? Didn't that scoundrel get drunk enough on Memorial Day?" the man asked with a laugh.

Gig Johnson was in his eighties and always had a ready smile on his creased face. He wore a pair of Liberty overalls and a Redman Chewing Tobacco cap over his salt and pepper hair.

"Nope, it's for me," Matt replied, taking a swig from the mason jar. He coughed and pounded his chest. It wasn't called "white lightning" for nothing. "Shit, I forgot how awful this stuff is." He took another gulp.

"Whoa there, son. You used to be able to drink your Pa and me under the table, but you haven't done so in quite some time. You'd better take it easy. And you sure don't need to be driving." Gig frowned.

Matt shook his hand. "Yes, sir. I'll take the rest of this home. I'm good. Well, maybe not *good*—I'm a Tyler, after all."

Matt drove around aimlessly for an hour, thinking about the past and his uncertain future. Then he hit a pothole, and the mason jar tipped and spilled over the floorboard.

"Damnation!" Just his crappy luck. He did a quick U-turn and drove to The Roadside Tavern.

Inside the dimly lit bar, Lucy Hargrove came over to wait on him.

"Hiya, Sis." Matt grinned at the bleached blonde, enjoying the look of shock on her face.

His half-sister was fifteen years older, and they rarely spoke. While they shared a parent, Pa had never married her mother. And Karen had refused to acknowledge "Loose Lucy" as family. It had once been a well-known rite of passage for a teen male in the county to meet up with Lucy and get to know her in the Biblical sense. It had been beyond embarrassing as a teenager to hear his friends talking about their experiences. As an adult, he rarely had anything to do with her because they had nothing in common except Pa.

Lucy's penciled-in eyebrows rose. "Hi, yourself. What would the congregation of Pine Bluff's First Methodist Church say if they saw St. Matthew here?"

"They'd probably say I'm headed straight to hell in the fast lane. My halo's a little too tight, Luce. Be a sweet sis and get me a bottle of Southern Comfort and let's see if that won't loosen it up a bit."

"Matt, you don't drink."

"I'm a Tyler; of course I drink. *And* I can hold my liquor."

Lucy rolled her eyes and poured him a shot.

Matt threw it back. A niggling thought flashed through his rational mind that this might not be a good idea. His alcohol-numbed brain countered that James Howell would never darken the doors of The Roadside Tavern. He ran a hand through his uncombed hair and scratched his five o'clock shadow as he looked around the dive bar.

"When you gonna fix this dump up?"

Lucy had owned the bar since the owner keeled over dead from a heart attack. Bobby Joe had been no loss to the community.

Lucy leaned across the bar and stared at him. "You look like hell. What's wrong?"

"Wrong? Nothing's wrong. This is my bachelor party." He motioned for another drink.

"Seriously, I'm a bartender. You can talk to me."

"I *am* being serious. I'm getting married tomorrow."

"What? Who? Does old man Howell know yet? What does Pa think?"

"Shhh, it's a surprise. Sam Morgan, she used to live around here…" Matt was silent for a moment. "As for Pa, I'm surprised he isn't the one marrying her. He likes 'em young—you and I both know that." He turned up the second shot and then reached for the bottle, downing more.

"This is crazy," Lucy replied, reclaiming the bottle.

"I'm a simple man with a complicated life." He grinned. "I could be a goddamned country-music song."

"Oh, brother. Matt, you're well on your way to being shitfaced. Let me drive you home. You've had enough fun for tonight. Hey, Jeff, I'll be back. Can't have this one drivin'."

The bartender nodded.

Matt narrowed his eyes to focus the two Lucys into one. "I'm fine. I'm not goin' home. I gotta go see Lizbeth. I gotta go see my baby and tell her the news. I'll tell Karen while I'm there. She oughta get a kick out of this."

"Fine, I'll take you. It'll be worth it to see your wife rolling over in her grave." Lucy grabbed her purse from under the bar.

He staggered to the truck with Lucy's help and grinned at her when she got in.

"You're the best sister ever…"

"And you're drunk as hell."

Pa hung up the phone as Sammie walked back downstairs from putting Luke to bed.

"Sonofabitch."

"Everything okay? That's gonna cost ya another quarter."

"No! That damn fool son of mine is apparently getting drunk off his ass. First he hit Gig up for some moonshine and now he's just left The Roadside Tavern. Thank God, Lucy's driving him. Take my truck, but don't ride the clutch. I'll stay here with the boy; you'll find them at the First Methodist cemetery. Lucy needs to get back to work but promised not to leave him."

Sammie drove to the church, unsure what she'd find. If Matt had a drinking problem, it was a game changer. She was tired of taking care of folks with problems. She found his truck parked in the parking lot. A bleached blonde stood next to it, smoking.

"Hey, I'm Lucy, Matt's sister. You must be the bride."

"Sammie Morgan. I used to live here, but we never had the pleasure." She shook Lucy's hand, a little in awe.

When she'd lived in Pine Bluff, her mother had made her cross the street any time they ran up on Lucy Hargrove. She was — in Sue Ellen's mind — a woman of loose morals who slept around. Not that Sue Ellen had room to judge…Lord knows she'd swung from being like a nun to throwing herself at a man for attention. Sammie remembered asking Matt what he knew about Lucy when they were teenagers. He'd become sullen and told her to shut up. At the time she'd wondered if he'd been involved with Loose Lucy. Later, Dylan had told her Matt and Lucy were half-siblings.

"You'll find him over there at the Howell plot. I'm gonna drive his truck back to The Roadside Tavern. Jeff and I will drop it off after we close." Dropping her cigarette, she hopped in and peeled out.

The moonlight made long shadows of the many tombstones, and it was definitely creepy. Sammie found Matt sitting with his back against an old oak tree, one knee propped up.

"Kind of a gloomy place for a bachelor party. It's nice, though. I need to bring Sue Ellen for a visit," she joked, wondering if he was a mean drunk. *He didn't used to be…*She stopped her trip down memory lane to focus on the present situation. Right now, she had to get him home.

He held his hand up, motioning her to stop.

Covering his eyes with his other hand, he mumbled, "Go away. Just go away and leave me the hell alone."

She knelt down beside him. "Come on, Matt, it's late. We need to get home."

"I killed them," he whispered hoarsely.

"Hush. Don't be ridiculous. It was a terrible accident." She rubbed his back.

Matt pulled away and wiped his eyes with the back of his hand. "No, you don't understand. Karen and I had a huge fight. I left to cool off, still angry. She was upset…"

He stood and staggered to the grave, pulling up the weeds at the base of the tombstone. Karen's name was carved on it with the dates and the words *Beloved daughter and mother*. Nothing about being a wife. He leaned his head against the marker, his shoulders shaking.

"Do you know what my last words to her were? I told her to go to straight to hell. She was my wife and the mother of my children, and I told her to go to hell." He turned and looked at her. "I'd even fought with Lizbeth at the dinner table that night. She wanted her ears pierced, and I refused. What kind of bastard fights with a little girl over getting her ears pierced? What the hell difference would it have made?"

He sighed. "Maybe James is right. I'm a terrible father; Luke would be better off with him and Lila. Hell, he'd even be better off with Karen's younger sister, Jinx. He loves her dog. The Howells can give him anything he wants. This past Christmas, I was so broke, I couldn't even buy him the bicycle he wanted. Not that he could've ridden it anyway; he was in the hospital."

He stood up, swaying.

"Matt, you're terribly drunk. This is the liquor talking. You didn't cause the accident. Telling Karen to go to hell and telling your daughter no to getting her ears pierced did *not* kill them. You're a wonderful father, and Luke loves and needs you! Now let's go home and get some black coffee," Sammie said firmly, helping him walk toward the truck.

Matt leaned on her, stumbling a few times. Finally, he actually fell and stayed down, wrapping his arms around her waist.

"I had to say goodbye…"

"I understand."

He buried his face in her T-shirt and sobbed. Sammie held him tight, her heart breaking.

When his tears were spent, he looked up. "I'm so sorry, Sam," he whispered.

"Everything'll be okay."

He hugged her one last time and stood, still swaying. Once in the truck, she managed to get him buckled in and drove home. It took considerable effort and cajoling to get him up the steps and into the house, where he collapsed on the couch and passed out.

"Should we try to get him upstairs?" she asked Pa.

"No, just leave him here."

"Pa, does he drink often? I mean, is this the norm?"

He shook his head. "Nope. I haven't known him to drink more than an occasional beer on the weekend since he was a teenager."

She placed a pillow under Matt's head and covered him with an afghan before turning out the light.

"Daddy, get up!"

Poked by a small finger, Matt opened one eye.

"Shh. You'll wake the dead," he muttered, rolling over. He rubbed his forehead. His skull was pounding like a jackhammer, and his mouth tasted like a sewer.

"I'm hungry." Undeterred, Luke pried open his eyes.

He blinked. "Where's Sam? You need to use your church voice. You're too loud."

"I *am*. You're not listening. She's still asleep and so is Pa."

"Well, then maybe *you* should still be asleep. What time is it?"

"Breakfast time."

Matt sat up and looked at the clock over the mantle. It was only seven. Gingerly, he stood and tried to get his bearings. Last night was a fuzzy memory. Moving like Pa, he made his way into the kitchen, started a pot of coffee, and handed Luke a half-empty sleeve of fig cookies for breakfast. It had fruit; how bad could it be?

"Go watch TV, but keep it low and don't wake Pa."

Surely Sammie would be up soon. Thankfully the wedding wasn't until this afternoon.

He made his way upstairs to brush his teeth, but when he looked in the mirror, he gasped. He was in desperate need of a shave, and his eyes looked like a roadmap. *Is that tree bark and leaves in my hair?* He prayed he hadn't done anything to embarrass himself or his family. *What the fuck was I thinking?* If Howell caught wind of this, he was a goner. Leaving the door ajar so he could hear Luke, he ran a bath and sank into the warm water. Standing for a shower was out of the question. His eyes drifted closed.

Sammie yawned as she wandered from her bedroom. Opening the bathroom door, she stopped short, finding Matt asleep in the tub. She blinked but couldn't look away. His tan chest rose and fell with his soft snores. Her gazed traveled down from the dark hair on his chest to his chiseled abs, and *oh my…*

She forced herself to look away and cleared her throat.

No response.

She sighed. *Do something, or you'll have to pee on yourself!* Counting the tiles above the sink until her breathing evened out, she sat on the side of the tub and felt the bath water. It was cool, so he'd been in here for a while. Impulsively, she splashed his face.

Matt opened his eyes and sputtered his outrage. "Fuck!"

"Fifty cents, Tyler," Sammie responded, laughing.

Rubbing his brow, he groaned, "Can't a man have any privacy?"

"You left the door open, and I have to pee. How long have you been in here?" She looked into the water. "Ain't you afraid it will shrivel up and fall off?"

Red-faced he sat up, attempting to cover himself. "And to think I once thought you were a nice girl. Oh shit, my head—I feel sick." He sank back and rubbed his forehead.

"Want to try for a full dollar?" Sammie used her toe to edge the garbage can next to the tub.

He glared at her. "You said ain't."

"Shoot, I did, didn't I? The stink eye doesn't work on me, remember? I have the power of the red hair. You look terrible. How long has it been since you drank like that?"

Matt closed his eyes. "Too long—twelve years, I guess."

"Do you plan on making this a habit? I don't like drunks. Turn your head. If I don't pee, it's going to be more embarrassing than peeing in front of you."

Matt closed his eyes and scowled. "How did I get home?"

"You don't remember?" Sammie smiled as she finished and washed her hands.

"No."

"You can open your eyes."

"I'm sure you'll take great pleasure filling me in on the missing details. I remember stopping by and seeing Dylan. Then I went to Gig Johnson's. Wait…Lucy…did I go to The Roadside Tavern?"

"You did. But it wasn't your last stop. I found you at the cemetery—you know, the one next to your *church*." She shook her head and clicked her tongue against her teeth.

"What?" Apprehension tinged his voice.

"I don't think you really want to know. Let's just say it wasn't a pretty sight."

"No. Tell me. All of it." Matt had a death grip on the sides of the tub.

She sighed. "Okay, if you insist."

Matt's throat bobbled, and his bloodshot eyes widened.

"You were dancing around the cemetery butt-ass-nekkid, singing 'Straight to Hell' at the top of your lungs. It was pretty pathetic; you never could carry a tune. Anyway, you were so loud the lights went on in the parsonage, and the minister came out and helped me get you dressed and back into the truck. He's sorry he can't marry us, by the way." Sammie examined her fingernails nonchalantly.

"Holy. Fuck."

She soon cracked at the horrified look on his face. It started as a giggle, morphed into a snort, and ended up with her doubled over laughing.

Matt's eyes narrowed. "Wait, he's out of town. That's why he couldn't marry us."

"Geezus, Tyler, that was too easy! I think you owe the cussing jar at least a buck and a quarter, maybe more. I wish you could've seen your face just now," she gasped between giggles.

"When did you become so mean, Sammie?" Catching her wrist, he yanked her into the tub. "But remember, there's always payback."

"Matt!" She splashed and squirmed, trying to escape his ironclad grasp. Turning to face him, she quit struggling when she became aware of his arousal. His lips curved in a sensuous smile, and a throbbing began between her legs. She couldn't stop staring at his mouth. *Kiss me!*

Using the side of the tub, she pushed up, and his gaze zeroed in on her hard nipples. Her breathing stuttered. He leaned forward—at last, her wish was about to be fulfilled. She closed her eyes and parted her lips…

Luke came tromping up the stairs.

Panicked, they tried to disentangle themselves and climb out of the claw-foot tub, but Sammie's gown might as well have been a rope. She fell back, and water splashed all over the floor. Matt somehow managed to climb over her and out of the tub. By the time Luke poked his head in the door, he had a towel wrapped around his waist. The boy stared quizzically at her and back up to his father.

"What are y'all doin'? How come Sammie's taking a bath with her clothes on?"

Sammie pulled her knees to her chest, wrapping her arms around them.

"I don't know, son. I guess she's not as smart as we gave her credit for," Matt replied with a laugh as he maneuvered Luke out of the bathroom, closing the door.

"Sonofabitch," she muttered, frustrated and aching.

Matt poked his head back in the door. "You owe the jar a quarter."

He ducked as she sent the bar of soap sailing past his ear.

Chapter Six

"**M**atthew Benjamin Tyler, we need to talk."

Matt groaned and stopped pacing, knowing full well he was about to receive a lecture. Pa wasn't the best father in the world, but whenever the notion struck him to impart parental words of wisdom, they were *always* preceded by the use of his full name.

"What in the hell's going on? You decide to marry on a whim and then get drunk off your ass? This isn't you. You're usually responsible and, quite frankly, kind of boring."

"Not now, Pa. Luke—"

"He's upstairs helping Sam get ready. Quit avoiding the subject. I'm not senile. Now tell me the truth. Is it about the sex? You don't have to marry, just be discreet. Don't make any more mistakes."

"This really isn't any of your business," Matt hedged.

"You're my son; of course it's my damn business. If you remember, we had a similar conversation back when you were a horny, reckless teenager, and I told you to stay away from Karen. That gal should never have come home from that fancy boarding school. But you weren't exactly thinking with the head on your shoulders, were you? I would've thought you'd learned your lesson by now."

Matt sank to the threadbare couch, feeling like a horny, reckless teenager as the image of Sam's hard nipples in her wet clothes surfaced.

His father cleared his throat. How did the man do it? He'd lived on his own since he was eighteen, and now, close to thirty, his father could still manage to make him feel like a fourteen-year-old.

"Karen and I loved each other—" he began.

"Shit, son. Karen may have loved you, but she married you because her fat-cat daddy told her she couldn't. You know it, I know it—hell, the whole goddamn county knows it. You were the forbidden fruit, the boy from the wrong side of the tracks. The two of you didn't have a damn thing in common except what went on in the backseat of a car." Pa held up his hand when Matt started to protest.

"Now, I know you've changed since then. You're all nice and respectable now. You quit drinking, smoking, and cuss a lot less. You even started attending church and went back to school to get an education. I'm sure you think you've done all this for the right reasons, but have you? Or are you just trying to make a silk purse out of a sow's ear? There ain't nothing wrong with being a plain ol' pig."

The fast-flowing metaphors compounded his headache. "Just what does this commentary have to do with Sam?"

"Be careful with her, Matthew. If you're genuinely in love with her, fine. Sammie's like us. She may not have the pedigree of the Howells, but she's got a hell of a lot of class. I've always been fond of that gal. She don't put on no fancy airs or look down her nose at people. I think you could be happy with her. I'm just saying I approve if this is *gen-u-ine*. But if it isn't, stop it now before someone gets hurt."

"Noted." Matt used his poker face.

Pa stared at him for a full minute.

Just when he thought his father was going to call his bluff, Pa added, "Of course, don't tell Sammie I like her. She'll try to run all over me, and before you know it, she'll have *me* acting respectable. Now straighten your tie."

Matt did as he was told and mumbled, "Who are you to give advice on marriage? Your track record isn't exactly great. Mama was what, your third or fourth wife?"

"Your mother was my *only* wife. I never married any of the other women, and you know it. Actually, Sammie reminds me of your Ma. She's got that same feistiness about her. Look, you knew her mother.

I have a feeling Sam's had a heap of hurt in her life; you can feel it hanging over her like a shroud. Be good to her."

Pa squeezed his shoulder and using his walker, returned to his room.

There was a commotion on the stairs. "You look pretty, Sammie," Luke's voice called. "Can Rufus and Rhonda come to the wedding, too?"

Matt's mouth dropped when Sammie appeared wearing an out-of-date white wedding dress. In one hand she held a pair of high heels. Her other arm cradled her mother's urn.

"I don't see why not. They're family, after all. Rufus looks nice in his bow tie."

Matt looked, and sure enough, the dog had a bow tie clipped on his collar. It must've been an old one of Pa's.

"Rhonda didn't like it."

"No, cats are persnickety," Sammie agreed. Pink tinged her cheeks when she looked over at him.

Matt closed his mouth. "You're in a wedding dress? And, er, is that Sue Ellen?"

"I-I think the dress might be too much. Pa had me get it and these shoes out of the attic. I didn't want to hurt his feelings and say no. And if it's okay with you, I thought my mother should be at the wedding." She placed the urn on the mantle. "If you don't like the dress, I can go change. The shoes are too small anyway."

"No, Sammie, you *have* to wear it," Luke protested. "You look like Ariel when she married Prince Eric. Tell her, Daddy! Pa said it was your mama's dress. It makes her look like a *princess*." He ran a hand down a wrinkle like a seasoned wedding planner.

"Yes, it does," Matt agreed.

His childhood fishing buddy did indeed look beautiful. It dawned on him he'd only seen a picture of this dress—the wedding picture sitting on Pa's nightstand. Mama had obviously been shorter than Sammie, as he could see well-worn tan tennis shoes with brightly colored laces peeking out from under the dress. His mother had apparently been smaller chested as well, judging by the strain on the seams.

"No, you look fine. Unless *you* want to change."

She'd applied more makeup than usual and attempted to tame her wild curls into submission.

"I guess it's okay…" She looked down, and her blush made her freckles stand out. "It's fine. It's a wedding, after all. Might as well make it look like one. You look really nice, too."

Luke grinned. "He's Prince Eric."

Sammie laughed. "Yes, he certainly is."

"Hold on a sec." It occurred to Matt that this probably wasn't the wedding she'd dreamed about either.

He darted out to the yard, picked a flower, and returned, handing it to her. "I should've bought you flowers. I'm sorry." He held it out, feeling like a teen going to prom instead of a grown-ass man getting married for the second damn time.

"I like this better. Thank you." She smiled and tucked the bloom in her hair.

Pa returned wearing a clean pair of overalls. He'd washed and combed his white hair, and his beard was free of crumbs for a change.

What a motley crew we make. This wedding was a far cry from his over-the-top first with Karen. She'd worn a designer gown strategically draped to hide her baby bump, and he'd been forced into an uncomfortable rented tux. They'd had twelve attendants and a reception at the country club in Harrisville.

"You look great, girl," Pa beamed. "Matt's mama would've been real proud."

To Matt's surprise, Pa wiped a tear from his eye.

The doorbell rang, and Dylan entered carrying a cake. His hair was pulled back in a neat ponytail, and he was dressed in a tailor-made suit—a far cry from his usual jeans and T-shirt. His family followed, with Jennifer in a lavender dress holding Rory, who was asleep. Wearing a pink dress, Angela hid behind her father's legs.

"Mrs. J sent the cake. Not sure what kind it is, but it'll be delicious." Dylan placed it on the kitchen table.

Jennifer walked over to Sammie with a wide smile. She was a beautiful woman with long, dark hair and bright blue-violet eyes. "Hi, Sammie. I'm Jennifer, Dylan's better half. It's nice to meet you. I know we'll be great friends; our kids are about the same age. This is Rory. Hopefully he'll sleep through the ceremony; he's a handful at times. And that's Angela. She's just a little younger than Luke. I have to confess, when Matt asked Dylan to perform the ceremony, I was a little shocked. My husband as a minister is a bit hard for me to grasp."

Angela stuck her tongue out at Luke, who returned the greeting. Sammie smiled. "Nice to meet you. And yeah, Dylan once threw a snake at me when we were kids; this is quite a turn for him." Sammie gave a small wave to the famous musician. "Hi, Dylan."

"Heya, Sam. Long time no see. You caught the snake, which impressed the hell out of me. What? No overalls today?" Dylan teased. "Unlike you, Jen, Sam used to love to fish and would even dig her own worms and bait her own hook."

"I like riding in the boat and relaxing, not working for my supper. And if you ever throw a snake at me, you're a dead man," Jennifer warned.

"Are we ready to get this show on the road? I'm sure y'all have better things to do." Dylan waggled his brows.

"Oh for heaven's sake, that's not very ministerial of you. I told you we should've seen if David would do this." Jennifer turned to Sammie. "David is our neighbor, and he has a daughter, Kenzie, who is also Luke's age. Luke and the girls attend Sunday school together—I mean, you know, they did before the accident...Anyway, unlike my heathen husband, David actually has plans to attend seminary."

"Hey now, don't be throwin' shade on my new job. And David would never have stooped to getting online credentials. Now, let's get these two married so they can get to the fun part, the honeymoon."

Matt felt his neck flush, and his tie seemed abnormally tight, which added to the discomfort of his pounding headache. "Uh, well, we're just staying here..."

He didn't want to get in to the fact that Luke shouldn't be left alone with Pa. It was embarrassing, and this had to look like a real whirlwind love affair turned marriage. Besides, the cost of going anywhere for a so-called honeymoon was out of the question.

"Don't be ridiculous." Dylan shook his head. "My wedding present to you is a stay overnight in Birmingham, complete with room service. And I've got Luke's situation all figured out. You'll ride on the boat back to our house, won't you, buddy?"

"Wow! Really? Can I, Daddy?"

Matt lifted a dubious brow, not even bothering to correct his son as he scanned the reservation Dylan handed him. "Sure..."

"It's a bit warm out, but if you're doing pictures, do we want to go outside?" Dylan asked.

Pictures? What else have I forgotten? When did Dylan add wedding planner to his résumé?

Matt glanced at Sammie. She shrugged, looking as clueless he felt. Years ago, at his first wedding, the photography had taken forever. All he'd wanted was for the day to end…

In that respect, some things never change.

Sammie mopped her brow with the back of her arm. Her hair was starting to curl again, and her mascara was now a bit smudged. "This is just a small wedding. And I'm already sweating like a ho in church on Sunday. Maybe someone could just snap a picture or two with their phone and be done with it? My pictures usually look like mug shots, anyway."

Matt laughed for the first time today. "Twenty-five cents, Sammie."

"Oops. Sorry." Her cheeks reddened.

"I've got this. Here, Mr. Tyler, if you'll hold Rory. I'll take pictures." Jennifer handed off the sleeping boy and pulled out her phone. "Angela, behave and stop sticking your tongue out at Luke."

The little girl gave Luke the stink eye instead, which he returned with an added sneer.

"So, we're here today to get you two married, for better or for worse, in sickness and in health, through no counter space due to makeup scattered everywhere and toilet seats left up. Trust me, most marital problems involve the bathroom, so y'all share nice, or even better — get separate bathrooms."

"Dylan!" Jennifer rolled her eyes.

"Wait, where's the music?" Angela asked. "You know, the here comes the bride song."

"That's a dumb song," Luke retorted. "Lemme have your phone, Daddy. I know a song."

Shrugging, Matt handed the phone to Luke. It had never ceased to amaze him how kids picked up so easily on technology.

"There it is!" Luke grinned and turned up the volume.

Billy Idol started singing about a white wedding and a shotgun. Dylan whooped, Jennifer blanched, and Sammie bit her lip, snickering while the kids bobbed in time with the music.

Matt rubbed his throbbing head, and when the song ended, he retrieved the phone from Luke. He wondered if Karen was somehow responsible for this.

"Interesting choice of music, Luke. Thank you. Let's continue," Dylan said.

Angela tried to hold Luke's hand. He snatched it away and wiped it on his shirt.

This time Sammie laughed out loud, and Pa chortled.

Matt silently urged Dylan to get this over with. Sweat poured down his back, even though they'd remained inside, and the pounding behind his eyes didn't help with his overall queasiness. When nudged by Pa, Matt repeated whatever Dylan said and then slipped the ring on Sammie's finger. It was a half size too big, but it made her gasp and smile. Her eyes actually shimmered when she looked up at him, as if he'd just placed a platinum and diamond band on her hand instead of forty-dollar ring from Walmart.

Sammie gripped his hands tightly and stammered her responses in a whisper. Before he knew it, Dylan was telling him to kiss the bride.

The entire ceremony had taken less than ten minutes. Rory woke up crying. Pa settled him by giving him his watch to play with and bouncing him on his good leg.

With everyone watching, Matt leaned over and gave Sammie a quick peck on the lips. She scrunched her nose and giggled, her face beet red. In an odd way, it helped his own nervousness to know she was uncomfortable too.

"You can do better than that," Pa goaded.

Sammie shook her finger. "We're keeping this rated G, old man. Kids are here."

After all the paperwork was signed, Jennifer insisted on snapping a few more pictures. Sammie shrugged uncomfortably in the tight dress as she lifted the skirt and clomped outside. Matt grinned. Pa was right—she never had put on airs. When she smiled at him, he impulsively kissed her forehead. Maybe they *could* make this work…

Surprised by Matt's kiss, Sammie spun her new wedding band, counting. She was beyond ready to shed the too-tight dress and get comfortable but was a little nervous about what happened next. *Honeymoon?* She and Matt hadn't discussed *sex*. Not that she was averse to it, but it didn't exactly factor into a friendly business deal, if that's what this was. Plus, she was pretty damn sure she'd qualify as a born-again virgin. The thought of sex added a whole new layer of apprehension to her anxiety. She had no clue what to expect or, more importantly, what *he* expected from her.

She glanced at her new husband. His face was pale, his smile strained as they kept up the pretense of being a happy couple through the photo taking. It occurred to her that he was probably comparing this marriage of inconvenience to his first one, the one he'd *wanted*.

After everyone feasted on Mrs. Jordan's cake, Luke packed a plastic shopping bag with his clothes, toothbrush, and favorite truck to spend the night with the McAthies. Dylan had promised hot dogs, s'mores, and fireworks if the rain held off.

She, Matt, and Pa watched from the front porch as Luke left without even a kiss goodbye, walking hand-in-hand with Dylan and Angela toward the boat dock half a mile away. Jennifer took Rory with her in the car.

"I'm afraid they're going to be camping inside." Sammie peered up at the gray sky.

Matt nodded. "Luckily they have a huge house, and Jennifer will make it fun."

"You two don't do anything I wouldn't do. Have fun and see ya tomorrow." Pa cackled as he made his way back inside with his walker.

Sammie bit her lip and waited.

"So, I guess we have a room…" Matt loosened his tie.

"Guess so. We don't have to go. It's up to you."

"No, it will make this seem more real if we go." Matt grimaced.

Sammie managed a smile, willing herself not to take it personally. "I can change first, right?" During the awkward photo session, she'd felt the seams in the top of the dress give a bit. And she needed a moment to collect herself.

"Sure, sure. I'm just waiting to make sure Luke doesn't back out at the last minute." His phone dinged, and a genuine smile spread across his face. Turning his phone, he showed her the video of Luke and Angela on the boat, waving. "A boat. I never thought of trying that. Too bad his doctor's office isn't on the lake." He pocketed his phone. "Uh, so, I'll change, and we need to pack an overnight bag."

"Okay." Sammie lifted the long skirt and plodded upstairs with him following. As she reached the landing, she remembered the countless buttons Luke had helped her with and stopped short. Matt ran into her from behind.

"Careful, now." His warm breath teased the back of her neck.

"Sorry. I don't know what to do. Luke helped me get into this thing, and he isn't here."

When Matt didn't move to help her, she glanced over her shoulder. He looked as if she'd asked him to put Rufus down.

She huffed. "Never mind. I'll manage and just sew the damn buttons back on later."

But before she could march to her room, he caught her hand. "I'll do it."

The look on his face was that of a cornered animal. Her insecurities flared again, but she took a deep breath, straightened her shoulders, and counted the slats on the hardwood floor.

Matt reached to undo the first button, hesitating as the memories surfaced. It seemed like only yesterday he'd taken Karen's blond hair down and kissed down her back as he'd slowly undressed her. He remembered being glad her morning sickness had abated in time for the ceremony. And that night, Karen had bemoaned the sparkling grape juice they drank instead of champagne.

His fingers shook as he unfastened each pearl button. As he worked his way down, he noticed Sammie's heated skin had a sensuous, spicy, floral scent. The freckles that slowly appeared beckoned to be kissed. She sighed, much like Luke did when he was bored and restless to do something else. His clumsy fingers brushed the satin of her bra, and finally he undid what had to be the seven-hundredth button.

"Thanks." Sammie held the dress to her chest and scurried into her room, closing the door.

Matt was relieved she hadn't looked back. Seeing her softly freckled shoulder, feeling her warm skin, and smelling her perfume had affected him in a painfully obvious manner. Closing his own door, he sank on the bed, elbows to knees as he pondered the upcoming night. *Why didn't we discuss this before now?*

His head still pounded, and the room was uncomfortably warm. He checked the window unit, but it seemed to be blowing cool air. Peering through the window, the sky was dark and gloomy with another incoming storm. It reflected his mood.

Chapter
Seven

The rain beat down relentlessly as Matt drove to Birmingham. Silence prevailed except for the squeak of the windshield wipers sweeping back and forth like a death knell. Sammie dug her nails into her palms and counted in time with the windshield wipers. *Seventy-eight, seventy-nine, eighty...*

Out of the corner of her eye, she watched Matt as he stared at the road, lost in his thoughts. He pulled into a convenience store.

"Why are we stopping?" she croaked.

"I need something for a migraine."

"I thought having a headache would be my line."

The joke fell flat. He slammed the car door and dashed into the store.

Sammie sighed. She had no idea how much farther they'd have to drive. She followed him inside and headed to the bathroom. When she returned, she found him pacing in the pouring rain, ranting expletives that would make his father proud and significantly increase Luke's college fund.

"What's wrong?" she yelled.

Matt slammed his fist against the car hood, whirled around, and roared, *"You locked the damn keys in the car!"*

"S-Sorry."

A drop of water hung suspended from his nose. Sammie couldn't help it. She started giggling. He looked like a bedraggled, rabid dog.

"Stop laughing. This is all your fault, Samantha Morgan!"

The ridiculousness of the situation made her laugh that much harder. She bent over, really glad she'd already peed. When she could speak, she gasped, "*Tyler*. Samantha *Tyler*. And what good is yelling at me? Just call a locksmith, moron."

"I *would*, but my phone is inside the goddamned *locked* car," he replied through gritted teeth.

Yeesh. Sure, she should've been more careful about the keys, but he was overreacting. And she didn't like it. Not one bit. It reminded her of Sue Ellen on the crazy upswing. She searched in her purse and handed him her phone.

Two hours later, the locksmith unlocked the car.

Buckling up she said, "Come on, Tyler. Someday we'll look back and laugh about this."

"I highly doubt it."

Feeling unsettled, she counted street lights as he drove, wondering if she'd made the biggest mistake of her life.

Matt opened the door and forgot to breathe for a moment at the size of the suite. It overlooked the city and included a living area with all the amenities, even a bottle of expensive champagne and chocolate-dipped strawberries. *Geezus.* This must've set Dylan back a small fortune. Matt hated being beholden to anyone, even if it was a gift.

"Wow! So this is how the other half live," Sammie commented, walking around the room. "Not bad. I could get used to this." She plucked a strawberry from the silver tray.

"You're going to be sorely disappointed then, being married to me." All he wanted was to get out of these wet clothes and sleep. His limbs felt like lead. Matt threw the suitcase down in the bedroom.

"Oh for heaven's sake, Matt. Lighten up. We're a little wet — no big deal. I said I was sorry. I'm going to shower." Sammie grabbed some clothes from the suitcase and shoved past him into the bathroom. "You're not so damn perfect, St. Matthew..."

Soaked to the skin, Matt adjusted the thermostat, sat on the side of the bed, and started channel surfing. When nothing captured his attention, he shut the television off. His teeth chattered. If he didn't get a hot shower soon, he was bound to have a case of literal blue balls.

The door opened, and Sammie wandered out in a T-shirt and shorts—a sharp contrast to the expensive French silk gown Karen had worn...Shoving the memory aside, he crossed his arms in front of his chest, trying to control his shivering.

Samantha tossed her glorious red hair and lifted that impossibly stubborn chin. "I told you I'm immune to the stink eye. It would serve you right if you caught your death by cold." Grabbing a pillow from the bed and a blanket from the closet, she marched toward the living area.

He followed fast on her heels. "Unfortunately for you, I wouldn't leave you a wealthy widow; you're not on my life insurance policy yet. What are you doing out here? Go get in bed." *Can this night get any worse?*

"It'll be a cold day in hell before I get in bed with you! And before you say I owe a quarter, the cussin' jar doesn't count when you're outta town." She lay down with her back to him and squeezed her eyes closed.

Fine. He marched back to the bathroom, swallowed a couple of Excedrin, and showered, but nothing helped the throbbing in his head and sore muscles. *What's wrong with me?*

He needed to apologize to Sammie. *We're friends. I need to quit being an ass. Luke's future depends on it.*

He found her asleep on the couch. An empty glass of champagne and a plate of strawberry stems sat on the table.

His guilt quadrupled. Feeling like crap, he hadn't thought to stop and get anything to eat. She had to be starving. It would cost a fortune, but the least he could do was order room service for her.

"Sammie?"

Her rhythmic breathing was the only response. Tenderly, he tucked the blanket around her, once again berating himself.

He crawled into bed alone.

The next morning, Matt towel dried his hair, careful not to jar his still-aching head. The shower hadn't done a damn thing to help his hangover. It had to have been the moonshine—maybe it was tainted. *I'm dying of arsenic poisoning. No, that's crazy. Gig's been making homebrew longer than I've been alive.* He rubbed his beard, deciding it would require too much effort to shave. Opening the bathroom door, he found Sammie sitting on the edge of the bed, dressed in a blue T-shirt and jeans. She was fingering her bracelets. They hadn't spoken since last night.

He shrugged into his shirt and sat next to her on the bed. His eyes felt like a sandpit.

"I'm sorry," he muttered.

As he bent to put on his shoes and socks, the room spun, and he felt sick to his stomach. Sweat poured down his back, and he got up and turned the air conditioner on high as he finished getting dressed.

Samantha crossed her arms. "For?"

"For everything." It was the standard husband answer. *Karen never bought it.*

"You're a jerk."

Apparently, Sammie didn't either. *Shit.*

He didn't have the energy to fight with her. "I'm sorry about last night. I have no explanation for why I acted like that. I truly appreciate all you're doing to help me and Luke."

"Matt, we need to talk. We rushed into this marriage without really thinking through how—"

"I don't feel like talking, Sammie. I just wanna go home." He hadn't tempered his tone and regretted it immediately.

Sammie's look darkened.

"I'm sorry. I'm just so tired…and with this headache, I literally can't think straight." Matt pulled her into an awkward side-hug.

Though stiff at first, she relaxed and patted him on the back. "We're going to argue; we did so as kids. But we need to work together." She frowned and placed the back of her cool fingers on his forehead. "Matt, I think you have a fever."

"Don't be ridiculous. I don't get sick. It's probably just stress or not enough sleep." He couldn't afford to be sick and miss work or school.

"No, I'm taking you to one of those doc-in-a-box places. You're sick."

Sweat trickled down his back, and his teeth started to chatter. He couldn't afford to pay for a doctor. "No. We're going home," he snapped.

"Fine. Don't complain if you die," she huffed. "But I'm driving."

Matt didn't argue as he handed her his keys. With a wry smile he said, "Just no stops. We can't afford another locksmith."

"Very funny."

The next thing he knew, Sammie was shaking his shoulder, which hurt. Everything hurt. He opened his eyes and had never been so glad to see his home. *I'm dying.*

"I'll get the suitcase; you go on in and lie down."

"No, I'll get it."

"Good God, Tyler. Is it your life mission to be a martyr? Aren't martyrs at least kind and good humored?" Sammie slammed the car door and marched into the house without a backward glance.

Great way to start a marriage…

As he slammed the trunk closed, Dylan walked up the driveway with Luke, who was licking a huge lollipop. Matt glanced at his watch.

"Really? Candy at ten in the morning?"

"It's a secret, Daddy. We can't tell Jennifer." Luke's face was a sticky mess.

"I parent by bribery. It works; ask my kids. You look like s-h-i-t. That must've been some night." He winked and grinned. "Although you're home early. Usually checkout isn't until eleven."

"Shut up, Dylan." Belatedly, Matt remembered he was an adult and needed to set an example. "I mean, uh, thanks for the room and stuff. It was nice." He turned to his son. "What do you say?"

"Thank you, Dylan. I had fun!"

"Anytime. And soon, we'll go for a ride in my race car, okay?"

Luke looked skeptical but didn't disagree. If Dylan could coerce Luke into a car without a tantrum, Matt would seriously rethink his own parenting style and give bribery a go.

As they went into the house, Luke regaled him with stories about his evening with the McAthies. Matt nodded, not really listening. It took everything in him just to put one foot in front of the other.

Sammie commandeered Luke into the kitchen and fussed good-naturedly about his stickiness as Matt made his way upstairs at the pace of an arthritic ninety-year-old. All he wanted was to crawl in bed and sleep off whatever this was. His body ached worse than it had after Bubba had beat the shit out of him.

Even his eyelashes hurt. *Do eyelashes have nerve endings?*

Sammie woke up in the middle of the night with the funny feeling something was wrong. She'd opted to sleep in her bedroom to keep from disturbing the cranky patient. Plus, they hadn't discussed the sleeping arrangements of this so-called marriage. She checked on Luke and tucked his covers around him.

She heard a whispered oath from Matt's room and scurried down the hall. He sat on the side of the bed, shivering.

She wrapped a quilt around him, frowning at the heat emanating from his body. His unshaven cheeks were flushed, his eyes glassy.

"I'm dying. I hope everyone's happy," he mumbled.

"Not particularly. You haven't changed your life insurance policy yet, remember?"

"You're cruel."

"I know."

"I can't get warm; I've never felt this bad in my entire miserable life. If I die, please don't let Luke find the porn hidden in my garage. They're on my workbench under a tarp and paint cans. At least not until he's a teenager." He rubbed his eyes with the heels of his hands, looking a lot like Luke when he was tired.

She laughed. "I'll burn them. I promise."

"No, don't burn them. Geezus, Sammie. Some of those issues are worth some money."

"Right, *oh-kay*. I'll look up their worth on the internet and sell them to help pay for Luke's college."

"T-Thank you. Although it'll probably be paid for by then at the rate the damn no-c-cussing jar is filling up. Buy him a car. A safe one. A t-tank might work."

"Will do. Now hush and let me take your temp."

She busied herself with the thermometer for a moment.

"A hundred and two! Matt, please let me take you to the doctor." She helped him back under the covers. He was still fully dressed except for his shoes.

"No, just get me warm," he whined, sounding a lot like his son.

"I'll be right back."

She returned and gave him more medication to bring down the fever and a cup of hot tea. He shook so bad he couldn't hold the cup without spilling, so she spooned the warm liquid into his mouth. When she'd finished, she gathered her things to go, but Matt reached for her hand.

"Don't leave," he whispered.

"I won't leave you, Mattie. Close your eyes and get some rest."

He pulled her in with him, spooning her butt and wrapping an arm around her waist.

"You're the only one I ever let call me that girlie name," he muttered. "Thank you, Sammie. Feels good. So warm, so good…" He slipped almost immediately into sleep.

"That's what friends are for," she whispered.

Chapter Eight

Leaving his room for the first time in a week, Matt wondered if he was having a temperature-induced hallucination. The house no longer looked ready to be condemned. Sammie had cleaned and organized the entire place. He hadn't even had to search for sock mates this morning; they were folded together in his drawer.

"Daddy's up!" Luke grinned as he ate his bowl of cereal.

"Good morning. Sausage biscuit?" Sammie asked, handing him a cup of coffee.

Hungry for the first time in a while, he nodded. "To go, please. I need to get busy. And thank you."

He frowned, slightly alarmed by how much money was in the no-cussing jar on the kitchen table. "Who's the main offender?"

"Luke," Sammie joked, handing him a sausage biscuit in a paper towel.

"Great. Hope you made sure he used them in the proper syntax."

"Of course. He's smart like his daddy. It's good to see you up."

"I'm pretty sure I was on death's door. I've never been that sick in my life."

Sammie snorted. "Man flu."

From the living area, Pa cussed loudly as his walker bumped into something. Matt frowned, confirming the source of the growing college fund. *Some things never change.*

"Sammie, I'm going to call Mrs. Jordan and see if she'll stay with Luke for an hour or so at lunch. James and his right-hand weasel, Travis, play golf every Friday afternoon. It's the best time to add you to my bank accounts."

"Okay."

He kissed Luke and headed out the back door.

"Wait, Daddy! Kiss Sammie! Pa said married people kiss a lot."

Wonderful. Pa's gone from dating advice to marriage etiquette. "Is that so? That's kind of private, son."

Sammie blushed and busied herself doing dishes, not making eye contact.

"You behave and help Sammie with the chores, okay?"

"Okay."

Matt hurried out to his shop behind the house and threw open the door. His mouth dropped. The tools were arranged on his workbench, and the place had been swept. To his dismay, his favorite faded and torn Crucified, Dead and Buried band T-shirt was in the pile of clean and neatly folded rags. There was even a new notebook with appointments for repairs—each numbered to go with the corresponding board now above his workbench, which featured numbered nails holding keys.

After lunch and a quick run to the bank, time flew as he tried to get caught up after a week off. He had to get work done so he could get paid. Wandering back toward the house for supper, he stopped, surprised to find Luke sitting on top of the car.

Squealing with laughter, Luke shouted in sing-song fashion, pointing at Sammie. "Nah, nah, nah, nah, you can't get me."

Stunned that Luke was anywhere near a car, Matt shot an inquiring look to Sammie.

"It's base. You know—the only safe place when playing tag." Laughing, she tagged him *it* and ran for the safety of the car. For the next thirty minutes, they played the silly game until Sammie declared it time to get cleaned up before supper. Matt picked up Luke and grinned at her.

The setting sun made her hair look like waves of fire. Her up-turned nose was pink, and a wide smile lit her face. In his arms, his son was relaxed and giggling like a normal little boy—one who hadn't been touched by tragedy.

A rare and welcome sense of peace settled in his heart as they made their way inside.

"Sammie?"

"Yes?" She paused at Luke's door, ready to flick off the light.

"Can I have another story?"

"No, it's bedtime. Daddy will be up in a few minutes to say goodnight."

"A song?"

Sammie smiled. "We already sang a song. Goodnight, Luke." She turned off the light.

"Did you know my mommy?" the small voice from the bed asked.

Sammie walked back and sat on the side of Luke's bed. "Yes. She was very pretty."

"Can I tell you a secret?"

"Of course." Something about his voice let her know this wasn't a stall tactic. She held his hand and gave him her full attention.

"Sometimes, I sneak into Daddy's room and look at Mommy's picture. It's in his dresser drawer."

"I see." *Where's Matt when I need him?* "You shouldn't be going through other people's things…"

Luke sighed. "Mommy used to say that, too—when I went in Lizbeth's room."

She gathered the child into her arms and held him tight. "I know you miss them."

He nodded. She sang "Silent Night" and tucked him back in.

Then Matt walked in and leaned over to kiss Luke on the forehead. Together they left the room.

"Christmas songs in June?" he asked with a chuckle, closing the door.

"I like them. They're comforting. Matt, we need to talk."

"Now?" His shoulders sagged. "I've been swamped with work, and I have a test I need to study for."

"It's about Luke—"

Matt smiled. "He's adjusting better than I ever dreamed. And supper was delicious tonight." To her surprise, he hugged her, but before she could respond, he darted into his room and closed the door.

Sammie took three steps toward his room and stopped. Memories of her mother's mercurial mood swings haunted her. Although her current situation was a far cry from her dreams, things were calm and harmonious. No way she'd risk upsetting this arrangement. She'd just find a picture of Karen and Lizbeth to give to Luke.

Matt kicked off his shoes and socks and collapsed on his bed, closing his eyes just for a moment. He'd made a good dent in his work this afternoon—which meant the bills would be paid—but he had a sneaking suspicion the uptick in business was related to curiosity regarding his marital status, not his mechanical expertise. Dylan told him he'd strategically let the news of the wedding drop at the Mug and Cone. Surprisingly, he hadn't heard from Howell yet. He sat up and grabbed his laptop to start studying. *Thank God for Sammie.* With her here, he almost felt like he could breathe again. This arrangement was working out well after all.

He heard Sammie in the hall and held his breath. He hated that phrase "we need to talk." In his experience, it never boded well. But the steps disappeared down the stairs.

Thank God.

Sammie was totally the opposite of Karen. His first wife would never have let the conversation go. He closed the computer, walked to the window, and stared outside. By the dusk-to-dawn light he saw Sammie sitting in the swing, strumming her guitar.

Quietly, he cracked the window and listened. He could just make out the chorus of "Angels We Have Heard on High."

Chapter
Nine

On Father's Day, Matt wandered downstairs, yawning and in desperate need of coffee. Things had settled into a quiet routine. He and Sam were learning to live together, but it was more as roommates than husband and wife. Apart from the one night she'd let him hold her to get warm when he was sick, she'd stayed in her room. He'd learned she was a morning person. She now knew he wasn't fully human until he'd had two cups of coffee.

This morning he'd overslept after staying up late working on a paper for school. Sammie had left the box of cereal on the table for him with a bowl and spoon, and there was still a half a pot of coffee. Next to it was a card from Luke. He smiled, looking at the card with two stick figures on it. Sammie must've helped him with the writing, as only three letters were backward.

Skipping the cereal, he enjoyed his coffee and walked toward the shop. He assumed Pa was still sleep, which was a good thing.

The day wasn't complete without Sammie and Pa getting into it about something. While it was mostly all in good-natured fun, Matt got tired of Pa making an issue out of everything. He'd always been a contrary old cuss, but he was much worse since his stroke.

From the back of the house, he heard Sammie calling for Luke. Walking past the car, he stopped when he heard a giggle. It took him a minute to realize it came from *inside* the car. Peering in the rolled-down window, he saw two mischievous dark eyes looking up at him from the floorboard of the backseat. *Luke's in a car?*

"Luke!" Sammie shouted from behind the house.

His son grinned and held his finger to his lips. Matt winked and turned around, leaning against the car. Samantha rounded the corner from the backyard. He sipped his coffee and waited.

"Lukas Matthew Tyler! Where are you? You better come out right now! I ain't playin' around no more." Samantha jumped when she saw Matt.

"Oh! Hello. I didn't know you were up. Happy Father's Day. Get that paper done last night?" Her gaze roamed the yard, and she started spinning her wedding band, despite the tape she'd used to try to make it fit.

I really need to get it resized for her. "Thanks. And yes, the paper's done. Where's Luke? I want to thank him for the card." Matt kept his tone casual, but it was hard to keep from laughing when Sammie's eyes widened.

"I, uh, well, I'm not really sure," she stammered.

Matt raised an eyebrow. "What do you mean, you're not sure?"

"We were playing hide and seek, and well…" Her thumbs tapped each finger repeatedly.

"Well what?" Matt shouted, trying his best to sound upset and not tickled.

"I can't find him!"

"Are you saying you've lost my four-year-old son?"

"I wouldn't exactly say *lost*…let's just say *misplaced*…momentarily. A-And he's almost f-five." She backed away as Matt marched toward her.

"How long has he been missing?" It was tricky, but he managed to maneuver their positions so her back was to the car.

"Um, well, not too long, maybe five, ten minutes tops…" Her voice trailed off as she continued to back away.

"He's just a little boy!"

"I'm sorry!"

"I guess you should be punished somehow. Yes, I think the sentence should be—" Matt reached around her, opened the car door, and shoved her onto the backseat in front of Luke. "Death by tickling," he shouted as Luke joined the punishment.

"Stop! Stop! I can't breathe!"

The level of panic in her voice startled Matt. Her face was pale and pinched, her breathing ragged. And then she started fighting.

"Whoa, stop, son." Amidst her flailing arms and kicks he managed to shove Luke into the front seat. Luke giggled, seeming to think it part of the game.

"It's okay, Sammie. Hold on." Matt backed out of the car, leaving a path free for her to escape.

She bolted and ran. Her hair fell loose from its clip, flowing behind her like a curtain.

"Sammie, I'm sorry!" Luke yelled, scrambling out of the car to go after her.

Matt grabbed his arm. "No, Luke. Give her a minute. We scared her."

"I didn't mean to."

"I know. I know. You run on inside, make sure the house is picked up the way Sammie likes it, okay? I'll go check on her. And thank you for the card. Being your dad is the best thing ever. I love you."

"Love you, too. Lots and lots. Tell Sammie I'm sorry!" He hurried in the house.

Matt found her sitting on the back step with her arms wrapped tight around her knees as she rocked back and forth. Her pupils were so large it was hard to see the blue of her irises.

He sat beside her and drew her into his arms. "Hey. You okay? I'm sorry we scared you."

She buried her face in his shirt, still shaking.

"I got you, Sammie." He rubbed her back and spoke softly, like he did when Luke woke up with a nightmare.

Nodding, she closed her eyes and curled in to him, holding his shirt tight. Her breathing evened out after a few minutes, and she looked up at him with a small smile. Her eyes returned to their luminous blue. "I'm okay. S-Sorry—oh my God!" She looked around and leaped to her feet. "Where's Luke?"

Matt stood. "He's fine, Sammie. More than fine. He was *in* the car." Matt still couldn't believe it.

"He was, wasn't he?" Sammie let out another deep breath. "I'm fine, too." To his surprise, she jumped into his arms, wrapping her arms around his neck, and hugged him. "Better than fine. No one can ever hurt me again. I don't have to be scared, anymore, do I?"

"I hope not. Who hurt you, Sammie?" He brushed a strand of hair out of her eyes. An urge to kiss her took him by surprise, but before he could act on it, she ran off to find Luke.

"Don't worry about it. It was a lifetime ago! Luke!"

That night, Sammie stared at the ceiling, hands behind her head. Matt was still downstairs studying. She never went to sleep until she heard him quietly come up the stairs and into his room. Every night, before Pa retired, he gave her and Matt a questioning look, which they pretended to ignore. Thankfully, he didn't ask *why* they were sleeping in separate bedrooms.

While she was happy here, she was lonely and in desperate need of someone to talk to. Living with her best friend should've been easy, except they never really *talked* except for superficial conversation. And this was compounded by two kisses and a few misses that had fanned the embers of her teenage crush into a forest fire of lust and other uncharted emotions. She wanted to be more than friends. And that was *her* problem. She wished she knew Jennifer McAthie well enough to talk to her, but even if she did, she couldn't very well tell her this wasn't a real marriage.

The car incident this morning had triggered a memory of one of the scariest nights she'd ever endured with Sue Ellen. When she was nine years old, she'd accidentally knocked the picture of her father off the shelf, shattering the glass. Carefully, she'd cleaned it up and placed the picture back, sans glass—praying her mother wouldn't notice when she got home.

But her mother *had* noticed. And she'd been off her meds.

That night, Sammie had awakened to her mother duct-taping her mouth shut and taping her wrists together. Terrified, she'd wet herself, but Sue Ellen hadn't swayed from her mission. Her mother had dragged her from the house and thrown her in the backseat of the car. As she drove to the deserted cemetery, she'd berated her for her "sins." Once there, Sue Ellen had hauled her from the car and ripped the duct tape off her face and wrists. To this day, she could recall in agonizing detail how her chafed cheeks had burned from her tears and the humiliating smell of her urine-soaked nightgown. Forcing her to kneel, Sue Ellen had hissed, "Pay respect to your father! Tell him you loved him! And pray for forgiveness; you're an evil little girl."

Her teeth had chattered more from fear than the cold night air. Her knees had bled from the sharp pebbles that dug into them. As her mother had paced back and forth quoting scriptures, she'd been forced to pray for forgiveness to a God she didn't believe in and apologize to the father she missed.

A terrified whimper pulled her from the past. *Luke.* Sammie bolted from bed and found the boy trembling and crying for his mother. She gathered him into her arms and rocked him, crooning in his ear. "Hey, hey. Wake up, Luke. It was just a bad a dream. You're okay."

He opened his eyes and clung to her.

"Everything is fine. Breathe in slowly and let it out all the way. Not so fast."

She demonstrated, and he slowed his breathing to match hers.

Matt appeared at the door, his face drawn and shadowed by pain. She felt awkward and intrusive. She wasn't the boy's mother. Did she have a right to comfort him? Matt came over and crouched beside the bed.

"Son?" His voice choked.

Luke reached for his father. Matt took him and walked back and forth, rubbing his back.

"Daddy's here. You're safe," he murmured.

"I miss Mommy and Lizbeth." The little boy's heart-wrenching sobs filled the room.

Wiping tears from her eyes, Samantha wondered how Matt was able to stand it.

"I know you do. But remember what I told you? Mommy and Lizbeth are always with you, right here." Using his finger, Matt traced a heart on Luke's chest and forehead.

Luke nodded and clasped his arms around Matt's neck. His crying subsided as Matt held him, whispering soothing words.

Luke's eyes grew heavy, and Matt tucked him back in bed with a kiss to his forehead. Silently, she followed him out of the room.

Matt didn't make it downstairs before collapsing on a step. Sammie sat beside him.

"You're good at that," she observed.

His brows knit together.

"Comforting your son—and me, making us feel safe. You have a knack for it."

He rubbed his face and took a moment before replying. "It's been several months since he had a nightmare. When he was in the hospital—after he wasn't so sedated—it was a nightly occurrence. The accident report claimed Karen ran a stop sign. An eighteen-wheeler hit them on the driver's side. Both kids were in the backseat, Elizabeth behind Karen and Luke in his car seat. The truck driver couldn't help it. He tried to avoid them. Karen and Elizabeth took the full impact. Karen died instantly; Elizabeth lingered for a few hours."

Matt rubbed his eyes with his palms. "They had to use the Jaws of Life to get them out. One of the first responders is a friend of mine. He said Luke kept calling for Karen, trying to get her to 'wake up.' He clung to her hair as they pulled him from the car…Lizbeth never regained consciousness and died right after I got to the hospital. It was as if she hung on until I could get there to say goodbye." Matt's throat bobbled. "When I got to Luke's bedside, I hardly recognized my son. He was covered in blood. His blood. Karen's blood. Elizabeth's blood. *There was so much damn blood.*"

Sammie placed her hand on his knee, not knowing what to say. Her heart broke just witnessing his pain. *How in the world had he stood it?*

"Sometimes I feel lost, Sammie…So fuckin' lost."

"You'll find your way," Sammie assured him, rubbing his back. Tears filled her eyes.

Matt didn't answer, unable to keep his shit together any longer. She kissed his cheek, and he wrapped his arms around her, drawing in her compassion, her strength. She was the only thing keeping him anchored lately. His body shook as he tried to contain his grief and fear, but it spilled forth in silent sobs. All of his inadequacies as a parent lay exposed like an open wound.

"I don't know what I'm doing. People say, 'Oh, Matt, you're doing so well,' and I smile, but it's fake. I'm barely hanging in here. Karen was a great mother. She handled everything...I'm finding out parenting is a crapshoot."

"Hush now, you're a good father. A good man. You're still grieving; this is all normal, Matt."

"I'm overwhelmed. I can't do this by myself."

"You're not alone. You have me. We're a team, Mattie."

He stared at her face, illuminated by the light downstairs. The need to connect with someone took hold of his rational thinking. Reaching over, he stroked her soft cheek and pulled her closer. His lips met hers, and she responded with a soft sigh. He deepened the kiss, not heeding the warning screaming through his mind. His hand moved from her cheek down her long neck. Exploring her body, he caressed her breast through the thin cotton gown, and her nipple hardened. She drew in a sharp breath but didn't stop him. He laid her back and kissed her frantically, wanting more...

The scrape of his father's walker downstairs penetrated his passion-drugged conscience and he pulled away, suddenly embarrassed. "I'm sorry. I don't know what I was thinking. W-We're just friends. Please... forgive me," he mumbled.

He bolted downstairs, unable to meet her eyes.

"It's okay, Matt," she whispered.

He turned at the bottom step and looked up, unsure he'd heard her correctly, but she was gone.

Sammie stood in Matt's doorway early the next morning. One arm lay over his eyes, as if he could hide from their strange new reality of being a family, but not a couple. His bare chest moved up and down with his rhythmic breathing. He didn't wear a wedding band, and it bothered her since he'd been wearing his previous one when they met. She was saving a dollar or two a week from their grocery money to buy him one. She fingered the simple band on her left ring finger. It gave her a small sense of belonging, though she knew *Matt* didn't belong to her. *He'll always be Karen's.*

Despite some therapy, she still struggled occasionally with feelings of inadequacy. She'd thought about looking up the local mental health center to schedule an appointment, but didn't, afraid it would give Mr. Howell leverage against Matt. He called several times a week to check on Luke. He was coolly polite before she handed the phone over to him. Yesterday, he'd choked up thanking Luke for the Father's Day card, and she'd almost felt sorry for him.

She found it strange that Mrs. Howell never called, though, and that they hadn't visited since she'd come into the family.

Anyway, if she couldn't seek outside help, she needed to process her feelings on her own. She began to list them. *Fear* when she thought Luke was lost. *Terror* when she was trapped in the back of the car. *Relief* when Matt had backed up and given her space. *Compassion* when she'd comforted Luke after his nightmare. *Desire* for Matt.

The last one shouldn't have been a surprise. In her dreams, she'd always held him as the standard for a man. And in reality, all other men had fallen short.

And last, but not least, *guilt* for wanting a man who was still grieving his wife.

Sighing, she left him to sleep and headed downstairs to start breakfast.

Matt stared at the pot of coffee, willing it to hurry up and brew. He needed to look into getting a new coffee pot — one of those instant brewers for jerks who needed instant gratification. *What the hell, dumbass? Kissing Sammie?* Things were great as is. They were friends. *Though with benefits would be nice...*

Matt spilled his first cup down his bare chest. Swearing under his breath, he reached to grab a quarter for the no-cussing jar, but was still in his pajama pants.

"That's what you get for running around half-naked," Sammie teased, walking through with a basket of clean clothes. She wore a pair of tight jeans and a blue T-shirt that did nothing to hide the curves of her generous breasts. Her red hair was piled on top of her head, exposing her long neck. His dick gave a morning salute.

Beyond embarrassed, he darted from the room to grab a shower and get a grip on things. *Literally.* When everything was under control again, he returned downstairs, fully dressed. He tossed a quarter in the jar for this morning and stuffed in an extra buck for his shower.

"You didn't have to put a shirt on for my sake," Sammie chided. "I *have* seen you without a shirt millions of times." As she handed him a fresh cup of coffee, a smile lingered on her full lips—lips he couldn't seem to stop staring at, remembering how soft they'd been. Thankfully she turned back to the counter, readying his breakfast.

"Hi, Daddy."

"Morning, son." Matt turned and greeted Luke, glad for the distraction.

Luke slipped Rufus half his biscuit under the table.

"I saw that, Lukas Tyler."

"How, Sammie?"

"I have eyes in the back of my head. Matt, if you want an egg, will you get them for me?"

Matt hoped she wasn't psychic as well. That kiss last night had unnerved him. By choice, he'd avoided women since Karen's death. He'd been appalled by how the women he'd known all his life—single, divorced, or widowed, it didn't matter—had descended upon him only days after the funerals. They'd cooked entire meals or special desserts and brought them to the hospital. Once he and Luke were home, they'd offered to take care of his son, run errands, and sew buttons on his shirts. His business when he'd returned to work had been comprised mostly of women needing minor or non-existent mechanical adjustments.

When Karen was alive, he'd rarely worn a wedding band because of his job. But after her death, he started wearing it everywhere outside the shop. Unfortunately, instead of a deterrent, it had seemed to be more of a magnet.

On the two occasions when he'd forced Luke to attend church, three different women had made eyes at him while fussing over the screaming boy. He'd been glad when their cooing attention hadn't helped, using it as an out to take Luke home. Three more times he'd tried attending on his own, which turned out to be a huge mistake. No matter how late he arrived or where he sat—in the back, middle, or the front of the church—an available woman found a way to sit next to him. They varied in age, and—ironically, since they were in church—morals. He'd confided to Pa that he felt like a dead rabbit, and the buzzards were circling.

He shook himself out of his memories.

"Do I go to school today?" Luke asked.

"No. We've discussed this. You're too young for elementary school, and I don't think we can afford preschool when it starts *in August*," Matt barked, tired of the daily question. *Fuck, stop being an ass!* For good measure, he shoved a quarter in the jar as Sammie pursed her lips. *Why is she staring at me? Does she know how she's affecting me?*

To avoid her searching gaze, he reached in the refrigerator and grabbed the carton of eggs.

Sammie stared at his red face and grew uneasy when he wouldn't look her in the eye. "Look, if you're upset about last night…"

Matt dropped an egg on the floor. "Dammit," he swore under his breath. He halfway cleaned it up, leaving the rest to Rufus. Digging in his pocket, he put another quarter in the jar. "I'm going broke."

Luke giggled. "Daddy's gonna get in trouble, and I'm gonna be rich!"

"If you're done eating, you and Rufus go outside and play, but stay on the porch," Sammie encouraged, shooing the boy and dog out the door. "Feed Rhonda, too."

"Okay, Sammie."

It was time she and Matt had a talk. She couldn't stand the weirdness between them any longer.

"For God's sake, Matt. It was a stupid kiss shared in the heat of the moment. We're only human. And we're married, so it's even morally legit if we give in to certain needs—"

"It shouldn't have happened. It isn't fair to you. I don't want to cross any boundaries or have any misunderstandings between us. I'm never going to love again."

That remark hurt. She tucked a loose strand of hair behind her ear, wishing for the millionth time it was blond. Pushing her feelings aside, she decided to lay out the facts to her obtuse friend/husband. "Well, that's just plain sad and asinine. Is that the example you wanna set for Luke? Why don't you just put a five in the jar to cover your expenses today?" She turned to straighten the silverware drawer.

"What did you say?" he asked.

"Love doesn't have a damn thing to do with it. You're the one in school. This thing between us? It's chemistry or biology…or some other subject, maybe human sexuality."

To prove her point, she spun around, grabbed his shoulders, and kissed him with all her pent-up frustration. Instead of pushing her away, Matt pulled her closer, wrapping his arms around her waist as his lips slanted over hers. His tongue explored her mouth. Closing her eyes, she pressed her body into his, her fingers playing with the waves at the nape of his neck.

This moment was the stuff of her dreams. Her knees would have buckled if his arms weren't supporting her.

"Ahem."

Startled, they jumped apart. Pa stood in the doorway, watching them, an amused grin spreading across his face. "Maybe it's time you two shared a bedroom. I can watch the boy while you get this out of your system."

Matt glared at his father and moved to the back door, nearly tripping over Rufus and Luke as they came back inside. "I'll be in the shop," he muttered. "I'm not hungry after all."

"Not for food anyway," Pa commented as he sat down. An amused glint flickered in his dark eyes.

"You're an evil old man," Sammie admonished lightly as she poured his coffee.

"You got that right. Stick with me, young lady, and you might learn a thing or two."

Matt busied himself with work. *What's wrong with me? It's finally happened; I've lost my fucking mind.* Getting caught making out with Sammie like some stupid, horny teenager had to be one of the most embarrassing moments of his life.

Maybe it wasn't quite as bad as the time Pa and Bubba Kelton found him in the hayloft with Janice Newton, but it was a close second.

A car pulled into the driveway, and Matt rolled himself out from under the vehicle he'd been working on. Mrs. Jordan waved as she parked. Hopping to his feet and wiping his hands on a rag, Matt went to see what she needed.

"Hello, Matt! How's everything going?" She smiled.

"Hi, Mrs. J, what brings you way out here? That timing belt isn't giving you any more trouble, is it?"

"No, just time for the oil to be changed."

"Sure. I can do it this afternoon. Need me to run you home? Your cake plate is in the kitchen. It was delicious and really nice of you to make a wedding cake for us. Thank you. I should've gotten it back to you sooner."

"You're welcome, and don't worry about the plate. There's no need to run me home. Jennifer's going to pick me up in a few minutes, and then we're headed to Birmingham. I'll visit with your family until she gets here. I made some fried apple pies and brought them. I remember how Luke loved them when he was in the hospital."

Matt strongly suspected this visit was more about curiosity, but Mrs. Jordan was a nice woman and a good friend. She'd been the one to stay with Luke while he and Pa attended Karen's and Elizabeth's funerals.

"Everyone's in the house." He escorted her through the front door, proud to show off the difference Sammie had made. The rugs were vacuumed, the floors mopped, and everything was dusted and polished. There were no old fast food wrappers or dirty dishes in sight, and the tantalizing smell of something cooking greeted them.

Yes, the house was perfect.

The inhabitants were another matter.

From the kitchen came a stream of profanity that shot Mrs. Jordan's brow upward. Matt wasn't even sure *he* knew the meaning of some of the words Sammie and Pa were shouting. Embarrassed, he hurried to see if there were any casualties and let them know company was here.

Standing on a kitchen chair, Luke jumped up and down, howling with laughter as Pa and Sammie argued. Matt guesstimated at least five more dollars had been added to the jar. Sam's blue jeans and T-shirt were covered in flour as she shook a wooden spoon at Pa.

"You can call me every name in the book, but it won't change my mind. You will *not* be served dinner at this table until you bathe and change those stinkin'-ass clothes, do you hear me?" Face flushed, her chest heaved with her exasperation. She dug in her pockets but came up empty handed and stomped her foot.

"I ain't bathin' for you or God Almighty himself! You're the orneriest goddamned woman I've ever met!" Pa dropped a quarter in the jar.

"Dammit, you haven't even got me started, old man. I'm not your frickin' maid, and I will *not* serve you in your room. You bathe, change those smelly clothes, and come eat at this table, or you can starve in hell, for all I care!"

"That'll cost ya two more quarters, Sammie!" It seemed Lukas was both refereeing and looking out for his college fund.

Sammie and Pa became aware of their presence nearly simultaneously. Sammie blushed, but Pa smirked.

"I'm sorry, Matt. I need to borrow a couple of dollars, please." Sammie glanced at the no-cussing jar. She shot Pa a withering look when he chuckled.

Matt didn't know whether to laugh or wash both of their mouths out with soap. It seemed Pa had finally met his match. He pulled out the only two dollars he had and handed them to Sammie, who shoved them in the jar.

"You'll have to put in an I.O.U. You're going into debt," he teased for lack of anything else to say. He glanced at Mrs. Jordan, who was biting her lip to keep from laughing.

Pa nodded. "Eloise."

"Leroy. Hello, Luke, Sammie."

"Make Pa get a bath," Luke shouted, still jumping up and down in the chair. "I think Pa owes money, too!"

Pa turned and shook his fist at his grandson. "Whose side are you on?" he growled.

Luke laughed even harder.

Sammie huffed her outrage and started in again. "Don't you dare talk to Luke that way—"

Matt decided to step in as head umpire. "Hold it, you two. Time out!" He helped Luke off the chair. "Mrs. Jordan brought you some fried apple pies. Why don't you take one to the porch?"

"It'll spoil his lunch," Sammie protested.

"I don't care," Matt replied.

"Thank you for the pies." Luke hugged Mrs. Jordan and headed to the front porch with Rufus following.

At least someone in this family has manners.

"How's the family, Ellie?" Pa asked.

"No one has called me that in a long time, Leroy." Mrs. Jordan blushed and patted her hair. "They're fine. Robert and Cathy just had an anniversary. He's as crazy about my daughter today as the day they married."

"Maybe I should find me another woman to court." He winked at Mrs. Jordan.

Sammie snorted and rolled her eyes. "Oh brother. No decent woman would want anything to do with an old man who's mean as a snake and stinks to high heaven!"

Leroy laughed as he made his way to the door with his walker. "You weren't listenin' to me. I didn't say I wanted a *decent* woman, just a woman. And she sure as hell wouldn't have red hair, either!" He flipped a quarter to Sammie. "Although, for Ellie, I might clean up."

She slipped the quarter in the jar, and Mrs. Jordan blushed, her eyes following his father out the door.

Matt's gaze met Sammie's. *No way...* he mouthed.

She shrugged and carried on with her rant. "So help me, Matt, that stubborn old man would try the patience of a saint—"

"Just drop it, Sammie." He shrugged apologetically to Mrs. Jordan. "I'm sorry about all this. Sammie and Pa can be quite colorful with their language—"

Mrs. Jordan interrupted, "Oh for heaven's sake, Matt. Don't apologize. I've known Leroy since we were children."

Sammie's eyes narrowed, and her breath hissed between her teeth. "Please excuse me, Mrs. Jordan. It was nice to see you again. That cake you made for our wedding was delicious; I'd love to get the recipe some time. As for you, Mr. Emily Fuckin' Post, I guess I'll go wash my own mouth out with soap now." With an angry flip of her braid, she stormed out of the room and tromped upstairs.

Matt pressed his lips together as he felt heat work its way up the back of his neck. He crossed his arms in front of his chest, wondering how he'd so completely lost control of his own household.

A horn outside beeped. Mrs. Jordan patted his arm, chuckling. "Honey, don't sweat the small stuff. It'll all work out in the wash." She left with a wave.

Pa walked into the living room as Matt closed the front door. "What were you thinkin' marrying Sam? She's too damn bossy for her own good. Tryin' to tell me to bathe in my own goddamn house—"

Matt took three strides toward his father and shoved a finger at his chest. "Don't start. Just don't start. If Sammie asks you to clean up, you do it or stay in your room!"

Pa gazed up at him. Matt kept his face impassive, hoping to bluff his old man. Without another word, Pa turned around and returned to his bedroom, quietly shutting the door.

Matt took a deep breath and ran his fingers through his hair. *One down, one to go.* Squaring his shoulders, he marched upstairs and found Sammie muttering under her breath as she picked up Luke's room. Matt leaned against the doorframe with his hands in his pockets, admiring the sight of her curvy bottom up in the air as she retrieved a stuffed bear from under the bed. He winced as she threw the bear in the toy box.

"I'm glad I'm not that bear," he commented dryly. "And Luke is capable of picking up his own room."

She stood and faced him. "Don't push your luck."

He weighed his words before speaking, taking in the difference she'd made in Luke's room. On his walls were two posters, one of Batman and one of Superman. Taped to his dresser mirror were pictures of Rufus, Rhonda, and Jinx's dog, Winston. And she'd placed a picture of Luke with his mother and sister on his nightstand.

"Look, I know Pa can be difficult. He's worse since this stroke. But you really need to learn to watch your mouth. You and I need to be an example for Luke—a good example." He smiled and added with a wink, "And I think you owe the jar at least another dollar."

"I'm sorry about my language, I ain't—I mean, I'm not used to being around kids."

"I said *we* need to be an example for Luke. I'm just as bad. I don't want to be like Pa. I want to be a good father, and you're his stepmother."

"Stepmother," she repeated thoughtfully, as if she'd just realized the concept. She rubbed her brow.

"You okay?"

"My head's pounding. And Pa ain't — isn't that bad."

In truth, it was the first time Matt had thought of her as Luke's stepmother, too. Sammie was part of his family now. He knew for certain he didn't want to go back to the way things were before she came. She made life bearable. More than bearable — it was comfortable.

"I'll do better, I promise." She held out her hand.

He shook it. "Me, too. Do you need something for your headache?"

"Nah, I've got something I can take. It isn't like the man flu." She flashed a saucy grin and walked out.

Matt watched her gracefully descend the stairs and wondered if she'd ever kiss him again.

Chapter
Ten

By the time the Fourth of July rolled around, the no-cussing jar contributions had slowed, much to Luke's dismay. And despite Sammie's apology and effort to cajole Pa to the table, he still ate alone in his room, watching television. She wasn't sure if he was holding a grudge or detoxing himself from the alcohol. Either way, it wasn't healthy for him to spend so much time by himself, and she felt bad now for taking such a hard stance about him cleaning up.

Sammie straightened the plate, placing it between the silverware and one inch from the edge of the table. The longer she stayed here, the worse her need for order had become. It wasn't quite where it had been when she'd sought help before Sue Ellen passed, but it was getting there.

She rubbed her throbbing head and considered using the I-don't-feel-well excuse to get out of the potluck tonight, but she'd promised Luke she'd be his date.

Yesterday, she'd found this china packed away in a box in the back of the pantry. Tired of mismatched dishes, she'd washed them and decided it was a shame not to use them. She adjusted the vase of wildflowers and called out that breakfast was ready. The plan was to eat a big breakfast and then this afternoon they'd go to the community potluck. Her pies were cooling on the kitchen counter. It would be her first time out with Matt and Luke as a family, although she knew gossip was already rampant from the stares and whispers she received whenever she went to Hudson's One Stop Grocery.

She smiled when she heard Luke chattering excitedly about the upcoming festivity as he came down the stairs. Quickly, she swallowed two Tylenol and an old antibiotic she'd found in her makeup case. She was pretty sure this was just a sinus infection.

To her surprise, not only did Matt and Luke arrive, so did Pa—freshly bathed. Although his hair and long white beard were still shaggy, he'd changed into clean clothes. She smiled at the old man and shocked him with a kiss on the little bit of his right cheek that was bare.

"I'm glad to see you, Pa."

He shrugged and brushed her away. "I decided I had to clean up so I could eat. Otherwise they'd find my dead, wasted body in my room. This family doesn't need any more scandals."

She'd made sure he had three square meals every damn day. But if this was his way to initiate a truce, she'd take it.

Luke bounced beside his chair. "Me too, Sammie. Kiss me, too!" She gave him a resounding kiss on the cheek. She loved this little boy.

"Kiss Daddy!"

She ignored the last request and placed the ham on the table as Matt brusquely told Luke to "hush."

"Sammie's gonna be my date for the fireworks and dance," Luke announced as she sat down at the table.

"Isn't she a little old for you?" Matt asked as he served Luke some eggs.

"I like older women. Pa likes all women," Luke replied.

Pa nodded. "Got that right."

"Good grief." Pulling his napkin out from under his fork, Matt frowned. "Why is this china on the table?"

"I found it in a box in the back of the pantry. I love the painted daisies. I decided it was a waste not to use them." She cut Luke's ham for him.

"Samantha!"

"What?" She looked over at Matt, startled by his use of her full name.

"Never, and I mean *never* use these dishes again."

"Why not?"

"Because I asked you not to."

"That's not an explanation." *Oh dear God, when will I learn to control my mouth?* She kept still and held her breath, waiting for the fallout. Sue Ellen had hated back-talk, and so did Matt.

The tension in Matt's face relaxed somewhat, and for the briefest second, she thought he might smile.

"I'm asking nicely," he amended. "Please, don't use these dishes."

"They're just damn dishes. Let it go, Matthew," Pa commented.

"Are Sammie and Daddy in trouble?" Luke asked.

Matt frowned. "Why would you say that?"

"I'm only called Lukas if I'm in trouble," he said.

Pa laughed. "The boy has a point."

"Nobody is in trouble. Just eat your breakfast," Matt replied.

A strained silence settled over the table, broken only by an occasional word from Luke about Rufus and the upcoming fireworks. Sammie shoved her eggs around her plate, unable to swallow around the anxiety lodged in her throat. She felt jumpy and agitated.

What's the big deal? They're just stupid dishes. However, self-preservation kept her from pushing him. If it meant eating off mismatched plates, so be it. She'd learn to deal. She was already planning on refolding everything in her dresser to calm down. Her therapist had once said this need to organize was a way of bringing physical order to relieve mental stress. She knew what that therapist had really meant. She was as crazy as a Bessie bug, just like her mother.

In her hurry to get the dishes done and packed away, she tripped over the leg of Pa's walker. She wobbled, trying to regain her balance, but hit the floor. Two plates flew out of her hands. Matt sprang to his feet.

The broken pieces blurred as she hurried to pick up the shattered plates. Looking up, she saw Matt standing over her. Instinctively, she tucked her head into her knees and covered her head with her arms.

"I didn't do it on purpose. I'm sorry…Please, don't…I'll buy you some new dishes."

Matt helped her to her feet. "Are you okay? You're bleeding; let me see your hand."

Slowly, Sammie raised her eyes and looked at him. He wasn't angry. In fact, he looked worried as he wrapped a napkin around her finger.

She let out the breath she'd been holding. "You aren't mad at me?"

"No, I hate those stupid dishes. Break all of them if you want to, but please be careful when you do it and don't hurt yourself."

"B-But you said you didn't want me to use them. I thought it was because they were so valuable, or held special meaning…Oh shoot, of course—they were Karen's. I'm so sorry; I didn't think!"

"No, I just hate those dishes. James bought them." Matt frowned. "Did you think I was going to hit you?"

Sammie lowered her eyes, embarrassed. Cupping her chin in his hand, Matt caressed her cheek, sending sparks down her body, swirling in the pit of her stomach.

"Sammie," he murmured.

"What?" she whispered, looking up.

"You know me. You know I'd never hurt you." He glanced over at Pa and Luke, who watched with wide eyes, then bent down to pick up the china.

Her heart flip-flopped.

After the breakfast dishes were done, Luke pulled one of her braids and giggled. "You look like Dorothy from *The Wizard of Oz*, Sammie!"

"Dorothy didn't have red hair, silly. *You're* starting to look like the cowardly lion with all these curls. Let's trim your hair before our date tonight." She ran her fingers through his dark hair.

Matt grabbed a bottle of water from the fridge.

"Cut Daddy's hair, too!"

Matt shook his head. "I don't have time for a haircut. I really don't have time for this potluck."

"It's a holiday, Matt. You deserve to take a day off and relax…"

"What's the matter, son? Scared you'll lose your strength if you get a haircut?" Pa cackled. "You might need it for some fun later on. I won't be home, ya know."

Matt shot his father a go-to-hell look before heading to the garage. Sammie raised an eyebrow. "You're first, old man."

She sent Luke upstairs to play while she waged a battle of wills and profanity with Pa. In the end, she was out a dollar, but she'd won. Pa's hair was cut, and she'd convinced him to let her shave off his beard. She'd grudgingly left his moustache.

"Well, well, well, what do you know? Underneath all that hair was a very handsome man!" she exclaimed as she crouched eye-level with Pa, checking to make sure his sideburns were even. Pa examined his face in the hand mirror.

"You nicked me, you little vampire," he shouted, pointing to a speck of blood on his neck. Sammie licked her lips and playfully kissed him on the other side of his neck. Pa grumbled and swatted her away. "Leave me alone, you she-devil!" He dropped two dollars in the jar.

Luke hurried back to the kitchen when she let him know it was safe to enter. His mouth dropped. "You look good, Pa!" He wore a pair of shorts without a shirt. "Me next, Sammie."

Despite his wiggling, she managed to trim his hair. Standing back, she looked him over carefully. "You're done. My goodness, aren't you a good-looking boy? You'll be a heartbreaker like your Daddy someday." She clapped her hand over her mouth.

Pa snickered.

"I need a shave, too," Luke replied, rubbing a hand across his baby soft cheek.

"You got a girlfriend you're trying to impress, boy?" Pa asked.

Luke nodded. "I have lots of girlfriends—Angela, Kenzie. And I'm taking Sammie to the Fourth of July dance."

"Yes indeed, I'm one lucky girl." She rubbed some shaving cream on Luke's face and gave him the hand mirror and a spoon to "shave" with.

"All right, boy. Move your mouth like this." Pa demonstrated as Luke carefully scraped his face with the spoon. Sammie left to get ready.

It seemed Sammie was right. The shop wasn't busy, so Matt shut it down early for the holiday.

When he returned to the house, he chuckled at the sight of his son "shaving" as Pa gave him careful instructions on the proper technique. He couldn't believe the difference in Pa's appearance. He looked at least twenty years younger. Come to think of it, Pa had been sober for the past two weeks, too.

"Stick your chin out, boy. There you go—" Pa looked up and growled, "What are you staring at?"

"You. You look real nice, Pa."

"I just did it to shut Sam the hell up."

"Sammie's gonna be my date, not yours, Daddy," Luke announced.

"Lucky boy. Oops, you missed a spot." Matt pointed out a place on Lukas's cheek and put a dollop of shaving cream on his nose.

"Jealous?"

"Shut up, Pa, and mind your own business."

The old man guffawed.

His father had to be the most exasperating man in the county.

"What's taking her so long?" Luke bounced around, waiting for Sammie to come downstairs. "We're going to be late!"

Every Fourth of July, the residents of Pine Bluff put aside football team preferences, family feuds, and class distinctions for a big celebration. A parade and street party started the festivities, which ended with a potluck dinner and dance held in the high school cafeteria. The night would end with fireworks sponsored by the bank.

"Calm down, son. Pick up that puzzle. You know Sammie doesn't like messes."

A horn sounded outside. "See you sometime tomorrow," Pa called as he headed toward the front door. For as long as Matt could remember, Gig Johnson and Pa had held a private July Fourth party with some of their cronies. It was a long-held tradition going back to when the men had been rowdy teenagers.

Luke shoved the puzzle pieces onto the board, sighing. "We already missed the parade because you had to work."

"It's called adulting."

"I'm not an adult; I'm a kid."

Matt closed his computer and helped Luke with the puzzle. He looked up and tried not to stare when Sammie entered the room. His heart pounded in his chest, and he hoped the blood stayed there rather than dipping south.

"Finally! How do I look, Sammie?" Luke did a turn in his blue shorts and red, white, and blue striped polo shirt.

She smiled and straightened the cuff on his shorts. "Very handsome! I'll be the luckiest girl in Pine Bluff to have such a good-looking date."

"You look pretty, Sammie. Doesn't she, Daddy?"

Matt stood up, still staring. He couldn't help it. The woman standing before him in a blue-green silky top and jeans didn't look at all like the girl who ran around in shorts and a T-shirt with her hair in braids as she played with Luke.

The top was totally modest in the front but when she turned to get her purse, Matt's mouth went dry. There was no back to the halter-style top. That meant there was no bra...He blinked and swallowed and looked again. *Nope...no bra.*

The muted light from the window caught the copper fire in her hair.

"Daddy! Doesn't Sammie look pretty?" Luke repeated his question, clearly exasperated.

"Beautiful," Matt managed to croak.

"Thank you." A faint shade of pink accented her freckles. "You look nice, too."

He looked down at his blue jeans and white shirt with the sleeves rolled up and felt a little underdressed. Sammie picked up his computer and placed it on the coffee table.

"Well then, are we ready?" Matt escorted his family out the door, mentally preparing himself for the real test. Would Luke get in the car?

To his surprise, after Sammie promised to sit in the backseat with him, he climbed into his car seat.

Matt looked in the rearview mirror and quipped, "Where to, Miss Daisy?"

"Duh, the party, Daddy!"

Sammie's gaze met his in the mirror, and she smiled. Luke chattered the entire way to the high school.

They entered the cafeteria, and Matt tried to ignore the questioning stares that greeted them. It was the first time he and Sammie had been out together. They placed the pies Sammie had made on the table and moved away from the commotion to stand in a quiet corner. Luke kept hiding behind him as Sammie repeatedly fingered her bracelets.

"Hello, hello! How is everyone? Luke, did you ride in a car? Sammie, you look stunning in that color. You and Matt make a gorgeous couple." Mrs. Jordan hurried over and gave them each a kiss on the cheek.

"Sammie's *my* date," Luke corrected. "Is Aunt Jinx here yet?"

Matt shrugged and held up his hands in mock surrender.

Mrs. Jordan laughed. "You're a lucky boy. I don't believe the Howells have arrived yet, and I know Dylan and Jennifer won't be here. They're in Birmingham."

As Lydia Meadows entered the gym, she narrowed her eyes and scurried toward them like a rat spying a piece of cheese. He swore the nosy cashier from Hudson's One Stop Grocery had radar built in to sniff out gossip.

"Oh dear. Please excuse me. I need to run interference." Mrs. Jordan turned and cut the woman off. Taking her by the arm, she walked her to a table across the room.

Thank God. Matt was glad for the help. Lydia, along with Bubba's sister, Frances, were in charge of the misinformation highway in Pine Bluff. And considering Lydia had been blatant in her interest in him after Karen died, he didn't anticipate her being kind to Sammie.

"Hi, Matt."

Matt turned and smiled at the tired-looking woman holding a baby on her hip. "Hello, Janice. How are you?"

He scanned the crowd for her husband. Matt always suspected Janice Newton Kelton had set him up fifteen years ago in the hayloft incident to make Bubba jealous. Even though Bubba and

Janice had been married for years with two kids, Bubba held tight to his animosity.

Matt re-introduced Sammie to Janice. Sure enough, Bubba crossed the gym as quickly as a three-hundred-pound man could. He rushed over to Janice's side, dragging Horace Kelton, Jr. with him, and threw an arm around Janice's shoulders.

Bubba eyed Sammie curiously. He was as nosy as his sister.

"Evening, Tyler. Who's this?" Bubba glared at Matt but smiled at Sammie.

"My wife, Sammie Morgan Tyler. She used to live here, remember? I believe she blacked your eye for bullying her when we were kids." He winked at her.

Bubba shifted and pulled his pants up. Without offering his hand, he gave her the onceover. "I'll be darned; you sure have changed."

Janice glared, and Matt could see this entire incident going downhill in a hurry.

"Come on, Sammie, let's go grab a table. Nice to see you both." He guided his family to a table in the corner where things were quieter. Luke settled on Sammie's lap and watched the crowd with his head tucked under her chin.

A little while later, with the potluck in full swing, Luke wiggled in his chair. "Everything tastes good except for that okra stuff. It's slimy."

Sammie laughed, trying to ignore the eyes around her. It felt like the entire county had been by their table to greet them.

"I agree, son. Unless it's fried, it's pretty gross." Matt chuckled and draped his arm around the back of her chair.

He played the part of a happy, newlywed man pretty well, until his laughter abruptly stopped. Sammie sat up straighter and fiddled with their dirty dishes as James Howell approached.

Beside Mr. Howell were his wife and Jinx, in town for the occasion and dressed all in black, looking decidedly out of place in a gym full of people dressed in red, white, and blue. A man who looked vaguely familiar joined them.

Matt stood. "James, Lila, Jinx." He pointedly didn't address the man.

"Lukas, my goodness, I swear you've grown six inches. How are you?" Mrs. Howell commented in a soft, breathless voice. "I'm sorry we haven't been by after church lately…" Her voice trailed off as she shot a look at Sammie.

Luke sprang from his chair and gave his grandmother a big hug and a kiss. "I'm fine, Grandma. Hiya, Aunt Jinx. Did you bring Winston?"

Jinx smiled and fist-bumped him. "Yes, he's at the house with Mae."

Matt started the introductions, and Sammie stood to face the firing squad. "James, you've already met my wife. Lila, Jinx, this is Sammie Morgan—"

"Tyler," she added.

"Yes, Sammie Morgan Tyler." His face turned red.

The handsome man standing next to Jinx cleared his throat.

Matt's jaw hardened. "Oh, and Travis Carlton."

"Hello, Sammie. How are you?" Lila responded softly. Unmistakable pain flashed in her eyes.

"I'm fine, thanks. Nice to see you again," she lied, feeling as welcome as a hair on a biscuit.

Travis's name did ring a bell, now that she thought about it. He and the Howell girls hadn't hung out with the kids like her and Matt when they were growing up.

Travis stared at her, and the tic in Matt's cheek became more pronounced.

Eighty-seven, eighty-eight… She went back to counting the bricks in the wall across the gym, hating being the center of attention. She squeezed Luke's hand so tight he pulled away, shaking the offended fingers.

Mr. Howell bit out, "You've yet to bring Luke over for a visit, Samantha, despite my numerous requests. Is it too much to ask that you let us see our grandson?"

Sammie looked over to Matt. Anytime she'd asked, he'd made up one excuse or another for her *not* to take Luke.

"We've been busy. And you haven't bothered to visit since I remarried," Matt retorted.

"Shh, gentlemen," Lila whispered urgently. "You're causing a scene and upsetting Lukas. We'll discuss this later. Let's just try to enjoy the evening. Come, James, I see George and Patsy."

James pointed his finger at Matt. "I'm watching you, Tyler. Don't ever forget it." Lila led him away. Jinx gave a Sammie a curious but sympathetic look before following her parents.

"Mind if I join you?" Travis asked with a pleasant smile, pulling out a chair to sit down.

"Yes," Matt snapped rudely just as she replied, "Not at all."

She looked at him and Travis. They were as different as night and day. Matt's dark, rugged looks countered Travis's tailored appearance. The hostility between them would've been apparent to a blind man. As Travis attempted to make pleasant conversation, she searched her memory for what might be the source of it. But other than Travis being one of the rich kids from across the lake, she didn't have a clue. Taking a deep breath, she focused on counting ceiling tiles.

"What brought you back to Pine Bluff?" Travis asked.

She shot a desperate look to Matt.

He leaned over and said, "Me."

The band took the stage and started playing, but it was merely background noise to the pissing contest going on at the table.

Beside her, Luke shrieked and jumped up, tugging her hand. "Come on, Sammie. Let's go. It's the Rhonda song! After you, I'll ask Aunt Jinx and then Grandma to dance. Is that okay?"

"Sure." Grateful to get away from the questions and tension at the table, she followed him to the dance floor.

Chapter

Eleven

Just before the fireworks, Luke started fussing and pouting, obviously tired from the day.

"Ready to go?" Matt asked, picking Luke up to go home.

"More than ready," Sammie said.

"Oh no, you two stay and watch the fireworks," Mrs. Jordan insisted. "I'll take him home with me. Would you like that, Luke? We'll make fried pies in the morning."

Rubbing his eyes, Luke nodded.

"I appreciate the offer, but that's too much trouble. Plus, he doesn't have extra clothes or anything," Matt replied.

"How many times did you and the McAthie boys spend the night at my house? Did you ever care about not sleeping in pajamas? Didn't I always have a toothbrush for you?"

Matt laughed. "Yes, ma'am. You have a point."

"Please, Daddy? I want to make pies."

Sammie shrugged. This was not her decision.

"Okay. But you can't back out at the last minute, understand?"

The boy nodded, and Matt walked him to Mrs. Jordan's sedan. Sammie transferred the car seat. She wondered if Luke would actually go through with it, but he happily climbed in, talking about pies, and waved goodbye as if it was the most normal thing in the world for him to ride in a car.

Matt watched until they were out of sight. "I still can't believe he's riding in a car." He grinned and picked her up, giving her an exuberant kiss.

She blinked, very aware of his hands on her butt. Their faces were so close she could see her reflection in his eyes.

"It must be the allure of fried pies. I'm surprised you didn't go, too," she joked.

He smiled as he eased her back down. "Well, they *are* mighty tasty. However, I guess I need to teach him it's rude to dump your date for another woman."

She attempted a small smile, stuffing the snarky retort. "I reckon I'll have to rely on you to take me home."

"Only if you'll dance with me." He wrapped an arm around her shoulders, but instead of looking at her, he glared at Travis as they walked back into the gym.

She shrugged him off. Had that spontaneous kiss been just for show? Was she just a pawn in whatever game he and Travis were playing?

"I need to use the ladies' room."

Disappearing into the bathroom, she took a moment to calm herself, washing her hands as she silently counted. It took effort, but she made herself stop at twenty-five rinses.

Janice Kelton walked in and looked at her in the mirror. "You're a lucky woman," she commented with a smile as she ran a comb through her hair. "Matt Tyler is a great guy. It's nice seeing him smile again."

"Yes, yes, he is." Nerves on edge, Sammie wondered where this was going. She dried her hands and applied some lip gloss.

"I'm not trying to butt in—I mean, this town is full of gossips, and I'm married to one of the worst—but if I was you, I'd be careful around Travis Carlton. He and Matt have a history. Travis dated Karen before Matt married her. Travis took it hard when Karen dumped him. Some say he never got over her. He's dated and stuff, but never married, and he's Pine Bluff's most eligible bachelor—and a player."

Janice put her comb in her purse and moved toward the bathroom door. Pausing, she added, "I'll say it again: you're a lucky woman. Matt's a good guy."

Sammie looked at her reflection and sighed. She didn't feel particularly lucky.

When Sammie returned from the bathroom, Matt pushed away from the wall and quit glaring at Travis. Alan Mitchell and his band had just launched into Simple Minds' "Don't You Forget About Me." He held his hand out to her and nodded toward the couples dancing. She looked less than thrilled but followed him.

"I'm not good at this." Her face reflected pure dread, and her palms were sweaty.

"That makes two of us. Just move with me and try not to step on my toes."

He laughed when she did precisely that. Holding her close, he closed his eyes for a moment, enjoying the feel of a woman in his arms again. Her skin was warm, and a loose curl tickled his nose.

Some of the stress from having to be civil to Travis eased as they swayed to the music. Matt wondered if she could hear his heart racing. He wanted to kiss her again, but making a spectacle of himself in front of the busybodies of Pine Bluff was not an option. He already regretted the kiss Travis had witnessed.

Knowing they'd be alone when they got home, a war raged between his desire and his brain. Matt withdrew slightly from her. She stiffened in his arms as he pulled away, and he wanted to kick himself.

"Ready to go?" she asked.

"No. I don't know...maybe. You?"

He looked up and saw Travis walking toward them. Behind him James glared, and Lila and Jinx looked sad.

"Yes, yes, let's get out of here." He took her by the hand and led her away.

"Where are we going?" Sammie asked.

"I don't know. The night's young, and we need to take advantage of being kid-free. Do you want to get an ice cream or—"

"Stop! Go back!" She turned in her seat, pressing both hands to her window as they passed The Roadside Tavern.

"The Roadside Tavern?" Matt groaned.

This was the last place he wanted to be. But it might be safer than being home alone with Sammie. He did a quick U-turn and prayed Lucy was off tonight.

As he opened the door to the seedy bar, his hand brushed Sammie's bare back, sending a bolt of electricity through his body. Maybe one cold beer wouldn't hurt. He'd just make sure to limit it to one. He nodded at some of the locals he knew, surprised by the number of people here, considering it was a holiday. As he pulled out a chair for Sammie, Lucy came to take their order. He cursed his luck.

"Hello, St. Matthew. Slumming it again tonight?"

Matt glared at Lucy and ignored her question. "What would you like to drink, Sammie?"

"A shot of tequila."

"Salt and lime?" Lucy asked.

"No. Straight up, no training wheels."

"Matt?" Lucy's attention remained fixed on Sammie.

"I'll be the designated driver, just water." He turned to Sammie. "Tequila straight up? You sure?"

"I'm not a teenager. I can drink, Matt," Sammie snapped with a defiant toss of her hair.

"I noticed," Matt mumbled as he drew his attention away from her to the drunk failing miserably with his karaoke rendition of "Heartbreak Hotel."

Lucy returned with a beer, a shot glass, and a half-empty bottle of tequila. Placing them on the table, she grinned. "C'mon, little brother, one beer won't hurt you. And any woman who knows how to order a shot of tequila isn't going to stop at one."

Matt sighed, afraid she was right. Sammie poured a shot, threw it back, and slammed the glass on the table, grinning at him. She pushed the shot glass toward him, but he waved it away.

He watched her do two more.

Her eyes sparkled, and she tapped the table in time with the music. She laughed with her whole body as she watched the drunks attempting to sing.

"This is fun! Do you come here often?"

Matt raised one eyebrow. "Sure, Luke and I hang out every Friday night. We shoot a little pool, throw back a few brewskis."

Sammie laughed again, and he grinned back at her. He loved her laughter; he always had. As a kid, her moods had been mercurial—quiet and reserved one minute, cussing and cutting up the next. He'd never forget the time she'd laughed so hard she peed on herself. The black eye she'd given him for laughing at her had hurt like hell.

Staring at her now, he wanted to know her secrets and how to erase the hint of sadness that haunted those aquamarine eyes. Without thinking, he reached for her hand and rubbed his thumb over her knuckles.

Sammie gazed into his eyes. His nearness made it hard for her to breathe. She liked the way the low lights in the bar softened the lines of worry in his face. She tore her eyes from his when Lucy took the mic on stage.

"All right, listen up. I'm gonna up the stakes and see if we can't get someone up here who can carry a tune. So, for the next thirty minutes, it's a contest. I'll decide who wins, and the winner gets a hundred bucks."

A hundred bucks! She swiveled to Matt. "I can win this!"

"Is that your talent or the liquor talking?"

"Probably a little of both!" She stood up, pausing to get her bearings as the room swayed. Running to the stage, she gave her request to the man working the karaoke machine. Three people ahead of her butchered the lyrics to different songs. At last it was her turn.

The music started, and she began singing "Making Believe" by Emmylou Harris. Her start was a little tentative, but she soon lost herself in the music and blocked out her surroundings. Pouring her heart into the song, she sang to her husband, not giving a damn about the consequences.

When she finished, the audience erupted, clapping and banging their glasses on the tables. Biting her lip, she smiled and did a clumsy curtsy. She searched the room for Matt, but the spotlight prevented her from seeing him. Lucy handed her the hundred dollars and gave her a hug.

"Wait, someone else might be better," she protested.

"Honey, no one in this place is gonna top that. Take it."

She hurried back to the table and squealed, "I won!"

"I know!" To her surprise, Matt stood and greeted her with a firm kiss. The cheers around them intensified.

Chapter
Twelve

At home, Matt opened Sammie's car door for her and held her hand as they walked toward the house, liking the way their fingers interlaced together. "You look really pretty tonight, Sammie."

"T-Thank you."

She stopped short, and he faced her, glad the dusk-to-dawn light was behind him so he could see her face. Fireflies flickered around them, and it was almost magical. He was a man, and she was a woman. And they were married.

There was no reason they couldn't move things out of the friend zone.

And a thousand reasons it would be a mistake.

My entire life is full of mistakes. Why change now? He lifted a lock of her hair and wrapped it around his finger. "The way your hair catches the light, it looks like fire. And your eyes are the prettiest blue I've ever seen. Or are they green? I can never decide..." He lowered his lips to hers, teasing, nipping, and deepening the kiss as he felt her respond.

She wrapped her arms around his neck and leaned into him. He backed away from the kiss, holding her face in his hands. "You're so sweet, so lovely, Sammie," he murmured as he raked his fingers through her hair, kissing her forehead, her soft cheeks, and her neck. He pulled her hips in closer to him.

"Matt?"

"Yes?"

"Can we sit and talk for a bit…um, first?"

Uh-oh. Talking means trouble. Talk about a mood killer… "Of course."

Sometimes he missed being an irresponsible teenager. He led her to the back steps, where they sat. *She's right. We're about to head into uncharted territory.*

"Do you remember the day we met?" she asked.

"Yeah, of course. You were beating the crap out of Bubba. It was great."

"Just before we moved to Pine Bluff, I got head lice. Instead of just treating it, Sue Ellen decided to also give me the worst haircut in the history of haircuts. I was mortified. Daddy told me it would grow back, but I heard him fighting with Sue Ellen over it after I went to bed. Usually they fought over money. Walking home from school my first day, Bubba threw a rock at me and started calling me names. He said no one could tell if I was a boy or a girl. I was so mad I started crying."

Matt didn't say anything. She wasn't exaggerating. He'd always wondered if she'd given herself the haircut. It had been chopped and uneven. "I'm sorry."

"I was already feeling outta sorts, getting uprooted from my school and moving here. So when Bubba started in on me, it set me off. I screamed every dirty word I knew and tore into his ass. I couldn't seem to stop; it was like I had oral diarrhea and all my anxiety and anger spewed out unchecked. I guess I took Bubba by surprise and somehow managed to black his eye. I'll never forget you standing up for me. You told Bubba you'd whoop his ass from here to Birmingham if he ever bothered me again."

Matt laughed. "I don't know that I did that much to break it up. You were like a honey badger or David facing Goliath. And that mouth. I was impressed. I'd never heard anyone swear as proficiently as Pa, until I met you."

She giggled. "You were my hero. After the Bubba incident, Daddy died and Sue Ellen went off the deep end. But you let me follow you around, even when some of the other boys got mad. You taught me to how to fish, skim rocks, and belch on command. Remember the time Dylan dared me to dip tobacco? You helped me clean up after I barfed my guts out, and you told Dylan it was an asshole thing to do."

She sighed. "And when Sue Ellen became too much to handle, I'd climb the tree outside your house, and you'd let me in to hide. At the time, you didn't realize what a sanctuary you were offering. Although I think Pa might've known. Did you know he came by my house one time and put a tire swing up for me? And he gave me my first fishing pole? Anyway, you just thought you were helping me bend the rules and learn to be a hell raiser like yourself. But the truth is, you were my best friend, Mattie."

"I never knew Pa did that." He'd never seen Pa through that lens before. "We did get in and out of some scrapes, didn't we? I knew your mother was...different, but I had no idea how bad it was."

He gave her hand a squeeze. Some of his best childhood memories had been made with Sammie. But when he fell for Karen, he'd turned all his attention toward her. Pa had called it the power of the pussy, and looking back as an adult, he decided his old man was probably right.

"I should've done more for you..."

"You couldn't have done nothing. Sue Ellen was sick. She'd go off her meds and it was like being on an out-of-control roller coaster. She'd either be way up and we'd have lots of fun, or she'd be really scary low, unable to get out of bed and tend to herself. Her self-esteem was terrible, and she didn't have any friends. Just me. I mean, you can't blame folks. It's hard to put up with crazy.

"Things changed when I was twelve. She started talking about her rich boyfriend who was going to make everything wonderful. We no longer went to the cemetery to visit Daddy for hours on end. We didn't have to be at church every time the doors were open. She'd tuck me in at night and disappear. Sometimes she'd be there in the morning when I woke up, sometimes not. At the time, I halfway suspected this so-called boyfriend was just a figment of her imagination. But I didn't care; it was a time of peace.

"Then one night I woke up and there was a man in my bedroom. His hands were under my pajama top...I screamed, and Sue Ellen ran him off. At first she comforted me, but then she snapped. She started screaming, blaming me for inviting him into my room. She made me kneel for hours and repent of my sins. If I sat back or swayed, she beat me with a belt. She wouldn't even let me up to pee, and I messed on myself. This went on for hours. I know because I watched the clock tick off every second and started counting to stay awake. I'd count as high as I could go and then start over because she'd beat me if I nodded off. Finally, after twenty-six hours and twenty-three minutes, she let me get a bath and go to bed. But it wasn't a good sleep. I was too scared.

"After that I couldn't sleep at all. I couldn't eat. Fear knotted my stomach all the time, and I was jumpy. I never knew which Sue Ellen would be around. I was afraid the stranger would return, but I was more scared of my own mother. I was in this constant state of hyperawareness."

"Geezus," Matt muttered.

"The lack of sleep affected me. My grades, which weren't great to begin with, fell into the sewer. I'd fall asleep in class. One of my teachers must've suspected something was wrong at home, because one day, a social worker came out to the house. Sue Ellen was furious after she left and called me a whore and a liar and beat me again. She didn't even give me a chance to explain I hadn't said anything…"

They sat in silence. He didn't know what to say, having difficulty taking in everything she'd just told him.

"I never told anyone," she whispered.

"Dear God, Sammie. You *should've* told someone," he choked out.

She shrugged, staring at the step. "I didn't know what would happen to me. I mean, even a known evil is less scary than the unknown. Things got a little better with time. I think the visit scared Sue Ellen, and she stayed on her medication for a while. We started having food in the kitchen, and I even got some new clothes. Somehow, we were no longer struggling. The next few years were pretty good. She wasn't worried about the rent, we weren't going to the food pantry or asking for handouts, and I had my best friend." She tapped his fingers one by one with her thumb.

He felt lost. *How could I have been so blind?* "But you left. One day you were just gone. I mean, I was wrapped up in my own life with Karen being pregnant and the wedding, but you never said goodbye."

Sammie withdrew her hand and looked down, tapping her fingers together. "I know. Sue Ellen got into some trouble, or something flew up her butt. One night she packed us up and said we had to go." She looked out into the yard. "I was fine with it…"

"But you never contacted me."

"You were busy with your life, Matt." A hint of bitterness tinged her words.

Matt rested his elbows on his knees, reflecting. "Yeah, I know. After Karen got pregnant, it got hectic. I'm sorry, Sammie."

"There's a reason I'm telling you all of this. My mother was mentally ill."

"I know. Everyone knew that—"

"Matt?"

"Yes?"

"I've always wondered—were you nice to me because you felt sorry for me?"

"What? No. You were my friend. Actually, it hurt that you didn't really say anything when I told you Karen was pregnant and we were getting married. I thought you'd be happy for me."

Sammie didn't reply. "After we moved, Sue Ellen got bad again. I stayed away from home as much as possible. I didn't cope well. I didn't have a sanctuary in the new town, and my problems got worse…"

"You should've come back to Pine Bluff."

"To what? You had your own life. I wasn't old enough to live on my own. My mother needed me. We did come back once, on my eighteenth birthday, to visit Daddy's grave."

"I wish you'd called me—stopped by or something…"

"We didn't even eat. Just visited the grave, then went to the bank and Sue Ellen added me to her lock box."

"That's weird. What's in it?"

She shrugged. "Who knows. She said it was my hope chest. Which at the time was pretty funny to me, as I felt *hopeless*." She looked up at the sky.

"For a time, I was cutting myself," she finally added.

Matt stilled. "What? Why?"

"It's hard to explain. It made me feel better. Somehow the physical pain relieved my emotional pain. I s-still have scars on my hip. I was careful to do it where no one would see. But Sue Ellen caught me. She may not have been the best mother in the world, but deep down, in her own way, she loved me, and she got me some help. For a while we were both better. But cancer beat us. I haven't cut myself in years, but you need to know, I still struggle with anxiety. I count stuff and keep things in order. It's my crazy way to maintain control. Is it healthy? No, but I figure it's better than cutting."

A tear slipped down her cheek, and she wiped it away. "So there you have it. I'm crazy like my mama. I should've told you this before we married. I'll leave if you want me to—" She stood.

He caught her hand. "In sickness and in health, Sammie. We promised."

"This ain't no real marriage, Matt. What if I go off the deep end? Maybe it would be best to end things now. This is a recipe for disaster. Have you asked Dylan to help you fight Mr. Howell? He's rich."

"If you take a dive, I'll jump in and save you."

He took a moment to collect his thoughts and looked at the beautiful girl before him. He'd always loved her. Was it that far of a stretch to think he could fall *in love* with her? He mulled over the past few weeks and realized life without her now seemed impossible. She made him laugh, she took care of him and his cantankerous father, and she loved his son. He ached to take her in his arms and hold her.

He stood and faced her. "I want you to stay."

"What if I'm more like Sue Ellen than I care to admit? I mean, you're like Pa in a lot of ways. I could ultimately harm you where Luke's concerned. I should've told you this stuff earlier. If Mr. Howell finds out—"

"I'm not like Pa," he protested.

She raised one eyebrow. "You're stubborn."

"Okay, fine, whatever. And fuck Howell. We can make this work. I want *us* to work. Stay, please?"

She gazed at him, and he held his breath, waiting for her answer.

"Thank you, Matt. I'd like that. If you don't mind, though, I think I need to be alone—just for a while. I'll soak in the tub...I've never told anyone but my therapist all this stuff." Her face was pale.

"I understand. Goodnight, Sammie." He kissed her hand, humbled by her resilience and her trust in him. Pa might've been a sorry parent, but he was a saint compared to Sue Ellen. And the bastard who had done that to her as a kid? There were no words foul enough to describe him. He'd kill anyone who hurt his kids.

Sammie kissed his forehead before going inside without another word. When the back door closed, he collapsed back on the step, covered his face, and struggled to breathe.

After a moment he stood and walked to his shop. In the corner hung an old punching bag. Taking a swing at it, he pounded it over and over. The dust and dirt flew around him as he pummeled. And when he didn't think he could go anymore, he took a breath and continued, fueled by a need to hurt something. He punched the bag until he couldn't stand because his legs felt like jelly. Dropping to the floor, he was drenched in sweat, his knuckles bruised and bleeding.

Eventually he looked up, suddenly aware he wasn't alone. Sammie stood in her gown and robe, her hair still damp, watching him, seemingly unafraid of the violence she must've witnessed. Regret seized his heart. He searched her face, hoping he wouldn't see fear. He'd never be able to forgive himself.

But there was no recrimination in her eyes. Instead, she knelt beside him and ran her fingers through his hair, rubbing his sweat-drenched back in soothing circles. He hung his head, spent, unable to move for a few minutes. When she held out her hand to him, he took it and followed her into the kitchen. She washed his hands, but never spoke.

"Thank you," he croaked. "I-I'm sorry, Sammie. I should've—"

She placed her finger over his lips. "Go get cleaned up."

Feeling numb, he trudged upstairs and stood in the shower until the water was tepid, wishing it was as easy to wash away his guilt. Drying off, he stepped into a pair of sleep pants and leaned against the sink. He stared at the man in the mirror.

You should've fuckin' been there for her.

He closed his eyes and sighed. All he could do was be here for her now. He vowed to protect her and make her feel safe.

She's my wife.

Matt flipped off the light in the bathroom and went downstairs. There was no way he'd be able sleep tonight. In the dark, he collapsed on the sofa. For the first time in a long time, he longed for a cigarette. He'd quit years ago, just before Elizabeth was born.

He rubbed his eyes with the heels of his hands and shoved the painful memories aside. There was only so much shit he could deal with tonight. He supposed he could go in Pa's room and scrounge up some liquor, but like a cigarette, it wouldn't solve anything. He closed his eyes. The couch dipped as Sammie sat next to him.

"Matt?"

He opened his eyes. In her hands were antibiotic ointment, gauze, and tape. He held his hands out to her, and she bandaged them. After she finished, she lay down with her head in his lap.

"Thank you. I'm grateful you're letting me stay."

"I'm not *letting* you stay. I asked you to stay because I want you to. Nothing you said changes anything. You're my wife."

She smiled. "And you're my husband. Ain't that somethin'…"

Chapter
Thirteen

"**D**ammit, son, we live in the middle of fucking nowhere. Why the hell did you lock the door?"

Matt stirred, hearing Pa pounding on the door, but he was trapped by Sammie on the couch. He didn't bother to move. Pa knew where the key was hidden. On top of him and still asleep, Sammie snuggled in closer, her head tucked under his chin. The front door banged open.

"Where is Luke?" James Howell snapped.

Startled, he and Sammie jumped up like guilty teenagers.

Pa slapped the irate man on the back. "Let's go to the kitchen and have a cup of coffee, Jim."

"You know damn well I don't go by Jim. Where's my grandson?"

"'Scuse me." Sammie scampered upstairs, and Matt stomped to the kitchen with James on his heels. He started the coffee rather than punching the man in his smug face.

"Luke spent the night with Eloise Jordan," he explained, trying to be reasonable.

"He rode in a car? Willingly?" James's anger deflated for a moment but escalated immediately. "I heard how you spent your evening at that dive bar, getting drunk."

"I had one beer. I've seen you drink a lot more. Hell, I used to deliver illegal liquor to your doorstep. That's how I met Karen," he goaded.

"Don't you dare mention my daughter. You weren't fit to be in the same room as her." Hatred filled his eyes.

"Hold on there, you happen to be talking about *my son*. Get the hell out of here!" Pa motioned to the door with his four-prong cane.

Sammie entered the kitchen now dressed, her face flushed and eyes narrowed. All three men turned and stared at her.

James pointed angrily at Matt's bandaged hands. "Did you get hurt in a barroom brawl? I know for a fact *she* had more than one drink. Is she a lush? You haven't changed one damn bit. You're still trash, Matthew Tyler."

Matt's vision blurred, and he grabbed James by the lapels of his expensive silk suit and threw him up against the wall of the kitchen, holding him there. Through clenched teeth he snarled, "I'm sick and tired of your shit. Don't you ever talk about Sammie like that again, do you hear me?"

"Matt, stop." Sammie tugged at his arm.

He backed away before he did something he'd regret.

"I think you need to leave, Mr. Howell," she said. "This is our home, and you're not welcome if you're going to be rude and insulting. If you want to see Luke, we'll arrange a time for him to visit."

"Who do you think you are? You can't keep me from my grandson."

"I'm his stepmother," Sammie replied calmly. "Now leave, or I'll call the law."

James straightened his tie and cuffs. "I'd like a word with you, Ms. Morgan. Alone."

"It's Mrs. Tyler now. Shall we walk to your car?"

"You don't owe him a goddamned thing! I, however, will be glad to give him a few choice words," Matt shouted.

Sammie smiled. "Matt, like it or not, we're all family now. Come, Mr. Howell. I'll give you ten minutes, no more." Head held high, she marched through the house with James following.

He moved to go after them, but Pa grabbed his arm.

"Let her handle it. She's the calm one."

"He's a sneaky bastard. I don't trust him."

"He's crazy, son. And if anyone can handle crazy, that little girl can. Sit."

Instead, Matt went to the living area and watched out the window, ready to intervene if needed.

"I don't like you," Mr. Howell announced, mincing no words.

"The feeling's quite mutual, I assure you. But we both love Luke. And he's what matters. Not how you feel about Matt, me, or Pa. Or how *we* feel about *you*." She crossed her arms but stood her ground.

To her surprise, tears filled his eyes.

"Parents never expect to bury their child. Or grandchild. On Sundays, Karen would bring the children over for lunch after church… W-We miss that. The house is much too quiet now. And Matt doesn't bring Luke by. And Lila and I can't abide the filth at Leroy's."

"If you'd been calmer when you got here, you might've noticed the changes. I'm a good housekeeper. And why would Matt want to go to your house? Think about how you treat him. I'm sure this is difficult for you. But continuing this quarrel with Matt isn't helping anything. He loved Karen and his children. Even if you don't like anything else about him, you *have* to acknowledge that. You have to accept that he's Luke's father. If you'd quit threatening him, he might be more inclined to let Luke visit."

"Lila and I could give Luke so much more…"

Sammie refused to engage. It was a trick she'd learned from dealing with Sue Ellen. "If you'll agree to be civil, I'll bring Luke over to see you and his grandmother. I promise."

Mr. Howell's shoulders sagged, and he stared at the ground. "This has been particularly hard for Lila. She withdraws, and it's been worse since Karen died. She and Eugenia aren't close…"

"What's her phone number? I'll text her to arrange a time for us to visit. Maybe tomorrow?"

He reached in his pocket and took out a business card, writing two phone numbers on the back. "Yes, tomorrow. Matt has our home phone. These are our cells. I expect you to follow through on your promise."

"I always do." Sammie pocketed the card and watched him drive off without another word. This time she wouldn't throw it away. For her family's sake, she'd be the peacekeeper.

Despite the early morning heat, she shivered.

Sammie practically ran into Matt when she opened the front door.

"What did he say to you?" he asked.

"Let's have some breakfast and discuss things."

They walked back into the kitchen and found Pa leaned against the kitchen counter, drinking a cup of coffee. He tossed a five in the jar.

"I'm covering your impressive string of words, son, as well as my own. Hell, this should even cover that asshole Howell's. Did you two have fun last night?"

"Not now, Pa," Matt sighed.

The front door opened.

"Daddy! Mrs. Jordan and I made some pies! I saw Gramps. Can I go visit him and Grandma tomorrow and take him some pies, too? He invited me! He said Grandma, Mae, and I can make cookies." Luke proudly showed off the heaping plate of fried apple pies. "Mrs. Jordan and I got up at six o'clock and made them, so the kitchen wouldn't get too hot," he explained.

Matt picked Luke up into a bear hug, holding him tight.

"Stop, Daddy." Luke wiggled to get down.

"What do you say to Mrs. Jordan?" Sammie asked.

"Thank you, Mrs. Jordan!" Luke grinned, but his attention had shifted to the hound dog meandering through the room. Luke followed him out the back door, babbling about pies and calling for Rhonda.

"He was very brave riding in the car. I left his car seat on the front porch. We passed James on the road, and he rolled the window down to invite Luke over…Everything okay?" Mrs. Jordan's curious gaze swept the room.

"Of course," Sammie replied smoothly. "He was disappointed Luke wasn't here when he stopped by. I'm going to take him to see the Howells soon. Thank you again for everything. I'd love to come over one day and have you teach me how to make fried pies."

"That would be fun, dear. I'd like that." Mrs. Jordan beamed.

Sammie walked her out of the room, thanking her again. She waved goodbye and closed the door.

Stalling for a moment, she took a breath, counting the flowers on the afghan thrown on the floor. What a strange twenty-four hours. She was still processing what Matt had said last night. Returning to the kitchen, she found him fuming, his bandaged hands fisted on the table.

Pa cleared his throat. "Anyone else left to visit? Seems like half of Pine Bluff's been here, and it isn't even nine o'clock in the damn morning. I'm going to sleep off this hangover." He squeezed Matt's shoulder as he left.

Sammie poured a cup of coffee for herself and Matt and sat next to him. "You okay? It's been a tough twelve hours…dealing with me and Mr. Howell." She looked over at him. "I know what all you said last night. Are you sure? I mean, now that you've had time to think on it. I'm *not* really mother material."

"I'd say that makes us a good match. My ex-in-laws say I'm not father material either." He nudged her shoulder.

"True enough." She smiled and nudged him back.

"This marriage of convenience…It isn't too far removed from arranged marriages in other cultures. And I've read they work out. We'll be fine." He pulled her into his lap, and she wrapped her arms around his neck, their foreheads touching.

"We sealed our marriage bargain with a handshake," she whispered. "I think I might need something more…"

"Yeah?" He grinned. "If I recall, there was a kiss in a downpour, too. And I agree, this deserves a whole lot more."

"You're right." Her soft lips met his. "It was a toe-curling kiss in a storm. But today, the sun is bright."

"Indeed. Like our future." His tongue teased, and she granted access. God, how this man could kiss…

The kiss grew more heated as his hands slid down her neck. Sammie shifted to straddle his lap, his erection lodged firmly where she wanted it to be, only without all these clothes in the way.

"No more separate bedrooms," he whispered.

She smiled against his lips. "I tend to hog the covers."

"That doesn't surprise me one bit." He kissed her again.

The back door slammed. "Ewwwww! Kissing." Luke made gagging noises, his nose wrinkled.

Matt groaned, and Sammie giggled.

"We'll finish this later, 'kay?"

Sammie nodded and crawled off his lap. The heat from her cheeks could probably cook breakfast. A side-glance to Matt revealed him listening to Luke with his arm strategically placed over his lap. It was going to be the longest damn day ever.

That evening, Matt closed his bedroom door and locked it. He smiled and desire lit his eyes. Sammie watched a drop of water from his dark curls drip down his cheek, drop onto his chest, and disappear into the towel wrapped around his waist. How she'd love to chase that droplet with her tongue.

But she remained still, wondering if he was as nervous as she was. Did guys get nervous? She looked down at her plain, blue cotton gown. It wasn't very sexy. Should she already be naked? Was married sex different from casual sex?

"Mrs. Tyler."

"Mr. Tyler." As much as she wanted to see him, the light made her self-conscious. She reached over and snapped it off.

The bed dipped, and Matt dove under the covers. His towel sailed to the floor.

"Ouch, my hair!"

"Oops, sorry, Sammie. Shit, I'm nervous."

She turned to face him. "You are?" *Nervous because it's me? Nervous because Luke's down the hall?*

"It's been a while…"

Sammie laughed and checked her runaway thoughts. "For me too. But I hear it's like riding a bike."

He chuckled. "Riding sounds good. C'mere. Don't let me fall off, 'kay?"

"What about Luke?"

"He's two doors down and sound asleep; I double checked. We're fine. Uh, birth control?"

"I'm on the pill. I've never done this with anyone else in the house. It's a little unnerving…"

Matt shifted over her, planting soft kisses across her jaw, nibbling on her earlobe. "You'll get used to it—and learn to be quiet. We'll save the wild, kinky stuff for when he and Pa spend the night elsewhere. Or go to the shop…"

Sammie giggled nervously. "You sound like a pro at this."

"I'm a little rusty, but we'll manage." He nuzzled her neck. "You always smell so good, spicy…and sexy…"

Her fingers tangled in the damp curls at the nape of his neck as she returned his kisses. "You make me sound like a taco." She stroked across his jaw, down his neck, across his chest, exploring his body. "Nice, you shaved."

"Mmmm, tacos are tasty. I'll avoid the obvious sexual reference. And skin burn, not good—ah, damn, that feels great…" Through her thin gown, he kneaded her breasts.

How can such a thin piece of material feel so confining? She moved from underneath him and wiggled out of her gown before maneuvering back on top of him.

"Better?" she asked.

"Much." His hands cupped her ass and squeezed. "Why didn't we do this sooner? Like a friends-with-benefits thing?"

Friends. Using the back of her fingers, she traced along his freshly shaven jaw. She suddenly wondered if this was a huge mistake. *I want more than friends. I'm in love. That's what he wants too, isn't it?* Doubt eased its way into her mind.

He flipped her back over, one hand wandering up her thigh, slowly stroking and teasing.

She'd loved him for a long time but had always been grounded in the reality that he loved Karen. What if he never loved her like he'd loved his first wife? Could she recover if he broke her heart?

"You okay, Sammie?" He stopped his exploration and stroked her hair.

"Yep. Just nervous," she admitted.

But she couldn't squelch the memory of the last time they'd been together like this.

On her sixteenth birthday she thought she'd finally found her opportunity to make good on her crush. Matt and Karen were eighteen, and Karen had caved to her Daddy's wishes and broken up with him.

He'd phoned Sammie, drunk, and told her he'd been dumped. She'd made the hasty decision to offer herself as a consolation prize. She'd thought it was her chance. After hurrying to his house, she and Matt had gone to the muscadine arbor in his backyard. Naïvely, she'd thought she'd be enough, that Matt would realize they were more compatible than he and Karen.

How wrong she'd been.

He'd passed out before things progressed beyond heavy petting. Disappointed and feeling foolish, she'd gotten up to go home. But Matt had stumbled after her into the house, apologizing. As she was leaving, the phone rang. He'd grabbed her hand to detain her as he answered, then paled as he sank into a kitchen chair.

"Pregnant?" he'd said.

In that instant, Sammie's dreams had shattered. It could only have been Karen on the line, and of course he'd return to her.

Yanking her hand from his, she'd gone home.

A week later, Matt had cajoled her into going fishing. She didn't know whether to be thankful or angry that he seemed to have no recollection of their encounter. He'd been over-the-top excited about the prospect of being a father, sharing his hopes and dreams even as hers evaporated.

Not long after, when Sue Ellen had decided it was time to move again, Sammie, with her heart broken, had put up no resistance.

And now I'm Matt's wife. Yet somehow, she still felt like that teenaged girl—like this might not be real, like everything could fall apart in an instant.

Karen had been Matt's first love, and she'd been gone less than a year.

"If you're having doubts…" He sounded as vulnerable as she felt.

"No, I'm fine." She willed herself to be present, to take this moment for what it was. She drew him closer, soothing his uncertainties with her body—and yet she couldn't find her way.

She decided to just give Matt what he needed and not worry about receiving. She faked her release. Surely it wouldn't be this way forever.

Chapter
Fourteen

Matt woke up the next morning feeling better than he had in months. Sammie's copper hair was a glorious, disheveled mess, which he pushed aside to kiss his favorite freckle on her shoulder. He smiled, happy for the first time in forever.

He needed her; he needed her as surely as he needed air to breathe. She was the bright light at the end of his tunnel, and he was close to coming out of the darkness. *Is this more than friendly love I feel for her? Lust? A combination of both?* He wasn't sure; he just knew she made him feel alive again, and he hoped she'd eventually feel the same way. He felt guilty that he'd enjoyed last night more than she had and vowed to correct that as soon as possible.

"What time is it?" she asked. Her phone dinged.

"Seven. Who's texting you this early?"

"Geez, she gets up early," she muttered, reading her message.

"Who? I'm going to go start the coffee. Sleep in, if you want."

"No, I need to get up. I know you're not going to like it, but I'm taking Luke to see his grandmother today. I, uh, texted her yesterday."

Mood ruined, Matt sat up and yanked on his pants. He *didn't* like it. Not one damn bit. "She probably won't say ten words to him. She's silent like a doormat. Is James going to be there?"

Sammie sat up, yawning. "I don't know. Did you want to go with us? Her text says to be there at nine. They're going to bake cookies. I assume Mr. Howell will be at work. It's the middle of the week."

"Oh sure, let me put on a suit and tie, and we'll go drink tea and pretend like we're one happy family," he replied, shrugging into his T-shirt. "It isn't like Lila will even do the cooking. Their housekeeper, Mae, does it. Lila's afraid she might chip a nail."

"Your attitude isn't helping the situation. You're as bad as Mr. Howell." Sammie climbed out of bed and began making it.

"Don't even go there," he snapped. "I'm going to work. Don't leave Luke alone with those people. They have the money to just take off with him." He slammed the bedroom door on his way out.

It seemed history was repeating itself. Here he was with his second wife, arguing about the same damn shit he'd argued about with his first.

Sammie and Luke arrived exactly on time. The front door opened, and Lila motioned them into a white marble foyer.

"Lukas! I'm so glad you're here." She smiled warmly at her grandson before turning her gaze to Sammie. The look on her face cooled.

Dressed impeccably in navy pants and a white top, Mrs. Howell looked ready for a luncheon at the country club instead of baking cookies with her grandson.

Sammie withstood Lila Howell's scrutiny with her chin lifted, shoulders back. She refused to cower. "Luke's been excited about seeing you today." She wiped Luke's nose with a tissue. "Wipe your feet before we go in."

Luke rolled his eyes and sighed. "I *know*, Sammie." He wiped his feet. "Grandma, can we bake some chocolate chip cookies and FaceTime Aunt Jinx? Maybe Winston will lick the phone!"

"If you like, dear. Although Aunt Eugenia is probably in class or at work." Lila's eyes filled with tears as she stooped to eye-level with Luke and cupped his face in her hands. "My goodness, you're growing up so fast. You may look like your daddy, but you have dimples just like your mommy and some of her same mannerisms..." She wiped her eyes. "I think Gramps would love to have some homemade cookies. We'll make some for you to take home, too."

She stood, her eyes filled with sadness. "Thank you for bringing Lukas over, Samantha. I've missed him terribly. Things have been... difficult."

"You're welcome. I, uh, know this is an adjustment for everyone."

Mr. Howell came down the stairs tying his robe, his hair damp but combed. Nodding his acknowledgment to Sammie, he swung Luke up in the air and gave him a big hug. "How's my favorite grandson?"

"I'm your only grandson, Gramps!"

James laughed, surprising Sammie. He seemed almost loving in his own environment.

"Not only are you my favorite grandson, you're my smartest grandson, too!"

Luke grinned even wider and held tight to his grandfather's hand once he was back on the ground.

"Good morning, Ms. Morgan. I decided to take the day off. I can't resist a homemade cookie." He ruffled Luke's hair.

And still the asshole baited her. "It's *Mrs. Tyler*. But Sammie is fine. Luke's looked forward to visiting." She toyed with her purse strap and gave the speech she'd practiced in the bathroom this morning. "I hope we can all maintain a level of civility for his sake. I don't want you to ever think I would stand in the way of your relationship with him. You're his family, and he loves you. I hope with time you'll realize his happiness is our common goal. That is, mine and Matt's—and Pa's..." Her voice trailed off, and she dug her fingernails into her palm as she breathed in and out, refusing to let her gaze waver under his stony stare.

"Of course."

A black woman walked in with a huge smile on her face. "There's my boy! You better come give me a kiss."

"Me-Mae!" Luke ran over and threw himself in her arms. His limp was getting better. "I'm here to bake cookies!"

"I know! Chocolate chip, your favorite." Holding the boy in her arms, she smiled and nodded at Sammie. "Mrs. Tyler."

"Just Sammie. Nice to meet you." Being in Karen's childhood home with her parents had her anxiety skyrocketing. She tapped her fingers to her thumbs.

"Would you like some tea or anything? Mae will be glad to fix it." Lila guided them toward the kitchen.

Three hours later, Sammie declined lunch, thanked the Howells and Mae, and herded Luke to the car with his bag of cookies.

Scrolling through the seven texts Matt had sent, she texted back that they were leaving but had to pick up a few groceries first. Matt replied that he had errands to run and would grab a bite to eat in town.

Luke chattered nonstop about the cookies and wanted to bake more when they got home.

"I think you really just want to eat the cookies," she teased.

When she parked at Hudson's One Stop Grocery, there was a cart next to the car. She tried to lift Luke into it, but he resisted.

"No, Sammie. That's for babies."

"Fine, but no dawdling. We need to get home and have some lunch. I bet Pa's hungry. And you need a nap."

"I'm *not* a baby. I hate naps."

Inside the store, he shuffled along beside her, picking up items they didn't need.

Nerves already shot from the visit with the Howells, she snapped, "No, Luke, put that back. We have toothpaste."

"But this is special toothpaste, Sammie. Look, it has sparkles."

"I said *no*." She replaced it and wheeled the cart to feminine products. She stood for a moment, searching for the tampons she'd need soon and tossed them in the cart.

"Hi!" Janice Kelton rounded the corner with Horace Jr. by her side and the baby in the cart.

"Oh, hello." Sammie smiled.

Horace Jr. stuck his tongue out at Luke behind his mother's back, which Luke returned in kind. Sammie shot Luke a warning look. While she and Janice exchanged small talk and cooed over the baby, the boys began to tussle and knocked over a display, spilling boxes everywhere.

The boys stopped wrestling and jumped apart with not-so-innocent looks on their faces. Sammie knelt down to put the spilled items back—making sure everything was lined up perfectly—while Janice fussed and threatened to tear up her son's rear end. The baby screamed, and Janice left, apologizing and tugging Horace Jr. behind her, leaving Sammie and Luke to clean up the mess.

"I'm sorry, Sammie." Luke handed her the spilled items so she could line them up, leaving precisely one-half inch of space between them.

"You know better," she noted as she put the last of the boxes back.

"Are you going to tell Daddy?" Luke's dark eyes, so very much like his father's, peered up at her as he chewed his bottom lip.

"Are you going to behave and help me carry the groceries into the house?"

"Yes, ma'am."

"Then I don't think Daddy needs to know." She tousled his hair and stood, realizing she sounded like a parent.

She received a grateful hug. When she started to unload the shopping cart at the checkout, he jumped up and exclaimed, "Let me! I want to help, Sammie!"

Nodding, she let him load the items onto the conveyor belt as she dug in her purse for her wallet. She smiled at Lydia, the frumpy, gossipy salesclerk who always looked bored and unhappy. Lydia picked up the last item Luke had retrieved from the shopping cart and giggled.

Sammie's smile turned to a horrified gasp, and she swore she could feel the blood drain from her face. She opened her mouth to protest, but nothing came out except an incoherent sound of distress.

The salesclerk now looked anything but bored. Pulling her glasses low on her nose, she looked Sammie up and down, focusing on her stomach. She blew a bubble and popped it loudly as she scanned the pregnancy test.

"No. No, that isn't mine," Sammie protested weakly, feeling as if she could pass out. "It must have fallen in the cart when Luke and the Kelton boy knocked over the display."

"Uh-huh. Matt Tyler must have some potent stuff." She guffawed, deliberately drawing attention. "Maybe he should've checked one aisle over for some condoms when he was in here last week."

Sammie was so mortified she wanted to slink away and hide.

"What does E.P.T. spell, Sammie?" Luke asked, peering at the box.

The people behind them craned their necks to see what was causing the hold up. Their quiet whispers and stares increased her paranoia.

At last, Lydia dropped the box into the grocery sack and pushed a button on the register.

"That will be $73.76," she said as she popped another bubble, a wide grin on her face.

Too mortified to ask that the pregnancy test be removed, Sammie glanced around, feeling the stares around her. Panic bubbled in her chest, and she felt lightheaded. Good God, she couldn't pass out—it would be like lighting a match to gasoline as Lydia's assumptions hung heavy in the air. She had to get out of here.

She shakily handed Lydia seventy-five dollars and grabbed Luke by the hand, fleeing the store and not waiting for her change.

Luke stalled when they reached the car and tugged his hand in hers, trying to get away. Her anxiety was contagious, and she could see the fear on Luke's pale, pinched face.

"No, Sammie, I don't want to get in the car!" He yanked his hand out of hers.

She threw her purse and groceries in the car and turned to face him.

"You have to!" Her agitation made her voice an octave higher than usual.

"No!" Tears welled up in his eyes, and he started to back away.

A large SUV began to back up, and she knew the driver couldn't see the small boy.

"Luke, get in the damn car!" she screamed. On the verge of tears herself, she grabbed his hand, jerking him out of harm's way.

"No! You can't make me!" He struggled to get away.

"Lukas Matthew Tyler, you rode in the car to get here without any problems…" She took a deep breath. "Stop. Please…" She lowered her voice and wrapped her arms around the boy as he flailed against her.

"Hey there, Luke. What's the matter, kiddo?" Travis Carlton approached and stooped down to make eye contact with the hysterical boy. He glanced up at her with a questioning look.

"I don't want to get in the car! I want Mommy!" Luke broke down sobbing and reached for Travis.

The man looked startled, but took him in his arms and held him tight. He rested his head against Luke's for a moment and patted him on the back, whispering in his ear until Luke calmed down.

She watched as he instructed Luke to take deep breaths. Travis smiled at her as he continued to hold the overwrought child, assuring him everything would be okay. Luke whimpered and laid his head on Travis's shoulder, hugging his neck.

"Mrs. Tyler, do you have perishables in the car?"

"No, just a few items. Please, call me Sammie."

"Sammie, it's time for lunch, and I'm starving. Would you and Luke like to join me? I'm afraid it won't be anything fancy, just burgers at the Mug and Cone. It's a couple of blocks from here, and *we can walk*." He winked at her as he continued to pat Lukas on the back.

"I hate to impose." Sammie glanced around at the people in the parking lot. All of them seemed to be casting questioning looks her way.

"Please, it won't be an imposition. I get tired of eating alone. Join me."

Sammie felt a little uneasy, but they were in a public place, and Luke knew him. After the morning they'd had, maybe a break was needed.

"They have good chocolate milkshakes, Sammie." Luke sniffled, hope filling his eyes.

"Well, I've never turned down a chocolate milkshake. Thank you, Mr. Carlton."

He grinned. "Mr. Carlton is my father. And even he prefers to be called George. Call me Travis."

He held Luke in his arms as they walked to the Mug and Cone, chatting about the weather and potluck supper on the Fourth. Impeccably dressed in a now tear-stained expensive blue suit, he was a handsome man. His light brown hair was trimmed short, and his steel gray eyes were kind and full of humor. Finding Travis easy to talk to, Sammie relaxed as they meandered down Main Street.

The bell jingled on the door of the Mug and Cone when they entered. The place was full of teens, local businessmen, and harried mothers with their children. The woman at the register looked up and nodded to Travis. Her eyebrows inched upward when she spied Sammie and Luke. She bustled to the table with three glasses of ice water, curiosity written all over her broad face.

"Hey, Travis. What can I get y'all?" Her voice was sugary sweet. "I'm Frances Kelton. You must be Sammie."

Sammie nodded, vaguely remembering Bubba's younger sister.

"What would you two like?" Travis asked.

"What do you recommend?" Sammie placed a hand on the bouncing boy next to her to get him to settle down.

"Get a burger and chocolate shake. They're the best! That's what I always get with Daddy."

"Where *is* your daddy, Luke?" Frances asked.

"At work. I made cookies with Grandma today. I want a hamburger with ketchup and pickles, no yucky mustard, and a chocolate milkshake."

"I'll have the same, thank you."

"Me too, but add mustard on my burger and an order of fries," Travis replied.

Frances grabbed the menus and hurried to the kitchen.

"So, Sammie, although you were behind me in school, I do remember you from years ago. Where have you been and what have you been up to?" He smiled and winked at Luke, who continued to wiggle beside her.

She lowered her eyes and shifted in her seat.

"Uh, well, I lived lots of different places before Sue Ellen, er, my mother passed. What about you?"

While technically not doing anything wrong by being here, she felt funny. Matt wouldn't be pleased. Or was it just the nerves from this morning that had her discombobulated?

He shrugged. "I went to college, graduated, and now I work at the bank. Not the most exciting life…"

"College sounds exciting to me. I never graduated high school."

"No? Why not?"

"My mother was ill, and I worked and took care of her."

"Ah. Understandable and admirable. I teach a GED class in Harrisville on Tuesday nights. You should come. It helps you prepare for the exam to get your high school equivalency diploma."

"I wish, but that isn't possible right now. Matt has class. But thank you. Was it your dream to work at the bank?"

"Well, my boss would want me to say yes."

"And what would the real answer be?"

"To have lunch with an exciting redhead." He gave a dramatic sigh. "And they say dreams never come true."

Heat filled her cheeks, and he chuckled.

"Yes, I find numbers fascinating. As well as redheads."

"I'm pretty good with math, but English is hard for me," she replied.

"Sammie counts stuff. She's like the Count on Sesame Street," Luke contributed.

Travis laughed. "He's my favorite. What do you like to do for fun? Aside from counting—which as a banker, I also find fun."

She shrugged. "I'm pretty boring."

"Sammie plays the guitar, too," Luke offered. He pointed at the door. A handsome dark-haired man walked in, holding a little girl all dressed in pink. "Look, Sammie. There's my girlfriend, Kenzie."

Sammie frowned. "I thought Angela was your girlfriend."

"I have two," he boasted.

"That's called being a player and could lead to trouble," Sammie offered. "You'll make them jealous."

Travis shifted in his seat, looking decidedly uncomfortable.

"Nah. Pa says don't settle for one when you can have two," Luke said.

"That just ain't right, Luke. One girlfriend at a time."

Travis held out his hand to the stranger when he approached the table. "Hi, David, Miss Kenzie. Sammie, this is David Patterson and his daughter, Kenzie. He's a teacher at the high school. David, this is Matt Tyler's wife, Sammie."

Sammie blushed and shook hands. "You live next door to Jennifer and Dylan. I've seen Kenzie at the McAthies'."

David smiled. "Right. Nice to meet you. Hey, Luke. Are you excited about Vacation Bible School? It starts Sunday."

"Sure! Can I go, Sammie?"

"I guess so…That would be up to your daddy." She rubbed her finger over and over the carved name in the table.

"Great. Hope to see you there. Nice to meet you, Sammie. See you around, Travis." David and Kenzie went to a booth and sat down.

"Like Matt, David's a single father. Uh, sorry. Obviously, Matt isn't single anymore," Travis corrected.

"It's okay." She laughed. "We're still getting used to being married, too."

She liked Travis and his easy manner. And she appreciated him helping her out with Luke during his meltdown. Her finger snagged a rough spot on the table and she winced. "Ouch, splinter."

"They really need to sand these tables down. Let me look. So, do you sing as well as play guitar?" Travis took her hand in his.

Matt Tyler stopped dead in his tracks across the street from the Mug and Cone. He'd come into town to pick up supplies and grab lunch before going back to the shop. He couldn't believe his eyes as he looked through the main window of the greasy hamburger joint. *Why the hell is Travis holding Sammie's hand? And why is she blushing and staring at him as if his shit doesn't stink?* Anger and jealousy blurred his vision.

He hurried across the street. Several turned to stare when he entered the diner. Taking a deep breath, he forced himself to calm down. No way he'd make a scene in front of all these busybodies and risk James's right-hand-man, Travis, reporting back anything negative. He placed his order at the take-out window, wanting to slap the smug expression off Frances's face. Behind him he heard Sammie laugh and Luke giggle. His blood pressure shot up at least thirty points as he wondered what the fucker had said that was so amusing.

Glancing over his shoulder, he took in Travis's flawless appearance and then looked down at his own work clothes. His jeans were filthy, the Crucified, Dead and Buried T-shirt he'd rescued from the rag pile had a hole in it, and there was grease under his fingernails. Old feelings of inadequacy surfaced, and he felt like he had in high school whenever Travis was around. He decided to leave with his food without speaking to them, but his plan was railroaded when Luke spotted him.

"Daddy!" Luke crawled out of the booth and darted over to give him a hug.

All eyes in the restaurant turned toward them. *Wonderful. Welcome to the show that never ends.*

"Whoa, son. You're gonna get filthy. I've got grease all over me." He tousled Luke's hair and walked over to the table to greet Travis and Sammie. He hoped to hell everyone's meals were getting stone cold since no one seemed to be interested in the lousy food.

"Samantha. Travis." He kept his voice as even as possible, suppressing the urge to drag Travis from the booth and smash his perfect face into the floor.

She looked up at him and began organizing the sugar and sweetener packets, chewing her bottom lip.

"Care to join us, Matt?" Travis asked.

He clenched his fist to keep from wiping the smug smile off Travis's face. "When hell freezes over. See you two at the house," he said softly. He gave a curt nod to his wife and son and glared at Travis. *That bastard.*

As he stormed out of the restaurant, he heard Luke giggling. "Daddy owes a quarter!"

He'd made it across the street before he heard Frances screaming his name. He reluctantly turned around.

"Hey! Matt! You forgot ketchup." She waved packets in her hand as she ran toward him.

He scowled.

"H-Here." She gasped for breath, and sweat poured off her flushed, full cheeks as she handed him the packets. "By the way, congrats."

He raised one eyebrow. "Congrats?"

"Well, maybe not. But let us know after she takes the test. I can fix a chicken finger platter for the shower, if needed." Her sly look slid into nosy anticipation as she waited for his response.

He now knew what deer felt like during hunting season. But curiosity got the best of him. "What are you talking about, Frances?"

"The pregnancy test. Lydia told me your wife bought one this morning."

What the hell? Everything went black for a moment as his world tilted upside down and sideways. Ketchup oozed from his clenched fist. Pulling himself together, he turned away from Frances and didn't bother to reply. Wiping his sticky hand on his filthy shirt, he marched toward his truck.

Through the roar of his own heartbeat pounding in his ears he heard his name again.

"Matt!"

He turned around and faced Sammie with a carefully composed face, aware that everyone in the Mug and Cone was likely watching them. *When did my life become a goddamned Lifetime movie?*

She darted across the street and caught up to him. "Whatever possessed you to be so rude? I was very embarrassed—" She frowned. "Is that blood? Are you okay?"

"Don't start in on me, Sammie," he warned.

"Excuse me? What's your problem? I'm the one who's had the day from hell. First at the Howells all morning, then Luke had a complete meltdown at the grocery store about getting in the car. Travis helped divert his attention by offering to take us to lunch. We're just eating. There was no reason for you to act like such a jerk! I think you should go back and apologize." Sammie's eyes snapped as she punctuated her words with her index finger pointed at his chest.

"Don't hold your breath. First off, *you* elected to take Luke to the Howells. *I* don't care if he ever sees them again. Secondly, I will *never* offer an apology to Travis. I don't like him, and I don't like my family being around him. Now quit pointing at me, because you have a hell of a lot of explaining to do yourself." Matt spoke quietly, not wanting to cause a bigger scene on Main Street than necessary.

He turned around, hoping she'd just let it drop. He should've known better.

"Don't you walk away from me when I'm talking to you! I *like* Travis. He's one of the few people in Pine Bluff I *do* like. I'm not going to let you dictate who I can and can't see. You're not my parent!"

Matt prayed the sidewalk would open up and swallow him whole to remove him from this shit show. He swung around and marched back toward her.

Holding the sack with his lunch in his ketchup-sticky left hand, he grabbed her at the nape of the neck with his other hand and pulled her close. Slanting his mouth over hers, he kissed her with all the expertise he possessed until her arms wrapped around his neck and she kissed him back. Her body pressed close to his, and she let out a soft moan. When he pulled away, her eyes were huge, her breathing erratic.

"I'll see you later, and you better have a damn good reason for buying a pregnancy test, Sammie," he told her as he turned and walked away.

Chapter
Fifteen

On her hands and knees, Sammie scrubbed the kitchen floor in meticulous circles. The repetition soothed her after this horrible day. Thankfully, she'd had no problem getting Luke in the car for the trip home after lunch. Matt had worked through supper and skipped his night class—something he never did—and she was worried. After she put Luke to bed, she'd tried talking to him, but he'd refused to quit working and come out from under the car.

Pa appeared at the doorway, and she sat back on her heels, pushing the hair out of her face.

"Be careful," she told him. "The floors are wet. Do you need something?"

"Girl, we could've eaten supper off the damn floors. What the hell are you doing?" He frowned.

"No, no, they're not perfect, and you owe the jar fifty cents," she replied as she returned to her precise scrubbing. *One, two, three…*

Matt sat at his workbench with his face buried in his arms and sighed. *Sammie's pregnant?* He'd been so upset, he hadn't felt up to talking to her when she came out to the shop.

Suddenly the silence was deafening. *Who the hell has the nerve to turn off Metallica's "Fade to Black"?* He lifted his head, hoping it wasn't Sammie again.

Using his four-prong cane, Pa approached.

It was still an effort for him to walk this far, and the fact that he'd come out to the shop didn't bode well.

"Not now, Pa. Just go away and turn the music back on."

"Why did you skip school, son?"

"I'm not fourteen; save the lecture — not that you ever cared when I skipped school." He dropped his head back to his arms.

"You only listen to this crap when you're depressed," Pa countered. "Why are you feeling sorry for yourself?"

Matt looked up and glared. "Feeling sorry for myself?" He stood, his fists clenched. "My life is for shit. I'm entitled to an occasional night of feeling sorry for myself!" He picked up a hammer and threw it against the wall.

Pa didn't flinch. "Nice. You'd spank Luke's ass for this kind of behavior. Are you through with your temper tantrum, Matthew?"

Matt sat back down. *Pa's right.* "Yes, sir. I have work to do. I'll see you in the morning."

"I didn't raise a quitter."

"You didn't do much in the way of raising me at all."

"True. But your boy needs you. And he needs a mother. *You* would've been better off if your mother had lived."

Matt turned and looked at his father. "Karen is dead."

Pa nodded. "I never cared for Karen, but she was a good mom. But as you said, she's dead. She's the past. That accident was a terrible detour in your life. Your dreams are still out there; you're just taking a different route, son. And you have a new wife. Sammie's good for you and a great stepmother. She loves your son, and she loves your ungrateful ass."

"Please spare me the life-journey clichés." Matt groaned, wondering if his father had been watching the Hallmark Channel.

"I heard what happened in town today. I had four phone calls before either of you got home. To be so damn smart with books, you're pretty goddamned stupid."

"What?"

"There's a stubborn redhead scrubbing your kitchen floors on her hands and knees. Did she make a mistake? I don't know. I do know none of us is perfect. Have you asked her what happened? I'm assuming since she married you, if she *is* pregnant, the father of the child isn't in the picture. If that's the case, she needs you more than ever right now. Genes don't make a parent. Being there for the kid does. Grow up, Matthew. Don't make my mistakes. You're a damn good father." Pa stormed out of the shop.

Matt cranked Metallica back up as loud as it could go and reflected on what Pa had said. Communication had always been his problem. Karen had often complained that he withdrew and didn't listen. That's what had caused the accident. If he'd just sat down and *listened* to her, maybe she wouldn't have left upset with him…

Maybe Sammie didn't know she was pregnant when we married. Or maybe this was just a scare, and that's why she bought the test. He stood and closed the shop, prepared to hear whatever Sammie had to say.

As he locked the door, he paused and looked at his home. Someone had left the light on for him. The back porch was warm and inviting—and not surprisingly, free of junk. Luke's trucks were in a basket, and Sammie had added a cushion to the rocker for Pa.

He'd been forced to move back to this house. Two mortgages had been too much for him to handle with the mounting medical bills. But now he was glad. This house had character. And Sammie had made it a home.

Our home.

It was time he manned up and treated her like his wife. He needed to apologize for his behavior and treat her accordingly, which meant *listening* to her.

Entering the back door, which had been left cracked open, he found her still scrubbing the spotless kitchen floors on her hands and knees. Her T-shirt was drenched with sweat, and pieces of her damp hair had fallen out of her bun. Her cheeks and nose were red, as were her raw hands.

She sat back, mopping her brow with her arm. Looking at his feet, her face fell. He followed her gaze to the dirt and grass he'd tracked in on the pristine floors.

"I, uh — sorry, Sammie." He kicked off his shoes and left them on the back porch.

She scooted to where he'd been standing and scrubbed at the muddy footprint.

"Sammie, stop."

"I'm almost done." Her voice was forced and a little too bright. "You need to fix the back door. Sometimes it locks automatically when it closes," she added, not looking up.

"I will."

She nodded and resumed her relentless scrubbing.

"Sammie, stop. That spot has been there as long as I can remember. It won't come out."

"No, I'll get it. I have to get it out!" Her voice rose and cracked.

She was disconnecting. He could feel it as surely as he could feel the hair on the back of his neck rising. Her fingers were bright red, and he'd lose it if she didn't stop the damn incessant scouring.

"Samantha, I said stop, and I meant it!"

He helped her to her feet and pried the scrub brush from her hand, placing it on the counter. Turning the water on, he gently rinsed her chafed hands and dried them. Her eyes seemed distant, her motions robotic. He cupped her face. She blinked as if just now seeing him. Her face changed, and it was as if he could see her soul return from whatever depths of hell it had gone to.

"What's going on?" Gently he added, "Are you pregnant?"

"What? No!" Lowering her lashes, Sammie looked at the floor, and her breathing hitched. "Is that why you've been so mad? This is all a huge mistake."

"Babies might be unplanned sometimes, but they aren't mistakes."

"I'm *not* pregnant."

"Then tell me about today, because I'm confused as hell." Matt held her hands.

She sighed. "The visit with the Howells went better than I expected," she finally began. "Luke enjoyed himself. Even Mr. Howell was pleasant. And Mae was fun; she's so down to earth. But I was nervous the entire time. After we left, Luke and I w-went to the grocery store, and he and the Kelton boy accidentally knocked over a shelf when I was looking for stupid tampons. Luke helped me pick them up, but a pregnancy test must've fallen into the cart. I didn't realize it until that witch Lydia Meadows scanned it and made a big production out of it. I wanted to die. I tried to tell her it wasn't mine, but she didn't believe me and said maybe *you* should've shopped one aisle over for condoms. I was so mortified, I left the store."

Matt raised his brow and bit his lip to keep from laughing.

"Luke was already tired, and I guess my anxiety was contagious because he refused to get in the car. He became hysterical and wouldn't listen to me in the parking lot. A car was backing up, and I didn't think they could see him. It scared the shit out of me, and I screamed at him. I ain't proud of that, and I'm sorry."

He rubbed her leg. "It's okay. I lose my shit and yell at him all the time. Maybe we should earmark some of the no-cussing jar funds for a therapist in his future."

Sammie hung her head.

Matt lifted her jaw and gave her a quick kiss on the mouth. "That was a joke. Go on."

"Well, Travis came by and was a voice of reason. He calmed Luke down and took us to lunch. That's it—until you came in and were rude and then kissed me on Main Street, adding to the rumors flying around."

"My turn." Matt moved to a chair and pulled her into his lap, wrapping his arms around her waist. "When I saw Travis holding your hand, it pissed me off." He shifted for a moment and dug out his wallet. Opening it he, threw a five in the jar. He grinned. "Just covering the rest of the evening for both of us."

"He wasn't *holding* my hand. I had a splinter in my finger; he was getting it *out.*" She held up her hand.

He slipped her taped wedding band off her finger. "I'm taking this to get it resized tomorrow. Moving on, I *assumed* he was holding your hand, because I have a long history with Travis that relates to Karen. I especially don't like him around Luke."

"Why? Luke likes him. Travis was great today during his meltdown. I know he dated Karen, but Matt, that was ages ago. Janice Kelton said he still carries a torch for her. You *married* her. If anything, you should feel sorry for him."

It will be a cold day in hell… Matt checked his irritation. Sammie had no way of knowing how deep his hatred ran. He continued his story. "After I left with my lunch, as you probably saw, nosy Frances got up off her ass and came running after me with ketchup packets. I knew it wasn't because she was concerned about me eating dry French fries. She's the one who told me about the pregnancy test. I was dumbfounded, and I admit, I wondered if you hadn't been totally honest with me when we married. So by the time you came outside to ask me why I was rude, I knew all eyes were on us, including Travis's. So I did a very male thing. I staked my territory and kissed you."

"Oh my God. This is like a really bad sitcom." Sammie giggled. "I guess I should be thankful you didn't pee on me on Main Street."

Matt chuckled.

"Not my kink, Sammie."

"What is your kink?"

"Apparently being a dominating asshole." He brushed a silky strand of hair out of her face. "Please forgive me for jumping to conclusions. I have trust issues that have nothing to do with you. I haven't truly given you a hundred percent." He shrugged. "I dunno…I think part of me is afraid to invest that much of my heart because it hurts so damn much when it's gone." He looked at the ceiling.

She placed her hand on his chest. "I get that. And I understand. We're still learning about each other. But you need to talk to me. Sue Ellen would act without thinking, and sometimes it wasn't good. I'm tired of living on the edge, always wondering if I'm doing something wrong. I can't live like that anymore. I'm *not* going to."

"I'm going to work harder at connecting with you on all levels. I hate to admit to any faults, what with my reputation as St. Matthew…" He awkwardly crossed himself and grinned.

"I thought you were Methodist." She snickered and cupped his face in her hands. "Go on."

He kissed her red palms. "I suck at talking. Especially about how I'm feeling, or admitting I need anything. Maybe it's because I grew up without a mom. Pa and I never talked much except to argue. Karen would get angry when I'd pull in instead of telling her what was wrong. Sammie, please…Don't give up on me. I care for you deeply, and I need you." He gave her a soft kiss.

"I need you, too. But I need you to lay things out for me. I don't do well with mood swings. If you're mad, tell me. If I'm upset, I'll tell you. We have to talk. It's the only way we can make this marriage work. I need honesty."

"I agree." He stood, holding her in his arms.

"What are you doing?"

"Carrying you to bed, Mrs. Tyler." He kissed her soundly. "To explore your needs."

Chapter
Sixteen

Sammie held her breath as Matt carried her upstairs, smiling into his neck. Could she dare dream that he'd one day love her as much as he had Karen? Was a second chance possible?

The door to Luke's room opened.

"Whatcha doin'?"

"Going to bed. Where you're supposed to be," Matt answered, frowning.

"I want some water."

"I'll get it," she offered.

"I'm trying to be romantic here," he groaned.

"I know," she replied, giggling. "But honestly? You need a shower."

"I thought you'd like me nasty and dirty." He winked.

"You thought wrong." She laughed and wiggled until he put her down. "Go clean up. I'll get Luke's water."

"Okay." Taking Luke's hand, he walked him back into his room as she headed downstairs. "Goodnight, son. Sammie will be back up with your drink in a minute, okay?"

"Okay, Daddy."

After checking to make sure the doors were locked, she returned and handed Luke his cup. She could hear Matt in the bathroom.

"Thanks, Sammie." Luke took a sip and settled back under the covers. Rhonda sat on the end of the bed looking smug.

She smiled. "Uh-oh. Did Daddy see Rhonda in here?"

"Yup." Luke reached down to pat the cat, which was being surprisingly tolerant. "I love you, Sammie."

Her eyes filled. "I love you, too." Tucking him in, she kissed his forehead.

She found Matt waiting for her in bed. She placed her dirty clothes in the hamper and lined up her shoes with his in the closet. She ignored his chuckle.

"How many times did you check to make sure the doors were locked?" he asked softly.

"Four," she admitted. "I can't help it."

"I know."

She sighed and slipped into bed, her naked flesh pressed against his hard planes. "It isn't fine. I need to learn to handle my anxiety."

He held her face in his hands and kissed her. "Put your worries aside for now. No counting…unless it's kisses." He then kissed each cheek.

"Three," she whispered.

"And many more to come."

His voice held so many promises. He turned out the light, and she let out the breath she'd been holding. Her body wanted him, no doubt about it. Her heart needed him.

Four, five, six… His lips traveled to the sweet spot behind her ear.

"Love me, Sammie. Trust me and let go. And be real with me."

Seven, eight… "What?"

He moved on top of her. "I'm scared shitless." His forehead touched hers, and he kissed the tears slipping down her hot cheeks.

Nine, ten… "Of me?"

"Of making a mess of this. I want us to have fun, Sammie. Like we used to."

"*Like we used to?*" she repeated. "Like when we were kids? We fished and cussed. We already do more cussing than we should."

"I meant I want the easiness between us we had before life got so damn complicated."

"I'd like that, too."

He ran a hand down her arm. "When we decided to marry, I wasn't thinking straight. I was out of my head with worry. I'm tired of being afraid—"

"Mr. Howell's threats were scary." She caught his hand and held it.

"It wasn't just that. I think I've been afraid of being happy, because in a split second it can be gone. I've been afraid of failing Luke, of not being enough. Karen…She was a good mom. She was the parent, the one who took care of the kids when they were sick, helped with homework, cooked, read stories, disciplined. Me? I worked all the damn time. I wasn't there for my family like I should've been."

"Matt, you're a good father."

"After the accident, I spent more time with Luke out of necessity. Honestly, the wreck was a wakeup call to what's important in life. My boy needs me. But quite frankly, I feel like an imposter. That's why James's threats scare the shit out of me. I don't know what I'm doing most of the time. I've always been kind of obsessed about money. Karen had champagne taste, and I had a beer budget. Those damn dishes? They were a sore point. She bought them, and I returned them because they were an expense we didn't need. So of course, James turned right around and bought them again, making a big production about giving them to her in front of me." He sighed. "After the wreck, the medical bills kept coming. Insurance only pays so much…"

He rolled to his back, clasping his hands behind his head.

Sammie rubbed his chest. "Karen probably couldn't help it; she was raised having whatever she wanted. You and me? We didn't have anything."

"I suppose. I'm telling you all this to say I don't regret our decision. I'm glad you're my wife. It's a well-known fact that I tend to be a high-handed asshole, but do you think you could love me? I mean, eventually? I know it'll take time." His whispered question was tinged with a vulnerability she'd never heard from him before.

Hope filled the emptiness she'd lived with most of her life. She moved over him, pressing her body into his, and smiled against his ear. "I reckon I could give it a go. I've always loved you, even though you are a high-handed asshole."

He chuckled. "Thanks. I've always loved you, too." One hand trailed up and down her spine, and his other cupped her face.

Stunned, she stared at him. *Do I dare hope he means it like I do?*

"Should we shake on it?" he teased.

Sammie rocked against his erection. "We could. Or we could even kiss…" She found his mouth and kissed him with all the love she felt. He shifted a bit and gripped her hips, lowering her onto him.

"Just one thing," Matt said.

"Yes?"

"If we're going to make this marriage work, no faking *anything*. I want to give you orgasms that will make you scream the roof down—only don't really…Luke…Pa. You know…muffle it." He smiled.

"Okay. You busted me. Now it's my turn to bust you." She waggled her brow and nipped his lower lip. Her fingers dug into his arms as she slowly moved up and down. It was the first time he'd let her be in control of anything…and it was liberating.

"Mmmmm, feels good. Feels so right, Sammie."

He kept one hand on her hip and slipped the other between them, rubbing circles on her clit. She leaned forward and kissed him, but it was too much. "Not…" She gasped.

He stopped. "You okay?"

"Don't stop." She ground against him. "Yes, no…I'm not coordinated enough to do this…ah, that feels so good…" She threw her head back, moaning as her orgasm built.

Matt sat up, repositioned her, and chuckled as he guided her to the sweet spot. "Shhhhh…" he whispered.

Faster and faster, her body seemed to be moving of its own accord until she couldn't contain the need for her release any longer. She muffled her pleasure in his neck as her body shuddered. Matt clenched his jaw as he came deep inside of her.

"Fuuuuck," he gasped.

He held on to her, panting. Their bodies were slick with sweat, and their harsh breathing was the only sound in the room.

She giggled. "If we do this every night, we'll go broke with the cussing jar."

"Totally worth it."

They rolled back onto the bed, facing each other.

"I see why they say honesty is the best policy." She rubbed her thumb across his lips.

"We can do this, Sammie." He pulled her even closer, kissing the finger that felt naked without her wedding band. "I'll get your ring resized tomorrow."

She settled in with her head on his chest. Her heart was so full it spilled down her cheeks. As she fell asleep, she counted his heart beats.

Four days later, Sammie daydreamed as she started the coffee. The past few days had been the happiest of her life. Her wedding ring was back on her finger and the perfect size. Matt had been attentive during the day, and more so at night. Even now she could close her eyes and feel his hands on her skin…

"Morning, Mrs. Tyler." He nuzzled her neck from behind. His jaw was freshly shaved, his hair damp, and he smelled so good.

Sammie turned and gave him a quick kiss, surprised to see him in a white dress shirt and black pants, his tie loose around his neck. "Good morning, Mr. Tyler. Look at you."

"Yuck. Quit kissing," Luke complained beside him. He wore a nice pair of shorts and a plaid shirt, his hair wet and combed.

"Why are you two dressed up?" She poured coffee and handed it to Matt. "What would you like for breakfast?" she asked Luke.

"Cereal."

She folded her arms and waited.

"Cereal, please."

"You don't need to make breakfast," Matt told her. "It's Sunday. And they serve it at church before Sunday school. Run upstairs and get ready. Vacation Bible School starts tonight. I thought we should make an appearance this morning. And tonight, we'll be down one in the house for an hour or so…" He winked. "Maybe I'll call Gig and see if he'll come get Pa."

Her mouth dropped. "You're shittin' me. Church?" She winced and pulled a quarter out of the drawer where she kept a roll. "I'm not going."

"Of course you are. You're my wife. We're a family."

She turned her back and angrily stirred her coffee. "I'm not going. And I'm not sure you're going for the right reason."

"Why not, Sammie?" Luke asked. "Pa says it's full of desperate women looking for something. You're a woman. What's desperate mean, Daddy? Is Sammie desperate?"

Pa entered the kitchen laughing.

"Pa, really. This is *not* acceptable. Luke, it means hopeless. I'm sure Pa meant people go to church to get hope." He glared at his father. "Sammie, you have plenty of time to get ready. I'll do the chores."

"I'm not going." Grabbing the dog food, she went out to the back porch and fed Rufus.

Matt followed. "Why not? It's just church."

She patted his chest. "You go have fun. Say hi to Lila and James. Will you be joining them for Sunday dinner?"

"What? Don't be ridiculous."

"I'm not a hypocrite; I'm not going. I do just fine talkin' to the good Lord on the back porch. Besides, I have plans with Sue Ellen."

"Plans with your mother?"

"I'm taking her ashes to the cemetery where my daddy's buried. I'm terrified she's gonna get knocked over and I'll have to clean her up with the vacuum cleaner."

"Do you want me to go with you?"

"No. I need to do this on my own."

"Okay. If you're sure."

She kissed him. "I'm sure. And thank you."

The church where her daddy was buried had burned years ago, and the congregation had rebuilt closer to the highway. The cemetery they'd left behind was quiet and deserted and not nearly as scary as it used to be in the dark. It took her a few minutes to find him, but she lovingly pulled the weeds around the simple marker. It wasn't even a real tombstone, just one her mother had made.

"Well, Sue Ellen. Here we are. You and Daddy can be together again. I hope you've found some peace. I didn't always like being your daughter, but I always loved you."

After pouring the ashes out, she hammered a wooden cross next to her father's marker. Pa had made it for her and carved *Sue Ellen Morgan* on it. Back in the day, her mother had visited the cemetery often and sat for hours, crying and talking to her father. She'd never understood why. Her parents weren't here. She hoped they were in a better place. Especially her mother.

No, the dead didn't hang out in cemeteries. They haunted your dreams and memories. Taking out her guitar, she played Christmas music. Matt would laugh when he heard her singing carols since it was hot as hell, but she found them comforting. Even when she was at her sickest, Sue Ellen had attempted to make things merry and have Santa pay a visit. Sammie blinked back her tears and softly sang "Joy to the World." Christmas was her favorite time of year and the source of some of her happiest memories.

The wind rustled through the trees. Closing this chapter of her life, Sammie left and headed home.

That evening, Matt pulled into the parking lot of Hudson's One Stop Grocery before picking Luke up from Vacation Bible School.

Sammie sighed. "I wish this town would get some other place to shop." She dreaded seeing the smirk on Lydia Meadow's face.

"If we're lucky, Dylan's done something to get on the front of the *National Intruder* and we'll be old news." Matt motioned her through the door first.

"I doubt that's happened. He's pretty tame now. Jennifer said he falls asleep in his recliner watching the news. I have to confess, I kinda miss seeing him on the tabloid trash. The best was when they reported he was in hiding with Elvis."

As they walked by, Lydia looked up from her register, popped her bubble gum, and smirked. Out of pure meanness, Sammie patted Matt's ass and hooked her hand in his back pocket. She wasn't sure who was more startled.

"If you're trying to pick my pocket, you're outta luck. I think I've got thirty bucks, tops."

She laughed. "Just my luck." Picking up a carton of milk, she turned around and shook her head at the frozen pie in Matt's hand.

"We don't need that."

"But it's *apple*." His whine sounded a lot like his son's.

"No, just milk."

He put it back and returned with a coconut cake.

"No. You're as bad as Luke."

"You're sooo mean," he said, perfectly mimicking Luke. "I do need to pick up a can of shaving cream, though. Meet you at the register."

She laughed. "Fine. Will you pick up a decongestant for me, too?"

"Will do."

"Hi, Sammie." Lydia smacked her gum and gazed pointedly at Sammie's stomach.

Before Sammie could tell her to quit being rude, Matt walked up behind her. He tossed a can of shaving cream, off-brand decongestant, and box of XL Magnum condoms on the belt in front of Lydia.

"We have about a half hour before we pick Luke up, right, Sammie?"

She bit her lip to keep from laughing out loud when Lydia practically choked on her gum.

Chapter
Seventeen

A month later, Matt picked up a box of chocolates while doing some errands. Life was good. Sammie and Pa still tangled at times, but for the most part, everything had settled into a quiet routine. His only regret was not being able to afford preschool for Luke. The boy was a sponge, wanting to learn and upset he wasn't old enough for kindergarten.

Pa raised his eyebrows when he walked in the front door. "For me? Shucks, you shouldn't have."

Matt shot his father a dirty look. Smirking, Pa went back to watching television.

He found Sammie upstairs, putting laundry away in Luke's room. He came up behind her and nuzzled her neck, squeezing her ass cheek.

She giggled. "Why, Pa, you dirty old man!"

"Good one." He chuckled.

She turned around and wrapped her arms around him, playing with the curls at the nape of his neck.

"Oops, my bad." She giggled.

"Hellion," he whispered, kissing the tip of her nose as he brought the chocolates out from behind his back.

Her eyes sparkled. "Yum! Thank you." She hugged him tight and gave him a quick kiss.

It occurred to him that a cheap box of chocolate would never have gotten this response from Karen, unless one of the kids gave it to her. Matt leaned over and captured Sammie's lips. The kiss deepened as her mouth opened to his. Growling deep in his throat, he slipped one hand under her T-shirt, knowing she wasn't wearing a bra. He caressed her breast until the nipple was taut, and she moaned.

"Daddy? Whatcha doin'?"

Matt yanked his hand out from under Sammie's shirt as if he'd been caught stealing a cookie. Sammie put the candy down and turned around, her face flushed. She began straightening Luke's drawers with shaking hands.

"What were ya'll doing?" Luke persisted.

"None of your business. What do you want?" Matt ran a hand through his hair and tried not to glower at his son.

"You're in *my* room," Luke pointed out. "Can I have a chocolate?"

Sammie snickered.

"May I," Matt corrected.

"*May* I have a chocolate?" Luke continued to eye them suspiciously.

Sammie laughed outright. "Sure. After you clean this room."

A little while later, Sammie put Luke down for a nap and went to find her husband — so they could finish what they'd started. She found him stretched out on the couch, dozing in front of a game on the television, his computer open in his lap. As she moved the computer, it came out of sleep mode. She looked at the article he'd been reading for school and didn't understand half of it. Placing the computer on the coffee table, she sat next to him and brushed a kiss on his cheek.

Matt stirred and pulled her on top of him with a sleepy, sexy smile. He cracked his eyes open and grinned. Inching forward, rubbing up his body on purpose, she lowered her lips to his. In turn, he rubbed her back in lazy circles as they kissed.

"Am I dreaming or is a red-headed imp seducing me?" His voice was husky and hinted of promises she wanted him to keep.

"Imp? You could've said *angel* or *seductress*." She pouted as she unbuttoned his shirt. Her lips followed each button, tasting his warm skin.

"What's the score?" Pa asked.

Startled, Matt jumped, causing Sammie to fall off the couch. Matt covered his eyes with his arm and groaned.

"Don't they make bedrooms for this kind of behavior?" Pa asked.

"Fuck," Matt swore.

"That one'll cost you fifty cents, son. Maybe we ought to let him in on our next game of dirty word Scrabble."

"Don't you need a nap, Pa?" Matt asked.

"I just got up from one."

Matt stood and helped Sammie to her feet. "Let's go."

"Where are we going?"

"Out."

"Out where?"

"I don't know, just out. Quit asking so many questions."

"When will you be back?" Pa asked with a knowing smile.

"Whenever," Matt answered as he practically dragged Sammie out the back door. "I now understand why people go berserk and kill their entire families. They're probably sexually frustrated," he muttered under his breath.

Sammie laughed so hard she had to stop and bend over to catch her breath.

"It's not funny," he complained, but his eyes crinkled, and a grin danced at the corner of his mouth. "I can't believe I just got caught making out by my father." He laughed and shook his head. "It's like being a teen all over again!"

"Pa's not as bad as Luke. I swear that kid has sex radar. Every time things get interesting, he needs a glass of water."

Matt tweaked her nose. "It's because you're loud. Come on." He pulled her toward the garage.

"I'm tired of the shop," she complained. "I still have bruises on my hips from last week, and it's so dirty in there."

"Okay." He changed direction and took her hand as they walked. Humidity hung heavy in the air, and crickets sang to them as they walked along the road where her car had broken down and brought Matt back into her life.

"Matt?"

"Hmmm?"

"Where are we going? Can we please slow down? I can barely keep up with you, and it's too damn hot to continue at this pace!" she grumbled.

Sweat trickled down her back, and she could feel her hair frizzing. She was pretty sure her antiperspirant had quit working.

"I thought I'd show you the lake. It's really beautiful," he replied as they turned off the road onto a trail through the woods.

"Oh for heaven's sake, I've been to the lake before. I hope we don't get poison ivy," she said, slapping some vines out of her face.

A hike to a lake she'd been to hundreds of times was about the last thing in the world she wanted to do. Sweating and stinking on a forced march through the woods? Not enjoyable. Lost in her thoughts, she ran into Matt when he stopped at the edge of the lake.

"Sorry—oh my. I'd forgotten how pretty it is." She admired the clear blue water lapping at the shore, so cool and peaceful. There were no houses and no boats to spoil the tranquility of the scene.

Kicking off her shoes, she ran a few feet into the water, which felt delicious around her feet and ankles. "Come on, let's cool off!" She splashed some water on her hot face. "We should've brought swimsuits."

She stopped splashing as she watched her husband kick off his shoes, peel off his shirt, and drop his pants.

"W-What are you doing?"

"What we used to do when we were kids." He dove in and swam past her, shooting up out of the water a few feet away. Slinging the water off his face, he grinned.

"I never went skinny dipping! Sue Ellen would've killed me. Matt, what if someone sees us?"

He looked around. "No one out here but us. Come on." He clucked like a chicken.

Still, she hesitated.

"Okay, Sammie, don't make me do it."

"Do what?"

"The ultimate."

Her eyes widened. "No. You wouldn't."

He nodded and grinned. "I triple dog dare you."

She stomped her foot. "Unfair, Tyler." Looking around, she quickly stripped off her clothes and dove into the water. Two hands grabbed her, and she surfaced, laughing.

"You look like the Little Mermaid, wanna fork?"

"Does this make you my prince?" she asked with a laugh. "You're right; this does feel good." She kissed him soundly, her legs wrapping around his waist, her arms around his neck.

A rebel yell and the sound of a jet ski froze them in place. She pressed as close to Matt as she could, and he wrapped his arms tight around her as Dylan and Jennifer rode by. Jennifer's smile widened, and Dylan laughed with a thumbs up as they circled them before driving off.

"Asshole!" Matt shouted, laughing.

Sammie snickered. "See? It isn't so deserted—"

He silenced her protests with a kiss and entered her swiftly. "This is easy; the water makes you buoyant." He peered down at her breasts and winked. "Must be the built-in flotation devices. Now kiss me, woman. You're already getting pink; I don't want you sunburned." He moved within her.

And any further thoughts of protest vanished.

Chapter
Eighteen

Sammie grinned all the way home, her hand firmly clasped in Matt's. They passed a field of sunflowers, and to her surprise, he stopped and picked a few.

"My favorite flower," he told her. "That sounds so lame for a guy to say. Don't judge me."

"I won't. They're mine, too." *Now.* She blinked back happy tears when he handed them to her. Maybe being like a sunflower wasn't so bad after all...

Matt opened the front door and frowned. The house was unusually quiet.

"Pa? Luke?" he called.

"I'll check out back. They may be on the porch." Sammie went to the kitchen and spied a notepad on the table. "There's a note in here." Smiling, she placed the flowers in a pitcher. This simple gift and the box of chocolate he'd given her meant more than he'd ever realize.

> Luke's spending the night with Eloise. She'll bring him home after church tomorrow. I've gone out. I'll be back "whenever." Have fun. Pa

Matt grinned. "Gosh, Mrs. Tyler, I guess this means we have the house to ourselves. What do you want to do? Watch TV? Play Scrabble?"

"Actually, Mr. Tyler, I'd be more interested in a game of strip poker."

"You'll lose the shirt off your back," Matt taunted.

"Wanna bet?"

He raised a skeptical eyebrow. "What are the stakes?"

"To be decided later, but they'll be mutually beneficial."

Matt hesitated.

"Unless you're chicken…"

"You're on. But remember, I grew up with Pa and Gig. I know poker." Matt found a deck of cards and went to the kitchen.

Sammie started up the stairs.

"Where are you going?" he called.

"To get into some dry clothes." *And put on some socks, a bra—what other clothes can I add?*

"Cheater, I know what you're up to. Don't bother. You're just going to have to take everything off when I beat the pants off of you—literally."

Sammie paused halfway up the staircase and smiled. *Busted.* She ran back downstairs and sat across from him. "Deal the cards, Tyler!"

Matt shuffled and allowed her to cut the deck. After deciding on five-card stud, he dealt. Sammie lost the first hand. Leaning over, she started to untie her shoe. Matt reached out and caught her hand.

"Winner gets to name the article of clothing to be removed." He was definitely leering. "Remove your shirt, sweetheart."

Sammie grinned and tossed her clammy T-shirt across the table to him. She tried to keep from blushing as Matt gazed at her bare breasts. Her nipples puckered, and his grin stretched. Preoccupied with staring at her, he lost the next hand.

She held out her hand. "Your shirt, *sweetheart.*"

Matt shrugged out of his shirt. She wolf-whistled and laughed as his face turned red. It wasn't long before they were both clad in just their underwear. The next hand would decide the winner.

As Sammie shuffled the cards, they heard a knock at the front door. She froze and stared at Matt. Another knock sounded. They scrambled into their clothes. Hers were still damp, and she had difficulty getting them on. She swore under her breath. The knocking at the front door became more insistent. Matt threw Sammie his shirt and told her to put it on as he went to answer the door, wearing only his jeans.

"Matt. How are you?" Pastor McClain smiled, obviously expecting to be invited in for a visit.

Forcing himself to be pleasant, Matt replied, "Hi. This is, er, unexpected." He continued to stand rudely in the doorway, refusing to budge or extend an invitation. "I'd invite you in, but we were just g-going out to eat," he stammered. He glanced heavenward, half expecting a bolt of lightning to strike him dead.

Pastor McClain raised one brow and looked him over.

Moron, you're standing here half-naked and you tell your minister you're on your way out?

Comprehension dawned on the minister's face. His eyes twinkled. "I see. Casual dining? Well, I just wanted to stop by and see if we could arrange a trade."

"A trade?"

"Yes. I know Luke wants to attend preschool, and we'd love to have him. He's a bright boy. The church van is getting old and needs some repairs. I thought maybe you could fix it and keep it maintained? Also, the woman who cleans the church is moving to be closer to her elderly parents. It's a once-a-week job."

Sammie poked her head out from the kitchen. "We'll take it! Matt can do the van stuff, and I'll clean the church."

Matt frowned. It sounded like charity to him.

"Luke will be so excited. Thank you!" Sammie called.

She's right. Luke wants to go to school.

He held out his hand. "Yes, that would be great. Thanks."

Pastor McClain shook his hand. "Excellent." Looking over his glasses, he stated more than asked, "I'll see you both in church tomorrow?"

"Uh…yeah…sure," Matt agreed, relieved the man was leaving. He shut the door, locked it, and leaned against it.

Sammie ran out of the kitchen wearing only his shirt and her minuscule panties. "This is wonderful, Matt!"

"You realize we'll have to attend church regularly."

"It's fine. It'll be worth it. I'll be honest; I have mixed feelings about church. While Sunday school with Mrs. Jordan offered a refuge when Sue Ellen was in one of her spells, my mother's religious fervor colored my thoughts on religion in general. And part of it was my shame at being the church's charity case." She looked away. "But that's childish thinking. I'm a parent now, and we need to do this for Luke. He's super smart, and preschool will help him. I don't want him to end up like me, an uneducated hick. And I want to fit in with the community—our family needs this."

Matt tilted her chin up with his finger and looked into her eyes. "You're a smart girl. Don't talk about my wife that way. And I love how you say *our* family. You're right. We need to do this for Luke."

Grinning, she added, "Plus you need to go to church and repent for lying to your minister, of all people. Just where are we going out to eat dressed like this?"

"To bed, Mrs. Tyler," he replied huskily. He nibbled her lower lip.

"Sounds good, but I'm actually kinda hungry, St. Matthew. And that's still a fib. You'd give Luke hell for lying, especially to a minister."

Laughing, Matt threw her over his shoulder. Walking through the kitchen, he grabbed an apple.

"Put me down! Where are we going?"

"Out! See? I didn't tell a lie!"

The back door slammed shut. He walked a few feet into the backyard and thoroughly enjoyed her sliding down his body to her feet. *Is there anything sexier than a woman in an oversized man's shirt?* Pulling her close, he trailed kisses down her neck and back to her full, inviting lips. His hands smoothed over her bare back under his shirt.

He bit into the apple and handed it to her.

She laughed and took a bite. "How Biblical of you, but shouldn't we be naked?"

"That can be arranged."

"Did you think to leave the back door cracked? It tends to lock itself when you shut it. Remember? I've asked you at least five times to fix it." She ran her hands up his bare chest and kissed him so sweetly her words didn't register for a few moments.

When they did, he turned to stare at the back door. "Oh shit." He walked over and tried the knob. Sure enough, it was locked. He'd made sure he locked the front door when Pastor McClain had left, too.

Sammie giggled, and Matt sighed, annoyed by life in general at the moment.

"Now what? Can you get us in?" she asked, her eyes dancing with amusement as she pointed to her hair. "Stop glaring—red hair power, remember?"

Matt surveyed the large magnolia tree next to the house. "What is it with you and locked doors? I haven't done this since we were kids." Going over to the tree, he began to climb.

"For heaven's sake, be careful!" Sammie warned as his foot slipped on a branch.

Grinning down, he cracked, "Still worried I haven't put you on my insurance policy?"

"Absolutely. I've gots ta get paid," she called, but worry creased her brow.

Opening the window to Sammie's old room, Matt decided he liked knowing someone was worried about him. With ease, he climbed into the house. Looking back out the window, he gave a convincing Tarzan yell and shouted, "Me Tarzan, you Jane. Coming up? Or are you going to take the easy way in?"

"When have I ever done anything the easy way? Sure!" She began climbing the tree.

Matt whistled at her. "Sexy girl."

"Stop it! You're making me—" The branch snapped.

"Sammie!" Matt reached for her, but she was too far away.

Her terrified scream as she fell to the ground sent him racing down the stairs. *Please God, no.*

He found her sitting up, cussing a blue streak when he reached her.

"Sammie! Don't move; you could have internal injuries. Breathe nice and slow for me, sweetheart. Let me make sure you're okay."

He carefully assessed her. While she was bruised, nothing appeared to be broken.

"You're okay," he said as he continued to look her over. "At least you didn't break your arm this time."

"Crap, that hurt. Why do we have this kind of luck?"

"Beats the hell outta me." He laughed. "Come on, I think it would be a good idea to have you checked out."

"Don't be ridiculous. I'm okay."

After supper, Matt studied while Sammie watched her favorite wedding show on television. Looking over at her handsome husband, she rubbed her wedding band, feeling quite content despite every bone in her body aching.

When the show ended, she turned off the television and admitted, "I ain't feeling so great. I don't know which is worse, this sunburn or the bruises. I think I'm gonna call it a night."

Matt looked up from his computer. "Sure you don't want me to take you to an afterhours clinic?"

"No, I just need to take it easy."

"Okay. I'll fix you a snack so you can take some ibuprofen." Matt gave her a kiss.

It took her an inordinate amount of time to bathe because everything hurt. Looking in the mirror, Sammie scrutinized her appearance and glowered at the sight of her sunburned nose and the large, dark purple bruises on her back. She was a mess. She carefully pulled on her nightgown and made her way to bed.

Downstairs was completely dark. The only light remaining came from Matt's room. *Our room*, she corrected. On the bedside table was a plate with a sandwich, a glass of milk, and two pills.

Matt sat with his back against the headboard, working on his laptop. His brow was furrowed as he typed. He wore a pair of pajama pants and his hair was damp. He must've used Pa's bathroom. Looking up, he smiled and closed the computer. Sammie's mouth went dry as she stared at his lips and her gaze traveled down his bare chest to the planes of his well-defined abdomen.

"Hungry?"

"W-What?" she asked, startled out of her daydream. She blushed and lowered her eyes, not wanting him to see the raw hunger she felt for *him*.

She giggled as he handed her the plate and glass. "Peanut butter and jelly? I hope it didn't put you out too much," she teased.

"I finished off the last of the pie. Sorry. Besides, my children claim I make the best peanut butter and jelly sandwiches this side of the Mississippi! It's all in the wrist as you whip the peanut butter and jelly together…" His voice trailed off, and pain flashed across his face. "Lizbeth lived on peanut butter and jelly sandwiches for the first six years of her life…"

"I did too," she replied, softly.

"Eat up. You need to take something for the pain before bed."

"I-I must look like a mess." She slipped under the covers and ate a few bites of the sandwich. Swallowing the pills, she winced as she adjusted herself onto her side.

"You're my mess. Are you sure you're okay? Do you want an ice pack?" Matt turned to face her with his head propped on his hand.

"No thanks."

"Are you counting or rearranging your closet in your head?" he asked with a gentle peck to her lips.

"Neither. I'm counting my blessings." Deciding her other side was less bruised, she carefully rolled over.

He pulled the covers up as he snuggled in behind her. "You're my blessing, Sammie Tyler."

She smiled and closed her eyes.

Chapter
Nineteen

Sammie pulled on a tank top and shorts and made her way downstairs. Coffee, toast, and ibuprofen sounded like a perfect breakfast. She was actually surprised to feel as well as she did. The bruising looked much worse than it felt. She found the note next to the coffee pot.

> Gone to church so God won't strike me dead for lying yesterday. Mrs. Jordan will bring Luke to church with her. He and I will pick up some chicken for lunch.
>
> xoxox Matt
>
> P.S. QUIT ORGANIZING/CLEANING AND GO BACK TO BED AND REST.

She decided to ignore Matt's edict and rearrange the cabinet with plastic containers. She opened it and cursed, wondering why the bowls were always separated from their lids. She was convinced they ran off with the missing socks from the dryer. Crawling deep into the cabinet, she dug into the very back.

"What the hell?" Pa exploded.

Sammie hit the top of her head on the counter. "Ouch! Dammit, don't scare me like that!" She peeked behind her and was shocked by the anger on Pa's face.

He pointed his cane at her back. "What happened to you? I leave you two fools alone for one evening and you look like you've been beat to hell and back."

"I fell out of the magnolia tree," she mumbled.

"You what? That's the most asinine excuse I've ever heard. Are you two into that weird sex stuff?"

"Pa! We got locked out of the house and had to climb in through the window to get back in, only I didn't make it. But I'm fine, just really sore and embarrassed."

"At least you didn't break your arm this time."

Sammie laughed. "That's what Matt said."

"For God's sake, girl, use the brain you were born with and throw that shit back in the cupboard and rest!"

"Without organizing it first?" She gasped.

Pa raised the eyebrow not affected by the stroke and managed to stare her down.

"Yes, sir." She threw the plastic storage containers in the cabinet and closed the door before they could spill on the floor again. She smiled as she realized she didn't feel the least bit anxious. "I did it!" She gave him a kiss on the cheek. "Hey, Pa?"

"Yes?"

"Can we pretend we didn't cuss? I'm broke."

"What Matt doesn't know won't hurt. Works for me."

The front door opened.

"Sammie!" Luke ran in and threw his arms around her waist. Flinching a bit, she hugged him back.

"Guess what? I made you a picture at Sunday school!" He proudly waved a picture of an airplane with two stick figures in it.

"It's wonderful! Uh, an airplane?"

"That's Jesus, and that's Pontius, he's the pilot," he explained.

"I see. Good job!" She placed the drawing on the refrigerator.

"Where's Daddy?"

"Right here." Matt placed the bucket of chicken on the table and loosened his tie. "Why are you out of bed? Do I have to beat you black and blue and tie you to the bed to keep you there?" he teased.

Pa snorted, and she bit her lip and winked at the old man.

"I was un-organizing the plastic container cabinet." She threw open the cabinet and the contents spilled out on the floor. "Ta-da!"

Matt laughed. "Well done. Now back upstairs to bed. You're supposed to be taking it easy."

"I'm fine. It's boring in bed," Sammie whined. She looked at Matt, batted her eyelashes, and mouthed, *"alone."* Matt turned red and darted a quick look at his father and son.

"You can look at books," Luke offered as he set the table.

"After we eat, Luke and I will clean up the cupboard mess," Pa said. "Why don't you two take *a nap* after lunch?" he suggested.

"Good idea, Pa. Only I'm not hungry." She grabbed Matt's hand and left the kitchen, pulling him behind her up the stairs.

Once inside, she slammed the bedroom door and locked it behind them. Her breathing was erratic as Matt stood with his hands on his hips, grinning at her. *Is there anything sexier than my husband in a suit with his tie loose?*

Yes, him naked.

She pulled off her tank top and launched herself at him. Wrapping her arms around his neck and her legs around his waist, they tumbled to the bed with her on top.

"Whoa, sweetheart. Slow down. What about your back?" he asked, his breathing ragged.

"Fuck my back—no fuck me." She pulled off his tie and tossed it to the floor, waggling her brows. She began unbuttoning his shirt. Leaning forward, she found his lips and managed to get him out of his shirt and jacket.

She saw her desire reflected in his eyes and smiled.

"You either owe the jar money, or I need to wash that mouth out with soap. Now slow down." He chuckled as he kissed her. "You're not the only one who wants this, but I have to know you're okay. I don't want to hurt you. *I refuse to hurt you.*" He waited for her answer, his hand resting on her cheek, his thumb grazing her lips.

"It's fine. It looks worse than it feels. Now fork me. Wait, I'm on top—maybe I'm forking you? I think it was the suit and tie. Mmmm, sexy."

He sat up, laughing, and kissed her deeply this time, his tongue exploring her mouth, his hand skimming down her neck, capturing her breast. He tugged her nipple, and she moaned.

"Shhhh, Sammie, we need to be quiet," he whispered.

"Okay," she whispered back, wrapping her arms around his neck.

She looked at him and took a deep breath as memories of a tall, lanky boy with hormone-driven passion lurked inside her head. Experience now tempered the raging hormones, but passion still burned in those dark, mesmerizing eyes. He lavished his attention on one breast and then the other. She began to shake with an overwhelming need to be one with the man she'd loved since she was a girl.

It took some maneuvering, and they both laughed as they tried to get her panties off. Finally, she stood up and removed them herself. Matt reached out and traced the scars on her hip. Embarrassed, she covered his hand with hers.

"Never again, Sammie. I never want you in this much pain again." His gaze locked with hers as he traced each line. "I'll do everything in my power to keep you from feeling this desperate."

"Never. I promise." She played with his dark waves, falling more in love by the minute. One work-worn hand found hers and gave it a reassuring squeeze, pulling her back into bed. He carefully positioned her on her side. And as he kissed her, one finger delved inside, bringing her to the brink over and over again. She whimpered and rubbed against him, needing more.

"Sshhhh," he said, laughing against her.

Being quiet wasn't an option. Not when his fingers toppled her over the edge of reason and gave her the release she'd been seeking. Feeling almost drunk, she smiled, spent and happy.

"Those are some talented fingers, Mr. Tyler."

"Thank you. They aim to please."

When she was able to raise her head, she giggled at the smug look on his face as he finished undressing.

Once her breathing regulated, she repositioned herself on top of him, her hands clasped in his.

"I like the way you think," he whispered grasping her hips. She lowered herself on to him and moved up and down his hard length. She rose and arched back, and another moan escaped her lips.

"Shhhh." His eyes crinkled into the laugh lines she loved.

Sammie leaned forward and whispered, "You think it's easy being quiet, Matthew Tyler?"

He shook his head and chuckled as his hands caressed her breasts—teasing, pulling, and pinching. She threw her head back and moved faster, building the tempo until she exploded once again. Moments later he followed, yelling a fifty-cent word and her name. She collapsed on his chest as they panted, catching their breath.

"Damn, Sammie," he murmured in her ear.

"Ditto, Mattie." She chuckled.

They froze as they heard footsteps in the hall outside the locked door.

"Daddy?"

Sammie raised her head and looked down at Matt. He laughed and whispered, "I told you to be quiet."

"Me? You're the one who yelled!"

"You moaned first!"

"Daddy!" Luke's voice was more insistent this time.

"What, son?"

"Whatcha doing?"

"Taking a nap."

"Why were you yelling at Sammie? You owe the jar fifty cents."

"Because she snores. I'll pay up later. Go downstairs and watch TV with Pa."

"Okay." He tromped downstairs yelling, "Pa! They're okay!"

Sammie rolled off Matt onto her side and curled into him, her head resting over his heart, which had slowed to a normal pace. She wrapped her arm around his waist, and they began snickering and laughing.

"One of the hazards of parenthood." Matt brushed Sammie's hair out of her face and kissed the top of her head. "What were the stakes in our poker game yesterday?"

She looked up at him and smiled as he kissed the tip of her slightly sunburned nose. "If I won, you would've had to make wild, passionate love to me."

Matt raised an eyebrow and grinned. "And if *I* had won?"

"I would've had to make wild passionate love to *you*."

Matt laughed softly. "A win-win situation. Well played, Mrs. Tyler."

He gave her a quick kiss and stood, pulling on a pair of jeans.

"Where are you going?" she asked.

"You need to rest. I'll take Luke fishing."

"I don't need to rest," she murmured with a yawn as her eyes closed.

Matt pulled the covers over her, tucking her in, and kissed her again.

He was out the door before she whispered, "I love you, Matt."

Chapter
Twenty

On Monday morning, the phone rang. Sammie had just finished the breakfast dishes, and Luke was with Pa on the back porch, shucking corn for supper.

She rolled her eyes at the caller ID.

"Hello?"

"Good morning, Ms. Morgan."

Sammie made a face at the phone and corrected sweetly, "It's Mrs. Tyler, but like I've told you before, just Sammie is fine."

She sighed. Mr. Howell called her Ms. Morgan on purpose. He damn well knew her name since he called twice a week to check on Luke, and she'd been taking Luke to see Lila and Mae weekly. Thankfully, preschool would be starting on Wednesday, and she'd have an excuse *not* to go.

"I'm sorry, Matt's working. May I take a message and have him call you back?" she asked.

"There's no need. I'd like to talk to you. I didn't have a chance to speak to Matt after church yesterday."

No, because I'm sure he hurried Luke to the car when he saw you approaching.

When she didn't respond, he continued. "The sermon was on forgiveness and made me think. I'd like to apologize for my past behavior. It's been very difficult for Lila and me to come to terms with our daughter's and granddaughter's deaths. I'm afraid I've been hard on Matt, and I'd like to make up for it."

"Then perhaps you should apologize to Matt, not me," Sammie replied crisply.

"Yes, and I plan to do that. But as I'm sure you're aware, Matt and I have a long history. It will take time. I was wondering, could you bring Lukas to the bank this morning? Say, around eleven? I want to give him a hundred dollars to open a savings account to celebrate the start of school. Please, Samantha, would you do this for me?"

She didn't trust him, but he sounded sincere. However, if he was so keen on helping Luke with his education, why hadn't he offered to pay for preschool? Not that Matt would've accepted it.

She sighed. But maybe he truly did want to turn over a new leaf. She could certainly understand how losing his daughter and granddaughter had been stressful. If she could get on Mr. Howell's good side, it might help ease the friction between him and Matt.

"All right, Mr. Howell. We'll be there at eleven. Thank you."

"Not at all, my dear. I look forward to getting to know you better."

"Matt?"

Matt looked up and wolf-whistled. Sammie was wearing a boho-type skirt and top. Her hair hung in loose curls instead of her usual ponytail or braids.

"Where're you going all dressed up? You look nice."

She twirled a lock of her hair around her finger. "That's what I need to talk to you about."

Matt dropped the hood of the car he'd been working on and wiped his greasy hands on a rag. "What about?"

"Mr. Howell called and wanted to know if Luke could come to the bank in an hour. He wants to give him money to open a savings account."

He swore under his breath. "You're meeting him in an hour? Meaning you already told him yes without asking me?"

"He's Luke's grandfather. Luke wants to go. He said he was going to ask you yesterday at church, but you darted out too fast."

Walking over to his workbench, Matt drummed his fingers as he attempted to rein in his anger. "Some teamwork, Sammie. No."

"No?"

"No," he repeated.

"Why not?"

"Just *because*," Matt replied through gritted teeth.

"Because why?"

"Because I'm too angry to talk about this right now." He sighed and then frowned. "What is he doing?"

She looked behind her and giggled. Luke had poor Rhonda up in the air as he warbled a chant from *The Lion King*. Rufus was howling along while Pa laughed, holding Matt's phone up.

"He's talking to Jinx and waiting on me to take him to see his grandfather while you and I argue over something petty."

Matt glanced over at Luke, who had put the cat down and wandered over to them. "Go in the house while Sammie and I talk."

"I don't want to."

"Life is full of things you don't want to do. It's my job to prepare you for disappointment, and don't back-talk."

Luke marched into the house, slamming the door for good measure.

Matt turned his attention back to Sam. "Petty? First, I refuse to take any money from that sonofabitch, and second, you didn't ask me!"

This was the same shit James used to pull with Karen. Why did Sammie have to be so bullheaded?

"Matt, be reasonable."

"I *am* reasonable. I've let you take my son to visit them every damn week. But I'm drawing the line here. Howell's flinging his money around to get his way. If you'd stop and think a minute, you'd see that. As a matter of fact, we're doing okay financially at the moment. Just stop the visits all together."

"Don't you dare use that tone of voice with me," Sammie hissed. "I gave my word, and we're going. Luke needs to keep visiting with them. He misses his mother; I can't replace her. Pa didn't particularly like Karen, and you're still so upset over her death you shut Luke down most of the time when he asks about her. You didn't even let him have pictures of Karen and Elizabeth in his room until a few weeks ago. Mr. and Mrs. Howell are Luke's only link to her, since Karen's sister doesn't live here. He likes to ask them and Mae questions about his mama. Don't deny your son his memories; it's not fair."

"And just when did you receive your degree in psychology? Did you take a correspondence course I didn't know about?" Matt demanded. "Or was it from taking care of Sue Ellen? James doesn't do anything without an ulterior motive, especially with me. And piling money on with it? Something's up, and I don't like it."

"I don't care. I gave my word. We're going."

"What?" He felt his blood pressure skyrocket.

"You heard me. You're not deaf."

"Why?"

"Just because," Sammie mimicked with a toss of her copper hair. "Life's full of disappointments, remember?" She turned to walk out of the garage.

"Where are you going?"

"I just told you. To the bank. And then to get school supplies."

Matt watched her slam the back door behind her. Good thing he'd fixed that damn lock. Angrily, he ran after her, taking the back steps two at a time. Pa sat in his rocker, whittling.

"Give it up, son." He handed Matt his phone.

Matt stopped and snarled, "Do you know what she's planning on doing?"

"Yup."

"You know how I feel about James Howell. And I don't want his blood money. I'd think you'd back me on this."

"Sit down, Matthew."

Throwing up his hands, Matt collapsed on the back steps. "All right, Pa. Give me your fatherly advice. You've always been such a shining example."

"Watch the attitude. I'm not so old and crippled that I can't wear that smart ass of yours out."

Matt clamped his mouth shut and stared out into the yard, waiting for the lecture. He tried to calculate how much money he'd need to move out of this house again. Maybe he could start over in Alaska, far away from the Howells.

"This isn't just about money. Do you remember when your ma died?"

He turned to look at his father. "Of course I remember when Mama died."

"But do you remember how you felt? Especially about a year later?"

Matt looked back out into the yard, not wanting to dredge up the feelings. Softly he admitted, "I felt abandoned. You were too busy staying drunk to have much to do with an eight-year-old. As I recall, you forgot my birthday."

Pa sighed. "I wasn't much of a father; I don't deny it. And you've done a helluva good job with Luke, much better than I did. But, son, do you remember the day you came crying to me because it was Mother's Day and you didn't have a ma?"

Matt didn't speak for a moment. He couldn't, because of the lump lodged in his throat. Finally, he nodded. "Yeah, I remember."

"Luke's a lot littler than you were when your ma died. You ain't wantin' him to go through that, are you? Now, I don't care for James or Lila any more than you do. But Sammie's right—they're his grandparents, same as me."

Sammie and Luke walked out and headed to the car.

"Bye, Daddy."

Pa stood using his cane and nudged Matt with it. Softly he added, "It would kill me not to be able to see my grandson, especially if my own son was gone. Seems to me, I'd want to see my grandchild even more—to see if I could see a little of myself and my son in him." Leroy went into the house without another word.

Matt waved goodbye to Luke, still fuming, but Pa's words struck home. He could well recall asking Pa, and even Lucy on the rare occasion she would stop by, to tell him stories about his mama.

Luke asked him about Karen and Elizabeth every day. And he always tried to circumvent the conversation, thinking it would cause more pain. Maybe he was wrong. Talking about Karen and Lizbeth might be what Luke needed to heal. But all that aside, he'd be damned if he ever took a dime from James Howell. He took out his phone and sent Sammie text.

We need to talk. Please don't take the money. I'm sorry.

Sammie finger-combed Luke's hair as they walked toward the bank. She was proud of him. He still didn't like riding in a car, and he still gripped his car seat until his knuckles were white, but it was getting easier. The meltdowns were fewer and farther between. His excitement about school made her glad to have picked up the job cleaning the church.

She frowned slightly when she noticed his chocolate milk mustache and licked her thumb to wipe it off his lip.

"Stop, Sammie. That's gross! Why does Gramps want to see me?" he asked for the fifth time as they walked into the bank.

"Uh, he just does. He loves you," she answered as she looked around the bank, wondering where they should go to find Mr. Howell.

"This way, Sammie!" Luke whispered as he limped toward the side of the bank where James could be seen in his glass-enclosed office, talking on the phone.

Luke stopped to say hello to Meka, one of the bank workers, and waved at his grandfather through the glass. James hung up and smiled, waving at them to enter.

"Hello, Lukas. I'm glad you came to see me today. And in the car?"

"Yes, sir."

"You're like a super hero, conquering fear." He pulled the boy into his lap.

"I'm Lukeman!" Luke gave his grandfather a high-five and began a thorough inspection of everything on top of the desk. James looked at her and motioned her to sit, his face a mask of pleasantries.

Sammie sat on the edge of the chair and folded her hands in her lap. "Luke's enjoyed seeing Mrs. Howell and Mae on Wednesdays, but school starts day after tomorrow, so we'll have to figure a new schedule for him to continue visiting. It seems odd to start on a Wednesday, but I guess it's in line with the real school schedule…"

Mr. Howell stared at her as if she were an annoying gnat. She stopped jabbering and started counting the file folders stacked on the credenza behind his desk, wishing she could straighten them. Her phone dinged with an incoming text, and she fished it out to read it.

"That's Mommy and Aunt Jinx." Luke pointed at a picture on his grandfather's desk.

Mr. Howell looked at the picture and back at Luke and smiled. Tears filled his eyes and he hugged the boy tight for a few seconds. "Yes, it is. You're very brave, Luke, and a smart young man. Your mommy would be proud of you. Now, would you like to know why I asked you to come see me today?"

Sammie bit her lip as she put her phone away. She'd missed three texts from Matt asking her not to take the money. "Um, about that—"

Ignoring her, James reached into his shirt pocket and drew out two bills. "I want you to save money, so you can go to college and come work with me. Would you like that?"

"Daddy goes to college."

James's mouth tightened for a second. "Yes, and I want you to go to college, too. Education is important. I'm giving you this one-hundred-dollar bill to open a savings account. When you put money in the bank, the bank gives you more money. Isn't that better than spending it and not having any money when you need it?"

"I guess so." Luke still didn't look too sure.

James laughed. "But it's nice to have a little money to spend too, isn't it?"

Luke's eyes brightened.

"That's not necessary…" Sammie protested, weakly.

"Here's a twenty-dollar bill to spend any way you want to."

"Thanks, Gramps!" Luke threw his arms around his grandfather's neck and hugged him.

Sammie felt her heartbeat pick up. *How can I fix this?*

James closed his eyes and his features softened. He seemed human in this moment, but Sammie always felt on guard in his presence. Being around him was like walking up on a coiled copperhead.

"Now, I have to get back to work. Travis will help you open your account, okay?" He buzzed to have Travis come into his office.

Travis entered with a warm smile. Sammie breathed easier, seeing a friendly face. He looked handsome in his dark blue suit, crisp white shirt, and red silk tie, but she decided Matt under the hood of a car in his blue jeans was a hundred times sexier.

"Well, Luke. Let's go open that savings account, shall we?" Travis opened the door with a smile and directed them to his office.

"Just a moment, Sammie."

She paused, noting that Mr. Howell had used the name she preferred, and turned around.

"The paperwork is already prepared. Please sit down and close the door."

Her breathing hitched. But it was a glass-front office, and there were people in the bank. Without Luke present, maybe she could stop the savings account transaction. Matt might not object to twenty bucks.

"It's very kind of you to offer the money for the savings account, but it isn't necessary," she said.

He stared at her for a few seconds and smiled. "It's more for my convenience than anything. This will make birthdays easier for Lila and me. She doesn't shop much anymore, and I frankly don't have time. Giving him money toward his education is important to both of us."

He cleared his throat and abruptly shifted gears. "What did your mother die from? I'm afraid I never offered my condolences. Lila and I were acquainted with Sue Ellen, of course, through church."

Sammie blinked. "C-Cancer."

"A devastating disease. It was just you and your mother at the end? She never remarried or…?"

Tears blurred her vision. "No, it was just the two of us. She, um, had other problems."

"I'm sorry. You must've felt very alone."

She nodded. "Thank you."

He stared at her for a moment, sort of like Matt did when they played poker, as if trying to read something in her face. At last he stood. "I'm afraid I have a meeting." He held out his hand. "I think this will be a new beginning for us."

Before she could protest the monetary gift again, he'd escorted her to Travis's office and left.

Sammie sank into the chair next to Luke and sighed. "Matt's not going to like this…" How she wished she could just start this day over.

Travis looked up. "Why? It's quite common for grandparents to open savings accounts for their grandchildren. They used to buy savings bonds, but that's gone by the wayside. It's never too early to learn fiscal responsibility. Let's see…I have Luke's birth certificate. Yup, we're done."

He turned some paperwork toward her. "James has already filled this out with Luke's information and, uh, he'll be on the account as well."

"How did you get his birth certificate? I think Matt should be on the account."

"It's just a technicality, because Luke's a minor. I don't foresee James running off with Luke's money. He has enough of his own." Travis smiled. "Matt would need to discuss that with James." He looked slightly uncomfortable, as if stuck in the middle.

She sighed and nodded. It occurred to her that she should've brought the key to Sue Ellen's lock box and looked inside it, but she'd do that some other day. Evidently they'd have to come back.

"What do you plan to buy with the twenty dollars?" Travis asked as he handed Luke an old-fashioned passbook.

"A milkshake!" he exclaimed.

"Great timing. I'm about ready for lunch. Would you two join me? I'm afraid it's still just burgers at the Mug and Cone."

"Oh, that really isn't necessary," Sammie replied. That might be the last straw with Matt today.

"You don't understand. All new savings account holders are treated to a free chocolate milkshake," Travis replied. He winked at Luke.

"I want a chocolate milkshake, Sammie!"

"Ahhh, if you're sure…" She didn't know how to get out of the invitation gracefully. It wasn't like she could just say *Matt hates you, no thank you.* Still, she didn't look forward to the conversation she'd have to have with her husband.

Travis shrugged out of his jacket, tossing it on his chair as he motioned to the door.

"I'm positive. Burgers and shakes can only improve this stinking hot day. I'll be glad when autumn arrives." Travis held Luke's hand as they left the bank, listening intently to the boy's excited chatter about starting preschool.

She smiled at Travis. He truly was a likeable man and very easy to talk to.

As they entered the diner, the air conditioning was a welcome respite after the walk in the oppressive heat. Once they sat down, Sammie dug in her purse and found a ponytail holder. She yanked her hot hair up off her neck.

Travis's face paled and then turned red. When he spoke, it was through clenched teeth. "What the hell?"

"That's a bad word! You need to pay the jar a quarter." Luke shook his finger.

"Luke! You don't correct an adult. Please apologize."

"But he said a bad word…" He bit off his retort when she gave him a look. "Sorry."

Sammie turned her attention back to Travis. "What's wrong?"

"What did that bast—" He stopped, took a deep breath, and evened his tone. "What happened to your back, Sammie?"

Oh, crap. She'd forgotten her blouse dipped low enough in the back to show the bruising from her fall if her hair was up. Matt had said her back looked tie-dyed. She pulled her hair back out of the ponytail. "It's nothing."

"That's a long way from *nothing!*"

"I fell out of a tree and got a bit bruised from the fall." She would've made up some outrageous story as a joke, but Travis already looked ready to combust. "Believe me, my ego was much more battered."

"Daddy said he was going to beat Sammie black and blue if she didn't rest and tie her to the bed." Luke's voice carried throughout the restaurant.

Mortified, Sammie placed a finger to her lips.

"What?" Travis's eyebrows shot toward the ceiling, and his mouth dropped.

Heat filled her cheeks as Frances hurried over to the table under the pretense of taking their order.

She looked almost giddy as she handed them menus. "What can I get y'all?" Her beady eyes darted back and forth between Sammie and Travis as she tapped the order book with her pen.

"A burger with ketchup and pickles and a chocolate shake!" Luke replied.

"I just want a glass of tea, please." Sammie counted sugar packets.

"You need to eat, Sammie." Travis's polite smile didn't reach his eyes.

"I'm *not* hungry," she replied, giving Travis the same phony smile in return.

"I'll have my usual, Frances," Travis replied without taking his eyes off her. He shoved the menus back at Frances.

The gossip beat a hasty exit to the kitchen, and Sammie sunk in her seat when she saw her reach for the phone.

It took her ten minutes to convince Travis she'd truly fallen out of the tree. But by the time the food arrived, he said he believed her. Luke went to work on his shake immediately.

"Have you thought any more about getting your GED?" Travis asked.

"I do want to, but I've got plenty to keep me busy during the day, and I can't do a nighttime class."

"What's a GED?" Luke asked.

"It's for people who didn't finish school. You won't have to worry about that, will you?" she replied.

"No. I'm going to school! I have a lunchbox, Travis!"

"You do? What's on it?"

"Batman."

"Good choice." He leaned forward. "I have an idea—a way you could get that GED."

She looked up, interested.

"Give me your phone." Travis reached across the table.

When she handed it to him, he quickly typed something in and handed it back. His phone dinged, and he pulled it from his pocket and smiled.

"There. You have my number, and I'll text you my idea once I check my schedule at work."

"I don't know…"

"Trust me! This will be great." He grinned at Luke. "Someone was hungry. Want more fries?"

"Yes, please. And thank you, Travis." Luke proceeded to eat the untouched fries.

Sammie glanced over at the register. Frances was so focused on their table that the customer in front of her had to clear his throat to get her attention.

Thankfully, before too long Travis had to get back to work. As she and Luke headed for home, she counted telephone poles, trying to find the words to explain yet another sticky situation.

Chapter
Twenty-One

Today had been a disaster, and Matt's mood reflected as much. *Everything* had gone wrong. To start things off, the part he'd ordered for overnight delivery had been lost in the mail, causing a delay in completion (and payment) for a major repair job. He needed this money because he was close to being late on his mortgage, something he couldn't risk since it was held by Howell's bank.

Washing up his lunch dishes, he'd realized the kitchen sink was clogged, and he'd spent half an hour clearing out the trap. This was interrupted by three phone calls reporting that his wife and son were at the bank with his despicable former father-in-law. Thirty minutes later two more phone calls hinted in a roundabout way that Matt had beaten his new wife, and finally, Pastor McClain stopped by with the church van and mentioned seeing Sammie and Luke with Travis at the Mug and Cone.

Now a power glitch, which had killed the electricity for all of thirty seconds, had obliterated the last ten pages of a paper for school. And like an idiot, he hadn't saved it. Matt covered his face with his hands.

"Daddy!" Luke ran into the kitchen, his new bankbook in hand.

In his hurry, he kicked the dog's water bowl and slipped on the spill. He fell to the floor with a wail.

Matt reached his side in seconds and helped him up. "How many times have I told you *not to run in the house?* Stop crying; you're not dying. Now clean this up and go to your room!"

"Really, Matt, I think you're overreacting," Sammie scolded, wiping Luke's tears.

"Quit mollycoddling him, and do *not* interfere when I'm disciplining *my* son! He's been told over and over not to run in this house," Matt snapped.

Sammie whipped around to face him. "I'm not mollycoddling him. I'm making sure he isn't hurt. I'm his *stepmother*, and I *will* voice an opinion if I think you're overreacting! What's wrong with you?"

"Don't even get me started," he snarled. "What were you doing eating lunch with Travis? *Again? Really?* Haven't I made it clear that I don't want you or Luke anywhere near him?" He raked his fingers through his hair, pacing back and forth. He knew he needed to calm down, but this was too much.

"Oh, for heaven's sake. We were in a public place. Your son was there. Even Pastor McClain was there. You act like Travis and I got caught having a torrid affair!"

Matt took a step back. It felt like he'd been struck.

"What's a torrid—" Luke piped in.

He threw a towel at his son. "Clean up your mess. We'll talk when I calm down."

It was either leave or do something he'd regret. He headed outside, slamming the back door in his wake. When he reached the muscadine arbor, he sat and covered his face, angry for losing his temper. This wasn't Sammie's fault. It certainly wasn't Luke's fault. He touted honesty with Sammie, but he hadn't been completely truthful with her.

And that was the catch. To do so would betray Karen.

He looked up when Sammie approached. She crossed her arms and stared at him, clearly displeased.

"I shouldn't have lost my temper," he said. "Is Luke okay?"

"Yes, but he said you were mean."

He hung his head. "I deserve that."

"You're not mean; you were worried. But you and I need to discuss the real issue. I got your text about the money, and I tried. But Mr. Howell pulled it out in front of Luke. I-I didn't know how to say no. Plus, he'd already set the account up in Luke's name—and his. I know you won't like that either, but Travis said you can stop by the bank and talk to Mr. Howell to be added as well."

She sighed when he didn't respond. "Mr. Howell said he did this so he can gift Luke money for his education on big occasions, like birthdays. I really don't see anything wrong with that. It's better than a getting a bunch of toys he'll grow tired of. The man seemed different today. He was pleasant and mentioned making amends with you. He even offered condolences about Sue Ellen."

"I don't trust him."

"I know. But like it or not, he's family. Regardless, you need to go to the bank to be put on the account. There's a hundred dollars in it. And he gave Luke a twenty to spend."

He sighed again. At this point, the bank account was the least of his worries.

"I don't like you with Travis."

"So you've said. Why? Why don't you like him? He's a nice guy." She looked around, biting her lip. "Never mind. I don't want to argue about this here. This place has too many bad memories."

Matt frowned. "Why does this place have bad memories?"

Sammie stared at the ground, tapping her fingers.

"Why are you counting? Look at me!"

Tears filled her eyes. "No, it's nothing. I'm being silly."

"Then tell me what you meant. I'm not a fucking mind reader."

"Fine! The last time we were out here, you were drunk. Karen had just dumped you, and I was foolish enough to think—I don't want to talk about this." She turned to walk away.

Matt caught her hand. A brief, fractured memory of a young, coltish redhead with braids danced at the periphery of his memories… She'd been kissing him. "Wait, you and me?"

Sammie crossed her arms, her fingers still tapping. The wind blew, mussing her hair, and she didn't say anything, as if searching for words. When she did speak, her voice was soft and flat.

"I was sixteen and madly in love with you. It's always been you, Matt. You were my best friend, my shelter, the one who protected me and could make me laugh. You made life worth living. Being with you was sunshine compared to the darkness at home. I dreamed someday you'd come to realize I wasn't just Sam, your fishing buddy, but Sammie, a girl who was head over heels in love with you." Her eyes sparkled with unshed tears.

"But you were in love with Karen Howell. And why wouldn't you be? She was everything I wasn't. Popular, blond, beautiful—but I didn't want to lose you as a friend. I might not have had your love, but your friendship grounded me. I didn't want to risk that."

She sat next to Matt and closed her eyes. "One night you called, terribly drunk and devastated. Karen had just broken up with you. Now that I know the Howells, I can feel sorry for her. I'm sure the pressure from her parents was unbearable. You were inconsolable, and it broke my heart to hear you crying, so I came over. I hoped I could get some food in your stomach and sober you up. You sang to me and called me Sammie." She smiled. "You never could carry a tune, but it's worse when you're drunk. We ended up out here…"

He tried again to remember, but the details were sketchy.

She took a deep breath. "You passed out after some fooling around. Before I could leave, Karen called to say she was pregnant. At that point, I knew you'd never leave her, so I went home. The next time I saw you, I kept waiting for you to say something. Instead, all I heard about was your marriage plans, and I realized you didn't remember. Part of me has been angry for years about that. But the rest of me has been relieved to avoid the embarrassment of throwing myself at you."

"I'm sorry, Sammie. Good God, I'm an even bigger asshole than I realized."

"We were *kids*. I was lonely and looking for someone to love. And you weren't really available. Karen was your world—"

"Matthew? Sam!"

Matt looked up, and his heart skipped at the desperation in Pa's voice. He grabbed Sammie's hand, and they took off running toward the house. They were out of breath when they reached the back porch.

"Where the hell have you been?" Pa demanded. "Luke's in the house coloring. I've got to go. Lucy needs me." He hobbled down the steps with his cane toward his truck.

"What's wrong?"

"She found her bartender dead. He overdosed, the dumbass."

"I'll drive you over there," Matt offered.

"I'll go with you, Pa. Matt, you stay and make things right with Luke. Do you want me to drive?" Sammie took Pa's hand and walked with him toward the truck.

"Hell no. B-But it might be best," he admitted.

She patted his hand. "Afraid I might ride the clutch?"

"I know you'll ride the clutch!" Pa handed her his keys and opened the door to the passenger side.

"Let me get my driver's license. I'll be right back."

Matt went with Sammie inside. She grabbed her purse off the kitchen counter and squeezed Luke before running out the door. Matt sank down at the table and watched Luke color. He felt shell-shocked.

"I'm sorry, son."

"It's okay." Luke continued to color. "I didn't mean to make a mess. Gramps gave me money. I'm going to be rich and go to school."

"I hope so." Matt tousled his hair and smiled. "How much do I love you?"

"Lots and lots. Want to color with me?"

"Sure."

Late that night, Sammie crawled into bed. Matt's back was to her and she snuggled in, snaking her arm over his waist.

"How's Lucy?" he asked.

"Pretty shook up, but she's okay. She's a strong woman. We brought her home; she's in my old room. Pa and I didn't want her alone tonight."

"And Pa?"

"He went to bed, pretty drained after dealing with all of this." She kissed him when he rolled over. "How are you? Did you apologize to Luke?"

"Yes. He's excited about school. He packed his backpack and looked at his lunchbox a dozen times before bed." He threw his arm over his eyes. Sammie rested her head on his shoulder.

"What are you thinking about?"

He didn't answer.

"You're not rearranging your shop or counting spark plugs, are you?" She ran her fingers over his perfect lips, wishing he'd smile.

"I'm thinking I'm the biggest asshole around."

"Personally, I'd still give that title to James Howell. Even if he was nice today, he's been horrible to you for a long time. I'm just saying everyone deserves a second chance."

"Why are you trying to make me feel better? I let a bad day and my hate of the Howells and that jerk Travis overrule my common sense. I yelled at Luke for a stupid mistake." He sighed. "And I took advantage of you when we were kids. It seems to be my MO where you're concerned: You give, I take."

"That last thing was a long time ago, and anyway I was the one putting on the moves. The past is the past, Matt. You give to me, too. It's called being in a relationship. Also, parenting isn't easy. You're not perfect. But you love Luke. He knows this because you tell him and show him every damn day. That's what's important."

Matt didn't say anything for a few minutes.

"Sammie…" He rolled back over and shifted on top of her. "I love you. I was a stupid kid, and I'm a stupid man. But I want to make up for lost time." He brushed the hair from her face.

"How much do you love me?" she asked, wrapping her arms around his neck.

He stared at her beautiful face. *This woman is mine…* It was amazing where life had brought them.

"Lots and lots," he whispered against her lips, kissing her.

"That's a helluva lot." She smiled, returning the kiss. "Will you give me something?" She grasped his erection.

"I'd be happy to."

He tore off her gown and ran his hands down the length of her body, exploring every inch, trailing kisses behind his hands. His tongue dipped into her belly button, and he nipped, kissed, and licked lower and lower—until he reached his destination and devoured her, tasting her until she panted with need and her hands fisted in his hair.

When she cried out her release, he smiled. Mission accomplished. He rested his cheek on the scars on her hipbone. After a moment,

Sammie tugged him toward her and pulled at his pajama pants. Shucking them to the floor, he caught his breath as she stroked him, gently at first and then with confidence. When her mouth followed, he watched, loving this woman who gave so much to him. He stopped her before he exploded and gently rolled her on to her back. He kissed her as he claimed her as his own, plunging into her and starting the rhythm that brought them together as one.

And as they spiraled toward release, she called his name. Matt shuddered and closed his eyes as he collapsed, fully sated. He didn't deserve her forgiveness or her love. But he accepted both, shoving aside his remorse for the past.

Matt rolled onto his back, and she curled against his side.

"Lots and lots is the best love ever."

"Yes, it is."

The next morning Matt woke up before Sammie. He smelled coffee and eased out of bed, worried about his father. He didn't think Pa would be up this early. He was *more* surprised when he walked in the kitchen and found Luke in Lucy's lap as she read to him. A pair of reading glasses covered her red-rimmed, tear-swollen eyes. Wearing a pair of Pa's old pajamas, with her hair pulled up in a loose ponytail and a scrubbed face, she looked younger and more vulnerable than she had in years.

"Your daddy loved Tigger, too." She took a sip of coffee and smiled at Matt. "Well, speak of the devil."

"Tigger is Tiggerific. Morning, Daddy! Aunt Lucy's reading me a story."

"Aunt Lucy?" Matt kissed his son on the cheek and gave his half-sister a look. She'd seen Luke maybe four times—and usually in passing—his entire life.

"What would you have the kid call me?" she asked.

"Her name is kind of like mine." Luke smiled up at Lucy.

"So it is."

She finger-combed his hair, looking wistful, and Matt wondered if she'd ever wished she'd had kids. He glanced down at the book and remembered Lucy reading the same story to him at the funeral home after his mother died. He placed a hand on her shoulder and kissed her forehead.

"Lulu. That's what I used to call you."

"Aunt Lulu!" Luke grinned.

Lucy smiled up at Matt, her eyes bright. "I like it. You haven't called me that since you were a kid."

He poured himself a cup of coffee and sat at the table next to the sister he'd never really known. It was time to mend at least one of the broken fences of his past.

"What are the plans for Jeff?" he asked.

"Cremation, no service. I guess I'll have a wake-type celebration at The Roadside." Lucy took a sip of her coffee. "He was a good guy, but troubled. He had issues left over from being in Iraq. I should've seen it coming. I tried to get him to go to the VA and get help. He was there for me after Bobby Joe died."

"You were a friend to him. That's what matters."

"A friend. Are you that naïve, St. Matthew? I'm the county whore—haven't you heard?" Her voice was bitter. She took off her reading glasses and rubbed her eyes.

"What kind of horse?" Luke asked, looking up from the book.

"Why don't you go watch TV? I need to talk to Lucy."

"Aunt Lulu."

"Aunt Lulu," Matt agreed.

Lucy smiled. "Thank you for keeping me company and letting me read to you, Luke."

"I have lots of books. Do you want to see them?"

Matt crossed his arms, and he huffed and crawled off her lap.

"Fine. I'm going. See ya!"

The sound of cartoons filtered in from the living area.

In a low voice, Matt cautioned, "Careful with the language around Luke."

Lucy stood and put her coffee cup in the sink. "I'll be out of here in half an hour. I know my presence here could put a black mark on your respectability score sheet."

"I didn't ask you to leave. Look, we've never been close, and I'd like to rectify that. I wasn't always fair to you, Luce. I'm asking that we do better at being brother and sister. We're *family*."

She sighed. "In all fairness, I was an embarrassment. Who wants to be related to the woman who's supposedly initiated all of your friends into manhood?"

Matt sighed. He couldn't deny his past feelings.

"I've always loved you, Matthew. And while I don't deny I've been around the block a time or two, you, of all people, should know half the gossip in this county is exaggerated."

"I know. You're right, and I'm sorry."

"You've had more than your share of problems. Pa has never been much of a father figure. Your ma died young, Karen and Elizabeth—but you can't let the Howells of the world dictate who you are. You can't relive the past or wallow in the memories. It's time to move on. You've got a great wife and a wonderful little boy. Quit demanding perfection out of everyone—especially yourself. It's okay to be imperfect."

Matt truly looked at his half-sister for the first time in his life and had to acknowledge that most of what she'd said made sense. Since the accident took his wife and child, his world had been turned upside down and his truths were no longer valid. He no longer knew who he was...But Sammie, Lucy, and Pa were there, trying to help him get back on course. His dysfunctional family had a lot going for it, because they had love. And lots of it.

"Thank you, Lucy. Stay as long as you need to." He took his cup of coffee and went outside. He sat on the back step next to Rufus. Rhonda wrapped in and out of his legs. He scratched the cat behind his ears, listening to the contented purrs.

After a moment, the back door opened, and Luke sat next to him. His son was his life. And his life was pretty damn good at the moment. He grinned. "Have I told you how much I love you?"

"You love me lots."

"Lots and lots." Matt hauled him into his lap and hugged him tight.

A few minutes later, Sammie joined them with her own cup of coffee.

"Good morning. Everyone okay out here?"

"Aunt Lucy said I could call her Aunt Lulu," Luke announced.

"I like that. It fits her. And how's Daddy this morning?" Concern creased the corners of her eyes.

Matt patted the stair next to him. When she sat, he wrapped his free arm around her shoulder and held his family close.

The sun was warm on his face. The birds chirped in the yard. Rufus snored beside them, and Rhonda chased a cricket. Happiness filled him.

"I can honestly say I have everything I want right here, and I'm the luckiest damn man in the world." He gave Luke a kiss on top of his head and kissed his wife.

"Ick. Stoooooop," Luke whined. "And that'll cost ya a quarter!"

Chapter
Twenty-Two

Although it was late September, the heat was oppressive, and Sammie felt sick as she left the car. It had been over a month since Luke started preschool, and she'd been coming to the library to study for her GED a few days a week after dropping him off. Matt was curious about where she went and what she was doing, but she wanted to surprise him with her certificate for his birthday.

Walking into the library, she headed to the back where there was a computer and a desk. Her GED test was soon, and she felt a bit overwhelmed. She was afraid she wasn't going to be ready. A few stolen hours a week wasn't long enough to study.

"Well, hello, Sammie."

Immersed in her studies, she jumped and looked up.

Travis smiled. "You're frowning. Is it me or whatever you're doing on the computer?"

Both. "Hi. I'm studying for my GED, but not very successfully. The test is in a few weeks, and I don't think I'm going to be ready."

"Just keep practicing; you'll get it. Want me to help?"

"Oh, no. I couldn't impose. I just wish I had access to the practice tests more than when I come here."

"No internet at home?"

"We have internet. But I'm doing this to surprise Matt. And the study guide I bought at the thrift store is old, with pages missing."

"Hold on, I can solve that. Be right back." Travis hurried out and returned carrying a new study guide.

"I keep extras in my car for my class because some of the students don't have internet or the money to buy the books." He sat down beside her and opened the book. "This is the latest edition, with all the pages. And you can sneak it home easily in that mini suitcase you call a purse."

She laughed. "Very funny. Thank you! I really appreciate this. I'll take care of your book and get it back to you. I keep my old book hidden in the back of the pantry." *In the box of dishes Matt hates.*

"I don't need it back. Keep it. Write down any problems or places you get stuck, and once a week, if you'd like, I'll join you here to help."

Matt would be livid. "Um, I appreciate the offer, but…" She shrugged, not wanting to hurt his feelings. "I'll manage."

"Well, my offer stands. Good luck." He smiled and headed back toward the shelves.

The next hour flew by, and Sammie left with the GED book tucked in her purse. On the way home, she called Jennifer.

"Hi!"

"Hey! How's the studying going?"

"Great! Travis gave me a newer study guide, so that's going to be a huge help."

"That's great. Starting next week, we'll get together for some more intense study sessions, okay? And Dylan and I are looking forward to our double date. A chance to be adults—Rory, get out of there! I have to run. See you Friday night. Bye!"

The phone clicked.

"Hey, Matt. Y'all ready to go? Jen's agreed to be DD tonight." Walking through the front door, Dylan shook Matt's hand and whispered, "Be afraid. She can't drive for shit."

"I heard that. You can walk home," Jennifer replied with a laugh. "The kids are all settled in at our house. Mrs. Jordan is a saint for sure. I needed this after taking care of three kids all week."

"Three? Is there something you haven't told me?" Dylan asked, his eyes dropping to her stomach.

"No, I counted *you* as one of the *three*."

Dylan frowned, and Jennifer laughed and gave him a kiss.

Matt ran a hand through his hair. He liked his friends but needed to stay home to study for his exam. However, Sammie had been looking forward to tonight, and he didn't want to disappoint her.

He looked up when she came tripping down the stairs in jeans and a green top with spaghetti straps.

"Wouldn't a T-shirt be more comfortable?" The thought of men ogling his wife made him edgy.

"I'm smart and laying the odds in my favor." Samantha tossed her hair with a saucy smile. "I really want that money."

"I get a 75/25 split of the winnings, right?" Dylan rubbed his palms together.

"75/25? Have you lost your mind?" Sammie gasped, outrage coloring her cheeks.

"Okay, 60/40. I'm trusting you on this. My manager is out of town, so we can't draw up a contract." Dylan winked at Matt behind her back.

"60/40? Why would you think you'd get a bigger cut than me?"

"I bring my name, voice, and expertise to the contest. I think it's only fair."

"Forget it, Dylan McAsshole, I'll get someone else. I'm not giving you more than a 50/50 cut of the winnings!" Sammie glared at him.

"I'd back off, Dylan. You're getting the stink eye." Matt laughed. He'd put his money on Sammie, hands down. She was tenacious. It was part of her charm.

"I could always enter the contest with you," Jennifer offered.

Dylan grimaced and shook his head. "Oh hell no. Please don't, angel." Turning to Sammie, he stage-whispered, "She couldn't carry a tune if her life depended on it."

Jennifer huffed and crossed her arms.

"I'm kidding, Sam. I'm doing this for you and to help Lucy. Even split, promise." Dylan flashed the smile that had mesmerized thousands of groupies.

Matt shot him a puzzled look but decided not to pursue why Dylan wanted to help Lucy. Some things were best just left alone.

"Hopefully Matt will sing as my competition. That will guarantee me a win," Sammie said.

"I'm not that bad," Matt protested.

"Neither am I," Jennifer added.

Dylan and Sammie snickered as they walked out the door.

The Roadside Tavern was packed. Everyone in the county loved Dylan and the gossip that was sure to follow wherever he went. Lucy hugged his neck and thanked him when he arrived, and she smiled at Jennifer, Matt, and Sammie.

"I appreciate you being here, Dylan. The money raised tonight will go toward a proper tombstone for Jeff."

"You look great, Lucy—younger or something," Dylan commented, ignoring his wife's elbow to his ribs.

Matt had to agree. His sister looked softer, and she had less makeup on. She wore her hair in a soft knot on top of her head, and it was a honey blond color tonight. She'd been to see Pa more lately and was embracing the role of Aunt Lulu.

"Thank you. I've saved a table for you. What do y'all want to drink?"

Jennifer ordered a Coke, and they got a pitcher of beer for the table. Sammie's eyes shone as she looked around the crowded bar. Matt worried she'd be ill at ease with this many people, but when he didn't see any of her usual signs of nervousness, he relaxed.

Lucy brought the pitcher, and Sammie picked it up to pour, tilting the glass.

"I like to give a good head—" she commented just as someone tripped on the plug to the karaoke machine, causing the room to go silent.

Catcalls, cheers, and wolf whistles sounded. Matt, Dylan, and Jennifer burst out laughing.

"—when pouring a glass of beer," she finished, blushing. "Y'all get your minds out of the gutter! It, uh, releases the carbon dioxide, and that makes it smell good and enhances the taste. Oh never mind!" She covered her face as several raised their glasses in toast.

Matt winked at her as he leaned in. "You do give good head."

She nudged him, her face burning.

Lucy stepped onto the stage. "I want to thank everyone for coming out tonight. I know y'all have heard, Dylan McAthie is in the house, and there may be a bit of a surprise later." She paused as the cheers rose and then died down. "All right, we're gonna start the contest. I've got two categories, solo and duet. Now y'all drink up—this is for Jeff!"

Several people approached the front and lined up to sing.

Sammie looked at Dylan. "Are you entering the solo contest?"

"Nah, I'd win!" he answered matter-of-factly. "Go on. Get in line. I want to hear if I'm going to be embarrassed by our duet," he teased.

Taking a sip of her beer, she wrinkled her nose. "Will you get me a glass of water?" she asked Matt. "This beer tastes off or something."

"Sure. You okay? Rather have a shot of tequila?"

"No, water is fine. I'm just nervous."

"You'll do great. But don't choose a Christmas carol. It might kill the mood."

She laughed and headed to the stage.

Perusing the selections, Sammie smiled when she came to just the right song. She waited for the girl in front of her to finish a halfway decent cover of Duffy's "Mercy" and walked up to the mic.

She took a deep breath, motioned that she was ready, and looked toward where Matt sat with Dylan and Jennifer. Closing her eyes, she sang "Landslide" by Fleetwood Mac. She'd barely finished singing before the applause started, and she squinted and looked to the table in the back of the room. Dylan and Jennifer were on their feet clapping, but she didn't see Matt. *Where did he go? Of all times to have to pee...* Disappointed, she left the stage.

Two strong hands grabbed her waist and picked her up, and she gasped as she looked down at the smiling face of her husband. She wrapped her arms around his neck, and he kissed her deeply and thoroughly. It was a full minute before either of them realized the spotlight was beaming on them. Matt broke the kiss and grinned at her. Laughing, he put her down and they made their way through the crowd to the table.

Before she could sit down, Jennifer hugged her, and Dylan gave her a quick kiss on the cheek.

"Okay, much as I hate to admit it, I'm really glad I'm not entering in the solo category. That would be one tough act to follow." He toasted Sammie with his beer.

Fifteen minutes later, Lucy crowned her the solo-category winner. She ran back to the table waving her prize money. "Where'd Dylan go?"

"To throw up—he gets stage fright," Jennifer replied with a laugh.

"No way!"

Jennifer nodded, and Sammie giggled. Who would've thought it? *He's famous.*

"I'm so proud of you," Matt said, squeezing her hand. Warmth filled her.

Dylan reappeared at the table, and Jennifer handed him a mint. He grinned sheepishly and escorted Sammie to the stage for their duet. The crowd stood before they'd even started.

"I don't know. Maybe I got a little too big for my britches…" she shouted in Dylan's ear.

"You'll be fine. It's just nerves. I get 'em before every performance. Let's win us a damn contest."

She'd let Dylan choose the song since he knew her vocal range and was pleasantly surprised by his choice of "Summer Wine" by Lee Hazelwood. When they finished, the crowd demanded an encore, and this time Sammie chose Johnny Cash's "Jackson."

No other duets entered against them, and she gratefully accepted the prize when they won. In the end, Dylan refused to take his half of the winnings.

When the night was over and they arrived home, Pa's truck wasn't there. Matt worried about Pa driving, but it was useless to gripe about it. Pa was gonna do what Pa wanted to do. He'd more than likely crashed at Gig's house after the poker game.

"Would y'all like to come in for coffee?" Sammie asked as they got out of the car.

"No! Uh, I mean, er…" Matt stammered and shoved his hands in his pockets.

Dylan laughed. "I think Matt has other plans. We'll head on home and relieve Mrs. J of babysitting duties. We'll return Luke in the morning."

"Thank you again for your help, Dylan," Sammie called.

"Anytime. Y'all don't do anything we wouldn't do." He yelped as Jennifer smacked his arm before she drove away.

"That was kind of rude, wasn't it? Basically telling them to go home," Sammie fussed as they walked up the steps.

"Yes, I suppose so. But Pa's not here. And Luke's spending the night over at the McAthies…" Matt's warm gaze undressed her, and his grin turned into a definite leer. She backed up, giggling, until she bumped into the front door. Matt leaned in and his finger traced along her jawline.

"You were wonderful tonight," he whispered as his lips sought hers.

Her knees felt weak as she returned his kiss.

"Wait here." He darted into the house.

A few moments later he returned with a quilt and a flashlight and led her to the muscadine arbor. She trembled as she watched him spread the quilt to the ground and turn off the flashlight. He lay down and held his hand out to her.

Immediately she joined him. So many memories, so many emotions swirled between them as they lay on their sides, facing each other. Matt brushed her hair out of her face, tucking it behind her ear.

"I want to make new memories tonight, Sammie. I can't erase the past, but I can promise a better future. I'm so sorry. I'm sorry for not being there for you as a young girl going through hell at home. I'm sorry for being selfish and marrying you to battle my former in-laws. I'm sorry I haven't always been a good husband—"

"Stop, Matt," she interrupted, putting a finger to his lips. "We're good. Lots and lots, remember?"

Matt kissed her finger and grasped her hand as he nuzzled her neck. "'Know you not that you are my sun by day, and my star by night? By my faith! I was in deepest darkness till you appeared and illuminated all.'"

She giggled, stroking his cheek with her fingers. "Yeah, yeah, that's what you always say."

Matt chuckled in return. "I'm trying to be all romantic and shit. I can't believe you aren't impressed with Alexander Dumas!"

"How do you know that quote?" She kissed the pounding pulse at the base of his neck.

"I had to do a paper for school," he admitted. "Impressed you, though, didn't I?"

"You did. I love you, too—ouch!" Sammie swatted a mosquito.

"You're just too sweet; everything wants to nibble on you, including me." He slipped his hand under her shirt and kissed her cheek. Sammie shifted, and Matt rolled onto his back.

"Dammit!" He sat up, dug under the quilt, and pulled out a pinecone. Sammie laughed and began unbuttoning his shirt, leaving a kiss after each button. She straddled him and pushed him back on to the quilt. He closed his eyes. "Mmmm."

"Matt?" Sammie stopped undoing his belt, listening. Something was moving in the woods.

"Hmmmm?"

"What was that?" Anxiety heightened her senses.

Matt opened his eyes. "Probably a raccoon or a possum. It won't bother us."

"A possum? They're hideous overgrown rats!"

He flipped her over on her back. "It's nothing, Sammie." He shrugged out of his shirt and kissed her, tugging gently on her lower lip, exploring her mouth with his tongue. He pulled the strap of her top down, kissing her shoulder.

"You always smell so good." He pulled her other strap down and kissed that shoulder, nipping it lightly. Freeing her breasts from her top and strapless bra, his warm hands tugged and tweaked her nipples.

"Matt? Something is out there!" She gasped with a combination of fear and desire.

"It's nothing." He bit and licked her nipples. And then jumped up with a howl.

Rufus barked, and Sammie burst into laughter.

"Geezus, I was really, really drunk the last time we were here. Did we have all these problems?" he muttered as he lay down beside her. "Rufus's wet nose on my back scared the bejeezus out of me."

"We were young and driven by hormones." Sammie sighed. "Does this mean we're getting old? I'd really rather be in the comfort of my bed instead of eaten by mosquitoes."

"I just wanted to do things right this time. I love you, Sammie…" He pulled her closer, his head resting in the crook of her neck, his arm wrapped around her waist. They held each other for a moment, listening to the night wind in the trees and watching the fireflies. Rufus scratched his ear, thumping the ground, and then started howling.

"This is crazy. Let's go back inside!" Matt stood and helped her up.

She adjusted her shirt and grabbed his as he gathered the quilt and flashlight. They held hands on their way back to the house.

"Matt?" Sammie paused before they went in and wrapped both arms around his waist.

"Yes?"

"Thank you. Tonight will be a nice memory."

Matt smiled down at her. "The night isn't over yet."

Chapter
Twenty-Three

"I hope I can carry it." Sammie eyed the no-cussing jar.

"Most of it's *your* money." Pa chuckled.

"The hell you say, old man!" Sammie grimaced. "Oh, shoot." Pa handed her a quarter from his pocket.

"How much is in there, Sammie?" Luke picked up his cereal bowl and slurped the milk.

"Probably enough to pay for at least one of your textbooks for college," Sammie replied as she finished making a sandwich for his lunchbox.

"But I'm not going to college."

"Why not?" Sammie closed the lunchbox and smiled as Matt entered the kitchen and headed straight to the coffee.

"Because I can't read good!"

"Does the coffee taste okay to you?" she asked Matt.

Matt took a sip. "It's perfect. You read well; give it time, son. You'll learn. You've only been in school for a little over two months. I think you're doing great."

Luke finished his breakfast and went upstairs to brush his teeth.

"I hope he's always this excited about school." Sammie smiled and gave Matt a quick good morning kiss.

"Just wait until he's fourteen and skips school like his father," Pa quipped.

"That's *not* going to happen; he has a father who will make sure of it," Matt retorted.

"Never say never," Pa cautioned with a laugh.

Sammie intervened. "I'm going to deposit the jar money in Luke's account after I drop him off at school."

Matt sighed. "I still don't like it."

"I know. You still haven't gone down to add yourself to the account."

Luke came back downstairs, and she helped him gather his things.

Matt laughed when Luke unzipped his backpack and checked it and then did the same with his lunchbox.

"I do believe this is a prime example of nurture versus nature, Sammie."

She stuck her tongue out at him and laughed as she walked out the door with her stepson.

Sammie lugged the heavy no-cussing jar into the bank after dropping Luke off at preschool. The bank was quiet, and only a couple of customers were in line. She glanced toward James Howell's office. She could see him through the large window that overlooked the lobby, talking to a gentleman in a suit. *Hallelujah, I don't have to deal with him today.* If she could just get this finished, she'd go home and lie down, skipping the studying. Something she'd eaten didn't agree with her.

Sammie approached the teller, whose nametag said *Rhiannon*. She placed the jar on the counter. "I'd like to deposit this in my stepson's account, please. Lukas Tyler."

"Account number?" The teller asked without looking up. She counted the bills in her drawer and added on the adding machine.

"I forgot to write it down. His name is Lukas Matthew Tyler."

The teller's mouth thinned as she typed a moment and then looked at Sammie, raising one eyebrow at the jar of change and bills. "You have to roll the coins first."

"But you're the bank. Don't you have a machine to do that?"

"This branch doesn't have one." She looked beyond Sammie, signaling the conversation was over and she wanted to wait on someone else.

Fighting the urge to just bail on the whole errand, Sammie pressed as politely as she could, "But you're a *bank*. I thought it would be part of the customer service."

"Look, Miss—"

"Mrs." Samantha interrupted. "Mrs. Tyler."

The teller shook her head and looked to the next person. "I already told you no. Roll them and bring them back. Next!"

Furious, but not wanting to make a scene, Sammie grabbed the jar off the counter. It slipped from her hands, and it was like watching a movie in slow motion as she tried to catch it before it crashed to the floor. The sound ricocheted in the cavernous lobby of the bank, and quarters rolled everywhere. She dropped to the floor to pick up the scattered money.

"Danny, please get a broom, a dust pan, and a box for Mrs. Tyler and help her pick up this money." Travis's gray eyes crinkled, and his lips turned up in a winsome smile.

"Yes, sir." Danny scurried away.

Sammie gathered the bills with shaking hands, sorting them carefully as she stacked. "I'm so sorry, Travis."

He shrugged. "It was an accident, Sammie. What did you do, rob Luke's piggy bank?" He squatted and helped her collect the scattered coins.

"No, it's the no-cussing jar. It was, uh, I'm ashamed to admit, full."

Travis laughed as he handed her a twenty-dollar bill. "Wow, Leroy's?"

Sammie blushed. Matt had dropped the bill in as a joke after an adventurous evening.

"Uh, no, that was Matt's."

"Who's contributed the most to the jar, Luke?" He looked away when she caught him staring at her chest.

"I'm afraid it would be a toss-up between me and Pa," she said.

Travis laughed. "I'm impressed. Leroy's known for his creative cussing. You must be good, too!"

Danny reappeared, and with the help of an eager little girl and her grandmother, the money was soon collected and placed in a box. Samantha gratefully gave the little girl a five-dollar bill.

Travis took the bills and deposited a hundred and fifteen dollars in Luke's account. He gave a low whistle as he handed her the deposit slip.

"Cussing is lucrative. If I were you, I'd take the coins to the Walmart in Harrisburg. They have a machine. They charge a percentage, but it's a time saver."

"Thank you, and I'm sorry," she apologized to the teller and to Travis.

"Not a problem, Sammie. However, I think you owe me a cup of coffee. Walk with me to the Mug and Cone?"

Sammie smiled. "Uh, no thanks. I'm not feeling well today. I need to get on home."

"Okay, I'll walk you to your car." He picked up the box of coins and followed her out.

Surely Matt couldn't object to Travis being polite.

"How are the practice tests going for your GED?"

"Pretty good. English is still my worst subject. Jennifer McAthie is helping me, though. She's going with me when I take the test for moral support. Plus, I have no idea where I'm going in Birmingham."

"The road construction and detours in that city are ridiculous. Good idea. Jennifer's from that area, so she knows it well." He smiled and waved as she pulled away.

Finished changing the oil in Jennifer's car, Matt slammed the hood. He tried to keep his face pleasant as Lydia drove up in her Chevy pickup. The smirk on her face spelled trouble.

"Hi, Lydia. What can I do for you?"

Lydia popped a bubble with her chewing gum. "I—er, I think it's time for my oil to be changed."

Matt sighed, stopped what he was doing, and walked over to Lydia's truck. He peered at the change oil sticker he'd placed on the windshield two weeks ago and then at her odometer. "You have more than twenty-eight hundred miles to go before it needs changed again."

He backed away, keeping his distance.

"Oh. Well, is Sammie home? I wanted to chat with her."

Matt frowned and waited for whatever gossip she was gearing up to deliver. "Sammie's in town running errands."

"Oh, so she's not back from her visit with Travis yet? Frances saw them talking at the bank. She said they seemed to be very good friends…" Lydia popped her gum again.

Matt kept his poker face on, refusing to let her know how she irritated him.

Lydia grinned and started her truck. "Well, I just came by to see if my oil needed changing. Bye, Matt."

He gritted his teeth and tried to sound pleasant. "Bye." *And good riddance*, he added under his breath as she peeled out of the driveway, already on her cell phone.

Why his area of the damn county had to have good cell reception was beyond him. It dropped everywhere else except in town. Annoyed, he pursed his lips at the thought of Sammie with Travis. Sometimes he really hated living in small town where gossip seemed to be the only pastime. She'd gone to the bank; it wasn't her fault the jerk worked there. Nor was it her fault he and Travis shared a painful history. He returned to work and shoved his jealousy aside.

Two weeks later, Sammie was at Jennifer's to help paint Angela's room.

She cracked open the can of paint and nearly threw up. Maybe she should've eaten breakfast this morning.

Deciding she'd let Jennifer stir the paint, she stood and asked, "What's Angela going to be for Halloween? Luke keeps going back and forth between super heroes. And even though it's two weeks away, Pa's already snuck in and eaten half the trick-or-treat candy."

"Dylan's my candy thief. And our dilemma is deciding which Disney princess Angela will be. David's having the same problem with Kenzie. It's the age. Rory will be a pumpkin. They're easy when they don't have a say in it. Are you nervous about your GED test tomorrow?"

"Very."

"You'll do great. You know this stuff. We'll review while we paint." Jennifer paused and looked uncomfortable as they draped dropcloths over the furniture in the center of Angela's room. "Um, Sammie?"

"Yes?"

"I don't know how to broach this. I mean…Okay, I'm just going to come right out and tell you. Because we're friends."

"What?"

"There's talk going around that there's something going on between you and Travis." Jennifer held up her hands. "Now I know that's just gossip. And I've heard there's bad blood between Travis and Matt. I think you need to tell him you've been going to the library and coming over here to study for your GED before things get out of hand. Trust me, Dylan and I have done the miscommunication dance. It's best just to lay stuff out, fight, and make up. The making up is the best part, actually." Jennifer waggled her brow, but she looked worried.

Sammie sighed. Matt had been asking where she was going lately, but she'd been circumventing the questions. Yesterday, Travis had stopped by the library for all of five minutes to wish her luck. But of course, she'd spied Lydia in the stacks as he was leaving.

"I bet it's that nosy Lydia Meadows. I can't stand that bitch. I'll tell him everything on Saturday; it's his birthday. I was going to tuck the receipt for my test in with his new wedding band."

"That will be fun. Does he have a clue you're having a surprise party for him?"

"Nope. I haven't even told Pa and Luke—one of them would blab. Plus it's small, just our two families. We're having pizza and Lucy's making a cake."

Jennifer poured the paint in the pan, and when the smell hit Sammie, she ran to the bathroom and threw up.

"I feel sick. I might have that stomach crud going around the preschool. Do you think we could do this after my GED, maybe next week?"

"Sure, of course…" Jennifer felt her forehead and handed her a washcloth.

"Is that a mom move or a nurse move?"

Jennifer grabbed her hand. "Come with me; painting can wait." They moved to the spacious kitchen, where Jennifer put a kettle on the stove. "Let's just have a cup of tea. Or would you prefer coffee?"

Sammie wrinkled her nose. "Not coffee. I love it, but I can't tolerate it lately."

Jennifer put the kettle down. "Wait, you didn't feel well last week, either. How long have you been feeling puny?"

"A few weeks."

"Are you late?"

"Late?" Sammie gripped the table and stared at Jennifer, mentally counting. She'd never been regular, but…"No, it can't be. I'm on birth control."

Jennifer slid into the chair next to her. "Didn't you have a sinus infection a month or two ago?"

"Yes. Why? A round of antibiotics cleared it right up."

"Sometimes they work against birth control. Didn't the doctor tell you that?"

"I didn't go. I had some left over and took them…" Sammie stood, her legs shaking. "I'll be right back. I have to run home for a minute."

"Okay. Are you well enough to drive?"

"Yes. I just feel nasty. I'm gonna brush my teeth. I'll be back in a few." She dashed to her car and drove home.

When she arrived, Pa sat on the back porch, whittling. Matt's truck was gone.

"That was a fast paint job."

"I'm going back. I forgot something." She ran upstairs, grabbed the pregnancy test from the cabinet over the bathroom sink, and stuffed it in her purse. After she brushed her teeth, she ran back to the car, not stopping to let Pa ask questions.

Twenty minutes later she handed the completed test to Jennifer, who whooped with excitement.

Sammie sank to the floor and covered her eyes as the realization sunk in. *I'm pregnant.* "Matt's gonna kill me."

Chapter
Twenty-Four

Matt looked across the kitchen at his wife as she tucked her phone in her purse. Sammie looked ready to cry.

"You okay?"

"Hmm? Oh yeah, I'm fine."

"Who texted you?"

"Jennifer. Rory's sick."

The purple circles under her eyes concerned him. She was also jumpy and nervous, and that made him suspicious. She was hiding something; he knew it in his gut. *Was that really Jennifer who texted? Karen used to get texts...*

Dammit, he needed to grow some balls and ask her what was going on. But he was afraid of what the answer might be.

"I'm going to be Batman for Halloween," Luke announced.

He turned his attention to his son. "I thought you'd decided on Superman." He sipped his coffee and motioned that he didn't need anything for breakfast—not with a stomach in knots.

"He changes his mind every day." Sammie straightened the salt and pepper shakers. "Are you done with breakfast, Luke? We need to get going."

"I don't like to drink the milk. It's yuck."

"That's wasteful, and you've always drunk it before," Matt snapped.

"I changed my mind. I don't like it."

"I agree with Luke. It's gross." She removed the cereal bowl and started washing the dishes. "Go brush your teeth. We have to go."

Mat watched her, feeling sad and helpless as Luke tromped up the stairs.

He returned in a few minutes and unzipped his lunchbox.

"I don't like pretzels." He scrunched his nose and made a gag- ging sound.

"Fine. Come on, Luke," Sammie urged, substituting a bag of corn chips. "We're leaving. And Batman, right? I'm buying the costume today. And the pumpkins we'll carve."

"I don't know. Maybe Superman is better?" he asked. "Which do you think, Daddy?"

Lost in dark thoughts, Matt didn't answer.

"Daddy, Superman or Batman?"

Matt blinked. "Batman."

"Okay! Batman, Sammie!"

Luke kissed him goodbye, and he received a perfunctory kiss from Sammie. Before she could get away, he cupped her face, searching her eyes for answers.

"Are you sure you're okay? Are we okay?"

She pulled away, not making eye contact with him. "Of course, but I need to go so Luke won't be late. Bye!"

As she herded Luke out the door, a feeling of déjà vu overcame him. Glancing at the clock, he realized she was leaving a half hour earlier than usual.

Sammie dropped Luke off at school and raced to Birmingham for her GED test. Her anxiety level soared as she merged into the traffic in the city. Even with GPS, she was afraid of getting lost and being late. She'd chosen Birmingham because the test was offered sooner than in Harrisburg—and because Travis wouldn't be there. She wanted this over with. She had enough on her plate at the moment. Starting with an unplanned pregnancy...

She parked, entered the testing site, made her way to the bathroom, and promptly threw up. Whether it was nerves or pregnancy, it didn't matter. She was miserable. After a few minutes she rinsed her mouth, pulled herself together, and took her spot at a desk in the testing room. When the test began, she was pleased to find the first answer obvious—and the second. After a few minutes she relaxed as the answers continued to come.

She left feeling reasonably confident and stopped to pick up the things she needed for Matt's party, some pumpkins, and a Batman costume for Luke. Then traffic came to a complete stop.

Checking her GPS app, she sighed. There was a wreck. Thank goodness Jennifer had said in her text that Dylan would pick Luke and Angela up after school. *Should I text Matt?* Not wanting to spoil her surprise, she didn't. An hour later than planned, she finally made it back to Pine Bluff, only to have the gas light flash on. Exhausted, she pulled into Bubba Kelton's gas station to fill up. But no matter how hard she tried to get the gas cap off, it wouldn't budge.

Already on edge, she burst into tears.

"Hey, are you okay?"

She looked over her shoulder to see Travis hurrying over. *Of all people...*

"I can't get the damn gas cap off, and I'm late!"

"Hold on, let me try. Wasn't today your test day? I just got back from a meeting in Birmingham. That traffic was horrendous."

"Yes." She couldn't quit crying. She just wanted to go home, soak in a tub, and go to bed.

Travis stopped working with the gas cap and patted her arm. "Hey, don't worry about the results. If you didn't pass it this time, you can try again."

"I don't care; I just need to get home!" She tried to move him out of the way so she could attempt to get gas.

"Step back. I've got this. It's not mis-threaded, I think a vapor vacuum has it stuck." He worked with it, and finally the cap popped. He began fueling her car.

"Thank you. Wait, stop—I'm only getting ten dollars' worth!"

He continued to pump the gas. "Don't worry about it."

She stomped her foot. "No! Matt's gonna be pissed enough as it is—"

"He's always pissed. What's one more reason?" Travis joked. "So which part of the test was easiest? Which part are you worried about?"

Sammie turned as Matt's truck raced into the station.

"Oh shit. Speak of the devil," Travis muttered.

Her stomach sank.

Matt got out and slammed the door. His dark eyes narrowed as he approached.

"I guess we have an irate husband to deal with. Are you up to it?" Travis asked.

"No," she said softly.

"Yeah, well, unfortunately, this isn't my first rodeo." Travis replaced the handle on the gas pump and screwed the cap back on. "Hey, Matt, what's up?"

"Shut up, motherfucker."

"Look, man, don't do or say anything stupid."

"I may be a fool, but I'm *not* stupid," Matt spat angrily. "This has been a long time coming, and you and I are going to have it out once and for all!"

"What are you doing here?" Sammie asked.

"Go home, *Samantha*."

She folded her arms across her chest. "You're acting like a jealous husband. And don't talk to me like I'm a two-year-old."

Matt looked at her as if she'd lost her mind. "I *am* a jealous husband!" he roared. "Now go home so I can deal with lover-boy, here."

"Lover-boy? Travis? That's crazy."

Travis looked mildly offended.

Matt glared. "I've heard the rumors. And Bubba phoned to tell me you were here and crying *with him*." He pointed a finger at Travis's chest. "What the hell did you do to make her cry?"

"If you'd listen to me, I can explain all of this," Sammie offered.

"Not now. Go home. I'm not going to tell you again."

"Don't talk to her like that," Travis shouted, stepping between them.

"Travis, this doesn't involve you," Sammie pleaded.

"I think it does. He doesn't deserve you."

"Don't talk to *my wife*," Matt bit out, the tic in his cheek on overdrive.

Through the window, Bubba watched them like it was the damn Super Bowl. Sammie glared at the busybody. To top off her embarrassment, she bent over and threw up.

"Now look what you've done!" The men shouted at each other.

Matt reached Sammie at the same time as Travis. He shoved the wife-fucker out of the way. "Sammie? Are you okay?"

"No, I'm not okay. I want to go home. I don't feel well."

"Being around Travis makes me sick, too," he offered.

"Stop! He's my friend, Matt." Sammie huffed.

Matt closed his mouth, fuming.

Bubba walked over. "Y'all need to clear on out before Sherriff Sanford arrives. You're creating a public disservice."

"That's public disturbance, you moron," Matt snapped. "And you're the one who called and told me to get out here." Turning his back on the jerk, he said, "I'll drive you home, Sammie."

"I can drive. I just need to pay for my gas. Travis put too much in there."

"It's all paid for," Travis said.

"Oh, I'm gonna make you pay for it. No doubt," Matt replied through gritted teeth.

"I am so done with this. I'm leaving." Getting in her car, she slammed the door and drove off without looking back.

Glaring at Travis, he returned to his truck. His thoughts swirled as he drove home. When he arrived, he sat in the driver's seat for a moment, thinking. This morning he'd gone looking for something to take for his headache and discovered the pregnancy test missing, he'd felt a stab of panic. He'd spent thirty minutes pawing through the garbage but hadn't found it. He didn't know whether to be relieved or angry. This afternoon Bubba's phone call had added fuel to the fire that had burned within him all day.

He could see Sammie sitting in the rocker on the back porch. He got out of the truck and walked up the back steps. Hearing the TV inside, he prayed Luke and Pa would stay put. His heart pounded in his ears. Taking a deep breath, he asked the question he didn't want to ask.

"What's going on between you and Travis?"

Don't say it, don't say it, don't say it…For Christ's sake, don't say you love him.

"What? Nothing's going on between Travis and me."

His world spiraled and crashed as the sound of rushing air exploded in his head. Memories of Karen from the night of the wreck taunted him.

"Don't be ridiculous, Matt. Nothing is going on between us…"

Karen had denied having an affair with Travis, too—until he'd flung the pregnancy test he'd pulled out of the garbage at her, telling her to go to hell.

Angry tears blinded him, and he turned his back to her. It felt like he was drowning. When he could breathe again, he faced her and softly asked, "How stupid do you think I am? Are you fucking him? What is it about that goddamned prick that makes him so desirable?"

"How dare you!" She jumped up from the chair and clenched her fist. But instead of hitting him, she began fingering her bracelets. Her eyes flashed and cheeks reddened, highlighting the freckles he loved. "Why would you think that?" she hissed.

"What the hell am I supposed to think, Sammie? You spend inordinate amounts of time away from home; folks are calling me, telling me you've been seen with Travis; and then this morning I find the pregnancy test missing. I have no idea where you went today, but you're never this late without texting me or leaving a note. Just when I'm worried something awful's happened to you, Bubba calls and says you're crying and arguing with Travis. And sure enough, I find you with him. Just fucking tell me the truth."

"Travis has been nothing but nice to me and is Just. A. Friend!" she retorted. Pointing at him she continued, "I need to talk to you, and I can explain everything, but right now I'm too angry. You, you…I can't even think of a word bad enough to call you right now!"

She stormed past him, stomping upstairs to her old room, slamming the door, and locking it.

Luke and Pa glared at him as he ran after her.

Matt jiggled the door handle. "Sammie?" His voice was thick with emotion as he leaned his head against the wall. He added hoarsely, "Please don't shut me out."

She opened the door. Her eyes were bright, her cheeks flushed. Walking to the window, she stared out, her arms crossed, her back to him.

He closed the door behind him and leaned against it. Drawing a deep breath, he admitted, "I hate Travis Carlton. I can't help it. I fuckin' hate him." Swallowing his pride, he continued, "But I love you, Sammie. And I'll fight for you. I won't quit. I won't give up."

"You're an idiot. There's nothing to fight about—"

"Then tell me why you were with him. Why were you crying? Whatever it is, we can work through this…" His voice trailed off, and he prepared for the news.

She sighed. "I'm pregnant."

He heard a car pull into the driveway. "Dammit." *How can I deal with a customer when I'm dying?*

Opening the door, he shouted, "Hey, Pa! Get the keys and ask whoever's here to leave a number and I'll call 'em later."

"It's Travis Carlton," Pa shouted back.

"Sonofabitch!" Matt tore down the stairs two at a time. "I should've killed him when I had the chance!" He raced through the house and was in the front yard in no time.

"I'm telling you once and for all, he's my friend!" Sammie ran after him toward the silver Porsche.

Matt grabbed the car door and pulled Travis out.

"I'm not going to tell you again to stay away from my wife!"

"Stop! I just came to check on Sammie—"

Before he could take a swing, water blinded him, and Travis swore.

Shielding their eyes from the stream, they looked up to see Pa holding the hose. He let up on the nozzle and threw it down. Luke turned the water off, eyes wide.

"You're interrupting *Jeopardy*, upsetting the boy, and making Sam cry," Pa shouted before grabbing Luke by the arm and going back inside, slamming the door.

Sammie wiped her tears and crossed her arms, watching them. The sun was setting, and the temperature had begun to drop. Matt shivered in his drenched clothes, and Travis's teeth chattered.

He hoped the sonofabitch's perfect capped teeth would crack and fall out.

"You might have seduced my first wife and gotten her pregnant, but I'll be damned if you'll take Sammie from me, too. I'll kill you, I swear I will," he threatened.

Sammie gasped, and her mouth dropped open.

"*You* stole Karen from *me* first. I loved her from the time we were in second grade, you goddamned—" Travis stopped mid-sentence and looked at Matt. He turned chalk white and reached for the car to steady himself.

Matt wondered if he was going to pass out.

"W-What did you say?" Travis asked, hoarsely.

"I said I'll kill you, you stupid piece of—"

Travis held up his hand, shell-shocked. "No, what did you say about Karen being pregnant?"

Glaring, Matt said, "Karen lied to me and told me there was nothing going on between you two. But the night of the accident, I found the pregnancy test. She finally admitted she was four months pregnant." He took a deep breath. "I knew it wasn't my child. Things hadn't been good between us for at least six months."

Shaking, Travis slid to the ground. He covered his face with his hands and rocked. It took Matt a few seconds to realize he was weeping.

"I didn't know she was pregnant," he choked. "Oh my God. Oh my God…"

Looking down at the man he'd blamed for his marital problems, some of Matt's anger dissipated. He'd assumed Travis had known. After all, Karen had been leaving him to go be with the bastard. Although it still hurt like hell, Matt finally accepted the hard truth. Travis and Karen had been in love. His wife had wanted to spend the rest of her life with Travis. They were having a child, and Travis had loved her.

Having loved and lost Karen and a child, Matt felt a strange, sympathetic connection and an understanding of his rival's agony. He left Travis alone to deal with his grief.

As he moved back toward the porch, Sammie came and wrapped her arms around his waist. Rising on tiptoe she whispered, "This is *your* baby, Matt. *Our baby.* Travis and Jennifer helped me get my GED, which was supposed to be a surprise for your birthday tomorrow. I was crying because I couldn't get the stupid gas cap off and my hormones are whack-a-doodle right now."

He kissed her. "Our baby?"

She nodded, smiling back.

It was like a weight had been lifted from his shoulders. An unplanned baby was a shock, but a gift. He turned and looked back at Travis, who sobbed.

"He needs a friend," Sammie said.

"Go." He squeezed her hand and made his way up the front steps as Sammie went out into the yard.

"What's wrong with Travis?" Luke asked from the doorway.

Matt sighed and watched as Sammie knelt next to Travis, cradling him in her arms as he wept.

He smiled slightly—it was so like Sammie to be compassionate. Hell, she fed every damn stray animal that came in the yard and so much more. With her love, a traumatized child was now a carefree, happy boy. An old, broken man enjoyed life again. And she'd even accomplished the impossible: she'd given him hope and brought light into his darkness. Sammie loved him; he knew that without a doubt. *And I love her.*

"Travis got some bad news. Let's leave him alone." He guided Luke away from the window.

Pa patted him on the back as he walked by.

Sammie straightened the silverware drawer. They'd agreed to wait until they were alone to talk, and she could hear Matt upstairs as he put Luke to bed.

Pa made his way into the kitchen with his cane. "I reckon I'm gonna go out for a bit." His gaze was kind as he looked at her.

She nodded, biting her lip. To her surprise, the old man engulfed her in a bear hug.

"Everything will be fine. You could talk the devil into serving ice water."

"Thanks, Pa." She hugged him back.

Five minutes after Pa left, Matt came downstairs. He collapsed in a kitchen chair and rubbed his face.

She sat next to him and held his hand as she looked him in the eye. "I'm only going to say this one more time, so listen up. I'm sorry you got the wrong idea about Travis and me. He's just a friend. He teaches a GED class in Harrisville, but it was at night. I knew you'd be suspicious of that, and you wouldn't like me working with him, so I've been studying on my own at the library or at Jennifer's. It's something I've wanted to do since Sue Ellen died. Although I did it for *me*, I also did it for our family. I want to be a good stepmother and be able to help Luke with his homework, and I wanted you to be proud of me, too.

"I haven't been feeling well for a few weeks. Just weird things, like coffee tasting off. And…" She blushed. "My boobs hurt sometimes when you touch them. On my birth control pills, I've always had light periods, and I just didn't pay attention when I skipped one.

"But yesterday, at Jennifer's, I got sick. She figured it out. Apparently, the antibiotic I took when I had a sinus infection made the pills not work. I came back here, grabbed the test, and took it back to Jennifer's. It was positive. I should've told you last night, but my GED test was today. And I was planning a little surprise birthday party for you tomorrow, so I thought I'd just lump all the news together. I'm sorry."

She paused, trying to gauge his reaction. "How did you know I was with Travis at the gas station anyway? Even I was surprised to see him there. Your turn."

"I knew this morning something was up. Around lunch time, I stopped by the bank to take the rolled coins in and get my name added to Luke's account. Travis wasn't there, and Meka mentioned he was in Birmingham. This afternoon, Pa told me Dylan picked Luke up because *you* were in Birmingham." Matt rubbed his eyes. "All day my imagination has been running wild. I made all kinds of assumptions, which wasn't fair to you. It was totally based on my past experience with Travis and Karen. I'm sorry, Sammie."

"I knew you hated Travis, but I thought it was left over from when you were teens. I never would've guessed he and Karen had an affair. You loved her so much...All this time, I've thought I was competing with the memory of Karen."

Matt tapped the table with his thumbs, not speaking for a moment. "I *did* love Karen. But our marriage had been falling apart for years. She was moody. She'd be up one minute and down the next. And she was secretive. I always felt like she held back on me—like she didn't fully trust me, or deep down she thought she could've done better. That's not to say we didn't have good moments. We *did*. We had two beautiful kids that proved it." His eyes shone.

She grasped his hand and squeezed it.

"Three months before the wreck, rumors were rampant that she and Travis were having an affair. I didn't believe them. But she was getting more and more distant and depressed. I begged her to go to counseling. She hated me for suggesting it. Lila had been institutionalized several times when Karen was younger, and in her mind, I guess counseling was a step in that direction. Honestly, I think James put Lila away because he didn't want to deal with her. I think those absences had a huge impact on both Karen and Jinx."

He looked up at the ceiling. "The afternoon of the wreck I was taking the trash out, and I saw the positive pregnancy test. I knew the baby wasn't mine. We hadn't had sex for months. I was devastated, and it resulted in the fight to end all fights. We'd never fought like that in front of the kids, and it upset them. So I left and went to class. At some point she must've decided to leave me. Their suitcases were in the trunk of the car, and she'd left me a note..."

Sammie didn't know what to say. She cradled her still-flat stomach and wondered what he thought about her news. *Does he blame me for not taking more precautions?*

"I'm sorry, Sammie. I'm sorry for projecting my past on you. Forgive me? I should've trusted you."

"Matt, love is hard. And trust is earned. Your marriage to Karen proves it takes work. We started as friends. We made a commitment to one another to fight to keep Luke. And I've always loved you, but I've fallen in love with you and can't imagine my life without you."

"You really love me, even after all of this?"

"Yes, silly." She kissed him and said against his lips, "Lots and lots. Here, open this."

He looked at the small package wrapped in birthday paper. "My birthday is Saturday," he protested, but he opened the box and slipped on the new wedding band. It fit perfectly.

"Thank you. It's perfect." He took a moment, trying to find the words. "I'm not a man with flowery words. I'm just a mechanic. But it seems inadequate to say *I love you*. It's more than that. You're my guiding light. My best friend and my wife. You're my lots and lots."

Sammie smiled. "I know this baby wasn't planned. I didn't think about antibiotics working against the pill. Jennifer's the one who told me what I did wrong—"

"Shhh," he said, kissing her. "You did nothing wrong."

"Well, I sure as hell didn't intend to tell you the way I did. But I hope you're happy?" Her voice rose with uncertainty.

He smiled. "All of my kids have been surprises. Even Luke. This is par for the course for me."

"You have strong swimmers," she agreed with a giggle. "And a long pole."

Matt laughed, and his cheeks flushed. "I'd sure love to have a little redheaded girl to take fishing with me and Luke."

"Or another dark-haired boy? And don't forget, I like to fish, too."

"I know. And you even bait your own hook. But you never clean the fish after you catch them."

"Because that's just gross."

"Sammie, it doesn't matter to me if we have a boy or a girl, as long as you're both okay."

He cupped her cheek and fell to his knees, looking up at her. "I love you, Samantha Morgan Tyler." Raising her shirt, he kissed her stomach. "And I love this baby."

She leaned over and held him tight. "I love you, too. Happy early birthday."

Chapter
Twenty-Five

Sammie gave her hair a final pat in the rearview mirror. In an hour she was meeting Matt for lunch before her first OB/GYN appointment. Luke and Pa were all kinds of excited about the baby, and Jennifer was already planning a baby shower.

Expecting a baby had made her think a lot about her own mom, so she'd decided to finally see what was in Sue Ellen's lock box at the bank. She could put her marriage license and Sue Ellen's death certificate in it while she was there and see what she needed to do to add Matt to the box. He'd given her a bunch of important papers he'd kept in a kitchen drawer to put in there as well.

Sammie entered the lock box vault and waited to be logged in. Meka, dressed as a bumblebee for Halloween, handed her the box and led her to a room to be by herself. Her antennae bobbed ridiculously as she closed the door behind her. Sammie smiled. Luke would've loved to see the bank employees all dressed up. They were having a party at his school today, and he'd worn his Batman costume.

Inexplicably, she felt nervous. Her hands shook as she opened the box. Inside she found her father's wedding ring and some pictures of him with Sue Ellen and some with her. She blinked back her tears. Would her parents have been happy to be grandparents?

At the bottom was a sealed, lumpy envelope addressed to her. She pulled out a note in Sue Ellen's handwriting.

> Samantha, I know I wasn't the best mother in the world. The Bible says we aren't given a spirit of fear, but of power, love, and a sound mind. But my mind's not sound, and I didn't do right by you when you were a little girl. I ain't proud of the things I've done, and I pray I don't go to hell. This is your insurance so you can live a good life. If he contacts you in any way, you have the proof. If he offers money, take it and don't look back. He's the devil.
>
> Love, Sue Ellen

Out of the envelope fell a silver tie bar with an H engraved on it and an old Polaroid photo of her mother with a man. She dropped them like she'd been burned.

The sounds from the bank grew distant, the room spun, and she felt sick to her stomach. Everything was suddenly painfully clear. The glimpse of her mother with James Howell wearing the tie bar was enough.

Memories of that night came crashing back through the filter of time. The terror, her mother's screams as she'd yanked the man away from her. Crawling under the bed to hide as they fought, she'd found this tie bar and held on to it. After the man left, her mother had returned to her room, sobbing hysterically. Sammie had tried to comfort her, only to have her scream it was all her fault. Sue Ellen had grabbed the tie clasp from her hand, and she'd never seen it again...until today.

When Sammie could breathe again, she threw everything but the tie clasp and Polaroid pictures back in the box and hurried out to the tellers.

"I-I'm afraid I'm late, and I-I don't feel well. I need to go. Can you put this back for me?" she asked.

Meka smiled. "Sorry. You have to go with me; let me finish with this customer."

Sweat prickled Sammie's scalp, and she felt trapped. She needed help, but her throat closed, and no sound came out when she tried to speak. Her hand shook as she took out her phone. She needed

Matt. But before she could send the text, Meka was leading her back to the vault.

"Are you okay, Mrs. Tyler? You look like you've seen a ghost. Of course, Rhiannon is dressed as a ghost." The bumblebee teller laughed at her own joke. She locked the box up and turned with a bright smile. "Anything else we can do?"

Sammie shook her head and hurried from the room, only to run into James Howell.

"Hello, Samantha. Will you be bringing Luke by to trick or treat this evening?"

"N-No!" she croaked, backing away from him.

"No?" He looked dumbfounded that she would dare defy him.

Before she could react, he grabbed her arm and pulled her into an empty conference room.

"Don't touch me."

"Is there a problem?" He let go, shut the door, and motioned her to sit at the long table.

His cologne was overpowering, and she sank into the chair. Spots danced before her eyes, and she was afraid she was going to pass out.

"I feel sick," she whispered.

He poured her a glass of water and stood over her. He was close. Too close…She couldn't get past him to the door; she was trapped. He held the glass out to her, and all she could do was stare at his hands. Those evil, vile hands.

"I know who you are," she squeaked.

His eyes narrowed. "Of course you know who I am. Are you on drugs? Or having a psychotic episode like your mother?" he bit out. "I'm Luke's grandfather. And Lila and I would like to see him this evening. I don't think that's an unreasonable request."

"No. I-I need to talk to Matt."

"This conversation is tiresome. And I'm a busy man." He glanced at his watch. "I have a meeting in ten minutes. Don't push me. I've done my research on you, my dear. Does your husband know about your mental health issues? The apple certainly didn't fall far from the tree, did it? Your mother was crazy, too."

Rage filled her. She knocked the glass out of his hand. "As well you should know. Don't you dare talk about my mother! How long did you fool around on your wife with Sue Ellen? Does Mrs. Howell know about your affair?"

His look was one of a cornered rattler. Thankfully, she wasn't scared of snakes.

"I don't know what you're talking about. You're as crazy as your mother was. Which makes you an unfit parent, like your *husband.*"

"How dare you! Matt's the best father, ever—" She stopped. She needed to talk to Matt about what she'd discovered. Taking a deep breath, she continued on a less confrontational course. "I'm not going to argue with you. I need to go."

James drummed his fingers on the table. "I've been thinking a lot about your *marriage.* Here's my take on it. I think he married you out of convenience, to thwart my efforts to get custody of Luke."

"He loves me—" She stopped again, realizing he was baiting her. "It's none of your business."

"It's very much my business. Luke is my grandson. My bank holds the mortgage on the Tyler place."

Dread crept through her veins. "Matt pays all of his bills. Your threat is unfounded."

"Actually, he's behind on his mortgage. But that can be managed… if you don't cross me."

Infuriated, she held up her chin. "You will do nothing to hurt my husband! And you'll never see Luke again if I have anything to do with it. I thought you were a parent grieving the loss of his child and granddaughter. I see now that my *husband* was right. You're a cold-hearted bastard through and through, and I know from experience you're evil. I pity you, Mr. Howell. You're going to die a lonely old man, full of regrets. I'll see to it."

Mr. Howell slammed his fist on his desk. "You *cannot* keep me from my grandson. I will fight you in court, you little bitch!"

"Go ahead." Reaching into her purse, she pulled out the tie clasp and showed it to him.

His face turned purple, and for a moment she wondered if he was going to stroke.

"Where did you get that?" he hissed moving toward her.

They circled the conference table, and she kept her eye on the doorway, hoping she could make it out—or raise enough of a ruckus that someone in the bank would help her.

"You're a dangerous nutcase just like your blackmailing mother was," he shouted. "Do you think I'll let you threaten me? Do you think you can take my precious Karen's place?" He reached to grab her but missed.

Her temper overruled her common sense. "And did you do despicable things to your *precious Karen*, too? Or just me?"

James flipped the glass-topped table, throwing her off balance. She fell backward, tripping on the chair and crashing to the floor. The glass broke around her, and the heavy metal base landed on top of her. She attempted to crawl, but it had her pinned. She held on to the tie clasp, the glass digging into her palms and arms.

He came after her, trying to wrestle the tie bar from her hand. When she refused to let go of it, he kicked her. She covered her face with her arms.

"My baby…" she whimpered.

She felt her body floating above the floor as James screamed obscenities and attempted to pry the evidence from her hand. Next thing she knew, people were yelling for him to stop, and every inch of her body hurt. She felt almost euphoric as she floated above the pain, the metallic scent of blood in the air.

"Sammie? Are you okay?" The weight holding her down was removed.

Why is Dylan here?

"Come on, Sammie. Don't you dare play possum on me."

She forced her eyes to open and met his worried gaze.

"I'm not." She tried to rise and promptly threw up. Someone eased her back onto her side. "It wasn't my fault," she whimpered. "I didn't do this."

"I know, Sam."

Around them, the bank was abuzz with activity.

Travis knelt beside her. "I called an ambulance. Oh my God…" He shrugged out of his coat and placed it over her.

"It wasn't my fault; I didn't do this," she repeated.

"You'll be fine, Sammie," Travis crooned as he held her hand.

"Please, Matt won't like this. Thank you, but I need to go." She struggled to sit up, glass digging into her palms as she held tight to her evidence. "Where's my purse?"

Dylan eased her back down. "It's right here. Look, you better be still. There's glass everywhere, and you're already all cut up."

Meka wiped her face with a wet paper towel. Sammie wondered what had happened to Mr. Howell. She cringed when she heard him shouting. Police rushed into the bank.

Her body shook, and in the distance, she heard the wail of a siren.

"Don't let him hurt me," she whispered.

"Breathe in nice and slow for me, Sammie," Dylan instructed. "You're safe now. Help's on the way."

"Where's Matt? I want Matt." *Matt! My God, Matt will kill James.*

"I'll find him, but first I want to make sure you're going to be okay."

"Hey, buddy. Did you eat too many sweets at the Halloween party?" Matt asked, buckling Luke into his car seat. Luke clutched his plastic pumpkin full of goodies.

Matt had received a call from the preschool saying Luke felt sick.

"My tummy hurt. But I think a chocolate milkshake might make me feel better," he replied. A hopeful glint lit his eyes.

Well done, son. I've just been played like a fiddle. Feeling relaxed and happy—and decidedly non-parental—he decided to cut Luke some slack. He was meeting Sammie for lunch before her first OB visit anyway.

"I know you're faking being sick. You do realize that's like lying, right?"

"I'm not—"

Matt raised one eyebrow.

Luke's face fell. "Yes, sir. I'm sorry."

"Want to explain why you fibbed?"

"The party was lame. They didn't even have Reese's. I want to go eat lunch with you and Sammie."

Matt laughed. Obviously, he'd overheard them discussing their plans for the day. "Today's a special day, so I'll let it slide this time. But don't do it again. We need to be able to believe you when you say you're sick. Anyway, if Pa hasn't eaten all of them, you have plenty of Reese's cups at home."

"I won't lie, promise."

"You can go with Sammie and me to the doctor. They're going to check on your new baby brother or sister."

"Hey, I thought you were going to lunch!" he accused. "I think I want to go back to school now, Daddy."

Matt pulled into the Mug and Cone parking lot. "We're doing both. And it's a doctor visit for Sammie and the new baby, not you. You'll be fine."

He helped Luke out of the car. His black Batman cape billowed with a gust of wind.

"I don't want to go to the doctor," Luke whined. "Can we go trick or treating instead?"

"Tonight." Matt paused at the door of the Mug and Cone when he heard the sirens. A murmur ran through the crowd on Main Street as the ambulance and police pulled up to the bank. Beside him, Luke started to shake, and Matt squeezed his hand.

"It's okay. The ambulance is going to help someone."

He wondered if the bank had been robbed. If so, he hoped the robbers had conked old man Howell on the head for good measure. He poked his head in the restaurant. When he didn't see Sammie, he glanced down at his watch. She was five minutes late.

He sent a quick text.

**Where are you? You're missing all the excitement.
Luke's with me. The party at school was "lame" lol.**

Frances rushed out the door, practically mowing him and Luke down. She hurried across the street and down two blocks to find out firsthand what had happened. Moments later, Matt was surprised to see her running back, waving her arms like a wild woman. His phone beeped with a text. But before he could look at it, Frances was screaming for him.

"Matt!" she gasped, her face red. She gulped in air and fanned her face with her hand. "You need to get to the hospital right away. Something's happened to your wife!"

Matt tried to comprehend her words. "Sammie?" he asked.

Frances nodded. Without a word, Matt grabbed Luke and ran to his truck. He was only slightly relieved to read the text from Dylan saying he was with Sammie.

Sammie felt movement and heard strangers talking. Struggling to reconnect with her body, she opened her eyes. "Matt?"

"No, it's just me," Dylan said.

"Hello, me. Where am I? My head hurts like hell." She sighed. "Oh shoot, don't tell on me for cussing. I'm running out of quarters."

"There was an accident. We're going to load you up in an ambulance and take you to the hospital to be checked out," a man with a red uniform shirt informed her.

Frowning, she turned her attention back to Dylan and tried to think.

"You know the tabloids will have me either responsible for this or a hero, if it gets out," Dylan teased, squeezing her hand. He looked pale and scared.

Sammie looked at the blood on her arms, felt her heart beat throbbing all over her body, and began to cry. *How did I do this? Mr. Howell did this!*

"Oh God, I c-can't breathe — my baby, don't let anything happen to my baby…" She struggled to catch her breath.

"Careful now, just breathe," the paramedic said. "How far along are you?"

"I don't know. I'm going to the doctor today."

"Let's put some oxygen on, and take slow, deep breaths. Everything will be fine."

"Do you think it's a boy or a girl?" Dylan squeezed her hand.

Dylan's face blurred with her tears. "Am I dying? My head hurts. I didn't do this, did I? Will my baby be okay?"

"You're going to be fine, and so is your baby. Sir, you can ride in the front or follow us."

"Don't leave me. Where's Matt?" she asked Dylan.

"He'll be here soon. I'll be in the front. You're in good hands."

As they lifted the stretcher and rolled her out, she closed her eyes and prayed for the first time since she was a child.

Chapter
Twenty-Six

"No, Daddy," Luke whimpered. He kicked the dash.

Matt cast a worried look at him but returned to the task of finding a damn parking spot. Why the ER only had six designated spaces was a mystery. He swore under his breath and went to another area to park.

Once he did, he tore out of the truck and threw open door. Luke sat in his car seat, crying. With an exasperated sigh, Matt undid the straps that Luke could easily undo on his own. "Come on, son. Sammie needs me. Get out of the truck."

Luke shook his head and pulled away. Matt sighed. He should have known the hospital would bring back memories of pain and separation. The boy was too frightened to reason with.

He tried to call home to reach Pa, but there was no answer. And Pa didn't have a cell.

That left him with no good options. Gently, but firmly, Matt reached in and hauled Luke out.

He knelt down and looked him straight in the eyes. "I know you don't like this place. I don't like it either. But we have to go in and see about Sammie. She needs us. Now be a big boy, and let's go."

"No!" His lower lip puckered, and he glared at Matt with the worst stink eye ever.

"But you're Batman! Batman's brave," Matt tried.

"I'm not B-Batman. I'm Luke," his son wailed.

Matt stood and looked down at his trembling son. *Now what the hell am I supposed to do?* Picking Luke up, he trudged toward the emergency room entrance as his son screeched like a feral child.

"Luke, stop. We're just checking on Sammie. I promise no one is going to hurt you. Dylan's here. He'll take you home."

A woman sat behind the admitting desk. Scowling, she winced at Luke's loud crying and shouted, "May I help you?"

"Yeah, I'd like to return him, please. Don't you have a money-back guarantee?" Matt cracked.

The woman raised an eyebrow. "Pardon me?"

Matt changed his approach. "My wife, Samantha Tyler. She was just brought in by—Luke, hush—by ambulance," he shouted over the wailing.

"Would you please try to control that child? This is a hospital!"

His temper flared. "Look, lady, my son is well acquainted with this place. He lost his mother and sister here less than a year ago. Now, could you please do your job and tell me where I can find my wife?"

"What did you say her name is?" The woman gave an annoyed sniff as she gazed at the computer screen.

Matt put his squirming, screaming child down. Luke buried his face in Matt's jeans. Over the boy's sobs he replied, "Samantha Tyler."

"I believe there's already someone back there with her. We only allow one family member to stay with the patient."

His patience wearing thin, he spoke through tight lips. "A friend is with her. I'm her husband."

"Well, you can't take that uncontrollable child back there," the woman huffed with a glare.

Matt leaned forward, his hands planted firmly on the admitting desk. "Lady, the sooner I can see my wife, the sooner my friend will come out and take my son home."

With a defiant, angry look, the woman placed a call to the nurse's station.

Matt looked down at Luke, who continued to cry and tremble. He picked him back up and held him tight. "Luke, you're fine. Remember how I told you hospitals are good places that help people who are sick?"

"No, they aren't! They hurt you and kill you! Mommy and Lizbeth got killed here!"

This was a perfectly logical conclusion from Luke's experience, and Matt was unable to come up with a reasonable response. He didn't want to rehash the car accident here in an ER waiting room.

Matt sent Dylan a desperate text. He rocked Luke in his arms, his sense of duty torn. He wanted to be with Sammie, but he needed to be with his frightened child, too.

At last Dylan came out of the back of the ER, ignoring the squeal of a teenager in the waiting room who recognized him. He smiled at everyone.

"Hey, everything's okay. I'll handle this…" He peered at the clerk's nametag. "Christa. What a pretty name. We good?"

The clerk blushed and gazed at him with stars in her eyes. "Um, sure…Everything's fine!"

"How is she?" Matt asked, patting Luke's back.

The boy's hysteria had subsided to soft sobs, but when he turned and saw the blood on Dylan's clothes, his crying intensified again.

"All kinds of scrub suits are checking her out. She's awake and talking. She'll be fine."

"What happened?" Matt asked quietly.

Dylan shrugged and looked away. "I don't really know. I walked in the bank just after the accident. There was a lot of blood…"

Matt's heart sank. He felt light-headed at the thought of Sammie and their baby being hurt. "Hush, son. Everything's going to be okay. The baby?"

"Sit down. You can't pass out," Dylan ordered. "Sam and that new kid need you. They have her hooked up to all kinds of monitors."

"I need to see her."

"Of course. Come on, Luke, let's get out of here." Dylan tried to disentangle Luke's fingers from his neck.

Luke pointed at Dylan's shirt, shaking, his color unnaturally pale. Dylan peeled off his shirt, tossed it in the garbage can, and again held out his hands to Luke. He didn't see the teenage girl quietly retrieve it and stuff it in her purse.

Luke dug his fingers into Matt's neck. Tears poured down his pale, pinched face, and Matt's heart flip-flopped. He looked very young and very vulnerable in his Batman costume.

"Come on, Luke. I hate hospitals too. Let's go outside," Dylan said, taking him in his arms.

"I'll be right back, son."

Dylan motioned to Matt that he had it under control and walked Luke out.

"Look for cubicle eight," the desk clerk said, buzzing him through.

The lure of Dylan McAthie must've done the trick; she even smiled.

The doctor stepped out of Sammie's room as he arrived. "Are you Mr. Tyler?"

"Yes. Is she going to be okay? Our baby?"

The doctor shook Matt's hand and introduced himself. "I'm Dr. Santos. We did an ultrasound, and the baby's heartbeat is strong. Your wife will be just fine. She has some bruising and cuts from the glass. Most are surface cuts that bleed and look worse than they are, but a few will need stitches. We're in the process of removing all the glass we can see, but there may be a few shards that work their way out later. Because of the baby, we're being conservative with medication, but she can go home later. I'm afraid she'll be uncomfortable for a few days." The doctor smiled reassuringly.

Matt nodded and thanked him. *Glass? Where did the glass come from?*

When he entered the room, he found Sammie positioned on her side with an IV in her hand and hooked up to several monitors. Under the bright lights, her skin looked like marble streaked with dried blood. She didn't *look* okay. A doctor and nurse worked to remove shards of glass from her arms and face. Blood was everywhere, and blood-soaked gauze littered the floor. A nurse motioned him to stand where Sammie could see him at her side.

"Sammie, your husband's here." The nurse stepped aside so Matt could be closer.

Her eyes fluttered open. "Hey. I'm okay," she murmured.

Matt tried to smile. "I know, sweetheart."

"He did this to me because I know..." She swallowed. "In my pocket—don't lose it."

"Lose what?"

"Get it!"

He dug through her clothes, which had been collected in a plastic bag, and pulled out a man's tie bar. *This doesn't make any sense.*

"This?" he asked. "I have it," he assured her as she nodded, her eyes closing.

"Okay." She whimpered as they pulled a shard from her arm. "What about Luke? What time is it? Do you need to pick him up?"

"I picked him up already. He's with Dylan outside. He faked being sick because he knew we were having lunch and the party at school was lame. No Reese's cups."

"Wow, that's *super* lame. I'm with him. What about trick or treating tonight?"

"I'm not worried about it. I'm worried about you and our baby."

"We'll be fine." She winced as the nurse worked, and a tear rolled down her cheek. She held his hand, fingering the wedding band she'd given him.

He squeezed her hand, too choked up to say anything.

"Why don't you take Luke home and come back?"

"I'm not leaving you. But I do need to check on him. He's upset over being at the hospital."

"I'm sure. Go. I'll just be hanging here with Elaine and the doc."

"I'll be back." He leaned forward and kissed her cheek. "I love you."

"Lots and lots?"

"Lots and lots." Reluctantly, he left her to check on Luke.

He walked outside and found Dylan holding Luke as he leaned against the wall, smoking a cigarette. He frowned when he realized his son held an unlit cigarette, pretending to smoke.

"Geezus, Dyl, he's four and a half. What the fuck?"

Dylan shrugged. "He's quiet. Don't tell Jen, okay? How are Sam and the baby?"

"Do another smoke ring, Dylan," Luke begged. "Daddy said the f-word. It's gonna cost him fifty cents, and I'm gonna be rich!"

"It got him to quit crying, and it isn't like I lit it or anything," Dylan said as he blew another smoke ring.

Luke clapped and dropped his cigarette.

"They're okay. I thought you quit."

"I sneak. It's our secret. Right, Luke?"

"Right! Women don't need to know everything! Are we going trick or treating now?"

Matt rolled his eyes. "Listen, about trick or treat—"

"Sir, I need to get your insurance information." The woman from the front desk had followed him outside.

Matt gnashed his teeth and sighed. "Luke, stay here with Dylan, okay? And no more cigarettes! Geezus, you're a worse father than I am," he grumbled.

"Hey, Christa? He's just gonna go grab the car seat from his truck, and then he'll be in to fill out the paperwork. I'm taking his son home with me."

"Okay. Just come straight to my desk when you get back, please."

Matt nodded and looked at Dylan.

"Jen's on her way to pick us up, and we're taking the kids trick or treating. Luke can spend the night with us."

"Okay, thanks." Matt sighed. "I really appreciate it."

"No problemo." Dylan looked at Luke and winked. "Hey, kid, wanna grab a beer later?"

"Dylan!"

"No, I want to go trick or treating!"

Matt returned with the car seat just as Jennifer pulled up. He thanked them and buckled Luke in, giving him a kiss. "Behave, okay? And have fun."

"I will, Daddy! Bring Sammie home."

"I will." He went back inside to the mound of paperwork that likely awaited.

Behind him, he heard his father's voice.

"Matt?"

He looked up, relieved, and accepted the hug Pa gave him, holding him tight for a moment.

"Luke's with the McAthies. They're going to take him trick or treating. How did you know I was here?"

"I was at Eloise Jordan's when Jennifer called. I saw them loading up as I pulled up to the ER. Good thing Jennifer's in charge. If it were up to Dylan, the kids would probably be drinking brown liquor and playing poker instead of trick or treating tonight." Pa laughed. "I always did like that McAthie boy..."

Chapter
Twenty-Seven

Hours later, Matt still sat next to Sammie's bed, holding her bandaged hand.

"What time is it?" she asked. "I want to go home."

"Eight. We're just waiting on the doc to sign off on your discharge."

She sighed. "Talk to me or something."

"What happened today? Where did all the glass come from?"

"Never mind. I don't want to talk about that yet."

He cleared his throat, but didn't push. He couldn't wait to get out of this place. Like Luke, he had nightmares about being here.

"How's this?" He sang the only Christmas song he knew the words to, making her laugh.

"Jingle Bells? Can't we get through Halloween first?" Pa asked, walking back in with his cane.

Sammie smiled. "Hush, Scrooge. I liked it."

Matt had tried to get Pa to go home, but the old man had stubbornly insisted on staying. "They let you back here?"

"I flirted with Christa. I've still got it. How's my gal?" he asked.

"The doctor was in a while ago and said everything was *fine*, whatever the hell that means." Matt sighed. "He doesn't even look old enough to be a doctor."

"I came back here to tell you I'm going to head on home. Walk with me to the parking lot, son."

"I don't want to leave Sammie."

"I might get mugged."

Matt rolled his eyes.

"Go. Maybe I'll be discharged by the time you get back." Sammie closed her eyes.

"If you're sure."

She nodded.

As they stepped out of the room, Pa grabbed his arm and ushered him into an empty room across the hall. "I need to tell you something, and I'm telling you here so you'll keep your cool."

In the hallway, Matt could see a nurse headed into Sammie's room with a policewoman.

"Wait, what are the police doing here? I think I need to be in there." Matt pointed, only halfway paying attention.

"Sam's fine. Look, I don't have all the details…but you need to know, Dylan told me James Howell was arrested for assaulting Sammie at the bank. I'm sure the police are here for her statement."

"What?" He felt like he'd been punched. He moved to go back to Sammie, but Pa grabbed his arm.

"Let go."

"No."

"It's a good thing they arrested him, because otherwise I'd kill him. Lila? Jinx? Do they know?"

Pa shrugged.

"Jinx needs to know. You know how her mother is — Lila will fall apart." He sent Jinx a quick text.

"I can't believe this." He felt ready to combust. His phone rang, and he gave Jinx a brief sketch of what was happening before he had to cut her off when he saw the doctor walking into Sammie's room.

He glanced at Pa and said through gritted teeth, "Don't you dare try to stop me." Racing across the hall, he returned to Sammie's side. Pa followed.

"All right, Mrs. Tyler, that's all we needed. Thank you." The policewoman smiled at Matt and walked out the door.

"Wait, what's going on?" He looked around wildly for someone with information.

The doctor glanced over at him and smiled. "She's ready to go. Just one more doctor to sign off and she can be tucked into her own bed."

"I'll tell you everything later, Matt. I want to go home," Sammie said. "Why's Pa still here?"

"But…"

"Walk me to my truck, son."

"No!"

"*Now.*" Pa had a surprisingly strong grip in the hand unaffected by the stroke.

Matt walked with Pa to the truck in silence. He kept his hands jammed in his pockets and literally bit his tongue to keep from screaming. The night was unseasonably warm with a slight breeze.

"Get in the truck, and I'll drive you to the door," Pa ordered as he climbed in the driver's side.

"I'll just walk back."

"Get in, Matthew. I don't want you doing anything stupid."

"I don't need a lecture right now, Pa. Sammie needs me. And I need to find out what happened."

"Just get in the damn truck."

Matt climbed in, slamming the door shut. Fed up, he crossed his arms and waited for Pa to start the car. "I'm going to kill that bastard. Sammie doesn't want to talk about it yet, so I have no information! Why would he do this?"

"Let the law handle this situation. Sammie wouldn't want you going off half-cocked. She needs you. This isn't about *you.*"

Matt looked out the windshield toward the hospital and didn't say a word for several moments. He hit the dash, swore, and turned to open the door.

Pa hit the locks and started driving around the parking lot.

"Let me out!"

"I'm not going to visit you in the state pen. That won't solve a damn thing. Now calm the fuck down." Pa drove in circles for a few minutes.

"Okay, okay." Matt leaned his forehead against his arm propped on the window and rubbed his brow. "God, I hate this damn place," he commented shakily. "For close to a year I've blamed myself for Karen and Lizbeth's deaths."

"Son—"

"I either need to talk or I need to hit something."

"Talk."

Matt pulled in a deep breath, his emotions all over the place. "Karen and I had the worst fight of our marriage the night she died. I'd found out she was pregnant with Travis's child…"

Beside him, Pa sat up straighter as air hissed between his teeth.

"I've never been so angry and hurt. I was afraid I was going to hit her. I'd never experienced such blinding rage before…Instead, I told her to go to hell and left for class. I had to get out of there. The kids were upstairs in their rooms, and I left without even saying goodnight."

He covered his face. "Karen was emotional. Looking back now, I know she was too upset to be driving. She packed a few things and took off with Luke and Lizbeth. She was leaving me." He swallowed. "I found the note on the kitchen table after they died. *I'm leaving and taking the kids with me*, it said. *We'll talk later when we're both calmer. I love Travis. We're done. It's over. We can't go on like this.*"

He dashed the tears from his eyes. "The thing is, she was right. We couldn't. But I wasn't ready. When I arrived at the hospital, she was dead, and Lizbeth soon followed—a part of me died that night, too. I blamed myself. I blamed Travis. I blamed Karen, and she was dead. I hated her, and I loved her. I lived with that guilt for months, and it ate a whole in my heart and pushed me into such a dark place I didn't know if I'd ever see light again. I went through the motions of pretending to have my shit together, but it was so far from the truth."

Pa reached out and took his hand. "Son, you're being too hard on yourself."

"No, *I'm not*. I'd obviously been a lousy husband. I moved back in with you, under the pretense of taking care of you. But I'm a lousy son, too. I resented you. I resented the responsibility on my shoulders. I questioned whether I was even a good person. I failed you and Luke so often—especially Luke."

He paused and scrubbed his face tiredly. "As you know, the Howells blamed me for everything. James was ratcheting up his threats to take Luke from me. And then boom! Out of nowhere, Sam Morgan, my best friend from before life got so fucking complicated, dropped back into the picture. I found someone who gets me, who loves me in spite of all my imperfections. She's the glue that holds me together. She makes me stronger. I love her, Pa."

"I know you do. She loves you, too."

Matt closed his eyes and leaned his head back against the seat, trying to keep his tears in check. "If anything happens to her or this baby...I don't know that I can survive another loss."

"They're going to be fine. C'mere." Pa pulled him to his shoulder and held him.

He wept in his father's arms, just as he had when he was a frightened little boy who'd lost his mother to cancer.

A nurse in blue scrubs came in and smiled. "The last doc has signed your discharge order. I just need you to sign here. Pretty much take it easy for a few days. No meds except some Tylenol, and follow up with your OB doc, okay?"

"Okay." Sammie signed the paper, and the nurse left. She missed Sue Ellen like she never had before. She rubbed her tummy. *I'll protect you, little one.* Had her mother ever worried over her like this?

She looked up when the door opened. Matt's eyes were red and swollen as he bent over to kiss her forehead.

"Are you okay? They're springing me free." She began counting, tapping her fingertips.

"Now that you're going home, I'm much better. What did the police want?"

"My statement. I'll tell you about it at home. Why don't you go get the truck?"

He pinched the bridge of his nose. "Okay."

As he stepped out, the nurse walked in with the wheelchair.

"Aw, Dad looks so tired..." she commented.

The nurse was right. Matt looked as if he'd aged ten years since this morning. And this was no time to tell him what she knew about

Mr. Howell. In his current state, he'd likely end up in jail or having a stroke. She'd wait until they'd both had some sleep.

After Matt got her settled in the truck, she closed her eyes, happy to be going home.

"Are you counting?" he asked.

"You know me well," she murmured.

"Count this." He kissed her wedding band.

"One. Thank you. Have you heard from Jennifer? Did Luke get to trick or treat?"

"Yeah. I think all the kids are in a diabetic coma by now." Matt pulled out his phone and handed it to her. She smiled at the pictures of the kids in their costumes. Jennifer was dressed up as a rock star and Dylan wore scrubs with a nurse's cap on. They laughed.

"I hate that we missed it," she said.

"Me, too. I hope Dylan doesn't steal all the Reese's. Will you tell me what happened?"

"Yes, but I'm starving, and I want a bath. Can it wait?"

He sighed. "Sure."

Thirty minutes later, after eating drive-thru fast food, Matt insisted on carrying her upstairs despite her protests.

"Hush," he grunted. "Let me do this now before you add eight or so pounds of baby."

She giggled in his neck. "You're being overprotective."

"That's what husbands and dads do."

He helped her with her bath, gently washing her hair and cursing as tiny shards of glass rinsed out with the bubbles.

"The nurse said this could happen for a while. We need to make sure we scrub the tub good before Luke gets in." Sammie purred as Matt massaged her scalp. "At first they wanted to cut my hair. I think I have haircut PTSD, so I refused."

"I think most of the glass is out of your scalp. Luke can bathe in Pa's bathroom, and I'll clean the tub. Sammie, I know James assaulted you. What I don't know is why? How?"

"Can we talk in bed? I'm so tired."

"You're stalling," he accused.

She kissed his cheek. "I am. Get cleaned up, but rinse the tub before you shower."

"You can only stall for so long, Samantha."

"I know."

"Get in bed. I'll be right back."

Fifteen minutes later, he crawled in beside her, still damp.

She rolled into his arms and snuggled. "This is my happy place."

"Mine too," he murmured against her hair. "Please tell me. My patience is wearing thin."

She sighed. "Mr. Howell isn't all that he seems."

"I beg to differ. He seems like an asshole, and he is an asshole. What was the tie bar? I saw the engraved H."

She decided to tell him part of the story tonight. The other could wait until they'd had some sleep. "You were right. He's a vile human being. He got mad when I hedged on letting Luke come trick or treat and totally lost it. He flipped a glass conference table and was screaming at me. I think he kicked me, too. But I'm okay. Our baby's okay. That's all that matters right now."

"But the tie bar, is that evidence? Do we need to give it to the police? I wish you'd strangled him with his damn tie. We could've been done with him for good."

"Nah, horizontal stripes on a pregnant woman, not flattering. We'll deal with this tomorrow. I need to sleep, Matt."

"But—"

She stopped him with a kiss. "Tomorrow, 'kay? Right now, I just want my husband to hold me."

At last he nodded, and safe in his arms, she fell asleep.

Sammie walked into the kitchen, still in her nightgown and robe. She'd been surprised to wake up and realize it was lunch time. She found Dylan eating a sandwich with Pa and Matt. All three looked grim. Before she could ask what Dylan was doing there, the phone rang.

"Who was that?" she asked.

"Jinx—warning me James is up to no good. The sonofabitch is out on bond. What a surprise. I've been summoned to the House of Horrors."

She stood and caught Matt's wrist. "Don't go."

Drawing her into his arms, he held her and kissed her forehead. "That bastard hurt you. He's not going to get away with this."

"Dylan, Pa, don't let him go."

"I've already put Matt in touch with a lawyer," Dylan offered. "And I gave my statement to the police. I agree Mr. Howell needs to pay for what he did to you."

Pa nodded.

"No. I mean, yes, he does, but going over there will make things worse!"

Matt's jaw hardened. "I'm going. I want to hear how he's going to try to weasel his way out of this, and then I'm going straight to the lawyer's office. I have an appointment before I pick up Luke. Your only job today is to rest."

"Please, promise me you won't do anything foolish. Promise me, Matt!" Sammie refused to let go. "His reputation is already ruined, witnesses saw what he did. Don't make it worse than it is."

"I need to do this. I won't do anything stupid, I promise." He gave her a kiss. Grabbing his keys, he walked out the door.

"Why didn't you stop him?" she asked Pa, sinking into a chair.

Dylan stood. "I'm going to go. You need anything, Sam?"

"I needed you to talk some sense into my husband!"

"He'll be okay. Chad's a great lawyer." He patted her shoulder and left.

"You should've stopped him," she snapped at Pa.

Pa stood. "When has he ever listened to me? While you eat you can tell me the whole story." He made her a ham sandwich and poured her a glass of milk.

She nodded and accepted the food. "Thank you. Something happened between Mr. Howell and my mother a long time ago. I found out when I opened Sue Ellen's lock box."

Sammie reached for her purse and pulled out the picture of her mother with James. "But that's not all, and if Matt finds out, I don't know what he'll do..."

Chapter
Twenty-Eight

Matt was unpleasantly surprised when Travis answered the Howells' door.

He stepped into the foyer and was about to shrug past him when the jerk placed a hand on his shoulder.

"Matt! Wait a minute. I want to talk to you."

He put his hands on his hips and glared. He might've come to terms with Travis being Sammie's friend, but he still hated the sonofabitch. "What? Don't tell me you're defending Howell. I thought Sammie was your friend."

"She *is* my friend. What James did was reprehensible. I just want you to listen to what my dad and Lila have to say and think about it, okay?"

Matt resisted rolling his eyes and nodded his assent as he turned. He hated this damn sterile house. Everything was white — white walls, white carpeting, white marble statues, even white soap in the bathroom. It had always reminded him of a mortuary.

As pale as her surroundings, Lila gave him a wan smile as he entered the den. "Hello, Matt. Won't you please have a seat? Would you like anything to drink?"

Matt rubbed the back of his neck as he sat on the edge of the couch. "No, ma'am. This isn't a social call." He glanced around the room. James was not there. However, George Carlton, Travis's father, was. This didn't bode well. He was James Howell's best friend. He was also a lawyer.

"How is Samantha?" Lila asked in a meek voice.

"Fine."

"And Lukas?"

"Fine."

The tension in the room was palpable; the silence deafening.

Feeling cornered, Matt stood up and began to pace. "Just what the hell is going on here? You don't give a damn about Sammie. How the hell did that bastard get out of jail? Oh, never mind. That was a dumb question. People like James Howell are above the law in this damn hick town—"

Jinx slipped into the room. Her short, platinum blond hair was a tousled mess and hung over her kohl-rimmed eyes. She glared at everyone but him, but the smile in her pale, pinched face didn't offer any reassurance. Without saying a word, she perched on the arm of the couch.

George Carlton cleared his throat. "Matt, calm down and hear us out. We asked you here to discuss the incident that happened at the bank yesterday—"

Matt whipped around to face George. "I'll tell you exactly what happened. James hurt my wife, sending her to the hospital. So don't you dare fucking tell me to calm down. I've had it with him. I'm encouraging Sammie to press charges, and I hope he rots in jail. Do you hear me?"

The room was silent except for Lila's soft crying. Travis looked out the window, gripping the back of a chair. Jinx stood up and applauded, which was strange. The entire vibe in the room was off, making him nervous.

George sighed. "Your, er, wife has been hurt. But James is not himself. He's not well."

Jinx began pacing, fisting and releasing her hands.

What is her problem?

"Eugenia, sit down, dear. You're making me nervous," Lila interjected as she cried.

"I think we can work this out without the publicity of a trial," George continued. "As it is, James has seriously damaged his reputation." He held up his hand when Matt started to interrupt. "Just hear me out. James is sorry for what he did. He lost control. As a matter of fact, he's had a complete nervous breakdown."

Lila's sobbing grew louder.

"Bullshit!" Matt closed his eyes, pinching the bridge of his nose. *Sammie was right. It was a mistake to come here.* He crossed his arms in front of his chest. "That man has been trying to ruin me ever since Karen and I got together. I have a whole laundry list of crap he's tried to pull. This is the last straw."

"Matt—" Travis said.

"Don't you say one goddamned word to me, motherfucker!" Matt wanted to punch something, and Travis was handy. He stuffed his hand in his pocket to keep from doing so.

Travis's face turned red, but he kept his mouth shut.

Lila's crying unsettled him, and Matt realized how old and fragile she looked.

He knew Lila had been the one to intervene and get James to be civil when he and Karen were first married. She'd been stuck in the middle of the long-standing feud for years. Matt took a deep breath, found her a box of tissues, and handed them to her.

She dabbed at her eyes. "Thank you, Matt. Please, just listen. What George is telling you is true. My husband isn't well. What he did was wrong. But think of the publicity. Let him retire quietly. He's not a bad person. It's just been so hard on us, losing Karen and Elizabeth. And Eugenia hasn't been around…" She looked pointedly at her youngest daughter. "I didn't realize just how hard this has been on James. He loves his family, his girls meant everything to him."

Jinx stopped pacing to clutch her stomach as if she felt sick.

He felt his anger boiling inside. If he didn't get out of here, Pa's fear would come true—he'd end up in jail. "I'm done listening. It's time for action. I'm going to get a lawyer." He stormed out of the room.

Slamming the door behind him, he marched toward the front door but stopped. Anger overtook reasoning, and he turned and marched upstairs toward James and Lila's bedroom.

He threw open the bedroom door with a crash and burst in. Everywhere there were pictures of Karen and Jinx at various ages, and photos of Lizbeth and Luke on the walls and bureau tops. Matt was not surprised to find no photos of himself. He'd always been the invisible man.

James sat in a chair, dressed in navy silk pajamas and a paisley silk robe. He held a glass of amber liquid as he stared through the large picture window that overlooked the lake.

Without turning to face Matt, he asked, "Would you like a drink?"

"No. Just answers."

James turned toward him, his face void of emotion. "Sit down, Tyler." James moved to his desk.

Matt remained standing. "You're a spiteful, mean old bastard, but you haven't had a mental breakdown any more than I have."

"Did George tell you my offer? To pay off your mortgage and cover Luke's college education?"

"No, we didn't get that far, and I'm not interested." He turned to leave.

Sammie was right; it was pointless to talk to him. If the jerk thought he could be bought, he was about to find out otherwise. He'd let his lawyer handle this crap.

"I didn't think you would," James called. "You've always been a fool." His self-righteousness was too much.

Matt whipped back around. "What did Sammie ever do to you? Why did you lose your shit yesterday? Was it the fact that we're having a baby? That I've moved on with my life? Answer me, dammit."

James paused. "I despise you with every ounce of my being. I always have and always will. You weren't good enough for Karen. She only married you to defy me. It was a simple act of rebellion that every teenager goes through. She also apparently lived to regret it."

Matt flinched and clenched his teeth.

James's smile didn't reach his eyes. "Karen was seeing Travis behind your back when she died —" The bastard had the nerve to raise his glass toward Karen's high school senior portrait, as if he were toasting her.

Matt squashed the urge to wipe that smug smile off his face. He was baiting him, wanting a reaction. He refused to let him have it. "I know all of this, and I've already dealt with it," he interrupted icily. "What I haven't dealt with is the fact that *you* hurt Sammie, sending her to the hospital, not to mention your ridiculous threats. I want you to pay for what you've done—and not with your filthy money.

"You've made my life a living hell, and that ends today. Yes, Karen and I had problems, serious problems. What you can't deal with, old man, is the fact that your precious daughter *did love me* at one time. She didn't have to marry me. As everyone in this damn town knows, you have more money than God. You offered her an abortion, adoption, any number of solutions to the *problem*. But Karen *loved me* and wanted to *marry me!*"

Matt paced to work off his anger. "You have some sort of sick vendetta against me, and now you've gone after an innocent woman, *my wife*. I'm done. We're going to court, and everyone will see you for the sorry piece of shit you are!"

"You know you won't win. I own this county," James taunted.

Matt glared, disgusted by the probable truth in his statement. The injustice of it all enraged him.

He turned to leave as Jinx burst into the room.

"I want to talk to my father." Her voice was tinged with hysteria, and her pupils were dilated so large her amber irises were barely visible.

James stared at his youngest daughter, looking bored.

"Jinx, your father and I have a long history of animosity. This doesn't involve you, and I don't want you caught in the middle. Please, go back downstairs. Your mother needs you." Matt tempered his anger for her sake. He reached over to escort her out, but she shrugged away.

"Stop it. I'm not a little girl anymore. Give me five minutes alone with *him*. I think I can solve this problem once and for all." The coldness in her voice gave him pause.

"Eugenia, baby girl—" James began.

"Don't! Don't you ever call me that! Get out, Matt," she said through gritted teeth. "Now!" Her eyes remained pinned on her father.

"But—" he protested.

With a scream, she shoved him out the door and he heard it lock behind him.

Ready to get the hell out of here, he hurried down the stairs, but before he made it to the front door, Lila caught up with him in the foyer.

"Please, Matt. James is paying for what he's done. He's lost his job, and you know the bank was his life! He's lost his respectability…"

Lila grasped his hand and wouldn't let go. "Travis told us about his affair with Karen. I had no idea anything was going on. If this goes to trial, you know all of these sordid things will be brought up whether we like it or not."

She closed her eyes for a moment. "I'm begging as a mother. Karen paid for her sins. She's dead, Matt. Please don't drag her name through the mud. Please. I know you loved her. For the sake of that love and for Luke, don't drag this family through a messy court battle—"

Lila's argument was cut short by a gunshot and a scream.

Matt caught her before she fell to the floor.

Chapter
Twenty-Nine

Sammie heard Luke pounding up the stairs and smiled. Hurriedly, she hopped back in bed before Matt caught her rearranging his closet.

"Sammie!" He bounced onto the bed. "You came home! You missed trick or treating! Mrs. Jordan gives the best candy. Please don't ever leave again!" He gave her a bear hug and kiss.

She hugged and kissed him back, not minding the discomfort caused by his exuberance. Her heart felt ready to burst with love for this little boy. "I won't leave you, Luke. I love you lots and lots. Where's Daddy? There must've been quite a line at the pizza place; you're late. What kind of pizza did you get?"

"Pa picked me up after school, and we went to the Harrisville Walmart. Look, I got some new cars. Then we went to get the good kind of pizza. We got pepperoni."

"All the way to Harrisville? Yummy. Why did Pa pick you up?"

"Daddy got *delayed*." He scrunched his face. "What's that mean?"

"It means he's running late." She frowned and crawled out of bed to slip into her robe. "Let's go help Pa."

"We're eating on paper towels. No dishes," Pa said as they walked into the kitchen.

"That smells delicious. I can do dishes. Goodness, I'm not help-less," Sammie offered.

Pa didn't look at her. He seemed nervous.

"Is Matt okay?" Her heart pounded. *Did he get into it with Mr. Howell?*

"Yep, he's just taking care of a little business. He'll tell you about it later." He shot a look toward Luke, who was happily tearing off paper towels to set the table.

Sammie forced a deep breath as she opened the box and counted the pepperoni on top of the pizza. Luke placed his pumpkin full of candy on the table.

"For dessert. But all the Reese's are mine," he declared.

She and Pa laughed, but it was forced. She picked at her pizza and noticed Pa did too. Only Luke seemed unfazed by Matt's absence as he chattered about trick or treating and school.

After they ate, she helped Luke with his reading. Proudly she showed him her GED certificate, which had arrived in the mail.

"That's great, Sammie! It means you're smart. Are you going to go to college like Daddy?"

"Maybe after he finishes."

After showering in Pa's bathroom, Luke crawled in bed with her to watch some TV. Her worried texts had finally gotten a response from Matt:

Home soon.

"Do those hurt?" Luke asked, inspecting her cuts and bandages.

"A little."

"Will you have scars like me?"

"I might. They're nothing to be ashamed of. We're survivors, Luke."

"We're superheroes!"

She let out a relieved breath when she heard Matt downstairs talking in a low voice to Pa.

"Think about how you break the news," she heard Pa say.

What news? In a few minutes, she heard Matt slowly climbing the stairs. He headed straight to the bathroom and turned on the water. Not wanting Luke to worry, she stayed put, counting the obnoxious number of times the laugh track played during the show.

At last, the water cut off, and in a few minutes, Matt entered the room with a towel wrapped around his waist. He looked beyond exhausted, and he hadn't shaved.

"Daddy!"

Matt held Luke tight, burying his face in his son's neck.

After a moment, the boy squirmed loose. "You're wet. Did you see the card I made Sammie?"

"Not yet."

"I'll go get it—be right back!" he hurried out the door and stomped down the stairs.

"Have you noticed his limp is better?" Sammie said.

Matt nodded, slipping into his pajama pants.

"You okay?"

Luke scurried back in, waving his card. Matt sat on the bed and smiled as Luke explained the picture. "Sammie said she might have scars like me. I'm Batman, and she's Wonder Woman!"

"I see." He looked at the card and grinned. "I like this one best." Matt pointed to the stick figure with the wild orange hair.

Luke laughed. "That's Sammie. And here is me and you and Pa."

"It's perfect. Why don't you go get in bed? I'll be there in a minute to tuck you in."

"In a minute, Daddy."

"That wasn't a request, son." Matt sent him a look that said *do it now.*

"Oh-*kay.*" Luke rolled his eyes and let out an exaggerated sigh before giving Sammie one last hug and kiss. "G'night, Wonder Woman."

"Goodnight, Batman." She held onto him for a moment and patted him before he left.

"Tell me he didn't just roll his eyes at me." Matt pinched the bridge of his nose.

"I didn't see a thing," Sammie replied with a grin. "Why don't I put him to bed. You look beat."

"You'll stay in that bed and rest, even if I have to tie you down!"

"Not tonight, dear. I have a headache," she joked.

He didn't even crack a smile. Sammie pushed the covers back to get up.

"Stay in that bed!"

"I have to put my shoes together, and I don't remember agreeing to obey you in the wedding vows."

Matt arranged her shoes and gently pushed her back in bed, tucking her in tight. "I have a lot to tell you. But let me put Luke to bed first," he croaked.

"Is it bad?" she whispered.

"Yes and no. We'll be fine."

Ten minutes later, Matt collapsed on the bed beside her and threw one arm over his eyes.

"Are you okay?" she asked, rubbing his chest.

"Not really, but I will be."

"I snuck some of the Reese's and hid them in the bedside table, if that will help."

He chuckled. "Sneaky."

"What happened?"

"Kiss me. Just come here and kiss me. I really need to hold you. You're my anchor," he replied with a heavy sigh.

Sammie curled into his arms and kissed his cheek. "Tell me; I can take it."

He didn't speak for a moment, just held her close, his hand rubbing up and down her back.

"George Carlton, Travis, and Lila were waiting when I arrived. James was upstairs. They told me he'd suffered a nervous breakdown. I told them that was bullshit and went to leave, ready to keep the appointment with our lawyer. But something made me go upstairs. I just wanted to beard the lion in his den. We started arguing, and the bastard tried to buy our silence—as if waving money would ever make what he's done okay. Next thing I know, Jinx bursts in the room. She said she could solve the problem once and for all, and she shoved me out. I'd had it by then and was walking out the front door when Lila stopped me and begged me not to drag the family name through the mud, to think of Luke. She said I hadn't thought about how all of this could impact him and then…"

He rolled over on his side to face her. "There was a gunshot—"

"Oh my God, Jinx?" she asked, covering her mouth.

He shook his head. "Not Jinx. James. Self-inflicted. He's dead."

Sammie gasped. "He killed himself in front of her?"

He nodded. "I'll never forget the sight as long as I live." His breathing stuttered as he attempted to control his emotions.

She stroked his hair and held him. "Oh my God, I'm so sorry, Matt."

He raised his tear-filled gaze to hers. "Please don't think bad of me. Part of me is relieved he's gone…But how am I going to tell Luke?"

"Shhh." Sammie covered his lips with her index finger. "We'll figure out a way. We can talk to Pastor McClain. Everything you're feeling—I'm sure it's normal. He was so hateful. He was sick, Matt. He was an angry man full of pain. He did despicable things to so many…"

She took a deep breath. "Also, I'm pretty sure it was him, Matt."

"Him?"

"When I opened my mother's lock box yesterday, I found a picture. I put two and two together. He was the man she hooked up with, the one who was in my room that night. I wanted to get out of there after I realized that, but he stopped me and asked about Luke coming by for Halloween. I told him no—I felt sick knowing what he'd done to me. Those hands…" She shuddered and handed Matt the photo from her nightstand. "Look, he's wearing the tie bar. I think it came off when he and Sue Ellen were struggling, and she kept it. When he wouldn't take no for an answer, I showed it to him and told him I knew what he'd done to me. That's when he lost it and flipped the table. He was trying to get the proof away from me."

"No." Matt sat up. "Oh my God. Karen would never let the kids be alone with him. Surely he didn't—no, this is all too disgusting. It's too vile, even for him…" He shook so hard the headboard rattled.

"It's over now. We'll be all right. Love will get us through this." She wrapped her arms around him and rocked as they both wept.

Matt held her tight. "I never want to let you go, and I promise never to take life for granted. I'm not a rich man, but if I could, I'd give you the moon and the stars and a life without any more pain."

"Matt, I never wanted the stars or the moon. I like them just fine right where they are, looking down on us from the night sky. Life is painful, but also joyful. We're rich in the things that matter—family, friends. We'll handle this; we have to, for Luke's sake. And we have to let go of the hatred or we'll never move forward. You've given me everything, Matt. With you, I can breathe again, free and easy."

"I love you, Sammie," Matt whispered. "Lots and lots. You leave *me* breathless with the depth of your forgiveness." He kissed her deeply.

"Try to sleep. Life's going to be hard for a while. But it *will* get better." She drew his hand to her stomach and held him, softly singing Christmas carols as he fell asleep.

Epilogue

Thanksgiving Day, Matt raked the leaves, watching Luke out of the corner of his eye. One year ago, their lives had been forever changed by the death of his mother and sister. He and Luke had visited the cemetery this morning to place flowers on their graves. The dirt was still fresh on his grandfather's grave nearby.

The boy had been quiet and sad since James's funeral. He'd asked questions Matt had no answers for. On the advice of Pastor McClain, he and Sammie had kept the explanation for James's death simple and vague. Jinx had fled the day after the shooting, despite his best effort to talk her out of it. Before she left, she'd given him Karen's diary. He'd read through it, and the words were seared in his brain — the trauma he never knew she'd endured because of the secrets she kept. The journal had given him a glimpse of his first wife that she'd never shared with him and explained so much of why she'd been the way she was.

He wondered if their marriage would've survived if she'd been honest with him. Living with the *what ifs* had plummeted him back into his grief. Sammie had made him talk through his feelings, which helped. And together, they'd sought counseling.

Sammie stepped out on the back porch. She was getting a baby bump now and was over the morning sickness. She waved at him, and her wide smile warmed his heart. They'd been to the doctor last week, and everything was going well with her pregnancy—which was the only good thing to have happened in forever. He'd wanted to know the sex, but Sammie wanted a surprise.

"Luke, can you help me set the table?" she asked.

"Okay." He followed her inside.

Matt sighed. Karen had started a tradition of them each saying what they were thankful for on Thanksgiving. Last year the only thing he'd been thankful for was his son still being alive. This year he had more, but it was still a damn hard day. Maybe they should've just gone to the Cracker Barrel in Harrisville. Or taken a trip somewhere. A car pulled up, and he was surprised when Lucy got out carrying a cake plate.

"Thank you for inviting me," she said as she approached.

Apparently, Sammie had done so, and he realized he was happy about that. His sister had been through hell this year, too. "I'm glad you could be here, Luce." He smiled. "What kind of cake?"

"Chocolate with Reese's. Luke requested it."

"Rats. I was hoping for coconut."

"I made you one for your birthday; quit pouting."

He laughed. "It will be great. Sammie's cooked enough food to feed all of Pine Bluff." He put the rake down and led the way inside.

The smell of turkey, dressing, and pumpkin pie filled the air, and Pa and Sammie were deep in a lively, colorful argument about who was going to win the football game. Luke held the no-cussing jar at the ready. Lucy laughed and took up the argument, siding with Sammie, much to Pa's disgust.

Matt leaned against the counter and smiled.

Sammie kissed Luke goodnight, hugging him extra tight before leaving to give him a few minutes alone with Matt. She heard Matt tell Luke a funny story about Karen and Lizbeth, and she smiled through her tears. Today had been tinged with sadness, no doubt about it. But after dinner, they'd played in the leaves and Luke had laughed. She rubbed her tummy. This time next year they'd have a highchair at the table. And hopefully over time, this season would get easier.

Matt stepped out of Luke's room, wiping his eyes. But his face lit with a wide smile when he saw her.

She held out her hand. "I've got a surprise for you."

He frowned. "Who left the light on in your old room?"

"I don't know. I'll turn it off." Opening the door, she shut the light off and pulled him inside.

Matt looked up. All over the ceiling and walls, she'd placed glow-in-the-dark stars and a gigantic glow-in-the-dark moon.

"Do you remember when you told me you wanted to give me the stars and the moon?"

"Yes. Because you've brought so much light into my darkness."

Sammie held her husband close. "Well, I wanted to make it a reality. And give you something in return." She kissed him fervently, melding her body as close to his as she could.

"Let me show you heaven," he whispered.

"In a minute. Turn the light on, Matt."

He flipped the switch and gasped. She'd painted the room a soft gray with white trim. And a beside the four-poster bed stood a crib in the corner with pink bedding.

He turned to her. "Pink? But how do you know? You told me you wanted a surprise!"

"I wanted to surprise *you*. You know how you met me for the appointment last week? I'd already had an ultrasound when you got there. The staff were in on the surprise after I explained that this was going to be a hard week and I wanted to do something to lessen the pain. I got dressed and met you in the waiting room. Didn't you notice the nurse snickering as we went back to see the doc?"

Matt laughed and held her close, kissing her brow. "A girl, huh? I hope she has red hair like her mama."

"I love you, Matt. Lots and lots." She smiled up at him. "Now, how about we go to our room, so you can show me heaven."

The End

Author's Note

Self-harm or self-injury involves hurting yourself on purpose. It is not a mental illness, but a behavior that indicates a lack of coping skills. Several illnesses are associated with it, including borderline personality disorder, depression, eating disorders, anxiety, or post-traumatic distress disorder. Self-harm usually begins in the teenage and young adult years, but it can happen later in life, too. People who have experienced trauma, neglect, or abuse are most at risk. The injury itself can stimulate the body's endorphins or pain-killing hormones and gives a false sense of "feeling better." But this rarely lasts and can lead to a vicious cycle of shame and guilt.

If you, or someone you know, is struggling with self-harm, help is available.

HelpLine: 1-800-950-NAMI (6264) or 1-800-273-8255

For further information: www.nami.org/Learn-More/ Mental-Health-Conditions/Related-Conditions/Self-harm

You are not alone.
Do not suffer in silence.
Don't be afraid to reach out for help.

Acknowledgments

As always, to my family, thank you for your sacrifices and support when I'm in the writing cave hiding in my dream world.

Jessica Royer Ocken, I appreciate your patience with me as I stress over a word or description. You always make my story better. Working with you is the best part of this journey.

Shannon Lumetta, I appreciate the fact that you don't laugh too hard at my cover ideas and that you always get it perfect in spite of my "helpful" suggestions.

Coreen Montagna, thank you for your line edits and beautiful formatting and tweaking—even after I've declared the book perfect and done.

Stephanie Phillips of SBR Media, thank you for your encouragement and support. I dream of the day we're in NYC striking a big deal or LA on a red carpet together.

Christina Santos, PA Extraordinaire, I know I'm OCD and difficult, yet you still put up with me. Thank you!

Cain Raisers, you are my "chosen family" and I love that we can have fun, talk books and be silly without judgment. You are the best, ever. I especially want to thank the Cain Girls who read and review my books and are my biggest cheerleaders.

To all the bloggers who have taken an interest in my books and helped spread the word, I couldn't do it without you. You truly are unsung heroes/heroines.

And to my SLOBS, you keep me honest, you make me laugh and you lift me up.

Gel Ytaz of Tempting Illustrations, you always bring by story to life with your beautiful teasers, thank you.

About the Author

During the day, Nancee works as a counselor/nurse in the field of addiction to support her coffee and reading habit. Nights are spent writing paranormal and contemporary romances with a serrated edge. Authors are her rock stars, and she's been known to stalk a few for an autograph, but not in a scary, Stephen King way. Her husband swears her To-Be-Read list on her e-reader qualifies her as a certifiable book hoarder. Always looking to try something new, she dreams of being an extra in a Bollywood film, or a tattoo artist. (Her lack of rhythm and artistic ability may put a damper on both of these dreams.)

Website: nanceecain.com
Blog: nanceecain.com/blog
Goodreads: goodreads.com/Nancee_Cain
Facebook: facebook.com/NanceeCainAuthor
Reader's Group (Cain Raisers): facebook.com/groups/Cain.Raisers
Twitter: twitter.com/Nancee_Cain
Pinterest: pinterest.com/nanceecain
Instagram: instagram.com/nanceecain
BookBub: bookbub.com/authors/nancee-cain
Newsletter: eepurl.com/bhFMtX
YouTube Channel: bit.ly/2xsU6Ad
Spotify Playlists: open.spotify.com/user/12184539074

Books by Nancee Cain:

Paranormal Romance (Angels)
Saving Evangeline
Tempting Jo
Loving Lili (novella)

Contemporary Romance (Pine Bluff Novels)
The Resurrection of Dylan McAthie
The Redemption of Emma Devine
The Rehabilitation of Angel Sinclair
The Redirection of Damien Sinclair
The Reinvention of Jinx Howell
The Reintroduction of Sammie Morgan
The Realization of Grayson Deschanelle

Contemporary Romances

pine bluff

Although each of the titles in this series can be read as standalone stories, this is the preferred reading order:

The Resurrection of Dylan McAthie
A Pine Bluff Novel

Maybe You Can Go Home Again

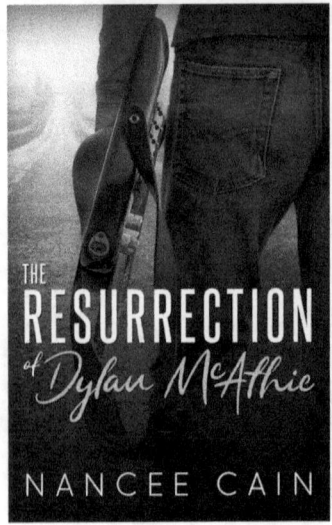

Hounded by paparazzi, Dylan McAthie—the former lead guitarist for Crucified, Dead and Buried—craves quiet anonymity to regroup and sort out his life. An accident leaves him dependent on the family he once ran from, with no choice but to return to the small town of Pine Bluff, Alabama.

Hired by Dylan's estranged brother, private-duty nurse Jennifer Adams remembers the charming boy Dylan was before fame and misfortune. And she notices he's developed a knack for blaming everyone else for his problems, rather than bothering with introspection. She's not having it.

Despite their clashes, as her patient heals, the chemistry between them grows undeniable—until scandal finds Dylan again, threatening to destroy the progress he's made and the couple's growing respect and affection. Can Dylan fix what fame has so easily broken? Or will his public resurrection mean the death of any relationship with Jennifer?

The Redemption of Emma Devine
A Pine Bluff Novel

A Little Shake-Up in Life Can Be Devine

Emma Devine is on the run and fighting to survive. Her tortured past makes trust difficult, especially where men are concerned. But she has no choice other than accepting the help of the man who catches her shoplifting on Christmas Eve.

When not stopping shoplifters, David Patterson leads a quiet life in Pine Bluff, Alabama, working as a high school teacher. His random act of Christmas kindness brings unexpected joy to his life, as he finds himself drawn to the mysterious Emma. When she leaves, his world is turned upside down, and his dreams are changed forever.

Four years later, Emma returns in search of long-overdue redemption. But despite an undeniable attraction between the two, trust is an even greater issue now—for both of them. Can they find their way to a place of understanding? Or have yesterday's mistakes destroyed their chance for a future together?

The Rehabilitation of Angel Sinclair
A Pine Bluff Novel

Love — the Hardest Addiction to Kick

Angel Sinclair arrives in Pine Bluff, Alabama, determined to make amends for his past and move on. But that changes after a chance encounter with a beautiful inn owner, and instead he finds himself pursuing two things that haven't been in his life for years: love and trust.

Still reeling from a bitter divorce, Maggie Robertson wants to focus on making her business a success. Getting involved with anyone in this gossipy little town is the farthest thing from her mind…until she finds herself tempted by a younger man.

Neither Angel nor Maggie can ignore the sizzling heat between them. But Angel's secretive nature soon fills Maggie with doubts about the man she's allowed into her heart.

Was she wrong to believe love could conquer all? Is their age difference an obstacle they can't overcome?

The Redirection of Damien Sinclair
A Pine Bluff Novel

Sometimes You Get What You Need

Acclaimed divorce attorney Damien Sinclair has witnessed more than his share of love's ugly aftermath. He keeps things black and white, preventing anyone from getting too close. But his illusion of control fades when an attempt on his life leaves him struggling with PTSD.

Enter Damien's childhood friend, the free-spirited Harley Taylor. Shrugging off the awkwardness of their teenaged fling and her broken heart, she appoints herself his caregiver. The man needs to learn not to take himself so seriously, and she's hellbent on snapping him out of his brooding funk.

After a decade apart, Harley and Damien find their attraction is stronger than ever. Could Harley's sunny disposition be the bright spot Damien needs in his life? Or will their differences overshadow any hopes of a future together?

The Reinvention of Jinx Howell
A Pine Bluff Novel

Can Love Unmask Their True Selves?

Hiding behind her wigs and heavy makeup, Jinx Howell masks her insecurities—which even she doesn't understand—with bravado, slashing through life with reckless abandon. Lonely, but unwilling to get close to anyone, she finds the ideal solution: a hook-up with the campus's most notorious heartbreaker.

In similar fashion, Mark "Two-Time" MacGregor protects his heart and keeps himself unencumbered through a string of one-night stands. A chance meeting with the edgy Jinx in a dark alley seems like destiny. She claims to want sex with no ties, making her perfect. *Like attracts like.* But this girl with a switchblade has more hang-ups than he does, which is a hell of a lot.

When tragedy strikes, Mark's hit-and-run lifestyle takes a backseat to his need to protect the broken girl whose secrets are unraveling. Along the way, both of them will find their truths unmasked. Can they forge a real relationship, or will they give up on their romance as jinxed?

The Reintroduction of Sammie Morgan
A Pine Bluff Novel

Can Life Get Any Crazier?

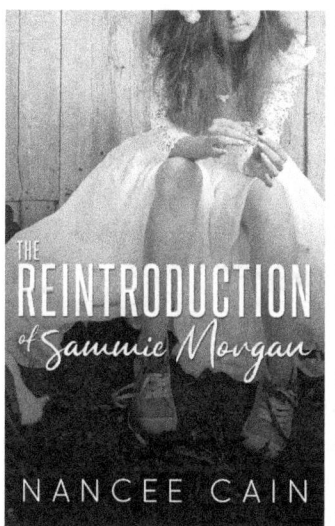

Still reeling from the tragic deaths of his wife and daughter, Matt Tyler trudges through life, caring for his young son, managing his cantankerous father, and working as much as he can. Despite his best efforts, bills are piling up and his vindictive in-laws seem determined to take Luke away from him.

Things change when he stumbles upon Sammie Morgan—with a car that won't run and her mother's ashes in the backseat. Best friends growing up, Matt and Sammie have spent years apart following very different paths. Now they've both run out of options. Without a dime in her pocket, Sammie has nowhere to go. And Matt lacks the stable home life he needs to fight his former in-laws.

Their hasty solution? A marriage of convenience.

But how convenient will this reintroduction be if it means Matt and Sammie have to relive the most painful parts of their past?

The Realization of Grayson Deschanelle
A Pine Bluff Novel

Sex, No Strings Attached

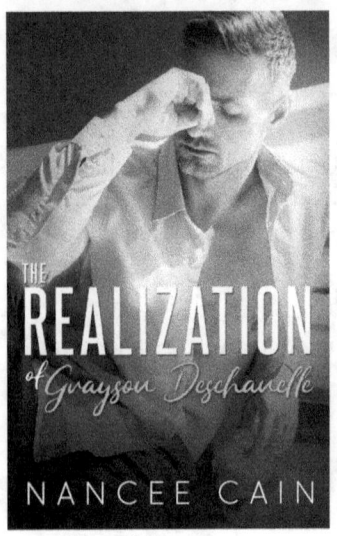

Despite a high-profile clientele, fashion photographer Grayson Deschanelle prefers being behind the lens, away from public scrutiny. After his movie star girlfriend dumps him, he flees to his stepbrother's remote cabin to hide from the paparazzi.

Caught by surprise, Grayson finds Lissy much different than the girl he's known for years. She's no longer a child—though her teenaged crush is still very much intact. Snowed in with her, he tries to fight his growing attraction. But being with Lissy brings what his life is lacking into sharp focus.

The ice melts, and they return home. When their families discover their secret, Grayson must decide what kind of life he truly wants—and whether he'll fight to keep Lissy by his side.

Paranormal Angel Romances

Although each of the titles in this series can be read as standalone stories, this is the preferred reading order:

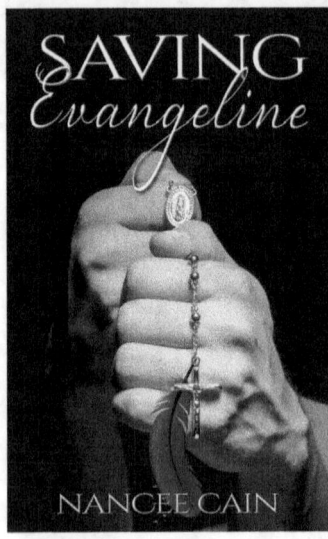

Evangeline is the town pariah. Everyone knows she's crazy and was responsible for the death of her last boyfriend. Even her mother left her and moved cross-country. Lonely and desperate, Evie decides to end her life.

Rogue angel Remiel longs to return to Earth, but there's just one problem. He tends to invite trouble and hasn't been allowed back since Woodstock. The Boss sends him to save Evangeline, but there's a catch: he can't reveal his angelic nature, and he must complete the task as *Father* Remiel Blackson.

Forced together on a cross-country trip, a forbidden romance ignites and love unfolds. A host of heavenly messengers tries to intervene, but Remiel and Evangeline are headed on a collision course to disaster. Will his love save her, or will they both be lost forever?

Forbidden love is hell…

Confident and quirky, Jo Sanford thinks her boss is God's gift to women — and she couldn't be further from the truth. Devilishly handsome, Luc DeVille will stop at nothing to lure his administrative assistant right into his arms — and bed.

Over Rafe Goodman's dead body…

Rafe, Jo's best friend, refuses to sit by and watch as Luc tries to win the heart of the woman he's always protected. After all, Rafe is her guardian angel. Suddenly, Jo's caught in the middle of a battle between good and evil. But the closer she gets to the fire, the hotter it burns. Now, Jo's going to learn that when love battles lust, Heaven and Hell collide.

Loving Lili (novella)

Their lovemaking is hot and dirty. Their break ups are nasty and epic.

Tired of taking the blame for every wicked thing that happens on Earth, fallen angel Luc DeVille decides to write a tell-all-book exposing The Boss.

Sharing a long and passionate history, Luc is shocked when Lili Nix arrives to interview for the job as editor. Immediately the verbal sparring begins, but the sexual chemistry remains combustible. Fascinated by this heavenly creature, Luc changes his game plan. After all, she's the only angel who has ever held his attention and understood his intentions.

Being in this world, but not of this world, is a lonely business. Can two lost angels connect and make it last this time?